THE RELUCTANT BRIDEGROOM

THE
RELUCTANT
BRIDEGROOM

★

GILBERT MORRIS

BETHANY HOUSE PUBLISHERS
MINNEAPOLIS, MINNESOTA 55438

Copyright © 1990
Gilbert Morris
All Rights Reserved

Published by Bethany House Publishers
A Ministry of Bethany Fellowship, Inc.
6820 Auto Club Road, Minneapolis, Minnesota 55438

Printed in the United States of America

Library of Congress Cataloging-in-Publication Data

Morris, Gilbert.
  The reluctant bridegroom / Gilbert Morris.
      p.   cm. — (The House of Winslow ; bk. 7)

   I. Title. II. Series: Morris, Gilbert. House of Winslow ; bk 7.
PS3563.08742R45   1990
813'.54—dc20   89–78389
ISBN 1-55661-069-6   CIP

To Daren and Teresa Reymeyer

God graciously gives us companions to help us bear our burdens and to encourage our hearts as we walk the narrow way toward the Celestial City.

None of my fellow pilgrims have refreshed my spirit more than you two—and your gift of friendship has made a place in my heart that will always be there.

GILBERT MORRIS spent ten years as a pastor before becoming Professor of English at Ouachita Baptist University in Arkansas and earning a Ph.D. at the University of Arkansas. During the summers of 1984 and 1985 he did postgraduate work at the University of London and is presently the Chairman of General Education at a Christian college in Louisiana. A prolific writer, he has had over 25 scholarly articles and 200 poems published in various periodicals, and over the past years has had more than 20 novels published. His family includes three grown children, and he and his wife live in Baton Rouge, Louisiana.

CONTENTS

THE
HOUSE OF WINSLOW

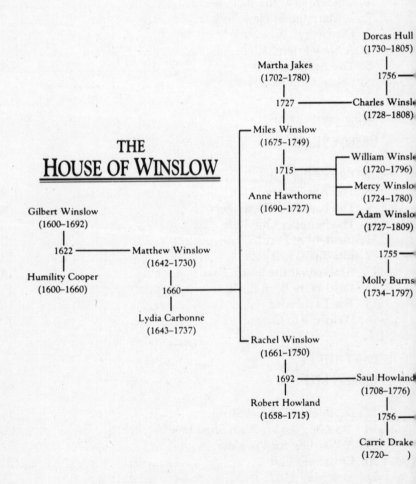

Dorcas Hull
(1730–1805)

1756 ——

Martha Jakes
(1702–1780)

1727 ———— Charles Winsl[e]
(1728–1808)

Miles Winslow
(1675–1749)

William Winsl[e]
(1720–1796)

1715 ——

Mercy Winslo[w]
(1724–1780)

Anne Hawthorne
(1690–1727)

Adam Winslo[w]
(1727–1809)

Gilbert Winslow
(1600–1692)

1755 ——

1622 ———— Matthew Winslow
(1642–1730)

Molly Burns
(1734–1797)

Humility Cooper
(1600–1660)

1660 ——

Lydia Carbonne
(1643–1737)

Rachel Winslow
(1661–1750)

1692 ———— Saul Howland
(1708–1776)

Robert Howland
(1658–1715)

1756 ——

Carrie Drake
(1720–   )

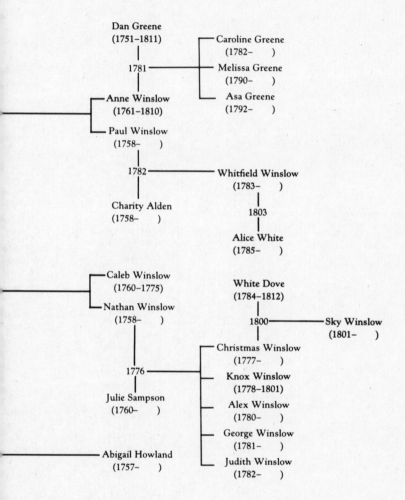

PART ONE

NEW YORK

★ ★ ★ ★

CHAPTER ONE

CINDERELLA AT THE BALL

★ ★ ★ ★

Heavy brass lanterns cast a pale yellow light over the carriages that moved slowly down the long driveway leading to the governor's mansion. The Governor's Spring Ball, traditionally held on April first of each year, generally enjoyed mild weather; but the winter of 1838 had been unusually severe. A late blast of northern air had swept down the month before, paralyzing the whole countryside. The snow had melted a week before the ball, but a raw, cold wind lingered on.

A rush of frigid air probed inside the ornate carriage standing second in line. Rebekah Jackson shivered at its icy touch. Across from her in the carriage sat her cousin Nora Bayless, watching Rebekah's nervousness with amusement and a hint of disdain in her greenish eyes. Nora's father, a wealthy factory owner and member of the House of Representatives, had spoiled his daughter all her life, which only encouraged the aggressive spirit she had inherited from him. Nora smiled at her cousin's obvious agitation.

"Are you cold, Rebekah—or just excited?"

"I—I think I should have worn my own dress, Nora." A thread of uncertainty ran through the young woman's voice as she looked down at her low-cut gown. "This is beautiful, but it's too—"

"Too daring?"

"Perhaps not for *you*, Nora. But I feel . . . almost . . . *undressed!*"

"Oh, Rebekah, don't be silly! It's not immodest at all! You'll see women wearing dresses far more dashing than that." Nora laughed at her cousin's flustered face; and as their carriage rolled up to the front door, she added, "*I'm* the one who ought to be worried! All the men will be so busy trying to meet you that I won't have a chance. Now—let's go. You just forget your staid puritan ways and be the belle of the ball, you hear?"

There was no time to argue. As soon as a black servant dressed in livery opened the door and helped them out of the carriage, Nora led the way inside where another servant took their cloaks. The foyer was ablaze with lights, and the enchanting music filtering from the large ballroom that lay beyond the double doors beckoned them toward its source. As they entered the room, filled with laughter and the steady hum of voices, Rebekah remained near the doorway, looking miserable and uncertain. Nora, however, was immediately swept into conversation with a group of her friends. Then noticing her cousin's reluctance, she broke away from them and came to stand beside Rebekah.

"Now, let me look at you one more time," Nora commanded. Standing back to admire her handiwork, she thought how strange it was that this simple girl should be here. She certainly didn't fit in with all the wealthy and important people there under the glittering lights!

Rebekah Jackson was the daughter of Nora's mother's brother, but the two had met only once, at a family reunion when they both were children. Nora had been angry when her mother had told her that she would have to take the girl to the ball. "But—Mother! I can't take that blue-nosed Puritan!" This opinion had been formed in her by her father, who invariably called his brother-in-law by that epithet.

Spoiled as she was, this was one time Nora did not get her way. "Your father doesn't want to offend my brother," her mother had shrugged. "It's a political thing, Nora. Rebekah's father is becoming quite powerful in his part of the state, and your father needs his help with the next election. Rebekah will only stay for a week, and it won't kill you to entertain her for that long—nor to take her to the ball with you."

"She's probably ugly as a toad!" Nora had grumbled, and had prepared herself to be as distant as possible to the girl. When her cousin arrived for her visit, however, Nora had been pleasantly surprised. Rebekah was quiet, but had a keen wit that lay just beneath the surface. In the two days before the ball, Nora had grown very fond of her, especially once she discovered that Rebekah had led a life more restricted than Nora could ever imagine. Nora knew that her uncle was a strict man, but when she found out that Rebekah had never been to a ball, did not know how to dance, used no cosmetics, and had never been left alone with a young man, Nora stared as if her cousin were an alien creature.

"That's *medieval*, Rebekah!" she exclaimed. "Why, you're not much better off than a slave!"

Rebekah said quietly, "Well, Nora, my sister—" She hesitated, then began again. "My sister Louise was wild. She ran away with a man, and it was terrible for my parents. Father *is* protective—maybe too much so. He just doesn't want anything to happen to the rest of us."

Nora was indignant, but held her tongue, determined to say no more—until she saw the plain brown dress that Rebekah had brought to wear to the ball. In an instant a scheme leaped into Nora's mind, and she vowed to make Rebekah's first ball one the girl would never forget. Plunging into the task with her usual enthusiasm, she insisted that Rebekah wear one of her own dresses and some of her jewelry. Rebekah had protested at first, but was soon caught up by Nora's eagerness—until now. Now she stood uncertainly, confused by the lights and the music, and wishing she'd never come!

Nora's critical eye surveyed the young woman of twenty—slender but well-formed, wearing a bright emerald dress that set off her abundant auburn hair. Rebekah's eyes were large and of an unusual hazel hue, which exactly matched the stone that hung on a golden chain around her neck. She had an oval face with a wide, provocative mouth, and her bare arms were smooth and creamy under the lights. *Beautiful!* Nora breathed, well aware that it was not the young woman's shapely figure nor her attractive face that made her so attractive, but the air of vulnerability that enveloped her.

"Come on, Cinderella," Nora laughed. "It's time for you to find the prince and set him on his ear!"

As they moved into the ballroom, Rebekah giggled. "If my father saw me wearing this dress, I wouldn't have to wait until midnight to become a poor, ragged girl! He'd take care of that!"

Nora led her around the room toward the large tables covered with food and drinks, her eyes scanning the room as they went. Nora soon found what she was looking for. "There's Robert," she said, and moved toward two men who were standing beside the tables, talking. Rebekah looked at them with interest, for Nora had talked of little else than the charm of Robert St. Cloud. *"He's going to marry me—but he doesn't know it yet,"* Nora had confided to Rebekah. Now she whispered, "I'll have Robert introduce you to that handsome man he's talking to."

"Oh no! Please!" Rebekah gasped, but it was no use. Nora pulled her up to the pair and introduced her to St. Cloud, who bowed and murmured, "A pleasure, Miss Jackson." He gestured toward his companion, saying, "Nora, you haven't met my new associate—Tyler Marlowe. Marlowe, this is Miss Nora Bayless and her cousin, Miss Jackson."

"A pleasure." Marlowe was a tall man of about thirty. He had a florid complexion and a pair of sharp black eyes. His lips were full and red under a trim mustache, and he smiled easily. "If I'd known the ladies of Virginia were so attractive, I'd have come here much sooner."

Nora responded easily, but the compliment had brought a glow to Rebekah's cheeks. She avoided his gaze, uneasily hoping that she could retire to a secluded corner. Instead, she heard Marlowe say, "Miss Jackson, may I have this dance?"

"Oh, I—I'm not a dancer," Rebekah stammered.

"I'm sure you're just being modest. In any case, I'm a good teacher." Somehow Rebekah found herself on the dance floor. Marlowe put one arm lightly around her, and she followed his lead as they moved among the dancers.

Nora and St. Cloud watched the pair until St. Cloud glanced down and caught Nora's expression. He laughed. "Nora, you're looking at Tyler as if he is the wolf that's taken your only chick."

"That's not far wrong, Robert. You have no idea how *green* that girl is. Her father's kept her locked up like a nun. If my father had done that to me, I'd have blown my brains out!"

"More likely you'd have blown *his* brains out," her friend chuckled. Then he glanced at the pair again and mused, "I don't know much about Marlowe. He's got some leases on land in Georgia that may turn out well."

"Well, *I* can tell you something about Mr. Tyler Marlowe," Nora said. "He's a man who chases women!"

"You think so?"

"Why, he almost drew a bead on Rebekah, didn't you see? I could handle him, but poor girl—she's never seen any like him."

Robert St. Cloud straightened up, nervously fingering his cravat. "Well, then, perhaps I'd better go give the poor girl some protection."

Nora smirked. "You! That'd be like letting the fox guard the hen house. No, I'll take Mr. Marlowe's attention from Rebekah."

"The devil you will!" said St. Cloud ferociously. "The fellow may be only the second best-looking chap in the room, but I'd still not trust him around my woman!"

Nora liked his possessive air and, allowing him to pull her to the dance floor, she observed casually, "Well, I don't suppose he can *steal* her, can he? We'll keep an eye on them." But despite her good intentions, as the evening wore on she lost herself in the gaiety of the party. From time to time she remembered Rebekah with a slight feeling of concern. *She's having a good time,* she told herself, catching sight of the pair laughing over something at the tables. *Let her shake off her chains for once!*

Marlowe's easy familiarity would have warned most women, but Rebekah was not like most women. Her inexperience with men prevented her from sensing the danger; she only knew that it was easy to talk with him, and she was having the best time of her entire life. Now as she looked up at him, her hazel eyes wide, she told him of how she had come to visit Nora. For his part, Marlowe found himself strangely drawn to her innocence. He was a man who knew women well; ordinarily he preferred women who were as wise in the ways of the world as he. But this girl fascinated him—more than most women he had met before. He redoubled his efforts to charm her, to win her over.

After all, it was a game to him, and he enjoyed the chase. If he lost, he lost with good grace—but he did not lose often.

Deftly he extracted her history, marveling that a woman of twenty could be at the same time so innocent and so beautiful. But innocent she was, which was further evidenced by the fact that she had taken three drinks with no idea that they had brightened her eyes and relaxed the rigidity which had bound her at the couple's first meeting. *Probably thinks it's lemonade,* he thought wryly.

Several times women in the room glanced at him with an expression he well knew to be an invitation. More than once he almost responded—but there was something about the girl that challenged him. Rebekah's simple joy in the party and her trusting eyes appealed strongly to him.

After many dances, he said, "It's warm in here. Would you like to get a breath of air?"

"Oh, I don't know, Mr. Marlowe. . . !"

"Tyler, not Mr. Marlowe," he corrected. "Just for a few minutes. It'll clear our heads."

He skillfully guided her through the French doors that led outside, to an extremely large room filled with many plants and a grape arbor—apparently a greenhouse. The music was muted as he closed the doors. Turning to her, he saw that she was shivering. "You're cold, Rebekah," he said, taking off his coat and putting it around her shoulders. It gave her an odd feeling to wear the coat as they slowly strolled along the wide walk.

She said little, but he spoke with ease, telling her of his travels, which seemed marvelous to her. They came to a cast iron garden bench, and he suggested, "Let's sit down for a while. You must be tired." He was careful not to touch her, but as he talked, he allowed his arm to go around the back of the bench and brush her shoulder. "Have you traveled much, Rebekah?"

"Oh no. I've never been anywhere!"

"I'd like to show you a few things." He smiled down at her. The moonlight reflected like silver in her eyes, and he had never seen anything more lovely than the line of her throat and her provocative lips. "You'd enjoy it, I think, in Venice. The streets are canals, and I'd like to take you down one of them. It's so beautiful there! The boatmen usually sing—nothing quite like it anywhere else."

"It sounds so wonderful!"

"You should see it—or rather you should let Venice see *you*!" With a single motion he reached out and pulled her around to face him. "I mean, Rebekah, a beautiful woman has no right to keep herself locked up. She needs to be seen—like a rare diamond!"

She dropped her eyes, not knowing how to respond. *First time a man ever told her she was beautiful,* he thought, and then she looked up and for one moment she was open and vulnerable. The drinks had broken down her natural defenses, and now in the moonlight she was stirred by a longing she had never before allowed herself to feel. The thousand cords of the strict code her well-meaning parents had placed around her loosened—and now, for the first time, she caught a glimpse of freedom she had not known existed.

Her lips opened slightly, and he saw her eyes filled with longing. Easily, he pulled her toward him and kissed her.

The power of his arms around her and the sudden touch of his lips stirred her with a mixture of fear and excitement. The few fleeting kisses of her life had been nothing like this, and she felt herself trembling wildly. She knew she should pull away, but instead she clung to him, kissing him back.

Finally she drew back, whispering, "Please—let me go!"

He released her at once, and found himself shaken as he had not been for years. The dewy youth, the innocent trust, and the hint of an eager passion that lurked beneath that innocence took his breath away, robbing him of speech.

She rose, saying nervously, "I must go inside . . ."

Instinctively he knew he had gone too far. He stood up and took her hands, saying contritely, "Rebekah! Please forgive me—I can't imagine what I was thinking of!" He went on speaking until she was calmer. "You must think I'm an ogre or something!"

"No, Tyler," she said with a hint of a smile. "Not an ogre. I just think that you're too—experienced for me."

He saw that she was intelligent enough to read him in part. Laughing, he nodded ruefully. "Tried and found guilty! But you must give me a chance to redeem myself. Let me see you again. You'll be here for a week?"

"Yes, but—"

"There's a concert tomorrow. I insist on taking you."

"Oh, I couldn't possibly do that."

"Why, certainly you can," he answered. He began to persuade her, and by the time he put her into the coach with Nora, somehow she had agreed to accompany him the next evening.

"I'll pick you up at seven," he said, then smiled and closed the door.

Nora remarked dryly as they drove away, "You and Mr. Marlowe became friends very rapidly."

"He's very nice."

Nora said no more until later that night. Entering Rebekah's room, she was caught by an odd sense of apprehension at the sight of the girl looking so small in an old-fashioned gown. Nora put her arm around her cousin and said, "Rebekah, be careful. Tyler's not your kind of man."

"You don't think I should go to the concert?"

Nora hesitated, then replied, "I don't see any harm in it. You'll be here only a week, and God knows you deserve a good time. I just say—be careful."

"I will, Nora. I'll be *very* careful." Rebekah was three years older than her cousin, but Nora felt a maternal protectiveness welling up inside of her. She wished the man had not been there, and she resolved to keep a close eye on Rebekah. Taking the kiss that Rebekah put on her cheek, she left the room, thinking, *It's only a week. Surely nothing can happen in a week.*

She slept poorly that night, wishing with all her heart that she had handled the affair better.

She wished it even more by the end of the week, for Marlowe had taken Rebekah out every night. Nora had tried more than once to tell the girl that it was improper, but there was always a quick defense in Rebekah's answer.

"It's only this week, Nora—then I'll be going home. I'll never see him again."

Nora had talked to Robert, but he only said, "I don't know what I can do, Nora. I don't know the man, really, except in a business way—and not very well at that!"

A sense of foreboding would not leave Nora, and she tried to warn Rebekah, who would not listen. "Oh, Nora, it's so sad! Tyler was married six years ago, but his wife died in childbirth—

her first." Tears gathered in her eyes, and she whispered, "He's so lonely, Nora!"

"He's too good-looking to be lonely, Rebekah."

"He is handsome, isn't he?"

It was all so awkward—and Nora felt responsible for at least some of the problem. Clearing her throat, she said, "Rebekah . . . I know you're a good girl. But Tyler's a man of the world. It would be tragic if you . . ." She floundered, then said angrily, "Well, has he tried to make love to you? I'd be surprised if he hadn't!"

Rebekah's eyes flashed, and she retorted defiantly, "Yes—he tried once. But when I told him that I couldn't do—such a thing, it never happened again!"

Nora gently laid a hand on her cousin's shoulder. "I'm just worried about you, Rebekah! You're so . . . so young!"

"I'm older than you are, Nora!" For once Rebekah spoke with a trace of anger, and she shrugged off Nora's hand. "I'm twenty years old, and very likely will wind up an old maid—unless my father marries me off to a rich widower with three children as he tried to do with Louise."

"Your sister? The one who ran away?"

"Yes." The anger went out of her, leaving a mist of misery in her eyes. "She writes every year, Nora—and my father tears the letters up without opening them." She sighed. "These few days are all I have, Nora. I'm going to go with Tyler until Friday. Then I'll get on a coach and ride out of his life. And I'll hate these days forever—because I never knew that life could be so—" She broke off and flung herself on the bed, weeping.

Nora stared at her helplessly, then left the room.

All week Nora yearned for Friday to come so that she could sleep again. But when Friday came, she was totally unprepared for what happened.

After breakfast Nora went upstairs to have a last talk with her cousin. Rebekah had been very quiet at the meal and her face was paler than usual. She found the girl all packed and standing at the window looking out at the blooming apple trees.

"All packed?" Nora asked brightly. She went over and put her arm around the other, saying fondly, "It's been so good to have you, Rebekah! I want you to come back very soon. I'm writing to tell your parents that we must—"

"Nora, I'm going to marry Tyler." Rebekah turned and her face was swollen from weeping. There was a sadness in her eyes, but a defiant light as well. Cutting off Nora's protest, she added, "We're going to New York to be married—and there's nothing you or anyone else can say to stop me."

Nora felt as if the world had suddenly dropped away. "Rebekah, this isn't right! Your parents—have you thought of them?"

"Yes. They'll tear up my letters—just like they tear up my sister's—but I'm in love with Tyler. Even though there's no way my father would have him as a son-in-law."

"But you don't *know* Tyler, Rebekah!"

"I know he loves me!" There was a sound of a carriage drawing up, and she looked out the window. "There he is—I'm going."

Putting her arms around her cousin, she said, "I'm sorry for putting you through this, Nora. It's awful of me—but it's my one chance at happiness!" She tore herself away, picked up her bag and fled from the room. Nora heard the front door slam and she went to the window. Marlowe stood waiting, and Rebekah ran to him. He put his arms around her, said something, then helped her into the coach. Nora could see that Rebekah was still weeping.

She turned from the window, feeling sick, and trembling so hard that she had to sit down on the bed. Tears of angry frustration filled her eyes. It was the first time she'd ever wept for anyone else, and all she could think of was: *Rebekah—you don't even know him!*

CHAPTER TWO

A MARRIAGE IN NEW YORK

★ ★ ★ ★

Rebekah looked down at the counter, comparing the items piled there with the list in her hand. "I think that's all, Mr. Laughton," she said. "What does everything come to?"

The storekeeper was a tall, thin man with a large nose and sharp blue eyes. He touched each item with a bony finger as he quoted the price. "Well, now, Mrs. Marlowe, the milk's two cents for the quart, two pounds of beef at six cents a pound, one chicken for eighteen cents, four pigeons at one cent apiece; the pickled herring comes to five cents, and the oysters exactly twelve cents." He tallied the figures on a pad quickly. "That comes to fifty-three cents. Will there be anything else?"

"Oh yes, I do need some ink powder."

"Ah!" Laughton turned and pulled a small green bottle off the shelf. "Now here's something you might like to try—bottled ink." He handed it up to her, adding, "Nothing I hate worse than mixing up ink powder! Always get it too thin or full of lumps. Only five cents for that bottle."

"What won't they think of next!" Rebekah marveled. As she held the bottle up to the light, the storekeeper gave her an approving glance. She was a good customer, quiet and uncomplaining. He remembered the first time she'd come into his store three months ago—a brand new bride. Her husband had brought her in and said, "You must let this lady have anything she wants, Mr. Laughton. We've just gotten married this morning, and she'll be a regular customer!"

She had been wearing a dowdy dress on that first day, Laughton remembered, but now she looked stylish in one of the outfits he had sold her from his own stock. The first three months of her marriage had already worked their magic, giving her an air of confidence she hadn't possessed before.

Today she had come in wearing a blue silk bonnet tied with ribbon under her chin and a sage green cloak, which she had set aside to do her shopping. Her bell-shaped skirt, made of dark linsey-woolsey, was stiffened by whalebone stays sewed into the skirt itself—without a hoop. Her green silk bodice was plentifully supplied with lace on the collar and the sleeves. The skirt was not long; it showed about three inches of leg above the shoe tops—a new fashion that had taken New York by storm. On her feet were delicate high-heeled shoes made of damask.

"Your husband still away on business?" Laughton asked, putting the groceries in a sack.

"Oh, no, he came back just yesterday." She put her cloak and hat on and left the shop. Walking briskly along the streets, she paid little heed to the noise and the bustle around her. It had taken her a few weeks to get accustomed to the big city, but Tyler had kept her at such a pace that now she felt at home.

For Rebekah, New York was a tremendous change from the quiet, even pace of her small southern hometown. She had accompanied Tyler everywhere, the two of them laughing over the wave of curiosities that were sweeping the city. They had gone to peep shows, wax figure displays, and dozens of other things. He had practically dragged her to see a "Female Samson," an Indian woman who, lying down, could support the weight of six men standing on her body. Another time they had viewed a creature that was billed as a "living alligator, four feet long."

She had quickly discovered that Tyler could not be still. She would have loved to spend quiet evenings at home with him, but he rarely would agree. He was an inveterate gambler, and Rebekah spent many evenings alone while he pursued cards, billiards and backgammon. Racing meets, horse races, bowling matches, cock fighting—he was interested in all of these. Concerned, Rebekah had asked once, "But, Tyler, you can lose lots of money gambling, can't you?"

"I don't lose, sweet—not in the long run." He had grinned at her, then given her a quick kiss. "I may lose for a time—but my luck always comes along, and I make a killing. Never fails!"

She turned off High Street with all its busy shops into a narrow lane lined on both sides with houses. The July heat had been soaked up by the bricks paving the street, and now they sent up waves that made the straight lines of the houses seem to quiver. As always, she had a quick surge of pride as she turned down the walk to her own house, which was as rigidly rectangular as a barn, without any projecting wings, bow windows, or architectural frills of any kind. Plain as it was, when Tyler had brought her from the hotel after a week and said, "This is your new home, Rebekah!" she had loved it. He had rented it for what seemed to her an astronomical figure, but laughed at her protests. "I'll have you in a palace one day," he'd promised.

Before she went inside, Rebekah spoke briefly to Mrs. Vander-Welt, who was working in her flower garden. The high-ceilinged rooms were cool, and she went straight to the large kitchen to put the groceries in the larder. Tyler was still asleep, but he would want a hot breakfast when he awoke. She started to make a fire, but after fashioning a small pile of shavings on the grate of the huge fireplace, she discovered that she had carelessly snuffed all the candles. "Oh, blazes!" she grumbled and rose to get the fire maker. Holding the flint over the lint and wood shavings, she pulled the trigger of the fire maker, which struck the flint, causing a spark to fall. She blew on the smoldering pile until a tiny tongue of white smoke curled up, then burst into flame. Soon the cedar was crackling, releasing a pungent odor.

While she waited for Tyler to awaken, she picked up a book and read at the oak table. It was a book one of Tyler's friends had loaned him, *The Nun, or the Perjured Beauty*, written by a woman with the unlikely name of Aphra Behn. Rebekah read for ten minutes, then snorted and put it down, "What nonsense!" Reaching into her pocket, she once again pulled out the white envelope that had arrived at the post the day before, and reread the letter inside with a sad smile on her face.

Replacing the envelope into her pocket, she roamed the

house restlessly for about an hour longer until it was time to awaken Tyler. He was stretched out on his back, his mouth open, and she had to shake him out of a deep slumber. He groaned, but finally said with some irritation, "All right, Rebekah! I'm up! I'm up!"

"Go shave and I'll have breakfast all ready by the time you have finished." She went back and made grits, battered eggs, and bacon. She put a bright yellow tablecloth on the table, then thoughtfully placed a bowl of yellow daisies in the center. Bringing the steaming plates to the table, she set them down and stepped back to admire her work, turning as Tyler came in. "Aren't the flowers gorgeous?"

"Beautiful," he said sleepily. "Just like you!" He grinned and came to give her a hug and a kiss. She recognized the smell of his breath—he had already had a drink that morning—but she said nothing. Stepping back, he reached into the pocket of his robe. "Got an anniversary present for you while I was in Boston."

"Why, our anniversary won't be until April!"

"This is for our third anniversary, sweet. Three months of gloriously happy married life!"

"You are crazy!" Rebekah smiled, but was pleased. "What is it?"

"You can take it out of my pocket."

She reached in and felt something with a rough hairy surface about the size of a fist. "What in the world—?" She pulled it out, then took one look and dropped it with a disgusted cry. "Tyler!"

He gave a whoop of laughter, scooped it up, and held it in one hand. "You don't like it? But it's a genuine shrunken human head from Brazil." He stared at the grisly article, adding, "Look at how perfect the features are! Wonder how they got the skull out?"

"It's awful!"

His eyes gleamed with humor as he put the head up on the mantel. Turning back to her, he pulled a small box from his other pocket. "Well, you've scorned my first gift—maybe this will please you a little more."

She took the small box, opened it cautiously, then looked up with wide eyes. "Why, Tyler!" She took out the large glittering butterfly shaped pin and stared at it. "I've never seen anything so beautiful! But you shouldn't have spent so much!"

"Had a good night at the card table in Boston," he informed her. Pinning it on, he took her in his arms and kissed her again. His hands moved along her back. "Never thought I'd get so foolish over a Little Puritan Maid."

That was his pet name for her—ever since they had left Virginia. He had used it on their first night when they stopped at an inn. He had asked for one room, but she had whispered, "Tyler—I can't stay in the room with you. Not until we're married!"

He had stared at her with mingled amusement and surprise as if such a thing had never occurred to him—which it had not! "My Little Puritan Maid! We'll get married soon—but we can't tonight."

For the rest of the trip she had steadfastly refused to share a room with him, showing him a side of her character that had brought him up short. When she had agreed to go to New York with him, he had remarked carelessly that they ought to get married—although he had no intention of actually doing so!

He had almost left her, but she was a challenge to him, and her fresh, delicate beauty had so drawn him that he had not been able to go. Finally, when he took a room in a hotel in New York and she had once more staunchly refused to share it with him, he stormed out angrily, leaving her alone. The next day he returned with a minister and a marriage license.

Now he thought of that with a smile. "It seems we've been married forever—but you're sweeter than ever, my Little Puritan!"

She lifted her face and took his kiss, and she, too, thought of that day when he had come with the minister. She remembered how happy she'd been—Tyler's careless attitude toward marriage shocked her. Having been reared in a home where adultery was something not even mentioned, Rebekah had never imagined anything but marriage was in store for her. When Tyler had returned with Rev. Lowell Johnson, she was tremendously relieved. Granted, the minister was a little seedy—Tyler explained that the man was just passing through on his way to New England. In any case, he had married them, and from that time on she had surrendered herself to Tyler with a reckless passion that had shocked them both.

Now he kissed her again, drew back and said, "The butterfly? Just a trifle, sweet." He sat down, and as they ate breakfast, he told her of his trip. He called himself an "importer," though Rebekah never understood his profession very well. "I buy low and sell high," he had laughingly explained once as she tried to figure it out. "Things are cheap in the Orient, and they're expensive here—so I buy there and sell here."

"It sounds so easy, Tyler," she had said in a puzzled voice. It all made her somewhat uncomfortable, for she was accustomed to stability. Her own father always went to work at nine and came home at six. His business did not change, and there was a rock-like security to it. But Tyler came and went with baffling irregularity. He would announce at breakfast, "I'm going to Philadelphia, Rebekah. Be back in a couple of days." At other times he would not work at all for a week, and the two of them would spend the time going to plays, races, or anything else that took his fancy.

The way they lived troubled her, and he knew it. But he also knew his own nature, and had quickly realized that although Rebekah longed for a world that had rules, he could not give it to her. Instead, he bought her things and kept her in a whirl of activities, hoping to distract her from the situation.

Now as he looked across the table, he saw that the gladness had once again gone out of her. "What's wrong?"

She shook her head sadly. "Oh, I got a letter from David yesterday." Her seventeen-year-old brother had written her several times since she had left. In his first letter he had explained how he knew where to find her: *Father tore your letter up—just as he has done with Louise's. But I pulled the pieces out of the trash and got your address. Father won't let your name be spoken, but I still love you, Rebekah.* She had no way to write him, but each time she got a letter, it numbed her spirit.

"No good news, I suppose?" Tyler asked. "Well, he'll change his mind when I take you back in diamonds."

"No, he won't." The words were stark, and he knew that she was speaking the truth. Not wanting to face it, he restlessly rose and said, "Get dressed, Rebekah. We'll go to the races—and there's a new troop of actors in town." He pulled her to her feet and kissed her gently. He had grown fond of her, and in his own selfish way, he longed to ease her unhappiness.

That week Rebekah had little time to think of home. Tyler moved around New York, spending money as if it were water, despite her protests. "Money is to spend," he told her. "When this is gone—why, I'll just make some more! It's that simple, so let me worry about money and just have a good time! There's my Little Puritan!"

The long, hot summer was rudely evicted in September by fall, and fled so abruptly that the wood-sellers were caught off guard. The price of firewood shot up as the temperatures went down.

One evening at dinner, Rebekah said, "They brought the firewood today, Tyler, but it cost us dearly."

When she told him how much she'd had to pay, his face grew livid. "I won't pay the thieves!" he shouted, cursing as he stalked around the room. "We'll leave this house—it costs a fortune to keep it up!"

"Oh, I'd hate to leave! We can cut down on expenses—"

"No, we've got to move!" he snapped. "We just rattle around in this big barn. I've already found us an apartment. Wanted to surprise you," he said, making an attempt to cover his anger. "I've found a nice little place over in the Bowery. You'll like it—you work yourself to death here."

"All right, Tyler," she replied quietly.

They moved the next week. She never let him know how hard it was for her to leave the house, for the apartment was small and in a section of town that was filled with working families—many of them foreigners. Saloons and gambling houses dotted the area, and Rebekah became afraid to go out after dark.

Tyler grew restless, and for the first time since their marriage, he became morose. Many nights he would not come home until almost dawn—and he was drinking far too much. From time to time he would look at her with regret, saying, "This is a rough time for both of us, Rebekah—but I'll pull out of it. I always have."

She realized his money problems depressed him, and she

asked, "Your business is going badly?"

"Rotten! Never saw anything like it!" He suddenly looked sheepish and bit his lip. "I hate to ask it, Rebekah—but I'm going to have to raise all the money I can for a big deal. I'll have to pawn your jewelry—just for a few days."

"Of course," she said, and got all the pieces he had given her—including the butterfly broach, which she hated to part with.

He took them, and his natural effervescence bubbled up. "Just wait until I get back! I'll put diamonds on your fingers you won't believe!"

"Maybe we can save a little," she smiled. He kissed her, and soon he was gone.

After he had been gone for three days, she ran completely out of cash. She had no money set aside for emergencies like this—Tyler never gave her much money at one time. Now she had no money even for food, and she was beginning to get frightened.

He came back the next day. She heard the door slam, and went to find him standing in the middle of the floor; one look told her that he was in trouble. His clothes were wrinkled and soiled, and his face was a sickly yellow-gray.

"Tyler!" she cried and ran to him, but was repelled by the strong smell of stale tobacco and whiskey. She put her arms around him. "Are you all right? I've been so worried!"

His red-rimmed eyes seemed to have trouble focusing on her. He licked his lips, and his voice was thick as he answered her. "Got to get some sleep!" Pushing her away, he stumbled to the bedroom where he fell across the bed, instantly asleep.

She undressed him and went out for a walk, knowing from past experience that he would not wake up until the next day. The chilling breeze stiffened her, but she walked for a long time, not knowing what else to do. She had no close friends, nobody to talk to—and she knew she could not approach any of those in their social circle for help.

The sky was gray and stiff; dead stalks were all that remained of the flowers as she walked along the street. The three days she'd spent alone had drained her natural buoyancy, and she dreaded facing Tyler the next day. What she had to say would not be welcome, she knew. For the first time since she'd left her home, she tried to pray, but could not form the words. Returning to the house, she went through Tyler's clothing and found a few dollars—enough to buy food. She spent the money carefully, then went back to the apartment to sleep on the couch for the night.

She slept fitfully, rising at dawn to make a fire in the small fireplace. There was only a little coffee, but she fixed a pot and drank the brew as she waited for him to awaken. It was nearly ten before she heard him groan, and she quickly made breakfast.

He came in from the bedroom, and she said brightly, "Come on, Tyler. Let's eat before the food gets cold."

"Gotta hava drink," he mumbled. Going to the cabinet, he pulled a brown bottle down and put it to his lips, not bothering to pour the whiskey into a glass. He shuddered, then took another drink before coming to slump down at the table.

She put the bacon and eggs on his plate, set it in front of him and patted his shoulder. "This will make you feel better."

He stared silently at her with bloodshot eyes. They ate the food, and she filled his cup with the last of the coffee. When he had finished, he laid his fork down. "I hit bottom, Rebekah." His hands trembled and there was a raw fear in his eyes that she'd never seen. "Do you understand? I lost everything!"

She tried to smile and reached over to put her hand on his. "It's all right, Tyler. We'll get by."

"Never saw such rotten luck!" He took several swallows of coffee nervously. "Don't know what to do." Dejectedly, he set his cup down, swept aside the dishes and put his head down on the table.

Rebekah was frightened; she had never seen her husband like this before. Still, he was her husband, and for half an hour she tried to raise his spirits, talking to him in low and soothing tones as he sat there with his head down.

Finally he seemed to arouse himself. Lifting his head, he gave her a crooked grin. "You're a good girl, Rebekah!"

She took a deep breath and said, "Tyler—I'm going to have a baby."

The grin evaporated, replaced first by disbelief—then anger. Cursing, he leaped up from the table and began pacing around the room before coming to stand over her, his face livid.

She said nothing, holding her head high as he raved on, until she heard him say, "We'll have to get rid of it. I know a man—"

"No! I'll never do that! Never!"

He stared at her, then said bitterly, "I should never have married you, Rebekah. How could you be so stupid! We can't take care of a baby—I may have to leave the country to make a living!"

"It won't be too hard, Tyler," she said. "I can work. We'll make it."

"You'll have to write your family. They've got money!"

"I'll never do that, Tyler," she answered softly, rising from the table. Tyler followed her around the apartment for an hour, alternately pleading and threatening, but nothing worked. At last he threw on his coat. "I'm leaving," he said in a tight, barely controlled voice. "When I come back, you'd better have your mind made up to do something about this little surprise of yours! I won't be tied down, Rebekah!"

The door slammed. She went to the window to watch him leave, his back stiff and his face a grim mask of anger. He did not look back once before he turned the corner. A sudden gust of wind loosened the dead leaves from the oak outside her window, and they fell heavily to the earth. She stared at them listlessly for a long time, then turned and left the window.

CHAPTER THREE

DISCOVERY

★ ★ ★ ★

On the fourth day of December New York was buried under snow. All night long, flakes large as half cents and almost as heavy dropped out of the skies; and when morning came, people had to burrow—like small animals—out of their homes through the shoulder-high drifts.

Rebekah got up at dawn, shivered in the aching cold of the small room as she hastily drew on her robe and slippers before going to the window. There the view of the glittering world outside drew a muffled cry of admiration from her; for the grimy neighborhood, stained with smoke and cluttered with leaning outhouses and piles of trash, had been transformed into a gleaming wonderland. The trash piles were no longer jagged with broken bottles; they were smoothly rounded hills, glistening like diamond fragments reflecting the rays of the rosy morning sun. The street itself was freshly covered, without a mark on its immaculate surface. Along the eaves of every house, glittering icicles pointed downward with dagger-sharpness to the pristine glory of the snow.

Rebekah sighed, then resolutely turned to make a fire in the tiny fireplace that served them for heat and cooking. She lit the wood shavings with a candle stub in a small lid that floated in a pan of water, adding tiny pieces of wood until a blaze began to crackle. Putting on two larger sticks, she noted that there were only five more in the woodbox—not enough to heat the room all day. Holding her stiff hands over the tiny fire, she glanced toward Tyler, sleeping soundly in the bed, and wondered if he had enough money to buy more wood and a few groceries.

Probably not, she thought as she rose and looked into the food box nailed to the wall. *He'd have told me last night if he'd won.* There were three eggs in the rough cabinet. *One for me, and two for him*, she decided. There was enough coffee for the day, but no bread. *Have to have crackers—there's a few left.*

The thought of their early days came to her as she put the meager breakfast together, but she resolutely pushed the memory away. Putting the kettle on the small grate over the fire, she waited until it whistled. "Tyler? Breakfast will be ready soon."

He groaned, opened his eyes, then shuddered as he threw the covers back and put his feet on the cold floor. He lifted them instantly, swore, and hunted for his socks among the bedclothes. "Your shaving water is hot," Rebekah told him.

"Why shave?" he grunted. "Nobody's going to see me."

Rebekah was tempted to suggest that he see if there was any work available, but she held her tongue. She had mentioned a job to him once, and he had cursed and slammed out of the house, coming back to the room only when he was so drunk he could barely walk.

He had been forced to sell most of his fine clothes—and hers as well. He kept only two good suits, putting one of them on each night before he went to the tables or the races. The diamond ring he had worn on his left hand was gone, replaced by a cheap imitation stone. Helplessly Rebekah watched their possessions being sold off, little by little, and now they had reached the end. There was nothing left to sell. The apartment that had replaced the house was luxurious next to the places they had later moved to. Now they were cooped up in one tiny room on the second floor of a shabby hotel in one of the worst sections of the Bowery.

"Have to eat crackers this morning, I'm afraid," Rebekah said, trying to sound cheerful. "We've got some of that blackberry jam you like so much, though—it'll taste good on anything." They had only one small table beside the bed. She put his plate and coffee on it, then got her own plate and sat down in the other chair. "The snow's beautiful, isn't it? We never had snow much in Virginia—not like this, anyway. . . ."

She tried to get him to talk, but he only finished his breakfast quickly, then lit up a cigar and picked up a week-old newspaper. "Cold enough to freeze hell over!" was his only comment. She ate more slowly, watching him. She could not help but notice how the man had deteriorated. He had been one of the most fastidious men she had ever known, but no more. He had not shaved in two days and there was, of course, no way to bathe in the single room. His fingernails were ragged and dirt grimed the creases of his hands. He had been in the habit of going to a barber shop twice a week, but now his black hair was stiff with a cheap oil, and hung scruffily on the back of his neck.

What concerned her more than his physical appearance was his loss of spirit; she had not heard him laugh in weeks. Day by day he got up, left the hotel, and came home only when he was too tired and drunk to do anything else. There was none of the exuberance and forceful determination that he had possessed when they had met. Hard times had pared him down, leaving him fearful and uncertain.

He dressed hurriedly. "Here's a few dollars—better see if you can get some food and wood," he instructed, then stalked out of the room without saying goodbye. She went to the window and watched as he made his way down the street, struggling through the deep drifts.

She looked at the money, and tried to think of how best to spend it, but there was no way to make the money stretch that far. She dressed, then huddled over the dying fire, savoring the last warmth. By ten o'clock, the room was unbearably cold, so she put on her warmest clothes and left for the library, which had become her refuge against loneliness. It was now a refuge against the cold as well, and she looked forward to the heat radiating from the huge stoves, well-stoked with oak.

The sun was out, but by the time she completed the hour's walk to the library, she was exhausted and chilled to the bone. The shop owners had cleared off some of the snow from the sidewalks immediately in front of their establishments, but Rebekah's feet were soaked from wading through the deep drifts between shops.

She entered the large Grecian building with a sigh, going at once to warm herself beside one of the stoves. Her legs were trembling with fatigue, and Mr. Mayberry, one of the librarians, hurried over to her. "Why, Rebekah Marlowe!" he chided, "you've soaked your feet! You come back to my office right this minute!" She followed him to a small room with a desk and chair and a small stove. Pushing the chair closer to the heat, the white-haired old man beckoned to her. "Now, you sit down here and thaw out."

"Thank you," Rebekah said gratefully and settled wearily into the seat. Mayberry studied her a moment, his bright black eyes thoughtful. They had become well acquainted, for she had often spent the whole day there; he had been helpful finding books for her, recommending his own favorites. Several times he had insisted on serving her tea.

And so it was not strange that he did so now, saying, "Now, you get those wet stockings off and put them to dry in front of the stove. By the time they get dry, we'll have a late breakfast— tea and some of my wife's cakes I took with me this morning."

His kindness brought tears to her eyes, which she tried to blink back, not trusting herself to answer him aloud. He pretended not to notice. "Hurry now! I'm hungry!" he said gruffly, leaving the room quickly.

She pulled off her soaked shoes and put them close to the stove and watched the steam rise for a moment before hanging her stockings on another chair to dry, then settled herself back into the chair, holding her feet up to the delicious warmth. Slowly she thawed out, and twenty minutes later, she was able to put her stockings and shoes on, warm and dry as toast.

Mayberry entered with a tray. "All dried out? Good! Now then, it's time for high tea." The two of them cleared a place on his desk, and as he poured the rich India tea, the sharp aroma filled the small office. "Try some of that marmalade on the cakes, Rebekah," he urged. "My daughter's recipe. Delicious!"

As they ate he carried on a lively conversation, and his sharp eyes took in every detail as his mind probed for clues. Mayberry was a man of books, but he was even more a student of the humans who read them. He noticed that Rebekah's cheeks, so full and rosy that summer, were now pale and slightly sunken.

She had lost weight, and he later told his wife, "I think Rebekah's in trouble, Helen. She used to dress in the finest styles—but lately she's been wearing the same dress every day. I'm afraid there's some kind of problem."

As they sipped their tea he tactfully began to find out what he could, but he soon discovered she was not one to complain. When he asked about her husband, she hesitated. "His business isn't doing too well, Mr. Mayberry, but we expect it to pick up soon."

Out of work, Mayberry thought. To her, he said only, "Well, times are hard, but come spring, things will begin to hum again." He talked with her for half an hour longer, then said, "Why don't you stay in here, Rebekah? It's more comfortable than in the reading room. I've got a couple of books I'd like you to read. Let me get them for you." Without giving her a chance to answer, he rose and went out of the room, returning with two books in his hand.

"Have you read *The Deerslayer*?"

"No. I don't know it."

"It's written by a man named James Cooper," Mayberry said. "High adventure about the noble redskin. It *is* an amusing diversion—though I couldn't say how accurately he portrays the savages." Putting the book down, he handed her the second book, thinner than the first one and bound in red leather. "Now *this* is more to my taste, Rebekah—real life adventure!"

Opening it, she read aloud, *"The Journal of Gilbert Winslow."* Looking up, she asked, "Who is Gilbert Winslow, Mr. Mayberry?"

"Oh, he was one of the firstcomers on the *Mayflower*. He never became very famous, like John Bradford or Captain Miles Standish, but he was quite a man, Rebekah—quite a man!"

Rebekah leafed through the book and smiled. "I've never read a journal before. It seems like such a personal thing."

"Ah, that's *exactly* why I like them!" The librarian's eyes sparkled, and he spread his thin arms wide with excitement. "All the fiction that's sweeping the country . . . it's all very well. But when you compare it with *this* book"—he paused to nod at the book she held—"why, there's more life in those few pages than in a hundred novels! The blood and sweat of real men—such adventure and excitement!"

Sheepishly she asked, "Is there a love story in it?"

He smiled. "Of course! Gilbert Winslow could have married the daughter of the most powerful noble in all of England, but he chose to marry a poor girl named Humility Cooper—though not before they had endured many hardships, you understand." He paused and a pensive look crossed his face. "This country has changed, I'm afraid. Gilbert Winslow and the others on that ship suffered a great deal in order to accomplish something they thought was worthwhile: to find a place where they could worship God as they chose. I'm not sure they'd be too happy with what they'd find if they were alive today."

"But, people are free to worship in this country!"

"Yes. And they're just as free *not* to worship," he answered. He looked at her sharply. "If I may be so bold as to ask—are you a Christian, Rebekah?"

"Why, I've been a member of the church since I was ten years old!"

"That's not necessarily the same thing, Rebekah," Mayberry said quietly. "Think of it: the Pilgrim Fathers gave up everything to follow Christ—and most of us today just sit and warm pews! No, Gilbert Winslow would be pretty unhappy with us, I'm afraid."

She looked down at the book thoughtfully. It would be wonderful to learn about the Winslows. Raising her eyes, she said, "I'd like to read it."

He smiled and said, "Consider it a gift, then. That's my book, not the library's." Ignoring her protests, he bustled off, leaving her alone. She read all morning; when he checked on her at noon she thanked him again, her eyes shining. "It's the most interesting thing I've ever read in my life!"

"Ah!" he said approvingly, "I knew you'd like it. Who knows—you may meet one of his descendants someday. There are quite a few Winslows around—most of them in Boston, I think. Their family goes back to Gilbert Winslow. The Winslow Fur Company was quite a successful business in its day, I believe."

He insisted on taking her to the restaurant across the street for lunch. "I hate to eat alone! Come along, now. You must humor a grumpy old man!"

They had a pleasant meal; then they went back to the library and she read until nearly four. When she left, he waved her thanks away. "Come again tomorrow. We'll have tea—and talk some more about the Winslows!"

The snow had not melted, and there was a hint of more in the steely skies above her as she made her way back to the room. She stopped and spent the money Tyler had given her for a few groceries and wood, then hurried to get home before dark. He was not there, so she built a small fire and read until the flame burned down. As the embers died away, the chill soon penetrated the room, and having no more means of heat, she crawled into bed for warmth.

For a long time she could not sleep. An unsettled feeling gnawed at her, worse than the icy cold that gripped the room. She tried to pray, but the words seemed to flow into empty air as though she were talking to herself. *Are you a Christian?* Mr. Mayberry had asked. She had always taken her religion for granted; it had been good enough for her when things were going well, but now it seemed thin and ineffectual. She thought of Winslow's journal, and of the Pilgrims who had fled in a small boat on the open seas, risking their lives for the privilege of worship; she knew they'd had something she did not possess.

She drifted off to sleep, awakening when Tyler came in. He did not speak, but took off his shoes and came to bed, smelling of tobacco and whiskey—and Rebekah thought she could detect the stale odor of cheap perfume.

The next morning they were aroused by a loud knocking on the door, and as Tyler scrambled out of the bed, fumbling for his shoes, Rebekah managed to rise and put on her shoes and robe. The knocking was insistent, and Tyler angrily flung the door open. "What the. . . !" He halted abruptly as a man pushed by him and strode inside the room.

He was a man of middle height, thin but well dressed. He wore a plum-colored square-cut coat that reached to his knees and flared out from the waist downward. His knee breeches were made of black broadcloth, and his vest was dark yellow silk with a floral design on it, with lace ruffles on his shirt front and at his wrists. The sword buckled around his waist was barely visible beneath his open coat.

Pulling off a three-cornered hat, the stranger regarded Rebekah with obvious distaste, then whirled to confront her husband, who was still standing by the door. "Well, Tyler?"

Carefully Tyler shut the door, his face as pale as paper. Turning to face the man again, his voice wavered slightly as he spoke. "Phil—what are you doing here!"

"I might ask you the same." His thin brown face had an authoritative expression as he shook his head, saying wearily, "How many times is this, Tyler? Three?—Four?"

Angrily, Tyler approached the man, who was much smaller than he. "Get out of here, Phil! Nobody sent for you."

Phil gave him a direct look that seemed to halt Tyler in his tracks. "Let's not go through any more of your stories," the smaller man said. "Angela wants you back—God only knows why! You'll have to go."

"I'll do what I please, Phil!"

"No, you'll do what *I* please, Tyler, just like the last time—and the time before that."

Rebekah had enough. "Tyler, who is this man?"

Tyler stared at her, opened his mouth, but no words came out. With a look of sick helplessness in his eyes, Tyler lowered his gaze to the floor and let the other answer for him. "I'm Philip Moore, his brother-in-law. And who are you?"

"I'm his wife!" she retorted.

Moore's hard expression softened perceptibly at her answer. He looked at her closely, paused, then said gently, "My apologies, ma'am. I thought—" He broke off, then shot a bitter look at Tyler. "I'm sorry, but you are not legally married to this man," he informed her quietly. "He's married to my sister Angela. They have two children, and he's deserted her twice before."

A wave of fear crashed over Rebekah, and she felt sick. "Tyler? His story . . . it's not true, is it?"

He met her eyes wordlessly, confirming her worst fears. Her legs suddenly gave out, and she sat down hard on the bed, horrified.

Moore broke the shocked silence when his hand shot out and caught Tyler's face with a sharp crack. "You dog! Why didn't you just pick up a loose woman as you always did before?" Moore's face was livid, and he cursed Tyler with unbridled rage. Tyler touched the print of Moore's hand on his cheek, but made no attempt to defend himself. "I don't know! God help me—I don't know!" he whispered.

Disgusted, Moore turned away from him and spoke to Rebekah. "I've come to take him back to Baltimore. He'll go, of course." He looked around the tawdry room. "He always does when he gets to this point."

With a quick movement he whipped out his sword and had it at Tyler's throat before the larger man could move. Moore held him there, his eyes deadly. "I don't make vows as a rule, Tyler, but I'm making one now. I'm taking you back to Angela—but if you mistreat her one more time, I'll kill you. I swear I will. Do you believe me?"

"Yes! Yes, Phil!" Fear raked Tyler's face, and he began to weep. "I'll never hurt her again, Phil! I swear it!"

Moore shrugged and sheathed his blade. "I think you will. And when you do, I'll kill you—and hang for it, probably." Then he said to Rebekah, "I'll leave you two for now. I'll try to help you if I can."

He wheeled and left the room, and Tyler staggered blindly to the window and stared out at the world.

"Why did you do it, Tyler?" Rebekah asked in a dead voice. Her face was white and her eyes stricken. "You said you loved me."

He wheeled and said in a tortured voice, "Rebekah—you must see that I—I'm not capable of loving anyone!" He moved toward her and would have put his arms around her, but she stood up and backed away. "I'm sorry, Rebekah," he uttered hoarsely. "Phil's probably right. I'll go back to Angela, and I'll be good for a while. But it never lasts. I'll never change—I can't."

She ignored his excuses. "What does your family think of all this? Or are they like that, too?"

"No!" he said, and held her gaze. "I'm the only rotter, Rebekah! My father died in the Revolution, but Mom always held the family together. I'm the only bad seed. But why do you want to know . . ." He looked up, startled. "You're thinking of the baby!"

"Yes. I have to."

"But, Rebekah!" he pleaded. "You *can't* have the child! How will you—"

She cut him off mid-sentence. "Tyler, don't say any more." Turning away, she added, "And I wish you'd leave now."

He stared at her, unbelieving. When he saw she was serious, he gathered his few belongings and put them in a bag. Trying to ease the weight of his guilty conscience, he remarked weakly, "At least there'll be no money problem now. Angela's family is filthy rich. I'll send you—"

"Tyler," she interrupted, "I want you to go. Now."

He ducked his head, then shuffled to the door. Opening it, he paused to speak, but one look at her face silenced him. After he had gone, she sat down on the bed, trembling so hard that she finally had to lie down.

She wept then, wept until no more tears came. Getting up, she washed her face in the basin and went to the window, thinking of everything—and nothing—all at the same time. She was still there an hour later when a cab drew up in front of the building, and Moore got out and entered the hotel. She saw Tyler slumped in the carriage, his face in his hands.

She opened the door at Moore's knock, stepping back to let him into the small room.

Moore's face showed strain, but his manner was composed, his voice even. "There's no easy way here, Miss Jackson, but I want to help as much as I can." Taking an envelope from his coat pocket, he extended it to her. "Go home," he said gently. "It will be difficult—but you have the child to think of."

She did not move. "Thank you, Mr. Moore, but I wouldn't feel right."

"Please," he insisted. "You must take it. It's not much, really. Just enough for your fare and lodging on the way back to Virginia. Tyler tells me your family is from there, though he couldn't tell me which part. Send me your address, and I'll see to it that Tyler does the right thing—financially, I mean."

He put the envelope down on the small table, then bowed slightly. "I must go." He hesitated, his hand on the doorknob. "Perhaps in a strange sense, you're fortunate it has turned out this way. He's made my sister's life a living hell. But you're young, Miss Jackson. Don't let this destroy you!"

He waited for her to speak: when he saw that she did not

intend to, he nodded understandingly. "I'm very sorry," he repeated, then turned and left the room. His steps echoed loudly on the stairway, and at last she heard the carriage drive away.

She was alone.

CHAPTER FOUR

A New Friend

★ ★ ★ ★

"Sorry, lady—but I got to have the money or you'll have to move out!"

The large man wearing a buffalo coat stood in the doorway. "Mr. Sandford," Rebekah pleaded, "if you'll just give me a little more time. . . !"

"Like to help you, miss, but business is business, see?" The owner of the hotel had heard so many hard-luck stories that Rebekah's words made no impression on him. He owned several run-down hotels and a number of houses in the low-rent district; several times a week he made the rounds, evicting people who could not pay their rent. He was not a cruel man, or so he told himself, but as he had said to his pastor: "Look at it my way, Rev'rend—if I let folks stay without paying, I'd fall behind on my own payments and lose my property. Who'd pay your salary then, I ask you?"

Rebekah's wan face and large eyes filled with fear tugged at him momentarily, but he was long past the stage of being influenced by such things. The story was plain enough. Her husband had left her and she'd have to go home to her people.

"You'll have to be out by tomorrow. I'm sorry for it—but I got others who want the room. You can leave the key next door with the Kellys." He felt a twinge of regret as he stared down at the young woman. *But I gave her a month!* he thought indignantly. *What more could she ask?* Nodding shortly, he turned and left before his good nature got the better of him.

Rebekah closed the door behind him, then went to sit down on the bed. Her throat was dry and there was a tight feeling in her chest. She knew the sensation well, for in the weeks since Tyler had left, it had come to her again and again: panic. Her hands were trembling, and as she squeezed them tightly together, she thought of the past six weeks.

Moore had left $50, which was a great deal of money, but Tyler had not paid the rent for October. After paying that and the rent for November, she had only twenty dollars left. Not once did she consider going back home; the only solution was to find work. Still, the search for a job had been a disaster, for she had no skills and not the vaguest idea of how to find a job. Sitting on the bed now, she recalled her conversation with Mr. Klein.

Going into the first shop she came to, she hesitantly inquired whether they had any work. The storekeeper, a short Jewish man, had compassion enough not to laugh. "Oy, miss, you want work? There ain't no work to be had in this city!" She turned to go, but he had stopped her.

"Wait! Miss, let me tell you something. I've got two daughters—nice girls, beautiful girls—just like you. Now, my eyes they tell me you've got troubles, right? Of course I'm right. And, if my daughters had troubles—God forbid—I would want that someone help them. So you will let me help you, yes?"

She could not refuse such kindness, and so she took the chair he offered her. His name, he said, was Sol Klein. Seating himself across from her, he had rubbed his balding head thoughtfully.

"I see all kinds and I can see quality!" he had said. "You're a nice young lady, but I think maybe you don't know what you're up against—trying to make it all alone. You got no help, am I right? Of course I'm right!" His eyes narrowed. "But there ain't no work, not even for them that got skills, and I don't think you've ever worked, have you?"

Warming up to his subject, he went on. "It was Andrew Jackson that started it all. He was a good man, a brave man—but a financial genius, he was not. Look at it—we got depression and thousands of banks closing all over the country! And if Van Buren is elected, is he gonna fix it somehow? No! No! There's millions out of work now, and it's gonna get worse!"

Now, sitting in the cold room, Rebekah heard all over again his well-meaning advice. "Miss, there ain't no work for a nice lady like you. Only a few schoolteachers work. So maybe you got a family? Go to them! This is no place for a nice young girl—there are plenty of bad men who'd like to take advantage of you! Listen to me, as a father. Your father will thank me. Go home, miss!"

No! I won't go back! Stubbornly, Rebekah rose and paced the floor, struggling against the fear that gripped her. Her mind flew back and forth as she sought desperately for some solution. Many nights she had lain awake, trying to think of a way to support herself. But even if she found work, what about the baby? More than once she thought of writing to Tyler, but could not bring herself to do it.

All morning she stayed in the room, and in the afternoon she went outside. Her clothes were too thin for the bitter weather, but she hoped for something to happen—anything! She had eaten nothing at noon, for she had no more money. When she got back to the room late that afternoon, she finished the last of the food she had in store: two pieces of stale bread and a spoonful of jam. There was enough tea left to make one more pot, and she sat down to drink it as she watched the sunset from her window.

There was now not even a stick of wood left; even the cooking wood was gone, so she wrapped a blanket around herself and shivered. The street outside was almost empty as the darkness fell. One old man pushing a cart went by, then later two young girls passed, bundled up against the bitter cold.

The room darkened, and she stirred herself enough to light the stub of a candle. Her eyes fell on the book Mr. Mayberry had given her, and she picked it up listlessly. Settling back in the chair with the blanket around her, she opened it and began to read. Her hands grew numb, but as she read she forgot them. She had gotten to the section of the journal where Gilbert Winslow told of what was called The General Sickness, and as she read, she tried to imagine it. She read the section dated January fourteenth.

Follows in order of deaths since landing: Edward Thompson, the first to die in the New World; Jasper Moore, James Chilton, and Dorothy Bradford, 11th December; Richard Brittermore, Christopher Martin, 8th January. Mrs. Martin the following day. Weather continues cold with snow and ice in abundance.

No two deaths are alike: Some of them rage and some slip away, like a child slumbering. Twenty dead already; less than twenty men and boys left to stand guard, build houses and hunt food.

Standish says we must bury the next ones at night, so the Indians won't know how few we are—but they must know already.

February 26. Seventeen have died this month. Unless God helps us, we will all perish. Do I believe He will come? Everywhere I look I see the gaps death has made in our ranks. Those of us still alive are sick and probably dying. The Indians wait, knowing we will soon be too weak to resist. There is almost no food. Will God come? My faith is small, for the circumstances are grim—yet I will believe God! He *will* intervene!"

A strange feeling came over Rebekah as she read the words: "Unless God helps us, we will all perish. . . . Do I believe He will come? . . . I will believe God! He *will* intervene!"

The room was dark and the bitter cold had numbed her fingers and her face—but now a peace flooded her heart. She had lived in the grip of fear and worry so long that she had almost forgotten what such peace was like. Nothing had changed, she knew. She still had no money, and no friends. On the next day she would leave the room with no place to sleep. No one to help with the baby.

But something *had* changed in her heart. The fears that had racked her mind faded, and she relaxed in the chair and closed her eyes, letting the book fall to her lap. For a long time she sat there, simply resting and allowing that peace to wash over her like a healing balm. There was a sense of security that could not be expressed in words—although when she thought of it later, if there *could* have been words, they would have been: "I have not forgotten you, Rebekah."

Finally she got up and blew out the candle, crawled into bed, and was asleep almost at once.

The next morning she rose in the cold and cracked the ice in the basin to wash her face. She dressed as warmly as she could; her few belongings went into one suitcase—she would ask Mrs.

Kelly to keep the blankets until she could come back for them. There was no wood for fire, and no tea to make in any case, so she cleaned the room and took a last look around. The bitter memory of her last scene with Tyler tried to rise, but she shook her head and bent to take her suitcase, then paused.

Impulsively, she dropped to her knees beside the bed. Not so much to *pray* as to *wait*. Once again she felt the peace that had swept over her the previous night, and again she was certain that she had not been forgotten. Finally she rose, took the blankets and the room key to Mrs. Kelly, then came back and picked up her suitcase, leaving the room without a backward look. She went down the stairs and out into the street; there she wavered for an instant. Right or left? It didn't matter. She turned left and walked away with firm steps.

In thirty minutes she passed along several streets, each a little more run-down and poverty-scarred than the last. The packed snow was dirty, and as she went farther, the cinders from the chimneys of factories fell like black snowflakes. Frame houses leaned against one another for support, ornamented by ragged washing that hung from lines in the barren yards, and by children of all ages who played in the streets. Some blocks were lined with ugly brick buildings several stories high, sparsely scattered with smeared glass windows. Most of them had large chimneys, and dirty clouds of coal-smoke rose heavily to foul the skies.

The people she met were all poorly dressed, and once a man came up and put his hand on her arm. She could smell the liquor on him. "Come on, now!" he grinned drunkenly. "Let's you and me have a li'l drink, sweetie!"

She pulled away, revolted, as he cursed and reeled down the street. For an hour longer she walked down the unpaved streets, and her feet were wet from wading through the dirty slush. It was almost ten o'clock when she came to the end of the industrial section. There was only one brick factory on her left, and six miserable unpainted shacks that seemed to huddle together for warmth. One woman was boiling something in a large black pot on an open fire, and an old man was being led inside one of the huts by a child.

Rebekah stood uncertainly, looking out at the fields where

cows grazed and a few small farmhouses lay back from the winding road that led east. She was very cold, and her arm ached from carrying the suitcase. She was thirsty as well, her lips dry and her throat thick with the sharp, acrid smoke that churned from the factories.

Wearily she turned, and would have made her way back, but she heard a voice call. Turning, she saw the woman who was stirring the pot lift a hand and motion for her to come. She hesitated, then walked across the street and into the yard that was littered with trash mixed with the mush of dirty snow.

"You look all tired out, dearie," the woman said. She herself looked quite worn; her body was thin beneath the shapeless woolsey dress, and her face pale except for two spots of red on her cheekbones. There were only traces of an earlier beauty left now; her hands were rough and reddened by hard work and by the cold, and her shoulders stooped. When she smiled, her teeth were yellowed and stained. *Somewhere in her thirties*, Rebekah decided. The woman's face was hardened by a rough life, but the kindness in her blue eyes warmed Rebekah.

"I'm a little tired," Rebekah admitted. Then she asked, "Could I trouble you for a drink of water?"

"Why, 'course you can!" the woman replied. "You stir these clothes, and I'll fix you a drink."

Rebekah took the stick the woman had used to stir the clothes in the big black pot. As she pushed them around she noticed that most of the clothes were for a baby.

"Take this now, dearie!"

Rebekah drank the water, then smiled gratefully. "Thank you. I was so thirsty."

"That's the smoke as does that. I'm Mary Sullivan. What do they call you, dearie?"

"Rebekah Jackson."

"My, what a pretty name!" She studied the girl before her openly. "You come all the way from downtown?"

"Yes. It's a long way."

"That it is. And it so cold and all—maybe you'd like to have some coffee and a bite of toast, and thaw out a bit before you go back?"

Rebekah hesitated, and the woman said a bit defensively,

"'Course, it ain't so fine, you know—"

"Oh no, it's not that!" Rebekah said quickly. "I just don't want to be a bother."

"Bother!" Mary scoffed. "Let me finish boiling these things out, and I'll make us a warm snack."

"Oh, let me do that!"

The woman looked at Rebekah strangely as she held out the washing stick. "That'll be a help." Quickly, Rebekah set down her suitcase and began stirring the clothes again.

Ten minutes later, Mary was back to say, "Let me wring these out, and we'll have our coffee."

"Let me help."

Mary protested, "You'll get your hands all red!" But Rebekah only laughed, and the two of them quickly finished the job. Then Mary said, "Come on now," and led her into the house.

It was dark, the only light coming from two small windows, and the floor was hard-packed earth. The small room contained a table and three chairs, an old mattress, a battered chest of drawers and a large box that had been made into a bed for a baby. The room was heated by a small fireplace, and the smell of fresh coffee and warm bread made Rebekah hungry.

"We'll hang them clothes later," Mary said. She went to pick up the baby, and holding him up said with a proud smile, "This is Mister Timothy Sullivan—ain't he a fine man now?"

Rebekah moved closer and the baby peered at her, then gave a loud belch and smiled toothlessly. "Oh, he's a fine boy!" she exclaimed. "Can I hold him?"

"Well—I can't make no guarantees, Rebekah," Mary said doubtfully. "He's about as messy as the next one."

"I don't mind." She took the baby and sat down in one of the chairs, pushing his fat cheeks with one finger, laughing when he made bubbles. She took his hand and examined it carefully, marveling at the perfect little nails.

She did not see Mary's intent gaze, and looked up in surprise when she asked, "You like babies?"

"Why, everybody likes them, don't they?"

Mary's face tightened and she said shortly, "Not everybody." Then she turned away and began to pour coffee into two mugs. She took two pieces of toast that had been browning over the fire in a wire grill, and set them on the table. "Let's have a bite," she offered. "Go ahead and put Timothy in his bed."

"Can I hold him later?"

Mary hesitated, and once again her eyes brightened. "Sure you can—but let's eat a bite first."

Rebekah put the baby in the bed, then came and sat down. "I always thank the Lord for the food," Mary said.

"I think that's good, Mary."

"Lord, we thank Thee for the food. Bless this guest and provide for all our needs. I ask it in the name of Jesus." Then she looked up and smiled. "Have some of this jelly. Made it myself from berries that grow in the bog."

They began to eat, and the toast and jelly was so good that Rebekah wolfed hers down. Mary noticed, and got up, saying, "I declare, I'm so hungry I could eat some more!" She made four more pieces of toast, but ate only one, saying, "Guess my eyes were bigger than my stomach—you'll have to eat the rest, Rebekah."

After they had eaten, Mary put some more coal on the fire and suggested, "If you're in no hurry, we might talk a bit."

"I'm in no hurry, Mary," she replied. "I don't have any place to go, anyway."

Mary's expression did not change. "What about your people?"

"I—I can't go there."

As they sat in front of the glowing coals, Rebekah found herself telling Mary Sullivan her story. It came out slowly, for parts of it were still difficult for Rebekah to talk about. Patiently the older woman listened, occasionally stopping her to ask a question. In less than an hour, Mary knew it all.

When Rebekah finished, she shook her head. "I didn't mean to burden you with my troubles, Mary. It'll work out somehow—but I guess I best be going now." She started to get up, but Mary stopped her.

"Don't go, Rebekah. I'm thinking we might be able to help each other." Mary took a sip of coffee. "I've got me a job at the factory down the street. It's hard work and it don't pay much, but it's more than lots of folks have. But I don't have nobody to keep my baby."

Rebekah saw that Mary's eyes were anxious. "Are you asking me to do that, Mary?"

She nodded. "I don't know if you're a Christian or not, but I've been praying for God to send somebody to help me with Timmy—and it comes to me you're the one He's sent." She chuckled. "We entertain angels unawares, Mr. Finney said."

Rebekah shook her head. "I'm no angel, Mary." Looking outside, she murmured softly, "I have no place to go—and now my baby won't have a father."

"Mine never did either," Mary answered, taking another sip of coffee. "I used to leave Timmy with a woman down the street, but she drinks terrible. I come home yesterday and she was passed out and him on the floor where she'd dropped him. I can't stand that!"

Rebekah said slowly, "I've been praying too, Mary. Maybe God does want us to be together." She rose and went to pick up the baby, then said, "I'm willing to do what I can."

Mary's eyes filled with tears, and she whispered, "Thank you, Lord Jesus! It's just like Mr. Finney said—God always hears our prayers!"

"Who is Mr. Finney, Mary?"

"Why—Rev. Charles Finney. Surely you've heard of *him*!"

"I don't think so."

"He is an evangelist, Rebekah," Mary said eagerly. "He made a church out of the Chatham Street Theatre and that's where I was converted. Now I try to go to church every night I can." She paused and smiled. "We'll go tonight, Rebekah—me and you and Timmy! You won't believe the preachin' of our pastor, Rev. Finney!"

CHAPTER FIVE

THE ANXIOUS SEAT

★ ★ ★ ★

The Free Church—an offshoot of the Chatham Street Chapel that had been established several years before—looked like any other church, but Rebekah could see that the people flowing steadily into the building were not the type who would normally frequent such a place. Most of them were poorly dressed factory workers and other members of the lower class.

"Come along, Rebekah!" Mary urged. "There'll still be some good seats if we hurry. Let me take Timmy."

"No, you just lead the way, Mary—I'm not tired." Mary's stamina amazed Rebekah. The two-mile walk to the church had been difficult, and they had taken turns carrying the baby. Rebekah wondered at the determination of her friend, who usually came alone—carrying Timmy both ways. Following Mary up the steps, she marveled at the light of expectation on the faces of those around her. Everyone seemed to be sharing some sort of glad anticipation at the service to come, just as Mary did. This was a novelty to Rebekah, for her faithfulness in attending services had been required of her by her parents. Uneasily she realized that her religion lacked something—whatever it was that put excitement on the faces of the men and women who moved eagerly to find seats.

"Now—this will do us fine!" The two women found seats

54

relatively close to the front. Mary took Timmy, and Rebekah stretched her aching arms as she looked over the crowd. The church was packed, and the place hummed as people talked and laughed together.

The platform was bare except for a few straight chairs and a stand with a pitcher of water on it. In front of the platform was a long, low bench that caught her attention because it was placed in such a way that no one sitting on it could possibly see. "What's that bench for, Mary?" she asked.

"That? Why, that's the anxious seat, Becky."

"The *what*?"

Mary laughed and squeezed Rebekah's arm. "That's what Rev. Finney used to call it." She had a sober light in her eyes as she recounted the story. "I used to go to Chatham Street Chapel when I was living a bad life. Went there many a time so drunk I could hardly stand up—and with some of the lowest men who ever drew breath." She had been blunt about the sordidness of her past life—and now the memory of those days came back to her, drawing her lips tight with regret. After a few seconds, her face softened. "But that's all under the blood of Jesus, praise God!"

"But—what's the anxious seat?"

"Ah, you'll see tonight, Becky. When Rev. Finney preaches the gospel, talking about how wicked sinners are and how they need to leave their sin—why, people start to get *anxious*! You'll see! First time, I just went to the chapel to hear Mr. Finney 'cause a friend of mine asked me. Had no idea of getting religion—not likely! I just come in, and we set right on the balcony. 'Course, I was just wanting it to be over so I could go get some gin. There was the singing—and then Rev. Finney stood up behind the pulpit and started preaching—and that was it for Mary Sullivan!"

"What happened?"

"Why, he preached about Jesus on the cross, and how the Savior was nailed to it for our sins. It was real strange, Rebekah! There was nigh onto a thousand people in the place—but all at once it was like he was talking right to *me*. He looked right up to the balcony and pointed at me—and he called out, 'Behold the Lamb of God that taketh away the sin of the world!'—oh, Rebekah, it just came near to *killin'* me! I started to cry, and all the time he preached I was just sitting there cryin' an' cryin'!"

Rebekah saw tears fill Mary's eyes. "What happened then, Mary?"

"When Rev. Finney finished preaching, he asked everyone who wanted to be saved from their sin to come to the front, but I couldn't do it! I was too bad! So I was just cryin' like to die, and this young woman come and put her hand on my arm and said kind of quiet like, 'Sister, let me go with you to the anxious seat. God wants to do a work in your life.' So I went down and it was a time, I tell you, Becky!

"The devil had me tight, and lots of people come to pray for me, but seemed like nothing worked—and finally Rev. Finney himself come and looked at me with them blazing eyes of his, and he prayed for me so hard—and as he was praying, I just sort of gave up—and soon as I did, the Lord came into my heart and I was saved!"

Mary's worn face, lined with fatigue, glowed; Rebekah wondered at the joy she saw there. "It was hard, Rebekah—after, I mean. Oh, it was hard! I'd been drinking a lot and running with a wild crowd! And I—I was carrying Timmy, though I didn't know it. I'd never worked, but the Lord carried me through it all. My job ain't much, but it's enough for Timmy and me—and now the Lord's sent you to me to help!—Oh, look, the service is about to start . . ."

Rebekah looked up to see a tall man in a black suit come out on the platform, followed by several others who seated themselves in the other chairs. "That's Brother White," Mary said. "He does the music."

White shouted, "Let us sing of the mercies of the Lord!" As he lifted his voice, everyone stood and joined in, and the sound of hundreds of voices filled the church and overflowed outside. It was a song that Rebekah had often sung in her own church, but it had never sounded like this!

When I survey the wondrous cross
On which the Prince of Glory died,
My richest gain I count but loss,
And pour contempt on all my pride!
Forbid it, Lord, that I should boast
Save in the death of Christ my God!
All the vain things that charm me most
I sacrifice them to His blood!

The sound rose like waves, breaking against the walls with a joyful triumph Rebekah had never heard before. The trained voices of the choir in her home church had been technically superior— but this was full of *life*! Filled with joy, she was moved to tears as the worshipful words rolled out:

See from His head, His hands, His feet
Sorrow and love flow mingled down!
Did ere such love and sorrow meet,
Or thorns compose so rich a crown?

The singing went on and on, at times triumphant and victorious, sometimes more quietly, but always the faces of those around her glowed with expressions of such peace and joy that Rebekah marvelled.

After several more hymns, the song leader stepped back, and another man seated in the chairs behind him stood up. "That's Rev. Finney!" Mary whispered. Charles Grandison Finney was a serious-looking, smooth-shaven man of medium height. Stepping forward to read his text, he paused, then looked around the church. His gaze was intensely electrifying, penetrating the crowd. Rebekah felt as if he were looking right at her, though she knew that was unlikely. As he read his text, the clear tones of his solemn voice carried easily to the farthest corners of the building.

This preacher followed closely the techniques that he had used during the revivals some years before. Rebekah later learned that Finney had practiced law in upper New York state, but left his profession to enter the ministry after a dramatic conversion experience. His powerful preaching drew thousands to the revival meetings, but his methods—or the "New Measures," as they were called—often brought him into conflict with established church leadership: He prayed publicly for people by name, permitted females to pray in public meetings, invaded towns without an invitation from the local pastor, employed the use of the anxious seat, conducted inquiry meetings, and called for the immediate admission of converts into churches.

Finney's evangelism ministry in "The Burned-Over District" of Rochester had been enormously successful. After two years there, he moved into New York City in 1832; his success as a pastor of the Chatham Street Chapel rivaled his victories as an evangelist. From the time he first took up the work, Finney insisted that the church should not be filled with Christians from other churches, but by new converts. As soon as the mother church was filled, a group was sent out to form a new one. There were seven churches in the area that had been planted by the Chatham Street Chapel, including the one they were attending tonight.

"My text is taken from Luke, chapter thirteen, the third verse," Finney announced. " 'Except ye repent, ye shall all likewise perish.' " For nearly two hours the congregation sat spellbound as he went from scripture to scripture, proving that men were lost and on their way to hell; that unless they turned from their sin to find forgiveness, there was no hope.

The man had a systematic method of preaching, each point being laid down in careful succession. Like someone building a house, he first laid a foundation, then raised the walls and finally capped it with a roof, so that it stood complete. The roof, in this case, was an invitation: Those who felt they needed to be saved from hell should come forward.

The reaction was immediate. From all over the room, people rose from their places and began moving forward in response to his invitation. His stirring message had deeply affected them, but Finney's attention was not directed at the men and women who swarmed the aisles. His eyes were scanning those who yet remained seated. Overwhelmed with compassion for the lost, tears streamed down his cheeks as he cried out: "God so loves the world—so loves *you*—that he sent Jesus to die for you! Will you reject that love? Would you not rather come and let the King of Kings and Lord of Lords come into your heart?"

Rebekah's mind reeled from what she had heard. She looked down to see that her hands were trembling, and she closed her eyes, holding back the tears that threatened to overflow. She had been in church every Sunday of her life and could quote large sections of the Bible. It had never occurred to her that her religion was lacking in any way—but now as she sat and listened to the cries of grief rising from those who pressed forward to the anxious seat, she was shaken to the very depths of her soul.

She had never considered herself a sinner; a "sinner" was someone who did things like Mary had done—living a life of drunkenness and immorality. Now she saw that she was in the same condition as the worst sinner, for the preacher had made it abundantly clear that there were no "good" sinners—only lost ones on the way to hell. Stripping away all her defenses, he pointed out that morality, church membership, baptism, good works could not save a soul from hell. She felt alone and naked before the eyes of God!

How long she sat there, she didn't know, but soon she felt Mary's hand go around her shoulder and heard her whisper, "You need Jesus as your Savior, Becky—don't you now?"

Rebekah could not answer, for there was a struggle inside of her. Part of her drew back from what was going on. Some seekers near her had fallen to the floor in an agony of grief, and she had been taught in her own church that such fanaticism was not of God. It was all foreign to her, including the cries of those at the anxious seat and the directness of the church members who moved from person to person, speaking to sinners and urging them to accept Christ.

But in spite of all that, there was a yearning in her heart to find the peace and joy she saw in others. She had found the words of the preacher disturbing, but they had offered her a hope that was very real. "Jesus never fails!" he cried out. "The world will deceive you; your own family may cast you off—but Jesus said, 'He that cometh to me, I will in no wise cast out!' "

I will in no wise cast out. In that moment, the thought of her own loneliness broke Rebekah's heart, and her eyes filled with tears, blurring her vision. "Oh, I need God!" she whispered to Mary. "But I'm so afraid!"

Mary squeezed her shoulder. "Let's go down and we'll pray for God to save you, Becky."

They made their way to the front, which was crowded with many seekers. Mary handed Timmy to a friend she saw there, then turned and said, "Let's kneel and pray, Becky!"

Falling to her knees, Rebekah could not think. Her heart was filled with grief, and she could not pray aloud. For a long time she knelt and listened as others prayed, hearing Mary's cries to God on her behalf—but she seemed to be paralyzed, and for a long time could do nothing but cry. Then she felt a firm hand on her arm, pulling her around.

"Young woman, do you desire Christ?"

She found herself looking directly into the eyes of Rev. Finney, whose gaze seemed to slice into the depths of her soul. She nodded mutely, and he said gently, "Don't be afraid, child! It's your time to find the Lord. Now, I will pray for you, and I want you to pray as best you can. If you can't pray out loud, then just call on God in your heart. Tell Him you're a sinner, and ask Him to forgive you of all your sins in the name of Jesus. Will you do that?"

"Yes, sir," Rebekah whispered.

He began to pray in a tone that was low but firm, giving Rebekah courage. He had been so somber in the pulpit, but as he knelt beside her, he spoke to God as a man would speak to his friend—very confident, very sure; and this assurance enabled her to pray as well: "Lord, save me for Jesus' sake!"

The moment she did, a peace flooded her, and she gave a glad cry of joy. Finney looked up and said, "You are converted, are you not? Jesus has come into your heart?"

"Yes! Oh, yes!"

"Glory to God! Now, you must ask God to fill you with His Holy Spirit—for you will need much strength for what lies before you." He noted her startled look and added hastily, "Oh no—I know nothing about you, except that the Lord has told me that you have a difficult path to walk, and He wants to give you a double portion of His grace. Will you ask Him for this?"

Although she did not understand fully what he meant, Rebekah bowed her head and prayed, "Lord, fill me with your Holy Spirit." She prayed this several times as the reverend put his hand on her head and prayed with her. In a few minutes, she felt a wave of joy rush through her, and she lifted her hands and began to praise God as she never had before! She was not conscious of the crowds around her—only that God had somehow touched her in a way that she had never thought possible. She leaped to her feet, her hands lifted and tears streaming down her face, and for a long time she just stood there, saying "Thank you, Jesus! Thank you, Lord!" over and over again.

Rev. Finney smiled at Mary, who was weeping freely for joy. "Sister—there's a new name written in the Lamb's Book of Life!"

By the last of February, the snow had melted, turning unpaved streets into rivers of mud and yards into quagmires. But the warmer weather cut down on the use of fuel, so Mary and Rebekah didn't complain.

Their lives had settled into a pattern. Mary went to work in the morning, while Rebekah stayed home and took care of Timmy and the house. She kept the house neat as a pin, and the baby filled her heart. Once she said, "Mary, I feel awful. You do all the work—and I stay home and do nothing."

"It's God's hand at work, Becky," Mary had replied. "Don't be faulting the way He does things."

The two of them went to the church almost every night; Rebekah had never known there was such joy in going to church. She had been apprehensive when she had first gone to pray for a young woman who was struggling with doubt, but the pastor insisted that it was the duty of all believers. The young woman had not been saved, but the following night, Rebekah prayed for another who was. Her work with the church became a joy to her, and she was happy.

Mary came home one afternoon with a newspaper one of the women had given her. As she sat down to eat the meal Rebekah had prepared, Mary had a peculiar look on her face. "Well, Becky, at least now there's always one thing we can do—to get husbands, I mean."

"Get a husband?" Rebekah looked up quickly, frowning. "What are you talking about, Mary?"

"Look . . ." She held up a newspaper with *Puget Sound Herald* emblazoned across the front. "Look at this—no, I'll read it to you." She found a notice in the middle section of the paper and began to read aloud:

"'Attention—Ladies of the East! If you are seeking a new life, Oregon is your answer. The men outnumber ladies fifteen to one, so the situation is desperate! Many fine men who would make wonderful husbands are wretched for want of comfortable homes, and would lose no time in allying themselves with the fair daughters of Eve if they would deign to favor us with their presence!'"

Rebekah laughed out loud at the last sentence. "He must have gotten that from a romantic novel, Mary! Nobody ever actually *talks* like that!" Then she cast an unbelieving look at the paper. "Advertising for brides! I never heard of such a thing!"

"Just you wait, now," Mary said quickly. "He goes on to say as how a man named Asa Mercer came east last spring and got over a hundred women to go to Oregon. 'Course, he made a call for *schoolteachers*—but everyone knew that was just for the looks of things. Says every one of them women got husbands, soon as they got there."

"You're not *really* thinking of going!" Rebekah stared at Mary in disbelief.

Mary dropped her head for a moment, then looked up and said, "Who'd marry me in this place, Becky? And what about Timmy? You've seen what this place makes of kids! They learn to be thieves and grow up to be drunks. I'm thinking maybe it would be different in Oregon. I—I'd be a good wife to a man if I had the chance."

Rebekah shook her head. "But to marry a man you don't even *know*! Why, Mary, I couldn't do it!"

"I'm surprised you've still got them romantic notions left, Becky," Mary said soberly. "I don't—had those knocked out of me long ago. All I want is a place for my son, and I'd work my fingers to the bone—and never look at another man—if I could find somebody who'd be decent to me and Timmy!"

Rebekah sat there, trying to fit the pieces together in her mind, but try as she might, she could not reconcile it with her ideas of marriage. "You're serious, Mary?"

Mary moved her finger down the page and said, "Listen to this, Becky. Here's another notice about a group that's going to Oregon next month:

" 'A group of responsible bachelors in the Willamette Valley of Oregon have formed an association to promote the institution of marriage in the area. Due to the scarcity of unmarried women in Oregon, the association will provide free transportation to Oregon City for any woman who qualifies. There are some positions open as schoolteachers and music teachers, but the primary purpose of the program is to bring marriageable women into the territory.

" 'Any woman who is healthy, unmarried, and who will consider marriage to one of our citizens may qualify. The virtue of all women who engage in this enterprise will be carefully guarded, and there will be a minister of the gospel to serve as a chaplain on the journey. There will be no pressure on any lady to marry any individual. Any lady who does not wish to remain in Oregon Territory will have her passage paid back to New York.

" 'Any woman interested in this venture can apply in person on March 15, 1839, to a representative of the association at the State Hotel in New York City. Space is limited, so membership in the association will be selected on a first come, first serve basis. Applicants should ask for Mr. Winslow.' "

Rebekah brushed the idea aside. "I couldn't do it, Mary."

Mary didn't argue. "We better hurry and eat. I don't want to be late to the meeting." She could see that the idea disturbed Rebekah, but her own mind was made up. As they walked toward the church, both of them were quiet. Finally, Rebekah spoke up. "I'd miss you, Mary—and Timmy; why, he's almost like my own!"

Mary smiled. "Best not to worry about it—Mr. Finney used to say we spend so much time worrying about what might happen tomorrow that we don't have the strength to bear our trials for today! I don't really expect it'll work out—but I'm going to meet that Winslow man! Anything that'll get my boy a daddy and a home—I'll do it!"

CHAPTER SIX

SPECTER IN THE CITY

★ ★ ★ ★

Just as the rigors of winter passed away from the city, a far more critical problem struck. Cholera in its most virulent form descended and struck without warning; young and old, rich and poor were equally defenseless against its onslaught. At first there were only a few isolated cases, like scattered drops of rain before a deluge, but by the first of March every block in the city knew the undertaker's carriage and had heard the agonized weeping of the survivors.

The rich took refuge in the country, but Mary and Rebekah had nowhere to go. Mary's meager earnings were scarcely enough to keep them going from one day to the next, so like the vast army of the poor, they remained in the city. Two families in their little cluster of houses were ravaged by the disease; despite the danger of infection, Mary insisted on going to help prepare the bodies. She had been adamantly against Rebekah's accompanying her, however, saying, "One of us has to be well to take care of Timmy."

The attendance at church grew as the plague claimed more and more lives. "It's a shame that people have to have trouble to make them get right with the Lord," Mary said one day as they got to church at their usual time and saw that all the seats were occupied. They found standing room only, but when the ministers came out to the platform, Rev. Finney was not among them.

Brother White, the song leader, came to the center of the stage and said, "We must be much in prayer. Brother Finney is ill." A murmur of dismay rose, but White put up his hand for silence. "It is time for the church to have faith. Our assistant pastor, Brother Reynolds, has been struck down as well. Tonight, I feel that instead of preaching, we should go to prayer for our pastors and for all others in our fellowship and in this city who are ill."

The church prayed fervently, but the next night, there was a somber look on Brother White's face. "We suffer loss, friends—Brother Reynolds went to be with the Lord early this morning. He died praising God. Now, we must pray for Brother Finney—pray as we never have prayed before for this servant of God!"

"It was so quick!" Rebekah said in a subdued voice when they got home. "Brother Reynolds was fine day before yesterday—and now he's gone!" She was dressing Timmy in his nightgown while Mary made his little bed. "I feel so helpless, Mary!"

" 'Our help cometh from the Lord,' " Mary quoted in a tired voice. "That's what the Scripture says, and at times like these all we can do is trust to God and His promises."

After Timmy was asleep, the two women sat at the table to read a chapter in the Bible and pray, as they always did. Each night one of them would select a portion, read it, and then they would discuss it briefly before praying. Mary opened her Bible and read Psalm 23, and when she had finished, she closed her eyes and began to pray. There was, Rebekah noticed, a weariness that crept into Mary's voice, and from time to time she would stop praying and sit there silently. *She's working too hard*, Rebekah thought.

Finally they sat with their heads bowed, praying silently. Tired to the bone, Rebekah was about to rise and go to bed, but a thought came into her mind, not once but several times. She knew it was a verse of Scripture, but she could not place it. Finally she said, "Mary, I keep thinking of something—and I think the Lord may be telling one of us something."

"What is it, Rebekah?"

"Well—it's a little like a Bible verse, but not quite. It's like someone was whispering inside me: 'Don't be afraid! I am the

Almighty God, and my arms are under you. Am I not the helper of the fatherless? I am merciful and gracious, and my mercy is from everlasting to everlasting, and my righteousness is unto my children's.' "

She stared across the table, her eyes troubled. "I don't know what it means. Is it from the Bible, Mary?"

"Some of it is." Leafing through her worn Bible, she came to a page. " 'Thou art the helper of the fatherless.' That's Psalm 10:14." She studied the page and said, "I guess that's plain enough. My Timmy is fatherless."

"And my baby will be too," Rebekah added quietly. "I think the part about not being afraid is for me. Even though I've found Christ, sometimes I get to thinking about how my baby will make it, and fear just rises up in me."

Mary reached over and squeezed Rebekah's arm. "I think the rest of what you said is somewhere in the Psalms too. Let's see if we can find it."

They started searching, and finally Mary said, "Here it is! It's in Psalm 103—in verses 8 and 17!" While Rebekah found the place, Mary looked at her thoughtfully. "The word of God has come to you, Rebekah! Look what it says in verse 17: 'But the mercy of the Lord is from everlasting to everlasting upon them that fear him, and his righteousness unto children's.' "

Rebekah read aloud the last phrase: ". . . and his righteousness unto children's." She looked up and tears glittered in her eyes as she said in wonder, "Why—that's Timmy and my baby, Mary! God says He'll take care of them!"

"If God says it," Mary announced, "then that settles it! I've been so afraid that this cholera would strike Timmy, but God says He's going to help the fatherless—and that's all there is to it! Glory to God!"

"I think that's right!" Rebekah answered happily. "I never knew God would speak to people like this! I'm not going to doubt Him anymore!"

Mary said slowly, "I hope you won't, Becky—but it gets hard sometimes. Right now we've heard from God, and we're feeling happy—but we have to remember times like these when things get bad." She paused, and her face brightened. "But God has given us a promise—and we'll help each other to remember it!"

For a week Brother Finney lingered between life and death, but on the next Sunday, March 6, it was announced that he was through the crisis, and the church went wild with joy. "I knew the Lord wouldn't take him from us!" Mary cried out happily.

The following Tuesday she came home from work early, her face pale with fatigue. "I'm feeling a bit down, dear," she said to Rebekah. "But I think if I lie down a bit, it'll pass."

Rebekah's heart sank, but she kept a smile on her face, saying, "It's probably just a bad cold. You get into bed and I'll fix you some warm broth."

But it was not a cold, and both of them knew it. Mary's fever rose and the diarrhea and vomiting began. By morning she was delirious, but in those brief moments when she was herself, she cried out to Rebekah, her eyes wide with fear. "My Timmy! Take him out of here!"

"He's over at the Satterfields—don't worry, Mary," Rebekah said. By noon she was worse, and one of the neighbors managed to get an overworked doctor named Gleason to stop by. The thin man was haggard, and his eyes were hollow from lack of sleep. Bending over Mary, he examined her briefly, then lifted his eyes to Rebekah. "You know what this is?"

"It's the cholera, isn't it, Doctor?"

"Yes." He hesitated. "Are you a relative?"

"No. I—I take care of her little boy."

Dr. Gleason bit his lip, then said, "Her family should be told."

"She has no one." Rebekah's heart filled with fear. "Is she going to die, Dr. Gleason?" she whispered.

He turned to look at the sick woman, who seemed to have dozed off into a fitful sleep. "She's very bad—very bad! I've seen worse cases recover—but it would take a miracle." He turned to leave, but paused. "I'll see that the boy gets a place to stay."

"The orphanage?"

"It's not a bad place," Gleason assured her. "Maybe it won't come to that. Give her the medicine. I'll stop by tomorrow."

He left and as soon as the door closed, Mary's voice caused Rebekah to move at once to her bedside. "What is it, Mary?"

"What was it he said—about Timmy?" Mary's face was a skull, the flesh stripped so quickly by the virulent fever, and her eyes were unnaturally bright. "He said the orphanage, didn't he?"

Rebekah picked up a damp cloth and wiped the perspiration from the sick woman's brow. "You're going to be all right, Mary. Don't worry—"

"No! Don't let them take him there, Rebekah!" Mary sat up and grabbed at Rebekah with frantic strength. "I was brought up in an orphanage! Let him die, God—but don't let him go to that place!"

It was all Rebekah could do to hold Mary in the bed, for fear had given the sick woman strength. Her voice rose, and she fought wildly—but it didn't last long. She fell back, pleading with Rebekah. "Don't let them take him—please don't let them!"

"I won't!" Rebekah took her friend's hand tightly in her own. "They won't take him, Mary! I swear it!"

Both of them were weeping, and finally Mary fell into a feverish sleep. Rebekah rose from the bedside and went to the basin, washing her face and hands. She was trembling all over, her heart beating wildly. Sitting down at the table, she rested her arms and hid her face on them, trying to get control. She tried to pray, but her mind whirled and it seemed to do no good.

All afternoon she cared for the sick woman, leaving only once to go see that Timmy was all right. The long day passed, and night came on. She lay on her bed, exhausted from lack of sleep. It was totally dark when she heard Mary call out. She got up from the bed at once, and found Mary awake, trying to speak through lips that were parched and dry. Rebekah quickly lifted the sick woman and gave her a drink, then lowered her.

"Get Timmy," Mary whispered.

"Mary, do you think—?"

"Quick—quick! I must—see my baby!"

Rebekah took a quick breath. "I'll be right back, Mary!"

She ran to the Satterfields and knocked on the door. Amy Satterfield opened the door and knew at once. "She's goin', Rebekah?"

"Yes—she wants to see Timmy." She took the child and ran back to put him in Mary's arms, knowing no harm would come to the baby because cholera was caught by drinking contaminated water. Mary's dull eyes brightened as she pulled the cover back from the baby's face. With a trembling finger she traced his tiny lips, his smooth cheeks. Tears ran down her face as she whispered so quietly that Rebekah had to lean forward to hear:

"I'll not be here to see you grow up—but you'll have a fine mother, Timmy. God has promised me . . . she'll take care of you—and she'll never let you forget me. . . ." Her voice faltered, and she turned her head to look at Rebekah.

"Becky—my Becky!" Her voice was weak, but her worn face was transformed by a look of utter peace. She reached out one thin hand to wipe away the tears that flowed down Rebekah's cheeks. "Don't you cry, dearie! Our Father has promised us, don't you remember?"

"Mary!" Rebekah cried. "What will I do without you?"

Mary's wonderful smile made her look years younger. "The Lord came to me just now—while you was goin' for Timmy. He said it was time for me to come and be with Him—but He said that you'd be a mother to both our babies—and that He'd never leave you."

Her eyes fluttered, and she settled back in her pillow. She gave Timmy's face one more caress, kissed him, and she said with her last breath: "So good of God . . . to care for . . . our babies. . . !"

And then she was still.

Rebekah bent down and kissed the hollow cheek, then picked up the baby. Holding him tightly, she whispered, "I'm your mother now, Timmy!"

The funeral was the next day. Rebekah was surprised at the crowd that came to bid her friend farewell. Amy Satterfield and another neighbor had prepared the body, and several of the men made the rough pine coffin. A minister from the church preached the funeral sermon, and many of the members of the church ringed the grave as the coffin was lowered into the earth.

Somehow Rebekah survived. She took the words of comfort that many stopped to give her, but it was caring for Timmy that kept her from breaking down. She did not leave him for one minute, and as Mary's body was lowered into the ground, she made a promise to God: *God, I'll keep my word to Mary. I'll be a mother to Timmy—and you must take care of us both!*

Three days after the funeral, a large man came by the house.

"I'm Mr. Simmons, from the orphanage," he said. "Dr. Gleason has told us about the boy."

"I'm going to take care of him," Rebekah assured him.

He regarded her a moment, then asked, "Are you a relative?"

"No, but—"

"Are you able to take care of him? Do you have work?"

"Well, not right now, but I can find a job."

He considered her uncertainly. "I know how you feel, miss—but we have to think of the boy."

"I can take care of him!" she insisted, but she saw by the man's expression that she was not going to win.

"I'm sorry, but you'll have to give him up," Simmons said. "You can take him in to the orphanage yourself—or we can send somebody by for him."

The shock was too much for Rebekah, and she leaned against the wall for support. "When do I have to take him?"

"As soon as possible. By the end of the week at the latest."

There was no use arguing. "All right." When he was gone, she knelt beside her bed. There was nothing to do, no one to turn to, and a bleak fear gripped her heart. She stayed there for a long time, praying for wisdom. At last she rose, fed Timmy, played with him for a time, then began to gather Mary's few things together. The rent was paid for a month, but that was no comfort. All she could think of was some means of keeping the baby.

She took all Mary's clothes and put them in a bag, but put Mary's Bible and a few tracts with her own things. She found a stack of papers and magazines on Mary's table and began to sort them out, throwing most of them in a waste box. Near the bottom of the pile, her hand fell on a sheet of newsprint, and her eyes fell on the message, capturing her attention.

Attention—ladies of the East! If you are seeking a new life, Oregon is your answer . . . men outnumber ladies fifteen to one. . . . Any woman interested in this venture can apply on March 15 at the State Hotel. . . . Ask for Mr. Winslow. . . .

For a long time she sat and read the words over and over—and then she closed her eyes and remained still. The silence ran on unbroken, so she opened her eyes and rose.

She walked across the room and looked at a calendar with a

picture of a farmhouse on it. Putting her finger on the date, she gave a determined smile and said aloud, "March, the thirteenth." Then she turned and her face was pale, but her lips were set.

"Mr. Winslow," she announced to the air, "you have a new volunteer for your association!" Then she ran and picked up the baby. Throwing him high in the air and listening to his delighted squeal, she cried out, "Timmy—how'd you like to go to Oregon?"

PART TWO

OREGON TRAIL

★ ★ ★ ★

CHAPTER SEVEN

PICK OF THE LITTER

★　★　★　★

A violent southwest wind rolled ragged black clouds over Oregon City as a wagon pulled up in front of Moore's Livery on Walnut Street. Swollen drops of cold rain formed a silver screen in front of the man and boy as they sat inside the protecting cover of the wagon, waiting. A short fat man appeared from behind the double doors of the livery. "Howdy, Sky. You want me to grain these horses?"

"Hello, Harvey." Sky drove the wagon inside and handed over the reins to the stableman. "Birdwell will want the furs moved to his warehouse tomorrow, I expect," he called over his shoulder as he and his companion left the stable.

The plank walkways across the street intersections were half afloat and sank beneath the weight of the two as they crossed over, turning right at the sidewalk. At two o'clock in the afternoon the kerosene lights were sparkling through the drenched windowpanes, and the saloons they passed exuded a rich blend of tobacco, whiskey, and men's soaked woolen clothes.

Five sailing ships lay at the levee, their bare spars showing above the row of frame buildings on Front. Beyond Seventh, in the other direction, the great fir forest was a black semicircle that crowded Oregon City's thousand people hard against the river. The raw, wild odor of massive timbered hills and valleys turned sweet in the rain and lay over the town like a blanket.

"Be good to get out of this rain, Joe," the man said. "Soon as we see Sam, let's eat."

"All right." The boy was bundled in a thick coat, and a fur cap was pulled low over his eyes. He looked across the street and said, "The pie is best at Holland's. Can we go there?"

"Your choice, Joey. I could eat my saddle!"

They hurried across another street as the rain dimpled the watery mud. Reaching a large frame building with a sign reading BIRDWELL'S GENERAL MERCHANDISE over the door, the two entered. It was warm inside, and Sam Birdwell came from behind the counter to greet them.

"Come in and thaw out!" He was of average appearance in most respects—neither tall nor heavy, though his balding head made him look older than his thirty-seven years. "Get up close to the stove, Joe. Cold as an Eskimo's nose out there! Coffee, Sky?"

"Won't say no, Sam." Birdwell poured the coffee—thick and black—then produced a can of milk and a bowl of sugar to lighten Joe's cup. As his visitors drank the steaming brew, Sam carried on the conversation, studying the pair unobtrusively.

Sky Winslow, standing with one shoulder tipped against the wall, looked rough, yet durable. At thirty-seven, there was no fineness or smoothness about him; his black hair had a trace of chestnut and lay in long rough-cut layers, framing high cheekbones and a pair of startling blue eyes well-bedded in deep sockets. A scar ran from the outside of his left eyebrow along his hairline, down to his ear, the relic of a youthful brawl. His expression was a mixture of sadness and strong temper. He stood a little under six feet, his body lean, like a distance runner; but there was a rounded quality to his muscle, a hardness that was not obvious at a casual glance. In fact, he seemed almost skinny until one took in the rounded neck that flowed smoothly to a torso that was thick rather than wide.

"Got your lessons all done, Joe?" Birdwell asked.

"Good enough, I guess, Mr. Birdwell." Joe Winslow was ten, and there was something of his father in this thin, wiry frame. He had blue eyes, dark skin, and his hair was brown. His face was sensitive, with features that were finer cut than his father's.

"Don't see no need of all that arithmetic," he muttered. He had obviously inherited his father's temperament.

Sky laughed and dropped a hand to the boy's shoulder. "We've been through that, Joe. Can't get by much nowadays without knowing how to do sums."

"Ah, Pa, I can shoot a buck, skin him out, and dress him. Don't take no figurin' for *that*!"

"More to life than skinning a buck, Joe," Sky said lightly; then to his host he added, "We're goin' to get supper, Sam. Too early for you?"

"I missed dinner," Birdwell admitted, taking off his apron and putting it behind the counter. He pulled on a heavy coat and called out to the young man who was stacking cans on a shelf, "Al—I'm goin' to eat. Be back when I get full."

"All right, Mr. Birdwell."

The trio left the store, heading directly for Holland's Restaurant. Like every other building in Oregon City, Holland's was built of rough lumber; the dozen tables inside were hand-built of pine slabs, as were the chairs. A potbelly stove in the center of the long room glowed with heat. The place was almost empty; two big men sat at a table against a wall, and one logger was wolfing down a steak at the far end of the room.

Mack Holland came bustling over to them. "What'll it be, gents?" Holland's stocky build was such that some would have considered him fat, but in reality his body was solid muscle. He had a huge handlebar mustache, and a pair of steady black eyes. And he was a fine cook. "Got some fresh beef, Sky—or maybe you'd like some chicken livers?"

"Livers for me, Mack," Sky said. "What about you, Joe?"

"Can I have one of your omelets, Mr. Holland—and what kind of pie you got?"

Holland smiled at the boy. "Omelet comin' up, Joe, and I got some apple pie I just took out of the oven." He turned and asked, "What'll you have, Sam?"

"Steak and potatoes, Mack." He looked around the room and asked, "Where's Stella?"

Holland frowned. "Got married." He slapped his side with a meaty hand and grumbled, "Paid that woman's fare all the way from San Francisco, Sam. She promised to work for a year, and the first logger that give her the eye—she runs off with him and leaves me with no help!"

Birdwell shook his head. "She was no beauty, Mack. And pretty long in the tooth at that!"

Holland sighed and headed for the kitchen. "Reckon most women would rather wait on one man than be a waitress and wait on a hundred of 'em!"

"Mack should have known better," Sky said as they waited for the food. "Scarce as women are in Oregon, he's not going to hang on to one for long—not even if she's ugly as a pan of worms."

Sam started to answer, then looked at Joe and changed his mind. He said instead, "How's things out on your place?"

"All right." There was a dissatisfied note in the words that made Birdwell look at him curiously. Sky shrugged and added, "Furs were good this year. They're at Moore's."

"Price is up some from last year," Birdwell murmured. "I'll have them moved tomorrow." He traced a pattern on the table with an air of concentration that caught Sky's attention.

"What's goin' on in that mind of yours, Sam?"

"Oh, just an idea. Tell you later."

Sky Winslow watched Birdwell carefully. The storekeeper was not impressive to the eye, but underneath that balding head lay one of the keenest brains in the territory. He was blessed— or cursed, as he himself complained at times—with a fertile imagination. Several times he had plunged into wild schemes that soon ran aground, but that same ability to see opportunities had made him a wealthy man. Besides the store in Oregon City, he owned controlling interests in stores in Olympia and Seattle, and had his hand in logging and furs. He was always looking for new ventures.

Sky grinned at him as Holland brought the food, and as they ate he tried to pry the secret out of the merchant.

Halfway through the meal, the two big men at the other table got up and started for the door. The taller of the two nodded at Sky and said, "Winslow—how are you?"

Sky held the big man's gaze steadily, then nodded. "All right, Poole."

"Don't see you much. Maybe we can have a drink later."

Matthew Poole, the mayor of Oregon City, was an easterner who had made a place for himself in the wilds of Oregon. He had come to Oregon City ten years earlier and gone into business, turning later to politics. His long frame was rawboned and had a cadaverous face and a shock of rough salt-and-pepper hair.

"A little later, maybe," Sky murmured, looking at the other man who had silently fixed his eyes on Winslow. "Hello, Rolfe."

Rolfe Ingerson was a burly man with a star on his vest. He was sheriff of Oregon City, but like Poole, he had a hand in other pies as well. He had curly red hair, and his powerful neck flowed into a massive torso. He carried a gun, but his fists were enough for most trouble; his small eyes were fixed on Sky with a steady dislike.

"Winslow, you got off easy last time. Walk soft when you're in my town."

He walked out, and Poole smiled ominously and spread his hands. "Rolfe is an unmannerly brute, Sky. Steer clear of him." With a final nod to the others at the table, he left the cafe.

"Fine pair of crooks!" Birdwell snorted. "But Poole's right about one thing; you'd better steer clear of Ingerson, Sky. He's been like a bear with a sore toe ever since you faced him down last month—he'll be looking for an excuse to bust you up."

"I'll try to oblige." Sky looked over at Joe, who had been taking it all in. "Finish up that pie, Son, then scoot off for your lessons. I'll be checking with Mr. Wilson to see how you've done." Bob Wilson had been a logger, but an accident in the woods had crippled him. Fortunately, he had some education, so he made his living clerking. He worked at his house, which was just off Main; Joe schooled with him as long as Sky was in town. "I'll see you in the morning."

"Watch out for that pretty little daughter of his, Joe," Sam grinned. "Mr. Wilson says she's got her eye on you."

Giving Birdwell an offended glance, Joe shot up out of his chair, grabbed his stack of books, and bolted from the restaurant.

"Musta hurt his feelin's," Sam observed, adding, "Boy don't get to spend much time with folks, Sky. Wish you'd leave him with me sometimes. I'm no teacher, but I could give him some pointers on business—and he'd be company."

"I'll ask him," Sky said shortly. Picking up his coffee, he took a swallow, then set the cup down with more force than necessary. He stared into his coffee, his lips tight. After a while he raised his head and gave Sam a bleak look. "I'm sick of the way we're living, Sam! Like hermits! Never see anybody, the place is never clean—and my cooking is worse than you'd believe!" He shook his head sadly. "It's makin' Joe into something I don't like, Sam. I've even thought of going back to the Mission."

"Hate to see you do that, Sky." Birdwell understood his friend's thinking, for Sky's father was a missionary to the Sioux in the North, and his mother had been half Indian. "Might be good for the boy, being around his kin and all—but I'd hate like blazes to see you go!"

"Can't keep on like this. I've got some bad memories back there, but Joe and me are at a dead-end here. Wish I'd never come!"

"You need a wife, Sky," Sam told him.

"I had a wife." The words were cut off short, and the dullness in Sky's blue eyes reflected an inner anger. "You know what she was like."

Sam bowed his head and considered his answer. He had known Sky Winslow for five years; his thoughts flew back to their first meeting. Sky had entered the store with his wife Irene; Birdwell still remembered how beautiful she was—how bright and outgoing—and how he had envied the dark young man. "We've got a place in the Willamette Valley," Sky had said. "Be coming in as often as we can for supplies."

Sam thought regretfully of the rumors that had come only a short time later—rumors about Irene Winslow. Sky had been out trapping most of the time, and one day a drunken logger had let Irene's name drop in a saloon. Oregon City was a small town, and word spread fast, though Sky never seemed aware of what everyone else in town already knew.

The rumors were further fueled two years later when Sky left Irene and Joe in town for a month while he went north into the hills for better furs. Irene had taken up with a gambler; the two of them openly carried on a romance. Sam had gone to Irene and begged her to show better judgment, but she'd ignored him.

And so, it had been Sam's job to meet Sky when he came back to Oregon City and tell him that Irene had left town with the gambler, leaving Joe with him. He would never forget the flash of rage that leaped from Sky's eyes, and he feared that Winslow would take off after them. "You've got Joe to think about, Sky," Sam had reminded his friend. "I'll help you."

Now Birdwell looked across the table at Sky and recalled a dinner they had eaten here nearly two years ago; after the meal, they'd walked back to the store to find a letter from San Francisco for Sky. He'd opened it, read it silently, then looked up to say, "Irene's dead, Sam." There had been neither hatred nor regret in his tone—only a sense of defeat.

"You know, Sam, this is why we left to come to Oregon in the first place." Sky had reflected aloud. "She never could leave the other men alone. But it sure didn't help to come here, ei-ther—did it?"

Breaking out of his reverie, Sam rose to his feet. "Let's get out of here, Sky." He paid his bill, and they both walked out into the cold air. "You got business to take care of, I reckon."

"Sure."

"Get it done, then meet me at the Rainbow later."

"Not much in the mood for that," Sky remarked quietly. The Rainbow was a noisy place, the biggest saloon in Oregon City.

"I'll get us a back room. We'll have a quiet game—just a few of our friends." Sam slapped Winslow on the back. "Come on; it'll do you good."

"I'll come for a while." Sky glanced up, saying distractedly, "Hmm . . . looks like snow tonight," then walked down the muddy street into the falling darkness.

———

The five men gathered in the back room of the Rainbow were a diverse group. Sitting out a hand, Sky sat loosely in his chair and considered the men around him. Each of them had the po-tential to greatly influence the growing town, he knew. It also occurred to him that there might be more to the meeting than just a friendly poker game. While there was nothing strange in the gathering itself—the men at the table were old friends of his, and it was a long-standing custom to have a game whenever he came to town—there was something watchful about them this night. He leaned back in his chair and studied them through half-shut eyes.

Judd Travers was the oldest, a tall skinny man with a craggy poker face. He was a crafty businessman; not a dog barked in Oregon City—or in the Willamette Valley, for that matter—that he did not know about. No one knew how much property he had, and those who tried to compete with him in business soon found out that his rustic appearance was deceptive, for his brain was as sharp as a razor.

On his left, Henry Sellers, the banker, was of a different stamp. The well-dressed fat man had brought the manners of the East with him. He was the only banker in Oregon City, and a man to be reckoned with; for those who wanted to do business usually had to go through his bank. He was a deacon in the Baptist church, and supported most of the benevolent activities of the town. His charity, however, stopped at the card table, for there he was a carnivore.

Clay Hill threw down his cards and glared at Sellers. "Blast you, Henry! You'll break your back trying to fill an inside straight someday." Hill, though not over twenty-five, was one of the sharpest lawyers in the territory. He had a thin face and a pair of sharp blue eyes. In the courtroom, he was a predator; he hated to lose, and would do anything necessary to win his case.

Sam laid his cards down and laughed. "An agreeable way to die, Clay." He took out his watch, looked at it, then snapped it shut and replaced it in his vest pocket. "You've won enough of my money for one night, Henry."

Sky started to rise, but Clay reached out and pulled him down, grinning. "Wait a minute, Sky. You don't know yet why we've got you here."

Sky sat back, looked over at Birdwell, and smiled slightly. "I'd guess it's another one of your wild schemes, Sam. I hope it's a far cry better than the one you had last year. Mink farming!"

A whoop of laughter filled the room, and Sam said loudly with a red face, "You just wait! Somebody'll do it one day, and it'll put you trappers out of business!" He waited soberly until the laughter stopped, then leaned forward and said, "Sky, this town is startin' to grow. The whole territory is going up—it'll be a state one day, and not too far off. But what we've got right now in this country is a mess!"

"You talking politics, Sam?" Sky asked.

"Partly. Matthew Poole may be polite, but he's crooked as a dog's hind leg, Sky! And he's in the saddle!"

"That's gospel!" Clay Hill spoke up. "I've been in politics all my life, and I've never seen a man get such a grip on a town in so short a time!"

"He sure gets the votes," Travers said.

"Yes, and when he can't get 'em honestly, he has Rolfe Ingerson tend to it!" Hill snapped. "Poole, Ingerson and Dandy Raimez have got a death grip on this town!"

"You fellows come here to make campaign speeches?" Sky asked.

"No—listen, Sky," Sam insisted. "We've got a good thing here in this country. Plenty of water, good farming, more timber than any place on the planet. But we're going to lose it if we don't do something about the way things are."

"Tell him your plan, Sam," Travers urged.

Birdwell glanced at the others awkwardly, and Sky could not imagine what was coming. He was fond of Birdwell, but wary of some of his ideas. "Out with it, Sam. Can't be completely crazy if you've got these three interested."

"All right, here it is," Sam swallowed. "What we need in this country is families. What we've got is a bunch of hard-nosed men. Got to have families to make a territory work, and . . . and . . ." He stumbled for a moment, then blurted out, "And you gotta have wives before you can have families!"

Sky stared at him. "Well, who's arguing with that?"

"Nobody, Sky—but nobody's doing anything about it, either!"

"And you've got some plan to get women here?"

"That's it!"

Clay Hill laughed shortly. "Sky, I thought it was crazy at first, but Sam's kept at me until I agreed to it."

"Nah—it's a good plan," Travers spoke up. "'Course, it's got its drawbacks—like all plans—but I'll back it."

"It all sort of depends on you, Sky," Henry Sellers explained. "The four of us can put up the money—but we need a man who can give some time and who knows his way around."

Sky grew irritated. "Look, why don't you just tell me what

this great plan is and let me make up my own mind?"

"All right, Sky," Sam said quickly. "Here it is. There's lots of men who want wives in Oregon—and lots of women back East who want husbands. All we have to do is fix it so as they can get together."

Sky stared, unbelievingly, then whistled softly. "This is *much* worse than mink farms, Sam!" He watched the serious faces of his friends closely. "I expect this sort of thing from Birdwell— but how in the world did he suck you fellows into it?"

"Let me explain," Sellers told him with the air of authority that usually clung to the banker. Sky had always respected the man, and liked the fact that his religion was not all talk, so Winslow leaned back and listened carefully.

"Sam is right about families. We must have them, Sky! I hate to see my own children grow up in a town like this—full of rough men! Now, what we propose is to form an association that will arrange for transportation to this territory for those women who would like to find a husband and a home. It will all be handled in a very businesslike manner, Sky." He saw a doubtful frown knit Sky's brow. "Believe me, I've asked myself most of the same questions you're thinking of. 'What kind of woman would come under such conditions?' Well, some bad ones I suppose, but I'm thinking that there are decent women who—through no fault of their own—have no home and can't get a husband. We'll screen them, though I recognize we'll make some mistakes."

"What if they get here and don't see a man they like well enough to marry?" Sky objected.

"Then we'll pay their passage back—with no hard feelings," Sellers assured him.

"It's going to be expensive," Sky remarked. He was only mildly interested, and could not see why they had asked him to sit in. "Passage around the Cape is high."

"Well, that's another matter," Travers said quickly. "I've come up with a plan that will get the ladies here free of charge. What we do is bring them here on a wagon train—making enough off of the goods we bring in the train to pay all expenses."

Sky gaped incredulously. "Judd, you're proposing to bring a bunch of women *by wagon train*? It can't be done!"

"Sure it can—if *you* lead the train," Sam responded simply.

"Me?" At first Sky thought he had misunderstood, but a look around the table told him he had not. "Why, you're all crazy!"

"You could do it, Sky," Travers told him confidently, his dark eyes alive with interest. "You've got your furs in for the winter, and you know the country better than any man alive, I suppose. And it would be to your advantage to have Oregon City become a more civilized place. You have a son who needs such things." He paused and suggested tentatively, "You might even find yourself a wife back East, Sky."

Everyone saw immediately that Travers had gone too far. Sam said, "Well, that's it. Think about it, Sky."

Sky got up. "It's not for me," he replied evenly and left the room.

"You shouldn't have said anything about his getting a wife, Henry," Clay said as soon as Sky was gone. "You know he hates women."

"Guess I did make a mess of it," Sellers admitted ruefully. "Well, he'll not do it now—but I don't think he would have gone anyway. Looks like it's all off, Sam. I wouldn't put money into a thing like this unless we had Sky."

"I'll talk to him, Henry," Sam said. "Maybe I can change his mind."

"Nobody else ever did," Clay shrugged.

Nobody knew better than Birdwell what a stubborn streak ran in Sky Winslow, so Sam said nothing for two days. Even then, it was Sky himself who mentioned it first. They were at Sam's warehouse grading Sky's furs when Sky brought it up. "I'm surprised at you, Sam. Thought you'd be at me to go bring those women here from the east."

Sam paused, stroked a beautiful black fox pelt. "Knew you wouldn't be pushed, Sky."

"Well, I've been thinking about it, Sam—and I've decided to do it."

"You *have*!" Sam exclaimed, tossing the fur aside and beating Sky on the back. "Well, thank God for that! It'll work, Sky, I'm tellin' you it'll work!"

Sky grinned at him, then sobered. "Well, I've got my own reasons for going, Sam. Not a wife, either."

"What you got in mind, Sky?"

"Some kind of housekeeper. A woman who can teach Joe and bring a little order into my house."

"You'd have to marry her, Sky," Sam commented. "Otherwise she'd have a bad name."

"I've been thinking of a way. What if I built her a little house, and she lived in it and just did my housekeeping and taught Joe? I mean an older woman, like."

Sam considered it skeptically. "It might work, Sky—but she'd better be old and ugly, or some woman-hungry logger will run off with her."

"Don't worry—I'll take care of that!"

Sam ducked his head and shuffled his feet. "Say, Sky . . . now that you're going . . . can I ask you to do something for me?"

"Name it, Sam." He put his hand on the smaller man's shoulders. "Listen, I've not forgotten how you stood by me when Irene left. Don't think Joe and I would have made it if you hadn't been there. Just tell me—what is it?"

"Well, I want you to find me a wife."

"You, Sam?" Sky stared at his friend in surprise. "Why, you could get any woman you wanted. You're still young enough, and you've got money—"

"It's just that—well, I've never been any good around women, Sky." Sam Birdwell looked at Sky painfully. "I've been turned down, see, more than once, so I'd just decided to give up the idea. But I'd give anything to have a home—and a boy, maybe, like Joe!" He paused and added, "She don't have to be a handsome woman, Sky. I don't care how plain she is! But I'd make a good husband for some woman—once I had her. It's just the courtin' and the askin' part that I can't face up to."

"Why, of course I'll do it, Sam!" Sky said. He looked down at the smaller man and assured him.

"Sam, you'll get the pick of the litter!"

CHAPTER EIGHT

THE APPLICANTS

★ ★ ★ ★

"Wonder what those dogs are barking at?!"

Christmas Winslow looked up at his wife from the table where he sat reading a worn Bible by the pale light of a lamp. He listened carefully, then got up. "Dunno, Missy. Might be something after the stock. Maybe I better go take a look."

He reached for his coat that hung from a peg in the wall as a loud knock sounded on the door. Twenty-six years of mission work had not tempered the watchful habits he'd learned as a mountain man—which was understandable; for those years had been spent right in the middle of the Sioux nation, where life was cheap. Smoothly, he pulled his Hawken from the wall, cocked it, and stepped to the side of the door. Motioning the woman to stand away from the door, he jerked it open with the rifle held steady in his right hand.

"Well—you gonna shoot me, Pa?"

Christmas yelled and with his free arm grabbed the figure that stepped through the door. He was a huge man, six feet three inches, and his grip at the age of sixty was still like a bear trap. "Sky! Look here, Missy!" He stepped back and replaced the rifle on its pegs as Missy came quickly across the room and took Sky's embrace. She was almost as tall as Sky himself.

"You rascal!" she chided with mock severity, "I ought to take a switch to you!" She bit her lips as tears came into her eyes, then put her arms around him again and held him close, unable to speak.

"Aw, Ma, don't take on," Sky said. She was really his stepmother, but Missy had been the best friend that his own mother, White Dove, had ever known. When the Indian woman died, Missy had promised to care for Dove's eleven-year-old son. Holding her now, Sky was grateful for the times in his childhood when this woman had loved him, nursed him, and disciplined him as if he were her own. He looked at his father, who was watching them with a smile.

"Well, for cryin' out loud, Missy, don't smother the boy!" Christmas reached out, pulled Sky's hat off and tossed it on a peg. "Get out of that wet coat, Sky, and set. Missy, it ain't too late to eat again."

Missy Winslow brushed her hand across her eyes, laughing. "I'll fry up some steaks from that doe while you two talk—but I don't want to miss anything, so you talk up loud, Sky!"

She busied herself with the food, pausing from time to time to look at the two men who sat at the table. Soon the tantalizing odor of fried steak filled the room, and the two listened avidly as Sky told them about Joe. It had been five years since they'd seen either Sky or his boy—from the time their son left with his family for Oregon; and they devoured him with their eyes. When Missy put the food on the table and sat down, Christmas glanced at Sky and bowed his head. "Lord, we're thankful for this food, for it comes as your gift. I'm grateful for your mercies on Sky and Joey. In Jesus' name, Amen."

Sky smiled broadly at the old memories this scene brought back. "You still don't waste much time blessin' the food, do you, Pa?" That had always been his father's way—short blessings and long sermons. He chewed hungrily on the rich meat, then said slowly, "I've missed your preaching."

Chris looked across the table and smiled. "Well, you'll get a double dose day after tomorrow. Still just about the same, Sky—turn or burn."

Sky swallowed another bite of the steak before he answered his father. "Nothing I'd like better, Pa—but I can't stay past that. Got to be in New York by March fifteenth."

"Why, you can't do that!" Christmas protested. "You've been gone five years—and now you blow in and stay for *two measly days*? Why, that's downright uncivil!"

Missy put her hand on his arm to stop her husband's flow of indignation. "Be still, Chris." With interest, she turned to her son. "What's the trouble, Sky?"

"Oh, it's not trouble, Ma. I've just got a job to do and the weather won't wait." He felt a pang of guilt. *I should have brought Joe with me,* he thought. But he had known that the trip would be too rough for the boy, and had left him with Sam. He knew that his son would be all right—but the disappointment in the faces of his parents hurt him.

"Sure would like to see that boy again," Christmas said wistfully. He and Missy had children of their own, two girls and a boy, but they were all married and gone.

"I'll bring him next year, Pa, I promise," Sky assured him. "This was just too rough a trip."

"No, we'll be there with *you*," Missy said firmly, glancing at her husband. "We haven't been away from the Mission for ten years—and your father's promised to bring me to Oregon next year. He'll do it, too, or I'll take a war club to him!"

"That's great!" Sky said. "Joe needs to know his grandparents."

"Well, what's this job, Sky?" Christmas asked.

"Now don't laugh, either of you," Sky warned. "I'm going to bring a wagon train of women from New York to Oregon—mail order brides, I guess you'd call 'em." He smiled at their reactions, and quickly explained the plan to them. Finally he said, "I need a little help, Pa. It's pretty risky crossing some of that country; I thought it might be safer if I got a few of the young men from different tribes to go with me as scouts and hunters."

"That's a good idea," Missy nodded. "You could take White Hawk. He still misses you."

"Sure, and Kieta would like to go," her husband added. "He's married a Sioux squaw, but it wouldn't hurt to have a Chiricahua Apache in the train when you cross Apache country." He named a few more and said, "It'll take a couple of days to get them."

"Just have them at Fort Kearney by the middle of April, Pa. It'll take me that long to get the women sorted out and the train put together. There's plenty of money, so they'll be well paid."

"Get the women sorted out?" Missy repeated. "How do you mean that?"

"Well, I'll have to talk to all the women who want to make the trip, and decide which ones to take."

"Be a little harder than picking out riding stock from a herd, won't it, Sky?" Chris asked innocently. "You going to get their weights and so on?"

Missy didn't smile. "I don't see how you can do it. If a woman comes and says she wants to go, and you tell her she can't, you could have a real problem on your hands, Sky."

He stared at her. "I never thought of that, Ma, but somebody's got to make the decision."

They talked long into the night, and when the fire burned low Sky got up to put another log on. He listened to the news of the Mission with interest—marriages and new babies and the like. It was only natural, for he had grown up among these people. "Five years is a long time," he commented after they had finished. "I guess some of the converts must have fallen away these five years I've been gone—some I grew up with."

"It's always that way," Chris said sadly. "But the Lord's blessed us with many real converts—the lasting kind." He smiled broadly. "Long Bow, for one."

"That reprobate!" Sky exclaimed. "He never did anything but steal and fight in his whole life!"

"Not anymore," Missy said. "He never misses a service. Wouldn't be surprised if he became an evangelist. He's won lots of his old friends to the Lord in the last year."

"Never thought I'd hear that."

Christmas took a deep breath and exchanged a quick look with Missy. "Sky, we've been much in prayer for you and Joe—since Irene died. How are you?"

This was his way, Sky knew, of asking if he was going to church, and he had to be honest. "Pa, it's ten miles to a church. But if this trip works, a lot of things will be different. I'll move to town, and Joe and I can go to church all the time."

He explained his plan to hire a housekeeper, and when he was through his eyelids were drooping.

"Let Sky get some sleep," Missy said quickly. "We've got all day tomorrow to talk."

After Sky had gone to the small room in the attic, Chris and Missy sat and talked for a time.

"He'll never marry again, Chris," she said sadly. "That woman hurt him so—he'll never trust another one."

"Too bad! That boy needs a mother."

They talked it over from every angle, and finally Chris said, "Nothing we can do but pray, Missy."

"There never is, Chris," she smiled and then they went to bed.

The next two days passed swiftly as Sky went around to meet his old companions. When he explained the situation, White Hawk said with a gleam of humor in his eyes. "I need wife myself, Sky. Maybe I buy one from you."

"You heathen!" Sky laughed. "They're not *mine* and they're not *for sale*."

"You just making a hard bargain with your brother," White Hawk scowled. "We look these squaws over good, eh, Kieta?"

The murderous-looking Apache nodded gravely. "I got one woman now. Brave warrior needs at least two."

Sky realized that they were laughing at him, and he grinned. "One look at you two, and the whole bunch will probably scream and run back to New York."

Sky felt much better about the train once they had agreed upon the wage he would pay the scouts. The rest of the time he spent with his father and Missy. At the Sunday service he sat with Missy and listened to his father preach. It was not a large group, not over a hundred—the fruit of twenty-six years—but he knew what a monumental task it had been, preaching the peaceful gospel of Jesus Christ to the fiercest tribe of Indians on the face of the earth.

Sky knew that his father's success among the Sioux was due in part to the fact that Christmas Winslow had been initiated into the Sioux tribe, and had married White Dove. Still, if he had not been a man of iron convictions and absolute honesty and courage, his ties to the tribe alone would not have brought these people around. Looking at the dark faces, he remembered many services when he was but a child, when the only ones at a service would be the family—not a single Indian. But the Sioux had gradually been won over, some of them at least, and now he was prouder of his parents than he had ever been before.

After the service they had returned to the house, and as he was packing his saddlebags, Missy came out with some dried meat and cakes. "Put these in, Sky."

"Thanks, Ma."

"You know, Sky, I've thought a lot about your mother lately." She put her hand on his arm, drawing him around, and there were tears in her eyes. "I loved her so much, Sky. Do you think of her at all?"

"Sometimes, Ma." He paused and thought for a moment. "I remember when she was dying, she told me you'd be my mother—and you have been. I'd never forget her."

Missy tightened her grip on his arm. "You're a man now, Sky, and you'll make your own way. But I want to say something to you—and you can't get angry with me."

He smiled and put his arms around her. "No chance, Ma. What is it?"

She said slowly, "Your mother was a Christian, Sky—and one of the last things she said to me was, 'I want my boy to follow Jesus.' I've told you that before, but it's been a long time."

"I remember."

"Sky?"

"Yes, Ma."

"One more thing—about Irene." At the mention of the woman's name, Missy saw his face harden, and she reached up to touch his cheek. "I know she cut your heart out, Son, *but you've got to forgive her*," she pleaded. "Not so much for her, Sky. She's beyond all that—it's for your sake."

"For me?"

"Yes, and for Joe. Because if you keep that hatred in your heart, the bitterness will poison you. And if that happens to you, Joe will drink it in; he'll be filled with hate just like you." She pulled him close and said fiercely, "Oh, Sky, don't let that woman drag you down!"

He felt her body shake with weeping, and held her awkwardly, not knowing what to say. She had touched on the truth. He had never forgiven Irene for her betrayal; whenever he tried, the memories burned inside him like hot irons.

Finally she drew back and wiped her eyes. "Your father and I have prayed for you—and we always will." She turned to leave, and then she gave him one smile. "God won't let our prayers fall to the ground, Sky—but you must fight this thing! It's the hardest thing a human being is ever called on to do—to forgive someone who's wronged him. But that's what Jesus died for—for all of us, for the way we've wronged Him!"

When he rode out of the Mission that afternoon, his last sight was Missy standing there, her eyes begging him to forgive.

————

"Do you have a room for Winslow?"

The desk clerk turned to find himself looking into a pair of blue eyes set in a bronze face. "Ah—I believe so." Looking into a book on the desk, he put his finger on a name. "Mr. Sky Winslow of Oregon City?"

"That's me."

"Yes—Mr. Sellers has made all the arrangements. If you'll just sign here, Mr. Winslow, I'll take you up to your room."

Sky took the quill and signed his name in careful strokes. "Is it always this busy in town?" he asked.

The clerk, a thin man with sleek black hair, smiled as he walked from behind the desk. "Actually, this is the slowest time of the year, sir."

"Hate to be here when it's busy," Sky commented. "Never knew there could be so many people in one spot."

"Ah—yes, indeed, sir!" The clerk led the way to a wide stairway, where a well-dressed couple stared at Sky as they passed. He felt self-conscious, for he still wore his trail clothes, and had neglected to take his pistol off. *Have to dress like a city man,* he thought as he followed the clerk to a room on the second floor.

"Room 206," said the clerk, opening the door and entering the room. "You also have room 208, which has been fitted according to Mr. Sellers' instructions. That is the door that joins the two rooms." The clerk gave him two keys. "I hope you enjoy your stay. We have a very fine restaurant downstairs if you'd care to eat with us."

"Thanks." Sky waited until the man left before he looked the room over. It was a large room, the nicest he'd ever been in. The walls were papered and there was a thick rug on the floor. An oak bed with a feather mattress took up most of one wall; and there was a washstand, a desk with a straight chair and an overstuffed chair as well. He opened the other door and saw that it was much the same except for the furnishings. The bed had been replaced by a dozen straight chairs neatly set around the room.

Closing the door, he walked to the window to stare down at the flow of traffic on the busy street. He watched the carriages, cabs, draught wagons, buggies, and delivery wagons as they rattled down the street. The sidewalks he watched even more closely, for he had never seen so many people. They were a mixed lot, and many of them were obviously foreigners. While everyone in Oregon City dressed in more or less the same fashion, the sidewalks of New York produced everything from a Chinese laundry man with a black cap and pigtails to a well-stuffed couple who strolled along in fine furs. Looking at the man's hat, Sky wondered if perhaps he had trapped the beaver it was made from.

Tiring of this, he washed and lay down to rest. The job of buying wagons, horses, and equipment for the trail had been hard work; and he had spent two weeks in Independence, Missouri, making arrangements for the trip west. The goods that his backers wanted had to be purchased, and he'd had to line up a dozen men to drive the wagons. He hired them in exchange for a small wage and free transportation to Oregon. One man, Dave Lloyd, seemed a higher cut than most, and Sky put him in charge of the men and the equipment.

"I'll be going to get our passengers tomorrow, Dave," he'd said on his last night. "I want to pull out as soon as I get back, so keep a tight rein on things."

Lloyd was a blond man with close-set blue eyes and a scrapper's jaw. He had been around a bit in his twenty-eight years, and had some of the scars of his education on his face, which was why Sky had chosen him to hold the train together. One of Dave's ears was misshapen, and his shuffling gait told Sky the man had done some professional fighting. His guess was confirmed when one of the drivers, a burly man named Simms, challenged Lloyd's authority and had been promptly put on his back with a single blow. Since then, the other drivers had walked carefully around Lloyd. Still, Dave knew a challenge when he heard one. "There might be some trouble, Mr. Winslow, with that many women—most of our drivers are a pretty hard-nosed bunch."

"Guess I already know that, Dave." Sky shrugged. "It's mostly losers who get to Oregon our way—rich people usually pay their own way. But I promise you, there'll not be much trouble over these women. I'll put a bullet in the first man who fools with one of them!"

"Better take plenty of ammunition," Lloyd answered dryly. "When you figure to be back?"

"I want to get out of Independence by the middle of April, so you're in charge of keeping the men sober about that time— oh, and by the way, you've got to find a preacher to go along."

Lloyd stared at him hard. "Mr. Winslow, that's a big order. Don't think there's many preachers waitin' to make a trip like this."

"I don't care what kind of preacher he is, Dave. But the notice said that we'll have a chaplain on the trip—so you best dig one up."

Lying there in his hotel room, Sky wondered if Dave had found a preacher, and was glad it was a problem he didn't have to face for a few days. He slept for four hours, then got up and went down to the restaurant. The food was strange to him, fancier than what he ate most of the time, but he enjoyed it. Afterward he walked around the city, stopping in at a brightly lit building that proved to be a mission building.

Inside, a short muscular preacher was working up a sweat, preaching to a poorly dressed group of thirty people. Sky thought about asking him if he'd ever considered going to the coast to preach, but decided against it. Walking out of the chapel and onto the street, he entered a saloon that had a bar longer than any two buildings in Oregon City. The light from the chandeliers dazzled him, and several times he was approached by women with brightly painted cheeks and fixed smiles. He turned them away quietly, and walked back to his room in the hotel. Looking at his watch, he saw that it was nearly eleven. The interviews would begin at nine, and he wondered if anyone would come. *Would be a big joke on Sam if nobody showed up!* he thought as he drifted off to sleep.

He rose at six the next morning, went downstairs and ordered a breakfast of pancakes and bacon, then drank coffee and read the New York papers while he ate. When he was done, it was a little before eight—still early. For an hour he walked the streets, returning to the hotel at ten minutes before nine. By that time, he was angry at Sam and at himself. *It's a fool idea—and it'll never work!* he grumbled as he climbed the stairs. Going into his room, Sky put his hat and coat on the rack, then squared his shoulders and went to the door. He listened and heard nothing, so he opened the door expecting to find the room empty.

To his utter amazement, all the chairs were filled, and at least six women were standing.

Covering his surprise, Winslow stood in the door and swept their faces with a quick glance. "Well, I'm glad to see you ladies—" Even as he spoke another woman came in, a thin girl, poorly dressed and very nervous. "Come in, miss," Sky said quickly. "We're just getting started."

He waited until the girl had shut the door before he continued. "First I want to tell you the purpose of the association. Some of you may want to leave. That's fine, of course. We're only interested in those who really *want* to go. After I've had my say, I know you'll have lots of questions, and I'll do my best to answer them. Then I'll want to talk privately to those of you who're still interested. All right?"

No one moved, so he went on. "Now, then, let me tell you about the trip and what you can expect. I'll give it to you with the bark on; it's not like going on a Sunday school picnic."

For the next hour he went over the problems they would face, both on the trail and after they got to Oregon. As he had promised, he left nothing out, and when he finished he said, "Now, I know that some of you may have changed your mind, and we'll give you time to leave before we go on." As he had predicted, five of the women got up and left the room quickly. After they had gone, Sky was quick to assure the remaining women, "Any one of you ladies can change your mind at any point—even after you get to Oregon."

Most of the women were poorly dressed and very plain, except for one. Sky had been acutely aware of her the entire time he was speaking, for she stood out like a peacock in a barnyard full of chickens. She wore a fashionable dress that was a bit gaudy over a figure that was full, and would soon be overripe. Her dark complexion was emphasized by too much makeup, and her bold dark eyes drew his, taunting him. "You mean if I don't find a man I like, you'll pay my fare back here?"

Sky saw that she was amused by the whole thing, and felt unsettled by it. "That's the way it is, Miss—?"

"Duvall. Rita Duvall." She must have known that the other women were staring at her, but she obviously didn't care. "Well, if it's question time, I've got a few."

"Miss Duvall, it's my job to get you safely to Oregon. I've got printed agreements here that you can take to a lawyer. They're very simple—and I'll do my best to answer any other questions you may have."

"Just one. What kind of men are in Oregon that causes them to get their women this way?"

He liked her audacity, and smiled in spite of himself. "Just men, Miss Duvall—some of them good, some bad. But it's a new country, and it's full of men who had to go alone. Now things aren't so rough, and they want wives and families."

"Are *you* one of those men, Mr. Winslow?"

Sky felt his face flush, and he knew that she was laughing at him. Her boldness told him one thing: if she wasn't yet hardened by life, she was surely on the verge of it. Sky waited until he could speak more easily.

"No, I'm not, Miss Duvall," he said calmly. "It's a long trip, but there will be no courtin' on the trail. All of the drivers are single men, and they've been told what will happen if they make any sort of improper approach to the ladies on the train."

A tall blond woman, not over twenty-five, raised her hand. Sky nodded to her, and she rose from her seat. "I'm Karen Sanderson. Excuse me, Mr. Winslow—but what *will* happen to a man who does anything . . . improper?" Although she was not attractive in the usual sense, she had a strong figure, Nordic blue eyes, and a pleasant face.

"I'll shoot him, Miss Sanderson." Her gaze did not waver,

and she smiled slightly and said, "I think those who chose our guide chose wisely."

The compliment caught Sky off guard, and he flushed again. Then a stocky girl with carrot red hair and freckles on her rounded cheeks asked, "Well, what *is* this 'improper behavior'?"

"Yes, tell us all about improper behavior, Mr. Winslow," Rita Duvall smirked.

Sky wished he were back in Oregon trapping beaver. "That will be defined by the clergyman who will be serving as our chaplain."

But he was not to be let off so easily. "And what will you do if one of *us* behaves in an improper way?" Rita asked pointedly. "Would you shoot *me*, Mr. Winslow?"

Sky felt like a fool when his face burned again, but he said, "I think, Miss Duvall, that those who are *chosen* to make the trip would not be guilty of poor behavior—but, again, that will be up to the chaplain."

The questions came at him hard and fast, and it was over an hour later before he finally could say, "No more questions? Well, then, I can't talk to you all at once, so we'll have to set up a schedule for the interviews. Excuse me while I get some paper." Going into the other room, he got a notebook from his bag. "Will one of you write numbers on small slips of paper?" he asked, coming back into the room and shutting the door behind him.

"I will." Karen Sanderson took the paper and followed his directions. When she had finished he got his hat and put the papers inside. "Take a number, please, and that will be the order in which I will see you." They took the slips as he moved around the room. "Allow each, half an hour I think. So if you've got number three, your turn will come in an hour, and so on. I'll be here for a couple of days, so there's really no rush. Who has number one?"

"I do."

A thin, middle-aged woman with work-hardened fingers held up a slip, and Sky said, "Please step into the next room. The rest of you can wait here or come back when it's your turn."

Several of the women left at once, but Rita Duvall sat back and held up her slip. "I'm number three, Mr. Winslow. And I can't *wait* for our little talk!"

Rita Duvall—you are one I KNOW won't be going along! he thought, but said only, "I'm looking forward to it myself, Miss Duvall." He turned into the room, well aware that her red lips were curved into a smile that made her look much like a cat considering a mouse she had just captured.

CHAPTER NINE

THE LAST TWO PASSENGERS

★ ★ ★ ★

By the end of the third day Sky had come to hate New York. He hated the talks he had to give, but the waiting room was filled with new groups each morning. The private interviews were worse. Most of the women he spoke with were pitifully eager to get away from a hard life in the city; he struggled to tell them they were headed for one that might be worse.

Some women were eliminated instantly, for physical reasons. At least five of them would have died before reaching the South Pass, and half a dozen more would not have lasted a year. One of them, a women of thirty with an obvious case of consumption, begged him, "Take me with you! At least I won't have to die in this place!"

A few he had refused because of their attitude. Three of them had been argumentative, fighting for their rights even before they knew whether they had been granted a place on the wagon. Sky had less of a problem turning these away, for he knew that they would make a train unbearable. *I'm doing some fellow a favor,* he thought. *A gal like this'd make a man go crazy in a week!*

Rita Duvall was harder. From the minute she swept into his room and sat down, she started her flirtations. He had tried to break the bad news gently, but when she saw that he had no intention of taking her, she threw her head back and retorted,

"What's wrong with *me*? Does a woman have to be plain and dull to go along?"

Sky had met her gaze evenly. "Miss Duvall, you're not fitted for this trip. Look, every one of the other women is headed to Oregon because they couldn't get a husband here." He looked down at her rich figure, taking in her well-dressed hair and full lips, then added dryly, "Obviously, that's not your problem."

Her anger dissipated at once, responding to his compliment. "I still want to go; I have other reasons."

"No, I won't take you. You'd be like a match in a powder keg to the men on the train; they'd be fighting over you in a week. I'd have to shoot all of them, pretty near." She continued to pout, and he got impatient. "Why don't you go by boat? You look as though you've got money. This trip is going to be hard, Miss Duvall. You'd be foolish to go overland when you could go around the Cape in comfort."

Her shoulders sagged, and she said nothing for a long moment, fingering the tassels on her blouse nervously before she finally lifted her eyes. "I—I can't go do that, Mr. Winslow. I can't tell you why, but please—I'm begging you to take me!"

He had almost wavered, for her appeal was very strong, but in the end he held firm. "Sorry, Miss Duvall. It wouldn't be good for the train—and you'd be miserable." She had stared at him silently, then left without further protest.

Sky thought about her several times as he sat at his desk on the last night with a twinge of regret, and wondered momentarily why she had been so persistent. At last he shook his head and picked up the list in front of him—the final choices.

Out of fifty-seven women who had answered the ad, he had spoken to forty-three—the others had been put off by his preliminary speech. Of those he'd interviewed, he had chosen twenty-seven. He ran his eyes down the list, wondering if he had made some bad decisions. For the past two nights he had slept poorly, never satisfied with his choices, but now it was over. Done.

He'd persuaded one stage company to add extra coaches on their Pittsburgh run, so that the women could travel together; he'd put a lady named Edith Dickenson in charge of the group. She was a small woman of twenty-seven with steady gray eyes, brown hair, and precise manners. He was not surprised to find out she was a schoolteacher, for in talking with her he could tell that she was intelligent and educated. He'd signed her on at once, giving her the money for meals and rooms for the group along the way to Pittsburgh, as he would not be traveling with them. At least that was one worry off his mind.

He had asked Edith, as he had the others, why she wanted to go to Oregon Territory. "I got left at the church, Mr. Winslow," she answered evenly. "I was engaged to be married, and the day of the wedding I got a note from my fiance, telling me he'd decided he loved another woman better. I want to marry and have a family, and I want to do it someplace other than here."

She'd be good for Sam, Sky had thought, though he'd also thought the same thing about Karen Sanderson.

Rising from the desk, Sky stretched his cramped arms and went to peer out the window. It was almost dark outside, and his mind was drawn to think of the days ahead. The trail west was rough and sometimes dangerous, but it was a world he was used to—his world. The city depressed him, and he wished he had taken the last stage, but there had been too many details to complete.

He left the room and went downstairs to eat, then stopped by the desk. "I'll be leaving pretty early. Might as well take care of the bill now."

The clerk looked at him strangely; Sky knew that the man was wondering about the stream of women who had come to the desk asking for Winslow. "Come back and stay with us again, sir," the clerk said, handing him a receipt.

"Not likely," Sky replied. "Seen enough people in these three days to do me for a lifetime."

He went back to his room, took off his coat, and settled down to read. About an hour later Sky heard a furtive knock on his door; laying his book aside, he stood up and—out of habit— picked up his gun from the top of the washstand. Concealing the weapon behind the door as he opened it, Sky found himself face-to-face with Rita Duvall.

"Please—let me come in!" she whispered, her large eyes fearful.

He stepped back and she came in quickly, closing the door

behind her. For the first time, she saw the gun in his hand, and the sight of it seemed to bolster her confidence.

"Sky, you've got to help me." Her voice quivered. "I'm in big trouble."

He noted her use of his first name, and followed suit. "What's up, Rita?"

She bit her lower lip, trying to control herself. "I've been living with a man named Nelson Stark for the last year," she confessed. "He's a bad one—I must have been crazy to take up with him—but he's got money, so . . ." She trailed off and began to pace the floor, and he saw her glance at the window. "He's a crook, big time. Last month he got caught and arrested. The police picked me up the same time—said if I didn't tell what I knew about Nels, they'd put me in jail for a long time, too."

She paused, and went to sit in the overstuffed chair by the bed. Her face was pale as death, and Sky hastily poured her a drink of water. "Take it easy, Rita."

She drank the water and put the glass down. "They let him out on bail, and me, too. Oh, Sky—Nels told me they couldn't do a thing to *me*, but I was scared. Then when the trial came, the district attorney had me picked up. Said he was going to send me up for life if I didn't testify against Nels."

"So you did—and now this man is out to get you?"

She nodded. "He's going to kill me. I've tried to get away, but he's having me watched. I know him, Sky! He likes to hurt people. He's playing with me, now—but when he gets tired of that, he'll have me killed and thrown into the East River!"

Sky's first impulse was to ask her to leave; she could see it in his eyes. He expected her to beg, but she had met men like Sky Winslow before, and knew that if she pressed him, it would only harden him against her. So she sat there quietly, biting her lip. He admired that—no matter what else she had done, she was a brave woman.

"Stay here."

She watched as he put on his coat, then slipped the gun into his trouser band. "Be careful, Sky! Nels has some tough ones working for him."

He didn't seem to hear her. "Don't open the door to anybody but me." Downstairs Sky found a different clerk at the desk—a sleepy-eyed young man who nodded to him respectfully.

"I'm Mr. Winslow. Been anyone asking for me?"

"There was a woman a few minutes ago. She went up to your room."

"Anybody else?"

"Well, not to see you." The clerk's eyes were alert now. "But a man came in asking about her—the woman who went up to see you."

"A short, fat fellow?"

"Oh no. Tall and thickset. He didn't go up, though. Just wanted to know about the lady."

"Thanks."

Sky went out of the hotel, turned west and walked briskly away. He saw the bulky figure of a man standing back from a streetlight in the mouth of an alley, but pretended not to notice him. Winslow turned the corner, then broke into a dead run. He passed several people, who turned to stare, but he paid them no heed. Reaching the exit of the alley on the next street, he cautiously turned into it and moved quickly toward the end. The alley was dark, and he inched along stealthily, avoiding the garbage and trash that lay in his path. It was a moonless night, but his eyes could see clearly in the dark. When he was close enough to make out the outline of the man who was waiting, he crept silently toward him.

There was still some doubt in his mind, for he did not *know* for certain that this was the man who was following Rita. He advanced until he was directly behind the man and saw that the streets were empty for at least a block. He pulled the gun from his belt, put the muzzle under the man's ear, and growled, "Don't make a fuss."

The touch of steel made the large man give a tremendous start. "Don't be a fool," he hissed at Sky without turning his head. "You can't rob me here!"

"Step back into the alley," Sky ordered. Keeping his gun trained on the man's neck, Winslow moved back and the man backed up slowly with him. When they were far enough away from the street to avoid detection, Sky reached out and shoved his captive around to face him. The man's face was thick and scarred, but there was no fear in his pale eyes. Sky said, "I'm tempted to send you back to Nels in pieces!" He saw instantly that he had his man, whose expression changed at the mention of Stark's name.

"What's the game?" The burly man demanded. He was a cool one; the gun in Sky's hand might have been a stick for all the attention he paid to it.

He'll have to go down—he's too tough to take water! Sky realized. He couldn't risk a bluff. Reluctantly, Winslow raised his gun with a swift motion and clipped the man across the head. It almost didn't work, for the big man had seen it coming and ducked. His soft hat partly cushioned the blow, catching him on the side of the head, just over the ear. He fell to his knees, and Sky struck him again as the man reached into his coat pocket.

He crumpled to the ground, and lay there without moving a muscle. Sky reached into his own pocket, removed his billfold, and put it in the unconscious man's pocket. Then he took the tough's gun from his inside pocket and put it beside his hand and ran across the street to the hotel. The clerk looked up at Sky, who said, "Fellow tried to hold me up. Can you get the police?"

In ten minutes it was over. The clerk had sent a boy for the police, and when the two uniformed men arrived, he introduced Sky as one of the guests. Sky led the police into the alley, where one of them bent over the form and exclaimed, "Well, Charlie! It's Benny Boudreau!" He stood up and gave Sky an odd look. "You took Benny by yourself—and him with his gun out?"

"Someone walked by the alley and distracted him," Sky shrugged. "He probably wasn't expecting me to have a gun."

"Pretty good!" the other policeman said with a laugh. "We've been tryin' to get this one for a long time."

"Be all right if I come to the station and press charges to-morrow?"

"Sure, Mr. Winslow," the first officer said. "That'll be fine. Here's your wallet. Be at the office about noon."

"He'll have a lawyer by then?"

"Not likely! We'll just have a little talk with Benny first. Law says 'within twenty-four hours' he gets to see a lawyer—and not a minute before!"

Sky went back to the room and knocked on the door. "Open the door, Rita." It opened and he stepped inside. "You don't have to worry about that one, anyway."

"I was watching from the window," she said slowly, looking at him with renewed interest. "You really did Benny in. Nobody ever did that before."

"It doesn't solve your problem. He'll be out tomorrow, I guess."

"Take me with you, Sky," she implored. "I won't cause any trouble."

He stared at her, making up his mind. "You probably will, but I can't leave you here." He pulled a blanket off the bed, then went to the door that joined the next room. "Stage leaves at five in the morning. Better get some sleep."

"Sky . . ."

He turned, his hand on the doorknob. She walked over to him and laid a hand on his arm. "Thanks!" She was very close, and the fragrance of her perfume made him a little dizzy. He hesitated, taken by surprise at this woman who was suddenly so open and vulnerable to him. He was not by nature a womanizer, yet a powerful desire rose up in him as she moved to put herself in his arms and turn her face up to his. He obeyed his instincts and lowered his head to touch his lips to her soft mouth, and the sensation made his head rush.

She drew his head down and put her lips against his ear. "You don't have to leave, Sky!" she whispered.

He had never known a woman could be so powerful. He almost moved back into the room—but something stopped him. A little roughly he pushed her away and took a deep breath.

"No, Rita," he said harshly. "You can go to Oregon, but just as another passenger. That's all!"

She took a step back. "All right, Sky." Then she cocked her head and sighed. "Wish I'd met a man like you a long time ago—things might have been a lot different for me."

Sky opened the door to the next room and nodded to the one that led out to the hallway. "Don't open that door. We'll pull out of here at dawn."

He shut the door and leaned against it for a moment, displeased with himself. He had been shaken by her kiss, and even more shaken by the hunger that kiss had stirred inside of him. He did not love her, he knew; it had been a purely physical reaction, but for an hour he lay in his blanket, unable to go to sleep.

The large clock down the hall had just chimed twelve times when a soft knock sounded on the door of the room where Rita slept. He was on his feet in an instant, and just as he plucked the gun from a chair, the door opened, and Rita whispered, "Sky—there's somebody at the door!"

He motioned Rita to step into the other room, but she paused at the door to see what would happen. "Who's there?" he called.

A woman's voice answered uncertainly. "Mr. Winslow? I need to talk to you."

He slid back the bolt and opened the door to find a young woman with a baby. By the yellow lamplight, he could see that she was slender with hazel eyes and curly auburn hair. She looked very small standing there, and he asked, "What is it?"

She shifted the baby to her other arm. "I want to go to Oregon."

She's got to be kidding. To her he said roughly, "Sorry, Miss. We've already got a full number for the trip. Maybe there'll be another group next year."

He started to close the door, but she put up a hand to bar the way, her eyes fixed on his. "Please, Mr. Winslow—let me talk to you . . ." He wavered. "Please—just for one minute!"

He rolled his eyes and stepped back so she could enter. Rita was standing just inside the inner door, watching the pair carefully. Sky said, "It's all right. You can go back to bed." The woman came in, casting an uneasy glance at Rita, who had taken her dress off and was wearing only a sheer undergarment. Rita's appearance seemed to bother the young woman with the baby more than it did her.

"In here." Sky led her to the adjoining door, and shut it after they had entered the room. He turned the lamp up, then turned toward her. She stood in the center of the room, holding the sleeping baby. "What's your name?"

"Rebekah Jackson." She was not over twenty, he decided. She was short, but she carried herself with determination; her short upper lip and full lower one were pressed together firmly as she held her head up to look into his face.

"Miss Jackson, you're too late—and we're taking only single women."

"I *am* single," she insisted.

He stumbled over his words awkwardly. "Well, what I mean is—we're not taking women with children."

"I've come here every day since the fifteenth, Mr. Winslow," she said. "But I was afraid. Now I've got no other choice—I'll do anything to get to Oregon! I'll work hard at any job. I'll wash clothes for you all—anything!"

Sky cursed himself for agreeing to talk with her, for he knew that there was no way he could let the woman bring a baby on the trip. No baby would tolerate that rough trip. But now as he looked at her, he found it hard to break off the conversation. He avoided her gaze and stared out the window. "It's a rule, Miss Jackson—for the protection of the whole group. Besides, the trip will be too rough for a baby. What if cholera hits? You'd lose your baby—and you'd blame us for it."

"No, I wouldn't." Her voice was firm, and he turned to look at her again. "And I'm going to lose him anyway if I can't get away from here."

"Lose him? How?"

"They—they're going to take him from me." She hugged the child tightly, in a possessive gesture. "I can't give him up! Please—let me go with you!"

The baby, her evasiveness—everything about the case told Sky to refuse the woman, and he set his jaw firmly, trying to think of a way to do it. Something about this woman made it much harder to turn her away than any of the others. As he sorted out his words, however, he realized why it was so difficult: Rebekah looked familiar; she reminded him of someone—someone important. He racked his brain to think of who it might be, and then it came to him. *Missy. Rebekah Jackson looks just like Missy.*

She was much smaller of course; his stepmother was nearly six feet tall and Rebekah Jackson was less than five. Nor did their two faces have similar features. As he studied Rebekah thoughtfully, it came to him—it was more her attitude and the expression in her eyes that brought Missy to his mind.

He had seen the same expression on Missy's face as he'd ridden away, and her plea for him to forgive his wife was fresh in his mind. It had hit him as hard then as it did now, for nothing had changed; the hate that had built up over the years was still a part of him. A new thought came to him. *Am I saying no to her just because I don't like women—and that makes it easier to stick to my plans?* The thought troubled him, and he shifted his feet and ducked his head, thinking.

When at last he raised his eyes, he said slowly, "All right, you can go—but I think you're making a mistake."

She did not thank him as he'd expected. She stood there, hesitant. "I said you could go," he repeated.

She took a firmer grip on the baby and said evenly, "There's something else you should know. I'm going to have a baby— about in July, I think."

His eyes widening, he studied her again. "You didn't have to tell that. I wouldn't have known."

She stood there mutely, making no response to his words. Recounting the dangers of the journey in his mind, he said, "It's another reason why I ought not to let you go."

"Please, don't leave me here."

She looks more like Missy than ever, he thought with annoyance. "The stage leaves at dawn. You got your things?"

She had waited with bated breath; at his word she replied quickly, "Downstairs. I'll go get them."

"I'll do it." Sky turned and opened the door and found Rita sitting on the bed. "You two will be traveling together. This is Rita Duvall."

As soon as the door closed, Rita said to Rebekah, "It's going to be hard for you." As Rebekah came closer, Rita saw the lines of fatigue on the newcomer's face. "Let me hold the baby. You lie down."

Rebekah could barely stand. Rita took the baby and Rebekah sank to the bed, her knees weak. Slowly she lay back and pulled her legs up, her eyes closing. Opening them briefly, she looked at Rita, who was walking back and forth, humming to Timmy.

"Are you with him? Mr. Winslow, I mean?"

Rita stopped humming and looked into Rebekah's drawn face. "No—I'd guess that nobody's with Sky Winslow." Then she smiled and said, "Go to sleep, Becky. It's a long way to Oregon."

CHAPTER TEN

THE NUMBER ONE RULE

★   ★   ★   ★

The stage had pulled out of New York just as the sun began
to send red streaks across the dull, gray skies. Sky had brought
the two women and the baby an hour earlier, and the last touch
of winter in the March air numbed their faces as they waited.
None of them spoke more than was necessary, but once as Rebekah pulled an extra blanket out of her bag for Timmy, Sky
murmured, "Cold for a baby just now. It'll be warmer a little
later." Finally the carriage had rumbled down the rough brick
street, and he'd helped the women on, then made sure that their
luggage was on board. Pulling himself aboard, he took a seat
between Rita and a large man in an expensive suit. Rebekah sat
beside a window in the seat opposite, with the baby asleep on
the seat next to her. A young couple occupied the rest of the
seat, the man looking out of the window at the sunrise. The
driver called out, "Yup!" and the carriage lurched as it left the
station.

Sky planted his feet on the floor, pulled his low-crowned hat
over his eyes and promptly fell asleep. As the carriage rumbled
on, Rebekah passed the time by watching him sleep and wondering what sort of man Sky Winslow was. Despite the uncomfortable conditions, she could see that he was completely relaxed, and that the long full line of his mouth had softened.

The air warmed as the morning went on, and as the first rush of sunlight slanted through the windows, the big man beside Sky took out a cigar. Lighting it, he dragged deeply on the smoke, his face growing blander and happier at once. Clouds of smoke spread through the coach, and he made an ineffectual effort with his hand to sweep them away.

The first smell of it awakened Sky. He opened his eyes and glared at the big man, who felt the weight of his gaze but avoided it by looking out the window. The steady gaze continued to smolder until the businessman sighed heavily, took three rapid drags on the cigar, irritably stared back at Winslow and held the glance defiantly—then pitched the cigar out the window. At once Winslow was asleep again.

All day they rolled along the foothills, stopping at noon for a bad meal at a run-down inn, then mounting the coach again for a long afternoon's ride. When they came to another inn at dusk, Rebekah's legs were so stiff that she had trouble getting out. She allowed the others to dismount ahead of her before she picked up Timmy and pulled herself to the door. The baby was in an active mood, and she nearly lost her balance as he yelled and pulled at the doorframe.

"Here—let me have him." She looked up to see Winslow holding his hands up for the baby, which she passed to him with a nod of thanks. The ground seemed to sway as she stamped her feet to get the feeling back, but out of the corner of her eye she saw he was smiling as Timmy pulled at the watch chain on Sky's vest. He looked up, saw her glance, and seemed embarrassed. "Fine boy," he murmured, handing him back.

That evening they sat down to a supper of boiled potatoes and tough steak. The large man's name was Clements, and he paid close attention to Rita during the meal, trying to find out more about her. Both Sky and Rebekah noted that Rita kept him at arms' length, while at the same time managing to keep him interested. *She knows how to handle men*, Rebekah thought. She'd seen nothing to change her first impressions about Rita, but preferred to make no judgments. Rita had been a help in caring for Timmy, and despite her boldness, she evidenced a real kindness.

"A walk might do us good," Winslow said as they finished eating. Rebekah looked up and saw that he was waiting for her and Rita. The three of them strolled slowly down the deserted road; Rebekah carried Timmy for a time until Winslow reached out and took him without invitation. "He's been good today," he commented, and added, "I've got a boy myself, but he's older than Timmy."

Both women waited for him to go on, expecting him to say something about the rest of his family, but he didn't. Instead, he walked a little faster until they reached a grove of huge oaks, where they turned and returned to the inn. "Better get all the sleep you can," he suggested as they approached the inn. "This is going to be a hard trip."

"How long will it take?" Rita asked.

"Four days to get to Pittsburgh. We'll take a steamer up the Ohio, then another stage ride for two days. Got to pull out of Independence by mid-April. The first trains out get the good grass, and that's when the water's good." Handing Timmy back to Rebekah, he added, "This part of the trip may be harder on you than on the wagons. You get to walk a lot then, and this sitting in a coach for ten to twelve hours is hard. I'll be glad when we get to Independence."

Rita ventured nervously, "I've heard a lot about the Indians, Sky." She pulled a lock of hair away from her forehead. "I'm afraid of them—and the awful things people say they do!" She saw with surprise that he was smiling broadly; it was the first streak of humor she'd seen in him. "What's funny about that?" she demanded with a trace of anger.

"Sorry, Rita." He pushed his hat back on his head absently. "Indians can be pretty dangerous—but I guess this trail will be safer than most in that respect."

"Why is that?" Rebekah asked.

"Because I'm an Indian myself, or partly." He grinned again. "Well, only a quarter Sioux—but even that helps a little when you're crossing their territory." Then he nodded to them both and said, "Get all the rest you can."

The two women slept that night in a cramped room on a mattress of corn shucks. It was, they soon discovered, one of the more pleasant inns they would stay in on the trip to Missouri. They rolled out the next morning at five, and the second day was much like the first—monotonous and hard on the muscles.

The second night, Rita and Rebekah slept in the attic of a private home, along with two other women passengers. "This is pretty hard going, Becky," Rita murmured as the two settled down. "I'll be glad when we get to Independence."

She lay still for a moment, thinking. After a while she asked dreamily, "Becky—Sky didn't say anything about his wife, did he?" She waited for Rebekah to speak, but saw that she was already asleep. Rita's lips curved in a smile and she reached out and touched Timmy's hair. Settling down as best she could in the cramped bed, she continued thinking about Sky.

The roads grew worse as they made their way west. Each day they endured the rocking of the coach for long hours, then fell out to eat whatever was to be had and to sleep until the next day. Winslow noticed with some surprise that Rita endured the hardships very well as the days passed. He had expected Rebekah to do well, but Rita had been accustomed to an easy life, and he did not expect her to stick with the bargain. *We'll see what she does when we get to Independence,* he thought more than once.

When they got to Pittsburgh, Sky found the other women at the hotel he had named. "Any trouble?" he asked Edith.

"No." She was calm, but thinner than Sky remembered her. "I checked on the steamer. It leaves at eight in the morning. "

"It'll be easier on you than a coach," Sky encouraged. "I've brought you a couple more passengers." He hesitated, then took her aside and explained the circumstances of each. When he was through, he said, "I should have said no, shouldn't I?"

She smiled. "You *do* surprise me, Mr. Winslow. My first impression of you was that of a much harder man. Now you put yourself in a difficult position just to help two women that most men wouldn't have worried about." The gleam of approval in her eyes made her almost beautiful. "I like you better for it!"

The trip was slow, but river travel was more interesting than the dusty road trip, and the food and accommodations were better. The women had long days with little to do, and within a few days they had sifted into groups and chosen a few close friends. Sky kept to himself for the most part. The captain had done two seasons of trapping on the upper Missouri, so he and Sky got along well.

By the time they finally pulled up to the crowded wharf at

Independence, April heat was in the air. Sky hired several coaches to take them all to the hotel, and when they pulled up in front of the building, Sky announced, "Well, we're here."

Rita got out and looked around, saying disappointedly, "So this is Independence. Not much, is it?"

"More than there was ten years ago," he replied, helping Rebekah out of the coach. "Nothing here then but a few log huts and two or three so-called hotels—and saloons, of course. It was the staging point for everything going down the Santa Fe Trail to Mexico. Come on, let's go to the hotel and get you ladies settled in."

From its ragged beginnings, Independence had grown into a richly roistering frontier metropolis of some 5,000 people, most of whom were transients journeying to and from various parts of the West. The original log huts had given way to an assortment of more refined structures: dry goods stores, barbershops, grog houses and emporiums that housed wheelwrights, blacksmiths, harness makers and every other sort of craftsman needed to outfit an expedition across the country.

After their luggage was put off, Winslow led the women inside the Walker Hotel, a three-story frame building. A clerk sat in a cane-bottomed chair, but got up at once as they entered the lobby. "Yes, sir?"

"I'm Sky Winslow."

"Ah, well, now!" The tall, thin man had a long face and false teeth that didn't fit well. "We've been looking out for you."

"Thanks. It was a good trip. Now, I'll need rooms for all these ladies."

"How long will your group be here, Mr. Winslow?"

"No more than two or three days. Tomorrow I'd like to get together with them. Any place we could meet—about thirty-five or forty of us?"

"The church on Elm Street would be your best bet, Mr. Winslow. Rev. Whitlow's the minister—a real accommodating sort."

"Fine," Sky replied, then turned to Edith. "Miss Dickenson, I'm going to be pretty busy—would you see that the ladies get anything they need for the ride out? There won't be many stores along the way, so any women things you'll have to get here."

"Women things, Mr. Winslow?" A humorous light glinted in

Edith Dickenson's eyes. "What sort of women things do you mean?" she asked innocently.

Winslow saw the grins of the others and knew Edith was poking fun at him. He grinned back. "How should I know, Edith? First time I've ever had to be keeper to a bunch of women."

"You may find it educational," she observed solemnly. "But I'll see to it this time. We'll be ready in no time."

Leaving the hotel, Winslow thought that his first impression had been right: Edith Dickenson would be a fine wife for Sam. It occurred to him that Edith might want more romance than the plain storekeeper could furnish. *But that'll be up to them*, he shrugged, and turned his attention to the more pressing problems of the trip.

He found Dave Lloyd at the stockyards on the edge of town looking at oxen. "Mr. Winslow—you made good time!" He gave Sky a hearty handshake in greeting. "Hope you're ready to go, 'cause I think we're about set."

"Figured you'd handle things, Dave." The two of them spent the day going over the stock and supplies for the trip west, as well as the other goods he had ordered for the investors. These were all stored in a small warehouse a few blocks from the hotel. "I let the men have the day off, Mr. Winslow," Dave said as they made their way toward the hotel at dusk. "They're a pretty hard bunch. You might want to cull a few."

"Won't fire a man because he's tough, Dave—only if he gets out of line. You get a preacher?"

Dave raised an eyebrow. "Well, I got one who says he *used* to be a preacher—but he shore don't look much like one now! Come on and you can decide. I got him watching the wagons."

Sky reserved comment. He had confidence in Lloyd, and knew that whoever he had dredged up was probably the best to be found. Lloyd led him to a large vacant area where the wagons were drawn up in order. "Brother Penny," he called to a man who got up from the wagon tongue where he had been seated. "This is Mr. Winslow. Sky Winslow, this is Lot Penny."

Penny was a muscular man of forty or so, with a balding head and a pair of wire-rimmed spectacles perched on the end of his nose. His hand was like a vise as he shook with Sky. "Pleased to know you," he responded in a high tenor voice.

"I understand you're a minister, Brother Penny," Sky said.

"Well, seems there's some argument about that," Penny answered, rubbing his chin thoughtfully. "I got converted under the preaching of Brother Peter Cartwright, and became licensed as a Methodist minister."

"My pa knows him well," Sky remarked. "Thinks highly of him—and my father is a Methodist missionary."

"That so?" Penny studied Winslow carefully, then shook his head. "Reckon I can't help you none, Mr. Winslow. Dave here told me you need a chaplain for all these brides—but don't see as I'm the man for you."

"Why not?" Sky asked.

"I got dismissed. Got no papers with the Methodists anymore."

"How'd that happen, Brother Penny?"

Penny lifted his head, and his thick shoulders squared. "Said I was a fanatic."

The idea tickled Sky, for he knew that the Methodists as a whole were branded fanatics by other denominations. If *they* labeled Lot Penny a fanatic, he wondered what it meant. "Well— are you?" he asked with a smile.

"Reckon so, accordin' to their views—and yours, too, maybe. When I hear from God, Mr. Winslow, I shout it from the housetops! No bishop can keep me quiet when the Almighty gives me a message."

"Don't see anything wrong with that," Sky shrugged. "It's pretty much the same way my pa preaches."

"Well, it wasn't just *that*," Lot Penny admitted. "Scripture says that God gives gifts to men. Well now, some people think all the miracles ended with the apostles in the book of Acts— but I don't! We ain't seen the last of His mighty miracles. Everything from healings in the body to the raisin' of the dead!"

"You've seen the dead raised, Lot?" Dave Lloyd asked.

"Don't matter if I have or not. It's in the Book, so it's so!"

Winslow studied the stubborn set of Penny's jaw and said, "I'd like you to come along, Brother Penny. We need a man who can lay it out plain, and I think you're capable of doing that."

Lot nodded. " 'Pears you're a-goin' to have trouble with some of the men no matter *how* plain I lay it out, Mr. Winslow. Some of 'em already been talking about what they're going to do when the women get here. If them men ain't converted, there's gonna be trouble for sure—but I'll go and preach for you."

"Good enough," Sky nodded. "They'll keep their hands off those women one way or another—either you convert 'em, Brother Penny, or I'll shoot 'em."

Lot Penny thought about that, then nodded. "Just like the Bible, Brother—either law or grace. Turn or burn—that's God's way!"

"He's a good blacksmith, too, Sky," Dave said as they walked away from the wagons. "'Course, his preachin' is pretty rough— got the bark still on it."

"You couldn't have done better," Sky complimented him. "It's going to be a rough trip, Dave. I reckon Brother Penny is just the preacher we need. Hope you did as well picking the rest."

"Like I said, they're tough, but I let one or two of 'em go that wouldn't do. Reckon we can find most of the rest in one saloon or another if you want to run 'em down."

"No, tomorrow's fine." By now it was about six, so he and Dave walked back to the hotel and ate supper at a small restaurant nearby. After they finished, the two rose and walked along the main street, past the steepled brick courthouse to the white frame church. They found the Rev. Ira Whitlow in the small parsonage behind the church building. He was a thin man with a hatchet face and kind eyes. "Certainly you may use the building for a meeting, Mr. Winslow," he responded to Sky's request. "Miss Dickenson came earlier, and I was most impressed with her." He shook his head, adding, "The whole town's talking about your venture. It's very—unusual."

"That's not as bad as I said when I first heard of it, Reverend," Sky grinned. "I said only an idiot would try such a crazy scheme—but here I am. A man never knows what he'll do." Then he added, "You may not agree with this—but I've asked Brother Lot Penny to be our chaplain on the trail."

"Ah, well, he's a strange man, Mr. Winslow. We've had some interesting theological debates—but despite our differences, I think he's a godly man. You could do worse—much worse." The men thanked him for his help and prepared to leave. "Glad to oblige, gentlemen. Come to services Sunday," Rev. Whitlow urged.

"We will if we don't leave earlier," Sky replied. "But I hope to leave on Friday at the latest."

As they made their way back through town, Lloyd spotted one of his favorite watering holes—a saloon called *The Wagonwheel*—and suggested, "Let's have a drink."

"Not for me, but I'll go along."

They went inside and took their places at the long bar. A burly bartender came to serve them. "Hello, Dave. The usual?"

"Sure, Tony." He took his drink and the two talked while he drank it, then ordered another. "There's Tom Lake, one of the drivers, Sky," he said, waving his glass at a man who was standing alone at the end of the bar. "You better meet him. Might be you won't want him along."

"What's the matter with him?"

"A drunk." Lloyd shrugged and added, "But he can drive a wagon, and he was the best I could do."

Sky followed him down the bar to where the man was bent over, looking into his glass. "Hey, Lake, this is the boss, Sky Winslow."

"Hello, Lake," Sky said and put out his hand. Lake looked at him through a pair of bloodshot eyes and took the hand with a limp grasp. Sky noticed that the man's hand, while not soft, was not calloused like most men's. Lake was a slight man of average height, with dark hair and eyes that contrasted strangely to his pallid complexion.

"Glad to meet you," Lake said. "Have a drink?"

"Not for me." Sky watched as the man waggled a finger at the barkeeper and downed the drink in one thirsty gulp, shuddering as the raw whiskey went down. Setting his shot glass down, Lake turned to face the two men. "Guess we'll be pulling out soon?"

Sky didn't answer right away. The man bothered him; while the thin, intelligent face was not the countenance of an evil man, Tom Lake could prove to be a liability. Better to replace him with a tougher man than have him play out on the way.

"Lake, I don't want you on this trip," Sky said bluntly. "You're in bad shape, and this is gonna be a rough trip."

"I can pull my weight!"

"I doubt it," Sky replied. "There aren't any saloons along the way—and even if there were, I don't need any man who can't handle his whiskey."

"I can leave it alone, Mr. Winslow," Lake protested, pulling himself to a more upright position. He wiped his sweating brow with a nervous hand. "I don't have to drink."

"You've been drunk every night, Tom—and most of the time while you were on the job," Lloyd interjected quietly. "I told you Mr. Winslow would have the final say about a job, and he says no. Sorry."

Lake's mouth twitched nervously; at Lloyd's words he dropped his head for a moment and studied the floor. There was some dignity about the man, Winslow noted, though his clothes were the poorest quality and his face was ravaged. He had taken a rebuff that would have angered most men, but now he faced them with pale lips and said, "That's right, Dave. I *have* been drinking a lot. But it stops the minute we pull out of Independence! If you see me take another drink, leave me at the first trading post."

"Can't trust you, Tom," Dave shrugged. "You better try to get a job here in town."

Lake's eyes did not waver. "I'm asking for a chance, Mr. Winslow. No more whiskey for me—and I'm the best man with sick stock you could get." He stopped then, his eyes begging.

Sky regarded him steadily, weighing the odds. He knew that the desert would try Lake's thirst in a way the smaller man could not imagine. He finally said, "You really know stock?" The other man nodded eagerly, saying, "Want me to name every bone and muscle in a cow?"

"That won't be necessary—but your staying off liquor *will* be." Sky nodded as he turned to go. "See you in the morning."

When they were on their way down the street, Dave said, "Didn't figure you'd take him, Sky."

"Probably shouldn't have—but then, I probably shouldn't be here myself, Dave. Every man deserves a chance to prove himself." Winslow's tone made Lloyd turn to catch a glimpse of Sky's face, but he couldn't read anything in its expression. "We'll try to get everything pulled together tomorrow, Dave. We'll bring all the drivers in with the women for one meeting tomorrow night, then pull out at dawn the next day."

"Be quite a meeting," Dave remarked as they walked into the hotel.

"No. Short and sweet," Sky returned, then amended that. "Well, short—but maybe not so sweet."

The next morning at breakfast he took Edith aside. "We'll pull out tomorrow, Edith. Have all the ladies at the church tonight at seven."

"All right." Edith considered him for a moment. "Are you worried, Sky?"

"Yes." The flat monosyllable spoke volumes, but he went on. "Everybody should be worried. It's a dangerous trip."

As Sky disappeared through the door, Rita cornered Edith. "Are we leaving today?"

"No, tomorrow—those who decide to go."

Rita gave the woman a quick glance. "That was for my benefit, wasn't it, Edith?"

"I think you ought to stay here. The rest of us are going because we have to—but you can get a man here."

Rita looked at her with a startled expression. "Why—that's just what Sky told me!" She lowered her voice. "Why is everyone trying to stop me? I'm not *that* much worse than the other girls!"

Edith put her hand on Rita's arm and said in a kind voice, "I'm not judging you, dear, but this trip is going to be difficult, even for those who are accustomed to a hard life. You're used to easy things and soft living."

"So are you, Edith!"

"Ah, you see that? But there's a difference between us."

"What difference?"

"You can get a man—and I can't."

The woman's blunt honesty struck Rita, and she stared at Edith, saying, "I don't believe that—about you, I mean. You're smart. Look how Sky picked you to be over the rest of us."

"He sees I'm efficient—but most men don't like that in a wife. I'd rather he'd look at me like he does at you."

"At me? Why, he hasn't spoken to me ten times on the entire trip!"

"You're attractive to men, and he's a man." Edith was tiring of the conversation. "We'll leave early, I think. Get what you need from the stores." She wheeled and walked away.

Sky was so busy that day he didn't take time to eat until Dave reminded him, "Boss, it's almost seven. Women will be at the church soon."

"All right. I guess we're ready for sunup, Dave." He raised his voice and called to the other men. "All right—time for the meeting."

He walked with Dave down the street to the church, nervous and tense. The dangers of the trail ahead did not bother him half as much as the speech he was about to make.

The church was brightly lit with lamps along the wall, and the women were all seated up close to the front as Winslow walked in, followed by the drivers. At a word from Lloyd, they sat down in the rear as Sky stepped up on the platform.

He saw May Stockton on the first row next to Karen Sanderson, who was as cool as ice as usual. Rita sat on the second row to his left, next to Rebekah, who was holding Timmy. A few of the others he knew, but most of them were just vague memories of a brief interview weeks ago. *I'll know them all pretty soon*, he thought grimly, then spoke up.

"This meeting won't take long," he began. As he described the journey ahead, he outlined the hard rules that must be followed, and warned them once again of the dangers. Rebekah only half listened to him, thinking, *I'll bet he doesn't know how handsome he is*. Glancing at the faces of the women in her line of vision, she knew that most of them were thinking the same thing.

For the first time since he arrived in New York, Sky Winslow had put off his city clothing; the tawny buckskins clung to him, clearly revealing the muscular outline of his body. His dark, wedge-shaped face was broken in the reflection of the lamplight into sharp planes, smooth and strong. Sky was not handsome in the same sense Tyler had been, Rebekah realized; he was too hard for that—the fishhook scar at the left corner of Winslow's mouth only emphasized his toughness. As she was thinking these things, Sky caught her eye; she knew he couldn't tell what she had been thinking, but she flushed anyway, forcing herself to pay attention to his words.

"That's about all—except for two things. It's still not too late for you to change your minds." He looked over the sea of faces in front of him, and added, "It was a tough trip just getting here; as you know, Miss Taylor went back to New York yesterday. This thing just wasn't for her. If any of you have any doubts, for any reason, just tell me or Miss Dickenson, and we'll see that you get back to your home."

He waited, half expecting one or more to take him up on the offer, but no one spoke. "All right—now the last thing. The trip ahead is going to be a long one, and we'll all get to know each other pretty well by the time it's over. But I want to make one thing very clear before we even start: There'll be no mixing between women and men on this train."

A stir went over the crowd, and May Stockton piped up, "What do you mean—'mixing'?"

"I mean, no walking together, no parties, no friendships."

"Don't you trust us, Mr. Winslow?" Karen Sanderson's face was calm, but there was a challenge in her husky voice, and a rustle went over the women at her question.

It was the challenge Sky had known would come, but he had expected it from another quarter. Aside from Edith Dickenson, there was no woman with the maturity that Karen had, and he wished another had spoken. Nevertheless, he turned to face her and said evenly, his voice edged with authority, "No, Miss Sanderson, I do not trust you." He waited until the gust of disapproval from the women died down, then added, "I don't trust myself either, nor any person in this room. Not under these conditions. I was against this trip from the beginning for this very reason. I can handle Indians—but no man can handle romancing on the trail—and I don't propose to let it happen."

"Reckon we're all grown-up!" A male voice broke across the room, and Sky glanced up to see Jack Stedman rise to his feet in the back of the room, a look of resentment on his face.

"I'm not going to argue about this thing," Sky announced. "We can discuss the other rules, but this one's not debatable. If you can't live with it—man or woman—don't be in the train when it leaves in the morning!" He looked at the women and asked, "Anything to say about this matter, any of you?"

Edith said firmly, "You know what to expect better than any of us, Mr. Winslow. If you say so, then that's the way it must be." A slight smile played on her lips. "Guess I want a husband as much as any of us do—but I can wait until we get to Oregon."

"I can hold out if you can, Edith!" Mary giggled.

As the women filed out, Rita stopped close to Sky and whispered, "You take care of the womanizers, Sky—but who takes care of you when *you* get romantic?"

"I'll lend you my gun, Rita," Sky responded. "You can shoot me if you see a romantic light in my eyes."

"I'll think about it," she said and filed out with the others. Outside, she caught up with Rebekah and laughed. "Never thought I'd be headed out with a bunch of men and a 'Hands Off' sign around my neck!"

"Like Edith said, it has to be that way, Rita."

"Oh, does it? We'll see how long rule number one lasts!"

CHAPTER ELEVEN

INCIDENT AT FORT KEARNEY

★ ★ ★ ★

For the first two weeks on the trail, rivers marked their progress. Sky chose to start out easily, so the first day they made only six miles, and by the time they crossed the Wakarusa two days later, a loose order had settled upon the train.

At four o'clock each morning Sky fired a single shot signaling the beginning of the day; in a short time slow-kindling smoke rose from the campfires while half a dozen men rode out to move the stock toward the camp. From six to seven breakfast was eaten, wagons reloaded, and the teams yoked. The fourteen wagons moved out promptly at seven, leaving the camping spot—so lately full of life—to sink back into the profound solitude that reigned over the broad plain.

Sky rode out scouting each morning, leaving Dave Lloyd in charge. There was no danger, he knew, so close to Independence, but he brought back meat every day, and it was good to keep the minds of the drivers and the women alert to the idea of danger.

At noon, the teams were not unyoked, but simply turned loose from the wagons while a quick meal was eaten. This was the time when Sky settled any arguments which may have arisen that morning, and when minor repairs were made.

By late afternoon the men and the beasts were tired, so Sky

would choose a spot to camp while there was still daylight. The drivers grew expert at pulling the train in a circle so tight that the hindmost wagon precisely closed the gateway, forming a barricade. Everyone joined in to prepare fires of buffalo chips to cook the evening meal, pitch tents, and prepare for the night. For the first week, almost everyone went to bed as soon as the meal was over, but as they toughened up, the sound of talk and low laughter scattered in the air as the women gathered in small groups, and the drivers carried on the inevitable card game beside their own fire.

They crossed the Kaw River, and a week later the Big Blue. It was May by the time they forded Sandy Creek and hit the Little Blue early in the afternoon. Rebekah took off her shoes and splashed across the stream, stopping long enough to dangle Timmy's feet in the water, laughing as he drew them up with a grunt. Swooping the baby up in her arms, she saw Sky Winslow riding back with an antelope across the pommel of his saddle. He unstrapped it and tossed it to Lloyd, who drove the first wagon, then looked up and saw her. Dismounting in an easy motion, he tied his horse to the rear of the second wagon and came to stand beside the stream just as she and Timmy came splashing up to the bank.

"We made good time today," he said with a hint of awkwardness. He had done no more than greet her in passing since the train had pulled out of Independence. Then again, he hadn't talked with any of the other women except for Edith Dickenson—and sometimes after supper with Rita Duvall. Rebekah knew that he was skeptical about her coming on the trip, but there was nothing she could say to make it appear better to him.

"Is it much farther to Fort Kearney?" she asked.

"Two days, I reckon." He reached out, saying, "Here—let me take the boy." He took Timmy as they walked slowly to the wagons. "We follow the Blue right in to the Platte. It's not much of a place—Fort Kearney, but they've got a store where you can get anything you might need."

"I don't need anything now."

He looked down at Timmy. "Well, I mean things for later—for when the baby comes, I mean." He seemed embarrassed, and hurried over his words. "If it's money, don't worry about that. We can settle it when we get to Oregon."

"That's very nice of you, Mr. Winslow. There *are* a few things that I'd like to have."

"Look, when you say 'Mr. Winslow,' I always check to see if my pa's around. Sky's good enough."

"All right." She smiled at him, saying, "I'm Rebekah."

The wagons raised a cloud of dust, and they moved off to one side to avoid it. Most of the women were walking, for the wagons were filled with goods. Sky had packed each of them so that there was space for two women to sleep in the rear, but most of them chose to walk during the day—at least for part of it. Their dresses made spots of color as they walked across the prairie, like the small, colorful desert flowers that carpeted the plain.

"Is it hard on you—all the walking, I mean?"

She looked at him uncertainly, then realized that he was thinking of her condition. "Walking is good for me." She reached down and pulled a few blossoms, then arranged them into a tiny bouquet. "Later I'll have to be careful, Karen says."

"She knows babies?"

"She had two. They both died of smallpox—and her husband, too. I feel so sorry for her!"

Sky marveled that a woman with her problems would have feelings to spare for another's grief. She didn't seem to worry about having a baby in the middle of Indian territory without a doctor—although he personally had some difficulty with the idea. Often he wished he had not permitted her to come, but it was too late to change that.

"Maybe we'll be at Fort Bridger—or at an army fort—when it's time for the baby. There'd be an army doctor."

"Don't worry about it, Sky," she said. "I know you feel responsible for me, but you're not. You've got the whole train to worry about. God will take care of me and the baby."

He shot a glance at her, then shook his head. "That sounds like my folks. Everything is in God's hands."

"You don't believe that?"

He weighed his thoughts. "I'd like to," he said honestly. "Maybe I better ride on and find a campsite now. I'll put Timmy in the wagon. He's too heavy for you to carry." He walked quickly to the second wagon, lifting the baby over the back gate onto the space reserved for him. "Be careful, Becky—don't do too much," he warned, then untied his horse and rode off across the flat plain.

"He's a driven man, isn't he, Becky?"

Rebekah turned to face Rita and May who had come up to walk beside her. "He's got too much to do, Rita."

"He's got time to talk to you, Becky," May grinned. "Wish he'd stop by and give me a kind word. He is one good-looking man, ain't he, now?"

"Better forget Sky Winslow, May," Rita said with a smile. "He's woman proof."

"No man's woman proof," May shot back. Her red curls danced in the sun as she tossed her head. "Just have to catch 'im off guard, that's all."

Rebekah liked May, though some of the other women said she was too outspoken. "How'd you do it, May?"

"Why, I'd just buy me a red ten-dollar dress, put some French perfume here and there," May confided. "And then I'd be real helpless and lean against him, innocent as a newborn lamb! I'd have that gent in front of a preacher before he knew what hit him, I tell ya!"

"That'd work with most men," Rita agreed, "but not with Sky. He had a bad wife, I think, so he's gun shy—he'll run like a deer from any woman who's thinking marriage."

"He told you about his wife?" Rebekah asked.

"Oh, he's never said a *word* about her. Talks quite a bit about his boy, though—and that's why I think she let him down." Rita shrugged. "His eyes got cold when I mentioned her, so I let it go—but he doesn't trust women. You can bank on that. I've been around a few men who had good wives, and you can always tell."

"Well, maybe I can't have our fearless leader," May said. "But I'll have a husband when we get to Oregon—even if he's cross-eyed and has only one leg!"

"You want a man that bad, May?" Rita asked curiously.

"I want a *home*, Rita," May responded, and for once she was totally serious. "Just give me a man who'll treat me decent, and give me some kind of house, and some babies. That's all I want."

She looked at Rebekah. "Fact is, I wish I was having the baby instead of you, Rebekah."

"You'll be having your own, May," Rebekah replied calmly. "And you'll make some man a fine wife."

"What about me, Rebekah?" Rita asked. "Think I'll find some man and settle down to washing diapers for the rest of my life?" Her laughter was hard. "Nah—I don't see myself doing that. You two will fall right in with some man—but I'm not like you, am I?"

"You'll feel differently when you meet the right man, Rita," Rebekah said firmly. "Don't you want a home and a family?"

Rita gave an angry shake of her head. "Can't see myself a nice obedient little wife!" She walked off rapidly before either of them could speak.

"Know what, Becky?" May queried as she studied Rita as she marched away. "I think she's gone on Sky. Notice how she manages to get him all to herself every night after supper? She's out to get him—and before we get to Oregon, she'll have him wrapped around her little finger!"

Rebekah changed the subject, but the scene lingered in her mind, and for the next two nights she noticed that every time they set up camp, Rita changed her dusty clothing for a fresh dress, and each night after supper she managed to engage Sky for a short talk. There was one brief flare-up when Jack Stedman stopped to grin at Rita, and she smiled back at him; but they had said only a few sentences when Sky walked by and observed the pair.

"Jack, get back to your own fire."

Stedman's face reddened. "You the only one who can talk to a woman, Winslow?"

"That's it." Sky turned to meet the challenge of the big man with an easy self-assurance. "You knew the rules before we left Independence, Jack. Now, you can either get back to your fire— or you can make your way back home. Tonight. Alone. Which'll it be?"

The challenge came so abruptly that Stedman was taken off guard. He thought about the pistol he had holstered at his belt, but Sky had one as well—and a reputation as a sure-shot to boot. But Jack Stedman was not one to back off from any other man, and for a brief moment, he stood there, weighing his options as the others held their breath.

Stedman glared at Sky, the desire to fight in his eyes and his hand hovering over the gun at his hip. But there was something about Winslow that made him suddenly cautious; with a curse he wheeled and walked back toward the fire where the other drivers had been watching.

A hum of talk rose up, and Dave Lloyd murmured to Tom Lake, "Stedman just about run his string out that time."

"He's a pretty rough customer, Dave," Lake responded, adjusting his spectacles. "Been pretty pushy since we started this trip. Might be too much for Winslow."

"No way, Tom! In a rough-and-tumble he'd probably be too much for Sky, but he'd get his ticket punched if he tried to pull that gun of his. He knows it, too." Lloyd looked at Lake's slight form and said, "Better stay clear of him for a few days, Tom. He'll be like a bear with a sore toe. Man like Stedman can't take a put-down like that without taking it out on somebody."

"Got no quarrel with Jack."

"Makes no difference. Just watch out for him."

The next day they reached the Platte, which Sky claimed was a mile wide and six inches deep. Rebekah walked over a rise beside Karen Sanderson; on the other side, the world flattened out before them as far as the eye could see. Rebekah had never seen anything like it; she had lived in a world hidden by trees and buildings and hills—a small world for dolls, where distance was something three blocks away. Now she saw the sky tilting to meet the flattened ground, and whispered, "Karen, look at it!"

"I know," the other woman replied quietly. "It makes me feel very small."

All afternoon they walked along, feasting their eyes on the panorama of sky and land, the borders of which met along a seam that was almost invisible. The next day they saw the fort, shining white in the afternoon sun high up on a bluff. Spotted below were white objects that they discovered were tepees. As they approached, two mounted Indians came out and met Sky, the trio forming an outline against the red sky. In a few minutes, he wheeled and galloped back alone to lead them to a spot outside the fort.

"It's not much, is it?" Rita looked around as they all walked eagerly inside the walls of the fort. There was a drab monotony about the collection of log huts that occupied the interior of the log ramparts. "At least I'll be glad to sit down on a *real chair*! I hope we stay here for a week."

"I heard Mr. Winslow tell Dave that we'd pull out day after tomorrow," Karen told them. "In any case, I doubt there's much in the way of entertainment here."

Like most western army posts, Fort Kearney had little in the way of elegance. Officers occupied private quarters, but enlisted men were crammed into barracks where rows of bunks stood head-in to the walls. Candles provided a flickering light, and a round iron stove offered a tiny circle of warmth. Privies were outside, and there was no bathhouse.

Colonel Malachi Kenyon sent word to Winslow shortly after they arrived, inviting him to come to his office. The colonel had been stationed in the North at one time, and had become friends with Christmas Winslow and his family. Sky remembered him as a trim lieutenant, but the years had added pounds, so that now he bulged in his uniform.

The colonel insisted on having some of the ladies in for a meal. "Not *all* of them, Sky," he said with twinkling eyes, "Can't fit them all at once. Just bring about five or six of the prettiest ones along."

Sky said ruefully, "Colonel, I'll have the others mad at me for the rest of the trip—but I'll do it."

He had avoided choosing by telling Edith of the invitation. "You pick out four of the women, and I'll ask Dave to come along."

Just before sundown, he found Edith waiting with Karen Sanderson, May Stockton, Rita Duvall, and Rebekah. They walked the short distance to the fort and went directly to Colonel Kenyon's house. The officer was a widower, and he greeted them at the door with a smile. "Come in! Come in, ladies!" He shook hands with each of them. "Fort Kearney is honored. Haven't seen such attractive ladies since I was back east ten years ago. Well, let's see what my cook has put together; then we can visit."

He led them to a dining room where a Mexican woman was setting a steaming meal on the table, which was covered with a snowy white tablecloth. Real china reflected the lights of the overhead lamps, and the gleam of silverware completed the picture.

"A bit primitive, I'm afraid," Kenyon apologized. "No ice to chill the wine."

"We'll just have to suffer, I reckon," Sky returned with a straight face, and Lloyd grinned impishly.

They ate course after course of the spicy Mexican food. Some of it was canned, of course, for the colonel was a gourmet. May picked up a morsel from a small plate. "What's this?"

Colonel Kenyon waited until she placed it in her mouth, then said, "That's escargot."

May chewed for a moment. "What's that mean, Colonel?"

"It's French for snail."

May's jaws froze and her eyes opened wide. Then she turned her head to spit it out in her napkin. "Some blamed fools would have *swallowed* that!"

The shout of laughter that followed freed the visit from any formality, and they sat around the table lingering over the delicious pie and coffee that followed. Kenyon was a highly intelligent man with a lively curiosity about their venture. He broached the subject carefully. "I don't want to offend, but sink me if I can understand why such attractive ladies as you would have to risk your lives to find husbands." He sat back and glanced at Sky. "Winslow—I'm afraid you've deceived me. You left all the homely women with the wagons, didn't you?"

"I chose these ladies, Colonel Kenyon," Edith spoke up. She was wearing a plain gray dress and no jewelry at all, but she was attractive in spite of that. She regarded the officer with a trace of humor in her gray eyes, knowing that his curiosity was the norm. "Everyone wonders why we're going to Oregon. It's quite simple, actually. There are many women in the East and few men, but in Oregon it's just the opposite. I want a home, and this is the way for me to get one."

"I see," Kenyon replied. He examined Edith carefully, and took a sip of coffee. "What about romance, Miss Dickenson? Do you suppose you'll find *that* in Oregon? I was under the impression that all women are entitled to it—expect it, in fact."

"My expectations fall in a different category, I'm afraid, Colonel," Edith answered. "I was engaged once, and my fiance supplied me with an abundance of romance." She lifted her head high and stared right into his eyes. "Then he left me at the altar. No, moonlight and roses and poetry are all very well—but there's more to a marriage than that."

"I don't think you really mean all that, Edith," Karen Sanderson smiled. "I want a home the same as you—but surely we can hope for a little romance as well?" Her blond hair was a crown of braids that framed her oval face, and a gentleness touched her broad lips as she added, "Does it have to be one or the other? Surely a marriage can have mystery as well as permanence and commitment."

Rita shook her head, her eyes set off by a dark green gown cut low to expose creamy shoulders. "Most of the marriages I've seen have been more business arrangements than moonlight and roses. Men are willing enough to play at romance for a time— but once the ring is in place, they put it away with the piece of wedding cake. Something to remember, but not to practice."

"Why, I'm surprised to hear you say so, Miss Duvall," Kenyon remarked, though he did not mean it. The woman stood out from the others in a glaring fashion. "If you feel so strongly, why would you cross a continent to enter the institution?"

The question caught Rita off guard, they all noticed, but May rescued her quickly. "Well, let me tell you *my* plan, Colonel," she interjected in a lively voice. "All my life I've had to take the leftovers as far as men are concerned. Always took whatever the pretty ones cast off—but it's going to be a different story in Oregon, you can be sure!"

"Going to be hard to get, are you, May?" Dave asked with a grin.

"That's the size of it. The man that wants me will have to whip at least a dozen other men to get me—just for starters. Then I'll let him hang around my door with a dozen roses every night for a month or so—maybe write some of that gooey poetry that I never got. Then, if he pleases me, I *may* agree to marry him—but you can bet he'll have to keep up some of the romancin' even after we tie the knot!"

"Bravo!" Colonel Kenyon cried out. Rising to his feet, he walked around the table filling wine glasses. "I think you should do *exactly* that, Miss Stockton—and all the rest of you as well! After all, if you're going to all the trouble of traveling to Oregon, it's the very least those bachelors can do. A toast—to all the bachelors of Oregon!" He raised his glass, saying with a grin, "May you ladies make them totally miserable—until you make them totally happy by taking their names!"

Resuming his seat, Kenyon noted that the final member of the company had said nothing. Thinking to include her in the light talk, he addressed her. "Now, then, Miss Jackson, tell me—are you determined to get a husband on the terms mentioned by Miss Stockton? Make them fawn at your feet?" He saw that the woman was embarrassed, and tried to soften his remark. "I suppose that you want to have a home and children?"

Later Kenyon wished he'd let well enough alone, for Rebekah lifted her face and looked at him with a quiet air that reminded him of the Scottish women he had met on his trip abroad. She was not flamboyant like Rita Duvall, nor was she as self-possessed as either Edith Dickenson or Karen Sanderson, yet he admired the natural beauty of her face.

"I have a baby, Colonel, and another on the way. I hope to find a man who loves children and will be a father to them."

A silence dropped around the table, and Colonel Kenyon cursed himself for being so clumsy, but redeemed the moment by saying gently, "I'm sure there will be that kind of man—especially when he will gain such a fine young woman for his bride."

Edith changed the subject quickly. "I've been worried about the Indians along the way, Colonel. Do you think we'll have trouble?"

"Always a danger of that, of course," the officer told her, relieved to be on safer ground. "But you've got a good man to lead you. No one in the West knows this country better than Sky Winslow. 'Course, if you were in a train of fifty wagons, it would be much better. Stragglers may get picked off, but Indians would never attack a train of that size." He smiled and added, "Which brings up a matter." Turning to Sky, he said, "There's a small group camped by the river, Sky—just four wagons. They dropped out of a bigger train that left last week, and they asked me to be on the lookout for another train for them to join."

"I don't think so, Colonel," Sky rejoined. "Ordinarily I'd jump at it—but this train is different. Don't think it would work to mix with another bunch."

"As you say, of course," Kenyon nodded. "You've got to think of your own train—but wouldn't it be possible for the two groups to travel together but camp separately? That way you'd both have the advantage of a larger train—more firepower."

"I'll think on it. Why'd they leave the other train?"

"Can't say. Some argument about leadership, I believe. But I have no vested interest in the group. Do as you think best."

The party broke up about nine o'clock and Sky asked Dave to take the women back to the wagons. After they had left, he talked with Kenyon about the trip that lay ahead. "You weren't telling it all about the Indians, were you, Colonel?"

"No. Didn't want to alarm the women. We've had reports that Spotted Elk is on the warpath in earnest. He says that he's tired of having his hunting grounds taken by whites, and that he'll kill anyone who tries to cross his territory."

"He's pretty tough," Sky replied quietly. "I met him once about five years ago."

"That might help—but if I were you, Winslow, I'd wait for the next train. Be easier to get through if you were in a train of fifty or so."

"Don't want to wait, Colonel—but I'll go check on the train you mentioned."

"You'll find them down by the river just beyond the sandstone outcropping."

Sky left and made his way to the river. He found the wagons with no trouble, and when he got close enough, he called out, "Hello!"

"Who's there?"

"Sky Winslow. Want to talk about joining trains."

"Come on in."

Sky found a small group of men and women seated around the large fire he'd spotted. A big man dressed in overalls stepped forward. "Git down and set," he invited in a deep voice. "Got some coffee left. My name's Albert Riker. These is my boys, Burt and Pete." He indicated two young men who had the same big build as himself, then introduced the man next to him. "That's Will Kent, my nephew."

The coffee was bitter, but Sky drank it down and said, "Haven't got long, Riker. Taking a train of fourteen wagons through to Oregon City. Colonel Kenyon tells me you might be interested in joining up with another train."

"Might be." Riker stared at Winslow, considering him carefully, "We broke off with the train we left with. The wagon master was a fool!" His voice grew angry. "Wouldn't even put out a guard at night! Can you believe that?"

"Wouldn't care to try that myself," Sky replied. Then he handed the cup back to Riker and said, "You better know what kind of a train we are." He explained the nature of his group. "It's hard enough to keep my drivers and the women apart; the only way I'd agree to join you is if you keep your people separate from ours."

Riker shook his head. "Never heard of such a thing—but it's your lookout, Winslow. All I want to do is get my family to the coast. Might not sound neighborly, but I'll find my own neighbors when we get to Oregon."

"You know this country, Winslow?" one of the sons spoke up.

"Been over it quite a bit."

"Done any Indian fighting?" the other son shot back. "That soldier told us a Sioux chief is on the warpath."

"I know the chief a little. May be a help."

He said no more, but stood there, waiting for Riker to decide. Soon the tall man nodded. "Agreed. We'll keep our own company, Winslow. You want to leave in the morning?"

"If that's not too soon for you."

"Not a bit! We'll meet you at sunup!"

"All right." Sky mounted and rode back to the wagons, wondering if he had done the right thing, but soon put the matter out of his head. He stepped off his horse and was met at once by Dave. "We got troubles, Sky."

"What's up?"

"Jack Stedman beat Tom Lake to a pulp. They got to drinkin' and kicked up a ruckus." There was anger in Lloyd's tone. "I'da shot him, Sky, but then we'd be short two drivers instead of one."

"How bad is he?"

"The women have been trying to work on him. You'd better take a look." He led the way to a wagon where Rebekah and Karen were bending over a still form.

"Let me see." Sky bent over to look at Lake's face and was shocked. Both the man's eyes were swollen shut, and his nose was obviously broken. One of his ears had been torn almost from his head, but was stitched. His lips were puffy and cut.

"Who did the needle work?" he asked.

"The army doctor," Dave answered. "He's got a couple of broken ribs, too."

"We can't take him on the trip in that condition," Sky said.

"You can't leave him here," Rebekah returned at once. Lake had driven her wagon and although he had not been much of a talker, he had revealed enough about himself that she knew how badly he needed to get to Oregon. "If we make a soft bed in my wagon, I can drive until he gets better."

Sky gave her a look, then agreed. "All right. "

He turned and walked away, headed toward the other fire, and Dave hurried along after him. "Watch yourself, now, Sky!"

Winslow did not appear to have heard. He walked up to where Stedman was waiting, flanked by his two drinking partners, Ralph Osmond and Leon Crumpler. All three were standing there like cocked guns, and Stedman said loudly, "Now you wait right there, Winslow! That fight was none of my doing. Lake called me a liar, and I don't stand that from no man!"

"That's right. Jack didn't have no choice," Crumpler nodded.

"Anybody else see this fight, Dave?" Sky asked, fixing the three men with a sharp gaze.

"Just a couple of soldiers."

Sky felt trapped. The three of them would stick to their story, and he could not continue the trip short three drivers. "Stedman," he said, "you're a sorehead and a troublemaker, but no more. If you lay a hand on any man in this train again, I'll cut you down."

The threat hung in the air, and Stedman said stubbornly, "No man calls me a liar!"

"Remember what I said," Sky reminded him and walked away.

"He thinks you were afraid to buck him," Dave said. "He'll give you more trouble, sure." He waited for a reply, but none came. "That feller Lake, he was doing real good, Sky. No drinking all the way from Independence, and now he's all done in. That Stedman. . . !"

Sky's reply was soft as the night air. "Oh, well, Dave, something may happen to him before this trip is over."

Surprised at the mild response, Dave looked over to see Winslow's face, and something he saw seemed to reassure him. "Yeah—reckon it might, Sky. Reckon it might!"

CHAPTER TWELVE

RITA TAKES A TRY

★ ★ ★ ★

Lake had a bad night, but Rebekah got a supply of laudanum from the army doctor. "We'll be using it for other hurts," she said as Sky stopped by their wagon before the group pulled out. She had asked Karen to take Timmy in her wagon until Lake got better, and now she pulled herself onto the wagon seat and took up the reins. "Ready whenever you are, Sky," she told him.

"Be a pretty bumpy ride on that seat," he said. He had noticed her thickening figure and wished there were another way. "I'll come and spell you after we get rolling."

He pulled his horse around, rode to the front of the column, and waved a hand at Kieta and White Hawk. The two slipped on their ponies and rode toward him. He grinned at the startled look on Dave's face. "Forgot to tell you, Dave, I hired us some guides."

"Them?" Dave asked in amazement. "But—they're *Indians!*"

"So they are. That's why I want them along."

"Don't know how it will go over with the others, Sky."

"If they don't like it, they can stay here." Sky rode along in front of the train, aware of the buzz of talk, but ignoring it as he discussed the trip with Kieta and White Hawk. When they got to the river, he saw that the Rikers were already in line waiting to join the train.

Riker started at the two Indians, and Sky said, "This is Kieta and White Hawk. Going to do some scouting for us."

A hard expression crossed Riker's face. "I don't trust an Indian, Winslow. They're all alike—treacherous."

Sky smiled. "Funny—that's what most Indians say about white men. But I know these two." He paused and added with no emphasis but with a light in his blue eyes. "Matter of fact, White Hawk here is my cousin."

The Rikers gaped and Malon Riker, the older of the boys, exploded, "Pa, we ain't gonna go on a train led by them savages, are we?"

Albert Riker plainly had some of the same thoughts, but he was anxious to get to Oregon, and the next train might not come for a month—and they might not want late additions. He chewed his lower lip as he thought it over, his big shoulders sloping. "Guess it'll be all right," he replied finally. "You say that one is a Sioux? Any kin to this Spotted Elk the colonel talks about?"

"Reckon they're some kind of kin," Sky shrugged. "Lots of different brands of Sioux, but they're pretty clannish. Spotted Elk is a Teton Sioux, and White Hawk is an Oglala. But it won't hurt us to have him along when Spotted Elk comes calling. Besides, these two will bring in all the meat we'll need."

"All right, Winslow. I told my people to stay clear of your train when we stop for the night. You know the way and we don't, so you're the wagon boss far as that goes."

"Glad you can see it like that," Sky answered. Then he threw up his hand and signaled for Lloyd to take the train on. He waited until Riker's wagons pulled in behind them, then said, "Guess we'll go get something for the pot. Don't expect Spotted Elk will give us any trouble—not till we get past Laramie." The three rode out and spent the morning hunting.

At two o'clock Dave saw a single horseman, and soon recognized Sky. He watched as Sky came closer. "Got some prairie chickens and a couple of small antelopes," called Winslow.

"Where's the Indians?"

"Oh, they'll come in when they take a notion. That's what an Indian likes, Dave. Prowling around and looking for trouble." Chuckling, Sky jumped off his horse. When Rebekah came by driving the second wagon, he tied his horse to the back of it and hoisted himself up over the rear. Lake was lying on a thick pile of quilts, and he turned his head toward Sky. His face looked worse than it had before, but that was to be expected.

"Who is it?" he whispered through his bruised lips.

"Winslow. How you feeling, Tom?"

"Well—there's a spot up high on my left arm . . ."

Puzzled, Sky touched the arm gently. "You mean here?"

"Yeah—well, I don't hurt *right there*, Winslow—but I do every place else."

"You took a bad beating, Tom. But there was nothing I could do about it. Stedman and his friends all say you started it."

Lake laughed, then gasped from the pain of the broken ribs. "Sure. Little Tom Lake jumped on the three of them!"

"What was it about, Tom?"

He hesitated. "They were talking wrong about the women on the train."

"Any particular one?"

Lake avoided his question. "Gotta thank you for bringing me along, Sky. Most men would have left me at Kearney."

"You have Rebekah to thank for that, Tom." He got up and said, "I'm going to spell her for a while. I doubt she's ever driven a wagon in her life. Sing out if you need something."

He leaped out the back of the wagon, landed lightly on his feet, then ran around to the front of the wagon and pulled himself into the seat. "I'll take the lines, Rebekah. Maybe you'd like to walk—or take a rest."

"Oh, I'm all right, Sky." She stretched herself, and turned back toward where Lake lay. "He's feeling pretty bad."

"A beating does that to you. Always worse the next day."

She observed quietly, "This is a hard country."

"Every place is hard. Guess there are people in New York who got beat up last night. The Bible says, 'There's nothing new under the sun.' " He sat loosely on the seat, his eyes the only alert thing about him as they constantly scanned the horizon. He was, she thought, like a wild thing, totally aware of the world, of his world—the trees, the hawk that circled in the sky, and the snake that coiled and struck at the wheel of Lloyd's wagon.

She asked, "Do you miss your boy much, Sky?"

"Yes." He turned to her and explained soberly, "Been worried about him. The two of us live a long way from a settlement, and he's getting too old for that. Needs to learn books and how to be with people." He broke off suddenly as though he'd been caught in some sort of error; she'd noticed that he often did that whenever he'd made a personal remark. *He's built a wall around himself a mile high,* she thought. *That woman must have hurt him terribly.*

Two hours later he called out, "Dave, pull in by those cottonwoods. There's a little stream there."

Soon the cooking fires were lit and Rebekah spent the time playing with Timmy. "He's such a good baby," Karen remarked as she watched. "Did you have a hard time with him when he was born?"

Rebekah hesitated, and for one moment she almost weakened. Then she replied, "He came pretty easy." That was what Mary had told her, so she was able to put the question aside without a direct lie or allowing any further questions concerning her life. She changed the subject quickly. "I think Timmy can ride in our wagon in another day. Tom felt pretty sick today, but he'll be better by then."

"He's no trouble. Look, the food's ready." They went to the cooking fire and found Sky squatting beside it with a small black pot simmering in front of him. "Didn't know you could cook," Karen smiled.

"Got some prairie chickens this morning. My ma always fed me chicken soup when I was sick. Guess this is about as close as we can come." He lifted the lid and sniffed it. "Smells pretty good. One of you want to see if you can wrestle some of this down Lake's throat?"

"I'll do it if you'll watch Timmy," Rebekah offered. She filled a pan with the steaming soup, found a big spoon, then made her way back to the wagon.

"She's a good nurse," Sky remarked.

Rita had come up in time to hear the conversation, and she stooped down beside Sky. "Well, there goes rule number one, Sky."

"Rule number one?"

"Sure. Women and men don't spend time together. Looks like Rebekah and Lake are spending all their time together. Can I have some of that soup, Sky? I'm tired of antelope."

"Sure—but about Rebekah and Tom, that's a have-to case."

"Oh, I don't mind," Rita replied as she took some of the soup and began sipping it hungrily. "But others might think it's odd."

"They can think what they like."

Sky got up and walked away, and Karen said, "You made him angry, Rita. He's got a hard job."

Rita shrugged. "I knew it'd never work. Men and women are going to get together. Sky can't stop it, and all Lot Penny's preaching won't stop it either."

Penny had wanted to have services every night, but there was little response, so he contented himself with the service each Sunday morning, and used his influence with greater subtlety during the rest of the week. He'd had one clash with Rita, saying to her, "Sister, you shouldn't wear such revealing clothes. It's distracting to the men."

Rita had been wearing a loose dress, the sleeves cut off between the shoulder and elbow, the neck low enough to reveal the curves of her body. "Let them look the other way, Lot!" she'd snapped.

"No, men are easy stirred. And no woman on this train knows that fact better than you. They can't help it."

"If they can't help it, neither can I," Rita had frowned. "And I don't want any more of your preaching!"

Later Penny tried to warn Sky about Rita, but Winslow had only said, "I'll keep the men away from her, Lot. That's about all I can do."

"What about you, Brother Winslow?"

"*Me?*" A look of surprise swept Sky's face. "I'm not looking for a wife, Lot."

"She's a mighty cunning woman, and you know as well as I do that she's got a knowledge of men. She's a deep ditch, Brother Winslow—be sure you don't fall into it."

As the days moved by, and the train made its way across the plain, crawling like insects under the enormous sky, Sky took Penny's warning to heart and kept himself aloof from the train. He went out each day, coming in early to help Rebekah with the driving, but took little part in the talk that went on over the campfire each night.

Day after day the train moved along the banks of the Platte

River. Three miles on either side the land rose in sandstone cliffs, higher and more broken as the trail moved west. Game was plentiful—antelope and coyotes, grizzlies and black bears, buffalo and innumerable prairie dogs. Sky told the people that the Platte valley lay in a kind of no man's land, with the warlike Pawnees to the north and the Cheyennes to the south. "We'll be in Spotted Elk's hunting ground soon enough," he added.

They crossed the confluence of the Platte's north and south fork, followed the north fork, and were forced to transport the wagons by chaining the wheels to the wagon boxes and skidding them with ropes to the bottom of the grade. The trail led through Ash Hollow, and as they began to move upward, the nights got colder.

On the first day of June, a Sunday, they reached a towering mass of stone west of the river. "Chimney Rock," Sky announced as the church service broke up. "Lots of people carve their names on it."

"Let's go do it," Rita suggested at once. She had been infuriated by the sermon, for Brother Penny had preached on the lusts of the flesh, and she had felt his eyes fixed on her. "Anyone care to go along?"

"I'd like to go," Karen responded, and several others spoke up. There was little to do on Sunday afternoons, and the fresh, cool air made them want some exercise. "Would it be dangerous, Mr. Winslow?"

"Might break your neck—but no Indians. Want to go along, Dave?"

"Sure."

"All right, we take the lightest wagon, unload it and ride to the base. But I warn you—it's a steep climb."

They made the trip quickly, and Sky said, "Dave, you go ahead and be sure nobody breaks a leg. I'll stay with the wagon."

"Don't you want to carve your name in stone, Sky?" Rita smiled. "It's kind of a permanent thing."

"Guess I'll just sleep, Rita. Here, you'll need a knife." He gave her his sheath knife, then watched sleepily as the women began to ascend the rock. It was at least 500 feet high, surrounded at its base by great mounds of debris. The slim stone shaft was something like a chimney, he thought as the figures grew smaller.

He crawled under the wagon and was instantly asleep. He had the knack of relaxing quickly and taking rest in chunks whenever he could get it. He slept lightly, aware of the call of a hawk and the scuffling of something in the shale around the bend from the wagon. But these were normal sounds, so he did not rouse himself.

Then he sat up—a voice was calling him! He came out from under the wagon to see Rita standing beside a pile of talus. She waved and called something he couldn't understand. He ran to where she stood, calling out, "What's wrong?"

"Oh, I twisted my ankle, Sky," she said.

He knelt to touch the foot she held off the ground, and she winced. "Can you move it back and forth, Rita? Now the other way?" He gently manipulated the ankle, then got up, saying, "Not broken. Let me help you to the wagon."

She held to him heavily and cried out as her foot touched the ground. "It hurts, Sky!"

"Well . . ." He looked down to the wagon. "Can't drive the wagon up here. I'll have to carry you."

He scooped her up easily and began walking carefully down the treacherous slope. She put her arm around his neck as he moved downward, holding her tightly. Several times he had to go to his right or left to find safe footing.

"Tough luck," he said. "You'll have to ride in the wagon for a day or two."

"You're always having to pull my potatoes out of the fire, aren't you, Sky?"

"Glad to oblige." Sky reached the foot of the rock, and began to walk across the level ground, but he was uncomfortably aware of her soft body pressed against his chest, and her face, which was very close to his own. There was no way to hold her loosely, but neither could he ignore the hunger she stirred in him.

He reached the wagon and leaned over to set her feet on the ground, but when he released her, she put her other arm around his neck with a deliberate movement and pulled his head down. Her lips were soft under his, and suddenly he put both arms around her and pulled her closer. She caressed the back of his neck, running her hand through his hair. When he lifted his lips from hers, she murmured huskily, "Oh—sweet!" and pulled his head down again. His blood was a riot in his veins, and nothing seemed real except Rita's lips.

He lifted his head and said thickly, "Rita—this doesn't mean anything."

"It means what it is, Sky," she whispered. "I want you and that's all that counts. Don't you want me?"

He removed her hands from around his neck and stood back. "Sure I do—but there's more to it than that."

"You've been listening to Lot Penny's preaching, Sky." She reached up to touch his cheek. "Preachers talk like that—and all the so-called 'good women' pretend they don't want a man, but we're all the same. I'm just different because I admit it." She leaned forward and said, "We're here for such a little while— got to grab whatever pleasure there is because it's all over so soon!"

Far off a coyote yelped. She pulled his head down again, and kissed him fiercely, then whispered, "Don't you love me, Sky?"

"Rita, wanting isn't loving," he said almost angrily, releasing her. "I had a wife once, and she said about the same thing you've just uttered—but she said it to other men. There's got to be more to love than just wanting, Rita!"

"There isn't, Sky!" she insisted. "Some men are the romantics, but when you peel down past the poetry and the flowers and the pretty speeches, it's just a man wanting a woman—and a woman wanting him back, like I want you. And you want me, too! Don't you think I know?"

"It's not like taking a drink of water when you're thirsty," Sky said bluntly. "If that's all love is, then we'd be better off without it!"

She looked at him with something like compassion in her face. "That's what I'm trying to tell you, Sky. That's all love is, just wanting. Nothing else." Then her eyes lost their light and she shrugged. "But you'll never believe that. You'll let the memory of that one woman poison you for the rest of your life. It's fool's gold, Sky—and when you get to be an old man, you'll think of times like this. You'll curse and say, 'I missed it all!' "

His face was carved in sharp planes, and at that moment he looked much like his Indian ancestors. Staring at her, he said quietly, "Maybe that's so, Rita—but at least I'll know I tried."

Disgusted, she grabbed the wagon wheel and lowered herself to the ground. Sky took a canteen out of the wagon and handed it to her, then walked away without looking back. It was two hours later before the others came back, gasping for breath. Karen took one look at Rita's face, then said, "Let me help you into the wagon." She saw that Sky was already mounted, and it was Dave who picked Rita up and deposited her in the back of the wagon. She held him tightly and said, "Why, thank you, Dave." Keeping her arm around his neck for just one extra second, her lips close to his ear, she whispered, "Sorry to be such a bother."

He flushed and said, "Why, it's no trouble, Rita." Then he turned and both Karen and Edith saw that the incident had affected him. Later on when they had gotten back to the train, Edith said, "There's gonna be trouble, Karen. Rita made her try for Winslow, I think. Now she'll have to have some man or lose face."

"Not Dave, I hope," Karen responded instantly, and Edith looked at her with surprise. Karen hastily explained. "He and Sky are such good friends—I'd hate to see Rita ruin that for them."

Edith studied her for a moment. "Karen," she murmured gently, "don't get too fond of Dave."

"Why not?"

"Because you know as well as I what an abnormal situation we're in. Out here, any man would go with any woman."

"Dave hasn't said a word to me, Edith."

"But you think of him, don't you?"

The question stirred Karen's face, and she looked off into the distance silently. "I don't know, Edith," she answered after a minute. "He's a good man, and I've had one good man. Maybe I shouldn't even think such things—be more like you. You never have problems with things like this."

Karen did not catch the flash of bitterness that touched Edith's gray eyes. "No, I don't have problems like that, Karen. But don't let Rita get Dave alone. It would mean that he and Sky would fight. And we can't afford to do without either of them."

The train pulled out at dawn; Lake was able to drive now, so Sky did not return as early as before. Rebekah saw that he was quieter, and she mentioned it to Edith, who said, "He's worried about Indians, I suppose."

They reached Fort Laramie on June eighth, but stayed only long enough to trade some worn-out oxen and buy a few supplies. Rebekah had been traveling in the wagon most of the time now. Her feet were swollen and she had felt ill for the past week. She was sitting in a chair in the general store watching some of the other women looking at the meager stores when Sky appeared and said, "Come along."

She rose heavily and walked outside with him. "Where are we going?"

"I want the army doc to have a look at you."

An hour later Dr. Schwartz, a short, thin man with a full set of sideburns, came out. "She's getting dressed."

"How is she?"

Schwartz stared at him. "She's not your wife, you say?"

"No, she—lost her husband."

"I see." He sat down and stared out the window so long that Sky thought he'd forgotten him. "I wouldn't take her if I were you."

"But we can't leave her here! She doesn't know a soul, Dr. Schwartz!"

"I know that—but she's likely to have complications when the baby comes." The doctor pulled a bottle of whiskey from the desk, took a huge swig, then shoved it toward Sky, who shook his head. "I'm just an army doctor, Winslow. Don't see many women. Haven't delivered five babies in as many years. I may be wrong about this. I hope so."

He stood up as Rebekah came out and said, "Thank you, Dr. Schwartz."

Sky said, "The doctor says you might be better off to stay here until the baby comes, Rebekah."

"But the train can't wait!"

"I—I could come back for you next year."

She smiled and put her hand on his arm, her face glowing with gratitude. "Oh no, I couldn't ask you to do that! I'll be all right." She gave a little laugh. "Women were having babies before there were doctors around to help. The Lord won't fail me. Thank you again, Doctor."

She turned and left the room, and with a helpless look at Schwartz, Winslow followed her. They walked in silence for a time; then she said, "You're not to worry about me, Sky. You have too many other things to think of."

"Can't help it."

"Yes, you can. I found that out not too long ago. A burden gets so big you just fall under it; but just before you do, the Lord gives you peace and you know it's going to be all right somehow."

The stars filled the heavens, and the path to the train was plainly illuminated. Sky stopped beside the wagon. "I wish you'd stay here, Rebekah. What would become of Timmy if you—if something happened to you?"

"Why, God would take care of him, Sky. He's the father of the fatherless, didn't you know?"

Sky stood there, and lifted his head. The stars glittered like tiny points of fire overhead, crowding each other in the velvet field. He said, "Look at that, Rebekah. Never see a sky like that without feeling pretty small. We're not much, are we, compared with all that?"

"Oh, I think so," she responded quietly. "Just one of us means more to God than all of those."

"Why? We're not as big."

"No, but they can't love Him—and that's what God meant when He made us, Sky."

Sky studied the stars again and murmured quietly, "My stepmother, she always said that." His eyes never left the sky as he told her, "You want to hear why I agreed to let you come on this crazy trip, Rebekah? I was all set to leave you behind, but somehow you reminded me of her."

"You love her very much, don't you, Sky?"

He could not bring himself to use those words, not even about Missy. "She was good to me," he said vaguely. "All right, you'll go, but I'm more worried about you than about Indians. You've got faith—but all the same, it seems to me that most of the good things in this life get busted."

He turned and walked away, and she went to sleep that night thinking of his stepmother—and feeling pleased that he'd said that she was one of the "good things."

CHAPTER THIRTEEN

AMBUSH AT THE SOUTH PASS

★   ★   ★   ★

The land slanted upward from Laramie, and some discouraged soul had left a crudely painted sign just outside the fort beside the trail: "You are now 640 miles from Independence, and not even one-third of the way to Oregon."

Dave read the sign aloud, then turned to Karen, who was riding beside him. "We've used up more than a third of our supplies—to say nothing of our patience. Wonder what we'll do farther on?"

She smiled at him. "We'll make it, Dave." It was the first time she'd ridden beside him in the seat, but Sky had asked Dave to go scouting with him farther ahead, and she'd volunteered to drive Dave's wagon while he was gone. As they rode along, waiting for Sky to appear, Karen watched the horizon. Dave stole one glance at her, then another, admiring the golden tan that she had gained over the summer. Her blond hair had become darkened with sun streaks, but her cheeks were rosy. She was a strongly built woman, full-figured and glowing with health.

Suddenly she turned, caught him watching her, and smiled. "You've thought about me sometimes, haven't you, Dave?"

"Well . . ." Her candor caught him off guard, and he could not frame an answer. He was never that much of a talker. Finally, he turned to look at her. "Yes, I guess I have, Karen."

"I'm not surprised. All of us must seem like a bunch of freaks—or worse, loose women out to grab a man with whatever it takes."

"I never thought of you like that."

"I believe you—but if you had, it would be natural. You know I was married once?"

"I heard that."

"My husband was a very good man. I had two children, too." Stealing a glance at her, he saw that her face was fixed as she stared out over the plain. "I still think of them all the time."

"That's tough." His words sounded weak and he hastened to add, "But you're a young woman; you'll have other children."

"I hope so, Dave." The intensity of her voice reflected the look in her eyes, and she gave her head a quick shake and asked casually, "You've never married?" Then she laughed, a rich, free sound on the morning air, and put her hand on his arm. "Oh, Dave, that sounded like a proposal! I'm so sorry."

He reddened and then laughed himself. "Better be careful, Karen. You might get snatched up before you get to all those rich merchants in Oregon City who can set you up in a fine house and give you everything. Be too bad if you crossed the whole country just to marry a poor ox driver!"

She did not smile, and her hand on his arm tightened just one instant. "Money and houses, they are not important."

He turned to face her and asked, "Then what is important to you, Karen?"

"Kindness. Sharing life. Caring for someone more than you care for yourself. Having children together. Growing old together."

He thought about that, then nodded. "Never heard it put like that. Sounds mighty good."

They were silent awhile, each lost in thought. Karen shook her head. "I'm worried about Rebekah. She is not doing well."

Dave looked back to where Tom Lake was driving his wagon. "Wish she'd had that baby in Laramie," he commented. "Sky's worried, too. Guess we all are." His tough face broke into a gentle smile. "Reckon we're her family, Karen. Got to take care of our own, don't we?"

"What a nice thing to say, Dave!"

He flushed at her praise, then saw Sky riding up on his horse. Handing her the lines, Dave said, "I'll see you this afternoon." He hesitated, then said, "It's—it's been nice talking to you, Karen. Roughneck like me doesn't often get a chance to talk to girls like you. Maybe we can talk some more?" he added as he got on his horse.

"Of course." She watched him ride off, and her lips softened as she thought of the brief encounter. Then she thought of Rebekah, and worry brought a wrinkle to her smooth brow. "Got to watch her," she said quietly to herself.

Dave rode along with Sky, listening to what he said, but thinking of Karen at the same time. "If Karen can handle the wagon part of the time," Sky said, "I'd like you to start scouting with the Indians and me. We're heading into Spotted Elk's territory, and the more of us screening the train, the more likely we'll be to spot his band."

"You think he'll hit the train, Sky?"

"He might. He's a tricky cuss, and mean as sin, but he's careful, too. Doubt if he'd risk a head-on battle, but it's just as well to double our lookouts." He turned in his saddle to look his friend in the eye. "If I go down, Dave, you'll have to hold this train together."

"Me! I don't know the way!" he protested. "'Sides, you won't get killed."

"Any of us could, Dave." Sky's head swiveled, methodically searching the horizon. "Snake could get me. Cholera's always a danger. Grizzlies can wipe a man out. And I've seen more than one man who's outwitted every Indian and varmint on the plain go out with a little rabbit fever. We're just here from day to day. Got no promises on tomorrow. That's what the Bible says."

Lloyd eyed his friend warily, but said nothing. He admired Winslow as he had rarely admired another man, but he did not understand the dark streak of fatalism that ran beneath the smooth surface. Nothing seemed to bother Sky—yet the man had few dreams and little hope that things would turn out well. Finally he gave up and said, "What's it like up ahead, Sky?"

"Uphill. We're through the easy part, Dave. Now it gets rough."

Dave was to find out what he meant in the days to come. The

land lifted, pulling the strength of the oxen down and sapping everyone's energies. They began to pass little piles of furniture and other goods that had been abandoned by earlier trains, forced to lighten their loads. Sheet-iron stoves, an anvil, a hand-rubbed claw-foot table, and other treasured items strewed the wayside as they doggedly urged the oxen up the slope.

The land was mostly barren. At long range the mountainsides looked like green meadows; up close they turned out to be dry sand and rock dotted by stunted clumps of sage and grease-wood. Finally they passed the Sweetwater (which was not sweet, they discovered!), and the scenery grew steadily more and more spectacular.

On the first day of July, they pulled in for the night and hurried to get the fires built. The mountain air cut like a knife, and Sky laughed as they huddled close for warmth. "Anybody like to be back in the desert, sweating?"

Edith pulled a blanket tighter. "No, but it's so cold here!"

"Maybe you'd like a glass of ice water?" Sky inquired. "I'm serious. Anyone for a glass of ice water?"

"I'll have one, Sky," Rita spoke up. She had barely spoken to him since the incident at Chimney Rock, but now she smiled and rose from her seat. "Where'll you get ice around here?"

"Come along—any of you—and bring a cup or a glass." He plucked a pick from a wagon and led the way to a spot close to a sandstone bank. The soil was soft, and he began to dig. The pick rang at once, and someone said, "Bedrock."

Sky cleaned the dirt away, raised the pick, and broke off a chunk of something and tossed it to Rita. "There's your ice—a little dirty, but ice all the same."

"Why, it *is* ice!" she exclaimed.

"Sure. This place is called Ice Slough. We're up seven thousand feet, and there's always ice about a foot deep, even in July."

The others fell to digging, and although the ice was liberally studded with gravel, they got enough chunks to take back and make drinks with.

Sky saw Tom Lake standing beside the fire, and made his way over. "How's it going, Tom? Ribs about well?"

"Sure." He turned his face toward Sky and touched his head. "Guess I'll always have a few scars, but a man gets those, doesn't he?" He dropped his hand and the corners of his mouth turned down with a worried expression. "Rebekah's not well."

Sky glanced toward the wagon. "We'll be through the South Pass in a couple of days. Then maybe we can make Fort Hall in a couple of weeks. Be an army doctor there, I think."

Tom shook his head. "Baby won't be that long coming."

Lake was an educated man, but an animal doctor—even a good one like Tom—was no match for the real thing. Sky looked at him with puzzlement. "How'd you figure that, Tom?"

Lake shrugged. "The women say so—and it's pretty plain." He shifted his feet and said nervously, "I wish she'd stayed in Laramie!"

"Well, she wouldn't—so we'll just have to do the best we can."

"How's the road after we get through the pass? Pretty rough?"

"Like a washboard." He glanced at Lake and added, "Not a road for a woman about to have a baby—but it's the only road there is. Keep an eye on her, Tom. When the baby comes, we'll pull up and wait until it's safe to move on—even if it takes a week."

There was something in his voice that made Lake look at him more carefully. "What's up, Sky?"

Winslow said slowly, "Don't say anything to the women, but we've got visitors, Tom."

Lake gave an involuntary look around, then asked, "Indians?"

"Reckon so. Keep your gun handy, and if trouble comes, you look out for Rebekah."

Sky went around the train, giving a warning to the men, and Riker asked, "You think it's that Sioux chief, Winslow?"

"I'd guess it's him, Al."

"None of us has seen a sign of an Indian."

"Nobody's going to see a Sioux unless he wants to be seen."

"Where's them tame Indians of yours?"

"Creeping around—just like Spotted Elk and his braves. They'll probably come in tonight or tomorrow. I want a heavy guard tonight. Half of us to watch while the other half sleeps."

"Me and my boys'll stand a watch."

Every man on the train was on a hair-trigger alert, and the women found out soon enough. There was little sleep that night or the next, and by the third night they were almost at the neck of the South Pass, and vigilance had relaxed.

Sky was standing beside Al Riker fifty yards out from where the wagons were circled. The big man was sleepy and yawned, "Whut time is it, Winslow?"

"I guess about two."

Riker strained his eyes to see, then said disgustedly, "I reckon it's a false alarm. Ain't no Indians hereabouts."

"Yes, there is."

The voice seemed to be right at Riker's feet, and a dark shape he had taken for a rock suddenly rose upright. Riker leaped backward, trying to get his gun in position.

"Hold it, Riker!" Sky barked. "It's White Hawk!"

The Sioux came closer and the two men could hear the laughter in his tone as he spoke in his native language. "If I were Spotted Elk, I would have two fine scalps to hang on my lodge-pole."

"That's the truth," Sky grinned, answering in Sioux. He slapped the Indian on the shoulder. "Guess I'm going deaf in my old age—but you always were a slippery one." Then he asked, "I reckon you've got Spotted Elk located?"

"Yes. He has followed you up the pass. Both Kieta and I thought he would attack, but he has gone on ahead."

"An ambush?"

White Hawk's teeth gleamed in the darkness. "He is a fox, Spotted Elk! You know a narrow place up there—outcropping on one side, sheer wall on the other?"

"I know it."

"Spotted Elk's braves are there, half on one side, half on the other."

"And when the wagons are in that place, all they'll have to do is stand up and shoot us like fish in a barrel."

The Indian grunted. "Good trap, is it not?"

Riker grew tired of being left out of the exchange. "Whut's he sayin', Winslow?"

Sky explained the situation, and Riker swore. "Any way around that pass?"

"No. We'll have to go through."

"Sounds like suicide to me!"

"That's what Spotted Elk is counting on," Sky said. "Let's get the men up. I've got an idea."

"Better be good," White Hawk responded as they went back. "He's got about twenty braves—probably his best fighters."

In ten minutes every man on the train stood around the fire, while the women remained in the background, listening. "It's really kind of simple," Sky explained. "Elk is smart. He knows we can't go back, and we can't go around, and we can't wait. He knows where we are, and if we don't show up, he'll get us here." He studied the fire, the angular planes of his face deepened in the flickering light. Lifting his head, he said, "We've got one thing going for us."

"I don't see what," Dave muttered. "Looks like he's got all the high cards."

"Thanks to White Hawk and Kieta, Spotted Elk doesn't know we're on to him. We'll have to make that our play."

"What're you thinkin', Winslow?" Al Riker asked.

"If we can knock Spotted Elk out, the rest will run. They believe in their medicine, Al, and when a leader goes down, they're pretty sure to turn tail. But it'll be hard to get at him. We'll have to send two scouting parties ahead and get in place behind them. Then when the train comes through in the morning, we'll pot the Sioux when they start the attack."

"Sounds like you're using us for bait, Winslow," Jack Stedman whined loudly.

"You rather go find Spotted Elk in the dark, Stedman?" Dave snapped angrily. "Keep your mouth shut and let the man talk!"

"Well, Stedman is half right. Those of you in the wagons will be sitting ducks if we don't get in place," Sky said.

"Who's going to go with you?" Lake asked.

"Just White Hawk and Kieta. I reckon only a Sioux would have a chance on sneaking up on another Sioux in the dark."

"Wouldn't care for the job myself," Riker commented. "When do we try this plan of yours, Winslow?"

"It'll have to be now, Al. I want some extra rifles, all primed and loaded and wrapped in blankets. And six pistols with full loads."

The extra arms were quickly assembled. "Get every rifle loaded and ready to fire," Sky continued. "I want one woman on each seat with the driver. When you hear a shot, you women grab the lines and drive the animals as fast as they'll go. You men start shootin' up at the rim of the canyon. You won't see much, but it'll be a little pressure on the Sioux." He looked around the circle and focused on Lot Penny. "Brother Penny, you might say a prayer for the train."

Penny took off his hat, and the others followed suit. "Lord, we are in a hard place. Those who lie in wait ahead of us are your creatures—but they stand between us and life. I don't know how to pray, for you love the Sioux just as you love all men. I ask you to favor us, and let there be little loss of life. And I ask this in the name of Jesus."

"Pretty good prayer," Dave murmured to Karen as Sky and White Hawk were swallowed up by the darkness. He looked down at her and asked, "You afraid?"

"Yes."

"Me, too. Guess everyone is—except Sky and them Indians. They take to this sort of thing natural, I reckon. Hope I don't show yellow."

"You won't." Karen's voice was sure, and she touched his arm lightly. "You'll be in the first wagon, Dave. Be careful." She hesitated, then whispered, "I don't want anything to happen to you."

Dave Lloyd was thinking about Karen the next morning as he sat in the wagon with May Stockton beside him. He glanced down at the three rifles at his feet and said, "That's it up ahead, May. Be ready to take these lines."

"I'm ready, Dave."

The silence seemed oppressive as they approached the high-walled pass, and every eye was searching the rim for the enemy. The only sound was the creaking of the wagon wheels and the voices of the drivers as they urged the animals up the slope. "Looks like the mouth of the canyon," Dave said quietly. "Reckon they'll let us get halfway in, then open up."

He was right, for when the last wagon rolled into the gap, a rifle shot broke the stillness, and a scream of pain rose up from one of the drivers.

"Haw up!" Dave screamed. Throwing the lines to May, he snatched one of the rifles from the floor and leaned forward, taking aim. The wagon careened from side to side, but he caught a glimpse of a red body on the rim to his left and took a quick shot. It missed, but the Indian dodged back as the slug hit the rock at his feet.

Rifle fire rattled from the rim. Glancing back, Dave saw Charlie Gladden drop his rifle and fall backward, his chest bloody from a bullet. Then Dave grabbed another rifle and tried to get off a shot, but the wagon was pitching so wildly that it was all he could do to keep from being thrown out. The other drivers were throwing fire up to the rim, and up ahead Dave saw the canyon widen. "If we can get there," he screamed to May, "we'll be all right!"

But the fire from the canyon rim was raking the train steadily, and he knew that they had taken losses. He fired the third rifle, then snatched a revolver from his belt, and while holding on to the canopy rim with one hand, he emptied the gun. One Indian grabbed his stomach and slid down the bluff, his body limp and bumping wildly as it hit the trail below.

Dave grabbed the other revolver and called out, "Keep going, May!" as he leaped to the ground. He stumbled and rolled to the dust, but was up in an instant. From the ground he could see the Sioux plainly, and he took a steady aim, zeroing in on one of them. On his fourth shot, the Indian's head flew back and he disappeared in the rocks.

As he fired the last load, a wild cry went up from the rim, and he glanced up to see an Indian cartwheeling down the slope, stopping abruptly as the body was almost impaled on a sharp outcropping of stone. At once the firing from the rim grew spasmodic, and Dave said to himself, "Spotted Elk, I'll bet!"

The rest of the train came through as the firing from the rim faded out and then ceased. Dave dropped his gun and ran to Lake. "You all right, Tom?"

"Yes—but we have some men hit."

Dave ran down the line checking the wounded as the wagons pulled to a halt. When he saw Karen step out of a wagon and fall to the ground, he yelled, "Karen!" and ran to her. "Are you hit?"

He pulled her up; she lifted her head, shaken but unhurt, and smiled tremulously at him. "Dave! I was so afraid for you!"

He knelt beside her, and impulsively kissed her. She put her arms around his neck. "We'd better see about the wounded, Dave."

He shook his head. "If something had happened to you. . . !" He didn't finish, but pulled her to her feet, and they moved to the next wagon where Charlie Gladden was being lifted out by Stedman and Penny.

"Took a slug in the chest," Stedman said. "Alive, but bad shot."

"Look—there's Winslow!" Penny had looked up to see Sky and the two Indians sliding down the slope.

Sky came running up, a gash on his forehead and blood running down his cheek. "How bad did they get us, Dave?"

"Don't know yet. Gladden is hurt bad, though."

They were soon relieved to discover that no one had been killed. Gladden was the most serious casualty, but Pete Riker, Al's youngest son, had a wrist shattered by a heavy rifle slug; and one of the women, Ada Cantrell, had a flesh wound in the calf of her leg.

"Could have been a heap worse," Dave said grimly to Sky. He started to say something else when he heard the sound of someone running along the trail. Both of them turned just as Karen, her hair disheveled, face pale, reached them.

"Sky! It's Rebekah! I—I think it's her time!"

Sky's lips pressed together grimly, and he voiced the sentiment that they all were thinking: "Two men hurt bad—and a woman about to have a baby. If either of you knows how to pray, this would be a good time to start!"

CHAPTER FOURTEEN

"YOU WERE BORN FOR IT!"

★ ★ ★ ★

Kieta appeared in the camp at dusk, like a ghost out of the shadows, his eyes obsidian. "No more Sioux," he told Sky. "All gone back to their camp."

Sky nodded. "Good work, Kieta. Better get some of that meat." As the Indian moved to pull a strip of roast ox off the fire, Sky said, "If it weren't for those two, we'd be dead by now."

"I believe it, Sky." Dave looked at the Apache by the fire for a long moment. "We're in a bad way, though. Gladden's not going to make it with that bullet in him—and Pete's arm is shot all to pieces."

Sky nodded and then groaned. "I've patched up a few bullet holes, Dave, but nothing like this!"

"Could one of us ride on to Fort Bridger, Sky—or maybe Fort Hall?"

"Thought about that—but it's no good. Wouldn't be a doctor at Bridger's place; it's just a trading camp—and not much of one at that. And Hall is at least two weeks away."

Winslow was well aware of the gravity of the situation, even more than Lloyd, for he had seen many deaths like this. He shook his head. "On the trail, a bad injury is just about as fatal as a bullet through the brain. Must be thousands of graves on the Oregon trail—and most of the folks in them would have made it if they'd had a doctor."

"I wish the women'd come and tell us something about Rebekah," Dave said nervously, turning to peer at the wagon that was pulled fifty yards away from the rest. "I heard her cryin' out a few minutes ago—and Rebekah's not a screamer."

"Guess we can go see."

They crossed the open space and found Karen and Edith standing beside a small fire. The men knew they didn't need to ask how Rebekah was; they could see from the lines of strain on both the women's faces.

"It's real bad," Edith said quietly. "Something's wrong with the way the baby's placed."

"It is hard." Karen wiped her brow, and her hand trembled. "It was not like this with my babies. They came easy—but she is in terrible pain."

"Can't you give her some laudanum?" Sky asked.

"I did—a little bit," Edith replied. "But that's no answer. She's got to deliver that child—or she'll die."

They all looked at Sky expectantly, and he felt the pressure. "Well, don't look at me!" he said angrily. "I don't know anything about babies!"

"We know that, Sky," Edith responded. "I guess we've looked to you for so long, it just comes naturally. But no one is blaming you—this isn't your fault."

"Sure it is. I let her come—I didn't make her stay in Laramie like I should have. It was my responsibility." His face was tight, and they all saw that he was controlling his voice only by a powerful exercise of his will. He looked around. "Where's Tom?"

"Why, I guess he went to get something to eat," Karen said. "He's been here almost all afternoon."

Sky felt the mounting pressure, set his teeth, forced himself to say quietly, "I'll ask Brother Penny to come over and say a prayer."

He left the three of them and went back to the train. Penny was with Pete Riker and his father, and the boy looked up anxiously as Sky came to stand beside him.

"How's it going, Pete?" Sky asked.

"Hurts like everythin'!" young Riker gasped. He clamped his

lips together and closed his eyes, but his limbs were trembling with the pain.

Sky knelt beside him, and put his hand on the boy's head sympathetically. "I know, Son. We'll see what we can do." Then he looked up at Penny and said, "Lot, I wish you'd go over and pray with Rebekah."

"I'll do that." Lot got up and touched the hurt boy's shoulder. "I'm believing God for you, Pete. Don't give up on God." He waited for a response, but the boy didn't seem to have heard.

Al gestured to Sky, who followed him out of Pete's hearing. Riker's square face was stern, but his eyes were fearful. "Winslow, Pete's going to lose that hand."

"You sure, Al?"

"Yes. It's got to come off—and quick." He peered at Sky's face closely, then asked, "Think you could do it?"

"Me!" Sky felt a wave of anger at the thought, but it quickly left as he saw the anxiety in the old man's face. *What if it were Joe?* he asked himself. *I'd be begging everybody I saw for help!* And so, with many misgivings, he said, "If it has to be done, Al, I'll take a try—but I've never done anything like that."

"None of us have." Riker bit his lip. "It's too dark now—but come morning, it'll have to be done."

"All right, Al."

Sky left the wagon with a sinking sensation in his middle. The thought of cutting into living flesh sickened him. Fear embedded itself in his gut, and sweat beaded his forehead despite the cold breeze that was whipping the canvas of the wagons. He wished fervently he'd never left Oregon.

Charlie Gladden was worse, which was what he'd expected. Rita was standing to one side, and she waited quietly while he listened to the report. "His breathin' is real shallow, Mr. Winslow—and the bleedin' won't stop. Just keeps seeping out," said Mack Malone. Malone was one of the drivers; now his eyes looked very large by the light of the fire as he wrang his hands and added, "He's going to die if that bleedin' keeps on."

"Do the best you can, Mack," Sky said, then turned to go away.

"What's going to happen, Sky?" He had stopped by the fire to get a cup of coffee and Rita stooped beside him. "I never saw anything like this before." Her face was pale and for once she was subdued. "There was always a doctor and a hospital close."

He didn't answer, but sipped the bitter black coffee and stared into the fire. His own nerves were jumpy, and he was tired of questions that had no answer. "They'll die, I reckon."

She flinched at the brutality of his reply. "Then it's like I said, isn't it?"

He stared at her. " 'Like you said?' "

"At Chimney Rock . . ." She looked at him steadily, but there was no anger in her eyes, only sadness. "We live and we die, and that's it, Sky. When Rebekah dies, she'll leave nothing. All the fun she's missed was for nothing."

He had only half heard her. Looking up from the fire, he said, "I don't know what to do, Rita." The vulnerability on his face evoked a tenderness in her, and she laid a hand on his shoulder.

"It's not your fault. Not anybody's fault. That's just the way things are."

He stood up and she stood with him. There was a bitterness in his face. "I wish Pa were here."

"He a doctor?"

"No—a preacher."

"We have one of those," Rita reminded him.

Sky rolled the cup in his hands and said slowly, "He's a praying man, my pa—and so's my stepmother. I've seen them pray—and things happened—things that were impossible happened, Rita!"

She asked quietly, "You still believe in miracles, Sky?"

"I don't know *what* I believe, but I know what I've seen," he replied through clenched teeth. "I saw my half brother dying of cholera one night—and I heard my pa and ma pray—and the next day I saw Thad running around like he'd never had a sick day."

"Well, I don't believe much in that sort of thing—but for your sake, I wish your folks were here," Rita returned. Then she cocked her head and stared at him in a peculiar manner, her eyes intent on him. "You're a pretty 'holy' sort of man yourself, Sky. Why don't you ask for a miracle or two?"

He searched her face, looking for mockery. Seeing none, he

said, "Don't feel like I've lived the right kind of life to be askin' for any favors from God, Rita. Always despised people who lived like they pleased, then ran to God when they were in trouble."

"So have I—but this is a little different, isn't it? I mean, it's not you who needs a miracle. It's these hurt people."

He stared back at the fire, thinking. Finally he spoke. "I'll go ask Brother Penny. Miracles are his department."

He made his way back to the wagon where Rebekah lay, and was met at the entrance by Lot Penny. The preacher's face was pale, and he seemed to have difficulty breathing. His usual piercing voice was thin and somewhat reedy, as if he were out of breath. "Brother Winslow, I wish you'd have a word with our sister."

"Me?" Sky asked sharply. "Didn't you pray with her?"

"Yes—but she's asking for you."

"Lot, this is out of control!" Sky's voice was agitated. He clamped his hands behind his back, astonished to find out they were not steady—it was the first time something had affected him like this in years. "These people are dying!"

"I know," Lot said simply. He looked old in the half light, and his plain features were haggard. "It's all in God's hands now."

"Well, what about these miracles you've been preaching about? Are they out of fashion or something? Is God on a vacation?"

The anger in Winslow's tone made Penny blink, and he said slowly, "God is always the same, Sky. Yesterday, today, and forever."

"Then why in the name of heaven can't we pray down some help for these people?"

"I didn't know you were a praying man."

"You *know* I'm not!" Sky shot back, the fear in him turning to anger. He knew it was unfair to blame his own failures on Lot Penny, but he couldn't seem to stop. "I'm just a sinner—but you're supposed to be a Christian—a preacher even! So start praying! And I'm expecting to see something more from your prayers than wind, you hear me, Lot?"

The anger that had exploded in him like a live charge drained out as he drew the cover from the wagon and looked inside where Edith was sitting beside Rebekah. The pale yellow light of the small lantern bathed Rebekah's face, and the sight of her shocked Winslow.

Rebekah's face was white, except for her eyes, which were hollow depths of blackness sinking into her skull. Her lips were pinched together, pale and bloodless, and the look of death on her hit him in the pit of his stomach.

She opened her eyes without seeing and arched her back, raising her swollen body off the wagon bed. Her lips opened in a silent scream, but she allowed no sound to escape.

He groped for a place to sit, his legs trembling with a sudden weakness. As she lay back with a gasp, her eyes focused and she whispered, "Sky—?"

"I'm here, Rebekah!"

"I . . . want you to take care of Timmy . . . and my baby."

He swallowed hard. "Why, you're going to take care of them yourself."

She shook her head. "Promise me? Please?"

"Well . . ." Sky looked up to see Edith nod, and he said, "Sure, I will, Rebekah—but you can't give up."

"I know." She paused and then her body arched again with pain, and Sky closed his eyes until it passed.

"You've got to pray!" Sky cried desperately. "Brother Penny is praying, but you've got to help."

She looked at him with cloudy eyes, and reached out a hand. When he took it, she said, "Will you pray for me? And for the baby?"

He held her hand and a weakness ran through him. He would have died before praying for himself—but her fragileness gripped him, and he dropped his head and choked, "Oh, God! I know you can do anything! You are my father's God, and he's not here—so I'm asking you to help this woman!" His voice cracked, and he waited, then ended the prayer in a whisper. "Not for me—do it just because you're the God of love! Do it in Jesus' name!"

He bent his head, his shoulders shaking, and she whispered, "Thank you, Sky! "

He stood up and stumbled out of the wagon, walking blindly, his eyes burning with unshed tears. He moved away from the train and walked along the road with his head down. He didn't come back to camp for hours.

The morning light was thin and gray as it dissolved the dark pockets of blackness shrouding the caravan. Here and there a few figures began stirring; every face was grim. Brother Penny busied himself around the fire making coffee. After finishing it, he poured a cup for himself and began drinking the brew. He looked up as Rita approached. "Any change in Rebekah?" he asked.

"No."

She took the coffee he handed her, then looked up to see Sky walking along the trail. "Guess he's been out praying for a miracle," she remarked quietly.

Penny did not answer, but stared at her tired face and drank his coffee. "We've got to cut off Pete's hand this morning."

A shudder ran through her. "Who's going to do *that*?"

"Sky said he'd do it." Penny shook his head sadly. "That young man's got too big a load to carry!"

They both watched as Sky stopped at Rebekah's wagon and asked Edith something, then turned and headed for the camp. He walked up to Lake's wagon and disappeared inside for at least five minutes; when he came out, he was holding a sack in his hand.

He approached the fire where they were sitting; his face was tense. "Seen Tom around?"

"Why, I don't think I've seen him since yesterday," Rita replied.

"Might be asleep in one of the wagons," Penny offered.

Sky said abruptly, "Tell Riker I'll be back soon as I can."

He wheeled and broke into a run. They watched with astonishment as he stopped, bent over the ground, and began running back and forth.

"He's tracking Tom!" Penny said. "I reckon he thinks Tom's lost."

Sky carefully examined the ground, but found nothing. He changed his position, going to the far end of the trail, and almost at once found some faint sign in the dewy grass. Head down, he followed the tracks until they left the road and led into a patch of scrub timber. He lost the trail more than once, but swept back and forth until he'd found it again. The scrubby growth gave way to a fir forest, making the trail harder to follow over the carpet of needles.

About an hour later, he came upon the limp body of Lake, crumpled beside a tiny brook. At first he thought the man was dead, but then he saw the empty whiskey bottle and breathed a sigh of relief. Picking Lake up by the shoulders, Sky dragged him to the creek and—holding him by the hair—plunged his face into the frigid water.

Lake began to buck at once, and Sky yanked the man's head out. "Wha—what's goin'—!"

"Shut your mouth!" Sky hissed and pushed Lake's face under again, holding the thrashing body down. Then he pulled him out and threw him down flat on his back.

Lake lay on the bank, gagging and coughing, until he was finally able to sit up and speak. When his head cleared, he cried indignantly, "You can't do—!"

Sky pulled his gun smoothly and aimed it at the man. "If you say any more, Tom, I'll blow your head off."

The shock brought reason to Lake's brain, and he sat there shivering until he couldn't stand it any longer. "Sky, what's going on? Just because I got a little drunk—"

"I'll tell you what's going on, Tom!" Sky snapped, his eyes bright with anger. "There are three people dying in that camp—*and you're the cause of it!*"

"Me! I didn't shoot them—and it's not my fault Rebekah's having a baby in a breech position!" The words leaped out, but he shut his mouth, realizing he'd said too much.

"A breech birth? I don't even know what that is," Sky said softly, menacingly. "But you do, don't you, Tom?" He picked up the sack he'd brought from Lake's wagon, put his weapon away and pulled out a small black bag. He tossed it to Lake, who caught it reflexively, then stared at it as if it were a deadly snake. "It's yours, isn't it, Tom?" Sky growled.

"It—it used to be."

"You're a doctor, aren't you?"

Lake's face crumpled and he dropped the bag and hid his face in his hands. "No more! I used to be—but no more!"

Sky waited until the man's shoulders stopped shaking before he moved to where Lake was slumped on the grass.

"Then why're you carrying the bag along? Tom, what happened?"

It all came out then, the whole story. His face ashen, Lake told how he'd been drunk and killed a woman he was operating on. "I always thought I could handle booze," he said in a thin voice. "But I killed her, just as sure as if I'd put a gun to her head myself!" He shivered. "Before, I was a doctor who was a drunk. Now I'm just a drunk, Sky. Don't kill anybody, at least. I still keep the bag with me—even if I don't dare use it. I don't know why."

"You've got to, Tom, and I mean *now!*"

"No, Sky!" Lake scrambled to his feet. "I knew you'd say that—but I can't! I haven't been a doctor in five years."

"Tom," Sky said evenly, "somebody's got to take Pete's hand off. If you don't do it, I'll have to. Somebody's got to dig that bullet out of Charlie Gladden. You may kill him, but if I do it, he's got no chance at all. And what do you think *I* can do with Rebekah? *You're murdering her if you don't do what you can.*"

For fifteen minutes Winslow pleaded with Lake but got nowhere. Finally, Sky glared at him and slowly pulled out his gun.

Anger flared in Tom's eyes. "You think I'm afraid to die, Winslow? I've prayed for death for years. Go on—shoot me!"

"I'm going to shoot you, Tom," Sky nodded coldly. "In the ankle—blow it to bits. Then I'm going to drag you back to the train and tell them about you. "

Lake flinched. "You wouldn't do that!"

Sky thumbed back the hammer and aimed at Lake's ankle. "I'll do it, Tom. There are three people dying back there, and I think more of any one of them than I do of a low-down cowardly dog like you! So you're going back, and you can amputate your own foot—if they don't shoot you like a yellow dog first!"

Tom Lake stared at the gun that was lined up on his ankle, imagining what the bullet would do to the fragile bones. He looked up into Winslow's unblinking blue eyes and knew that there would be no reprieve—the man would do as he said. Tom dropped his head and stared at the ground.

Sky kept the gun trained on Lake's ankle, and knew as well that he would shoot. An icy wave of violence washed over him, for Winslow knew only too well what was at stake. He waited to let the man decide whether to live or die.

The sun was rising, and a gray squirrel ran out on a limb over their heads, chattering at them angrily before retreating inside the trunk. The sweet smell of pine and balsam was fresh in the cold air, and the creek bubbled over the stones, making tiny fists of white foam that reared up when the water hit a stone.

Finally Tom lifted his head, and there was a light in his eyes that Sky had never seen. "Let's go."

"All right, Tom."

Lake picked up the bag and trudged out of the glade with Sky behind him. The squirrel popped his head over a branch, his bright beady eyes inquiring; he came down and frisked his tail, staring down the trail where the two disappeared.

By the time they got back to camp, everyone knew that Lake had left and that Sky had gone after him. The people had gathered together in a group, and as the two men approached and stepped into the center, a quiet fell across the company.

Tom Lake looked haggard as he stood in the middle of the circle and looked around. His face was puffy and his eyes were bloodshot; nevertheless, they saw that something had changed.

"I used to be a doctor," he announced in a clear voice that carried easily over the area. "Then I began to drink, and killed a woman I was operating on. That's when I became a real drunk." He let that sink in, then added, "I haven't been a doctor for five years, but I'll do what I can."

Al Riker stepped forward, his tired eyes gleaming hopefully. "Lake, help my boy. He's bleedin' bad!"

"I'll do what I can, Al. No guarantees."

"I know, Doc," Riker replied quickly. "Just do what you can."

"Is there someone who can help me?" he asked.

"Yes. Edith," Sky said quickly. "Karen, go get her and then you stay with Rebekah."

When Edith arrived Lake began. There was a new authority in his voice as he gave orders. "Edith, give Pete ten drops of that laudanum. By the time I finish with Charlie, he ought to be ready."

In twenty minutes Lake had extracted the bullet from Charlie's stomach and stopped the bleeding. "It's a good thing I got in there," he said quietly to Edith, who was helping him. "That bleeder would have killed him today." He treated the wound, then went to amputate Pete's hand.

The operation on Pete Riker took much longer, but those who watched saw that the man knew exactly what he was doing. After it was over, he said to the Rikers, "He'll have a good stump. I left a good cushion of muscle, and it won't be long before he'll be able to wear a hook."

Mrs. Riker began to weep, and Al said in a husky voice, "Thanks, Doc!"

Tom said quietly, "Sorry to be so late. Should have done this before."

Sky had stood by during the procedures. Now he accompanied Lake as they hurried toward Rebekah's wagon. There was admiration in his face as he said, "Well, Tom, you're a slow starter—but you're a real sure-shot once you let the hammer down."

"I feel like a man again, Sky!" Then he added soberly, "It's not going to be so easy with Rebekah, Sky. It's a little different from digging a slug out."

"You'll do fine, Doc," Sky reassured. "You were born for it—a natural!" He dropped a hand on Lake's thin shoulder. "An angel unawares, as the Good Book says!"

Lake grinned in embarrassment. "Nobody ever called me *that* before—an angel unawares."

"Well, you'll do till one comes along—now do your stuff!"

Lake had been right, for Rebekah had not been as easy to deal with as the others had. All day long the train sat still, the men and women milling nervously around, asking each other unanswerable questions.

At suppertime, Dave sat by the fire with Sky, Rita and Karen. The four of them were absently picking at their dinners when a cry tore the air and all of them scrambled to their feet.

"That was a baby!" Dave exclaimed.

Edith came out of the wagon and ran toward them, crying, "It's a girl!—and Rebekah is fine!"

Sky pulled his gun out of his holster and emptied it into the air with a yell—then stood stockstill and looked around with a sheepish expression on his face. "That was a dumb thing to do!" he muttered.

Rita had a wondering smile on her face. "Well, I guess a little salute for a miracle isn't too foolish, Sky."

CHAPTER FIFTEEN

THE LAST FROLIC

★ ★ ★ ★

Fort Boise was no better than Fort Laramie or Fort Hall—but it was on the last leg of the Oregon trail, so there was a lighter spirit on the train as it rolled westward toward the Blue Mountains.

A hint of winter was already in the winds that came down from the north, though it was only mid-September. As wagons wound around the crooked trail, Edith and Sky marched along, keeping pace easily with the plodding oxen. Since they had left the South Pass, this had become a habitual thing, for with sick people in the train, Sky had found her to be capable of judging the speed of the march.

"Seems like a year since we left the South Pass," she mused. The wind stirred a lock of her brown hair, blowing it across her eyes, and she carefully replaced it.

"You've done a good job," he commented.

The compliment colored her cheeks, and she answered, "We've done well, haven't we, Sky?"

"Better than I'd have thought," he admitted. "That day at the Pass—I was just about a gone coon, Edith. If Tom hadn't come around, there would have been three graves, I reckon."

Rebekah had recovered slowly, but with Lake's care, she was up in a few weeks, able to walk for short periods beside the wagon, and now was strong as ever. The baby, whom she'd named Mary, had a little trouble at first from the long birthing, but now was growing stronger every day, with no apparent complications. Pete Riker had made a swift recovery, and would before long be able to wear a shiny steel hook on his left hand. Lot Penny had already forged one for him while they were resting up at Fort Bridger, and when Al Riker saw it he said, "Pete'll be prouder of that hook than of his hand, I reckon. Says women love novelty—and it'll be handy in a fight!"

Charlie Gladden had not fared so well. He'd never regained his strength, and they had been forced to leave him at Fort Hall with the army doctor to care for him. Sky had paid Charlie's bill, and left enough to pay his way to Oregon City with one of the trains that would be coming through later.

Thinking of all this, Sky looked back to where Lake was sitting on the wagon seat beside Rebekah. "Looks like they're having fun," he remarked.

"Tom saved her life. I suppose he's got a vested interest in her now." Edith studied the pair and said, "Tom's not the same man that started this trip." She walked along silently, then added, "*None* of us are—except you, Sky."

He looked at her, admiring the trim figure and the quick, intelligent eyes. He had long ago felt that she would be the perfect wife for Sam, but had not known how to approach her concerning the idea. At first he had thought it would be best simply to introduce the pair, but he knew that the women would be swamped with offers the day they got to Oregon City. It made him uneasy to think that Sam, because he was not impressive on the surface, might be passed over for another man with much less to offer.

"Not far to go now," he said, mulling it over. "We'll follow the Snake about 300 miles, cross the Blue Mountains, then take a little boat ride down the Columbia—and that's it."

"How long, Sky?"

"Oh, maybe a month, if the weather holds." He hesitated, then asked, "You ever have any second thoughts, Edith—about coming on this trip?"

"Sure—lots of times."

He didn't know exactly how to take that. "You gettin' cold

feet about the end of all this? Marrying a man you don't even know?"

She glanced at him, but he was looking out across the horizon and didn't notice. "Why, I've had a few bad thoughts about that, Sky." She laughed shortly, adding, "It's not like picking out a new bonnet that I can throw away if it doesn't please me."

"What sort of man would please you?"

She looked at him again, and this time their eyes met. He had the steadiest and the bluest eyes she'd ever seen in a man, or perhaps they just seemed so, the way they were set in his bronze face. She felt the weight of his attention, as she had several times in the past, and finally answered, "Oh, that's hard to say!"

"Tall? Short? Dark? Fat? Thin?"

"You know, those things don't matter," she replied. She was quiet for several moments longer before she answered. "I want a man who's honest. If he's honest with other men, he ought to be honest with a wife. And one who's steady—not moody." She thought hard, then added, "And he's got to like children."

He waited for her to continue, but soon saw that she was finished. "Not a long list, Edith." He smiled. "Must be plenty of men like that."

"No. Good men are almost as scarce as good women."

He looked puzzled, and asked, "I can't figure out who you're tryin' to insult with that—men or women?"

"Oh, neither one, Sky!" She laughed and asked, "Why are you so interested? Going to give inside tips on the new brides to your friends in Oregon City?" She saw his face change, and instantly regretted her hasty words. "I didn't mean that, Sky. I'm sorry."

"No apology necessary, Edith." He walked along silently, then said, "Edith, would you ever—"

He broke off and she prompted, "Would I ever *what*, Sky?"

He stooped, picked up a smooth stone, and after studying it sent it sailing through the air. "I guess I feel a little bit skittish about all this, Edith," he admitted. "But please let me ask you to do something—just between us."

"What is it?"

"Don't make up your mind about a man right off. I mean,

when you get to Oregon City, there'll be a hundred fellows trying to turn your head. Some of them will be pretty flashy, Edith, making us ordinary fellows look pretty slow. Some of them will have enough money to dazzle a woman, and they'll all be promising you the moon with a fence around it."

"Sounds very enticing, Sky."

"Yeah, I know—that's why I'm asking you to wait." He almost spoke the truth, but held back. "Just don't jump into anything too quick. I'll have more to say to you about this later, Edith."

"I'll wait until you tell me, Sky."

He left her then and Rita came up to walk beside her. She glanced at Edith's glowing cheeks with a smile. "You look like a girl who's just been asked to a dance. What's our fearless leader been spilling in your shell-like ear?"

"Oh, nothing."

Rita studied her carefully. "Edith, take a tip from a girl who's spent a lifetime getting to know men, will you?"

"Why, I guess so, Rita."

"Sky Winslow's not going to have a wife. "

If Rita had any doubts about Edith's being in love with Winslow, the woman's reaction settled it. Edith's eyes flashed with denial, and she gave an involuntary shake of her head. "Rita, you're cynical! He's not as hard as you think." Then she retorted, "He may have turned you down, Rita, but just because a man isn't looking for a quick romance with no ties doesn't mean he's not ready for something more real!"

Rita didn't take offense, but shrugged philosophically. "Well, I *did* make a try for him. And he turned me down, you'll be glad to hear." She touched the other woman on the arm. "Believe it or not, honey, I'm on your side. You're a good woman—but you're headed for a fall. God knows I've taken enough of those to know what it's like! Still, I hope you're right. I'd like to see you marry Mr. Sky Winslow and live happily ever after—just like in the story books!"

For the next week, the train crawled slowly along the Snake River's high, boulder-strewn south rim. Just getting water to drink meant clambering down a precipice into the gorge of the river, then toiling back up again.

"By the time a man gets back to the trail, he needs another

drink," Dave complained, returning to the wagon with a flushed face. "How long before we get out of this, Sky?"

"Hang in there, Dave," Sky shrugged. "When we leave the Snake, we've got to scramble up the Blue Mountains—that'll be worse, I reckon."

"Can't be worse!" Dave growled, but he took his words back when they got to the mountains a week later. They were forced to cut timber to make a way for the wagons, then in many places had to rig a windlass to haul the wagons up the steep grades.

After one such haul, Sky called a halt for a two day's rest on the flat land at the top of the bank. By then the oxen were sore-footed and the men were almost past going, so everyone sighed with relief, and that night there was a festive air in the camp. Game had been plentiful, but up till now there had been little time to cook it. Besides, no one had the strength to catch it, so huge fires were built from fallen timber, and one of the weaker oxen was butchered and set to turning on a huge spit. There were a few delicacies left, and everyone brought out what remained. The women found enough dried fruit to make pies, and they used the last of the coffee. "We can get more in Walla," Sky nodded.

"What about the Rikers, Sky?" Dave asked. "They're not too well fixed for grub—but they say it's your rule to keep the trains separate."

Sky hesitated, then said, "I guess we can bend a rule now, Dave. I'll go give them an invite."

He found the Rikers beginning to make their meal, and said, "Al, bring your bunch, and let's celebrate making it to Oregon."

Riker looked up in surprise. "What about your rule?"

"Figure we can bend it a little. We've had a hard trip."

"Well, we ain't got much to put in the pot—"

"We got plenty, Al."

By dark the smell of barbecued beef was rich in the cool air, and for once the drivers and the women mixed freely. Sky sat back and watched, his eyes alert for trouble. Someone brought out a fiddle and soon there was a couple here and there dancing.

"They're sure enjoying themselves." He looked around to find Edith standing beside him. She was dolled up in a clean blue dress he hadn't seen before, and there was a ribbon in her hair.

"They deserve it," he said. "Sit down and watch the frolic." She sat beside him as he silently watched the scene. "I'll probably regret this," he remarked glumly. "There's still lots of time for trouble between the men and women."

"I guess you can handle it, Sky." She smoothed her dress, and they talked quietly, enjoying the music and the festive air. Finally Lot Penny called out, "Come and get it!" and they went to get some of the food. He walked with her back to a spot at the edge of the clearing where they sat down and ate hungrily.

Sky listened as she told him about the train—how this woman had this problem, how Timmy was cutting a tooth—little things out of their microcosm of a world. As she talked, Sky suddenly made up his mind.

"Edith, I started to tell you something once—before we hit the Snake."

"I remember." Edith's hands went to her throat nervously. "Are you ready to tell me now, Sky?"

"Well, Edith, I've been thinking about you ever since I met you in New York." He smiled at her and added, "I guess you're just about the most able woman I ever met."

"Thank you," she murmured quietly.

"Well—it's like this—I know you can get just about any man you want in Oregon City, but I'd like you to think about . . ."

He floundered, and Edith smiled and put her hand on his. "Think about what, Sky?"

He stared at her hand, confused; Edith was not a demonstrative woman. Then he squared his shoulders and plunged ahead. "Edith, the best man I know is a friend called Sam Birdwell. This trip is all his idea, and he got it up mostly because he wants a wife. He asked me to look all the women over and see if one of them would do for him." He paused and gestured with both hands. "Edith, Sam's not much for show, but he's solid gold!"

She sat as still as a stone, her face stricken. "This—this is what you've been trying to ask me all this time, Sky?"

"Well, yes. It's asking a lot, Edith, but you're just about the best woman I've ever seen, and if you could just hold off until you get to know Sam a little—"

"Excuse me, Sky—I don't feel very well." Edith got up hastily, and he scrambled to his feet and walked with her until she said in a tight voice, "You stay here, please. I—want to be alone."

He stopped and watched her go to the wagon she shared with May Stockton, climb inside and draw the canvas. *Sure did upset her,* Sky thought. *Guess she thinks I'm pretty bold, asking a thing like that.* He shuffled back to the fire, depressed and wishing he'd said nothing to her.

The dancing was in full sway, and he moved over to stand by Lake, who was holding Timmy and talking to Rebekah. "Where's Edith, Sky?"

"Got to feeling a little woozie, Tom. "

Lake handed him the boy and said, "I'll just have a look. Hold this captain for me."

As he walked away, Rebekah looked puzzled. "I talked to her earlier, and she seemed fine, Sky."

"Came on pretty sudden. Probably not serious." He looked at her carefully. "You got a new dress. Looks good on you."

"It's one of Rita's." Her attention focused on the dancers. "Look at her, Sky. Isn't she beautiful?"

He turned and saw that half a dozen of the drivers were lined up to take their turn for a dance with Rita. She was wearing a bright green dress, and her face glowed with enjoyment. "She sure can dance," he commented. Then he turned and began to dangle Timmy. "Mary all right?" he asked Rebekah.

"Healthy as a horse—and eats like a pig," she laughed. She kissed the baby and held her up for him to see.

"Looks like you," he smiled. Then the music slowed, and he looked around quickly. Dave was standing close by, talking with Karen, and Sky suddenly handed the boy to him, then reached out and took the baby from Rebekah, who stared at him, bewildered, as he gave the child to Karen. Then he turned back and held his hands out.

"Care to dance, Rebekah?"

She took his hands shyly and he pulled her to her feet and into the circle of dancers nearby. As the pair moved around by the firelight to the tune of the fiddle, Dave watched them, saying,

"Don't know what to make of that. Wouldn't even think Sky could dance. Somehow I always think of him as fighting or killing something. Guess he's got his weaknesses like the rest of us."

Karen frowned. "I'm not sure it's good, Dave."

"What? Her dancing with Sky?"

"I'm worried about her. What will happen to her when we get to Oregon City?"

"Why, she'll find a man and marry him. Just like—" He broke off and looked at her strangely. "Just like the rest of you."

"A woman with two children? It won't be so easy—even in Oregon City."

They talked a while and then Lake came from the wagons and stood beside them. He watched Sky and Rebekah dancing, and said quietly, "They make a good-looking couple."

Something in his tone drew Karen's gaze, and she shook her head as Dave opened his mouth to agree. They all watched until the dance was over; then Sky brought Rebekah back. "How's Edith, Tom?"

"Just a little stomach upset. I gave her something for it to make her sleep."

Sky started to speak, but a loud commotion at the edge of the clearing distracted him. "That's trouble!" he said, running quickly across through the crowd, followed by the other two men.

At the edge of the circle just beside the trees, they saw Jack Stedman. He was holding the arm of May Stockton, who was struggling to free herself. At his feet lay Mack Malone, who was holding his face and twisting in pain. Stedman lifted his foot to kick the small man in the head, but Sky called out, "Don't do it, Stedman!" The big man instantly wheeled to face him.

"Better see to Mack, Tom," Sky ordered, and as Lake went over to pull Malone's hands from his face, Sky demanded, "What's this about?"

"He tried to cut me out with this gal," Stedman said sullenly.

"That's a lie!" May jerked free from his grasp. "Stedman pulled me into the woods and was making free with me. I screamed and Mack came and told him to turn me loose."

"It was none of his business!"

Lake stood up and helped Mack to his feet. "He's got a broken nose. I'll have to work on it."

"Get it done fast, Doc," Sky said. "You're going to have another customer right soon—in a lot worse shape."

Silence fell like a weight, and Stedman's eyes narrowed. "I ain't got a gun, Winslow!"

"I brought mine along."

A streak of fear ran through the burly Stedman. "You can't shoot an unarmed man!" he protested.

"I could—but I'm not going to shoot you." Sky took off his gun belt and handed it to Dave. "Just cripple you up enough so that you can still drive a team—but you won't be bothering any more women on this trip."

The pronouncement hit Stedman hard, but he sized up Winslow's body, which looked frail compared to his own bulk, and growled, "Try it, Winslow. I'll bust you up for good!"

He was fast for a big man, and his lunge almost took Sky off guard. Stedman's massive fist grazed his head, the brutal force of it turning him around and driving him to the ground. He rolled to one side and doubled up to protect himself from the kick he knew was coming. The numbing blow caught him in the flank, but he managed to grab Stedman's foot and twist it enough to send the man heavily to the ground.

Sky was on his feet instantly and waited until Stedman was up, then hurled himself at the man, smashing him in the soft flesh under the ear. Stedmen fell to the ground, with his mouth wide open, sucking in air.

Sky knew the man would not give up that easily. He waited until Stedman came up with a howl of rage, clawing to get at his enemy, then stepped aside and lifted a knee, driving it into the man's groin. As the huge arms dropped, he broke Stedman's nose with one head-on blow. Stedman cried out and covered his face, then recovered quickly and, with a spiderlike jump, tried to carry Sky down with him. Sky bent and caught Stedman on the hip, clamping the man's thick neck in the crook of his forearm. He swayed until he felt the cartilage of Stedman's neck grind, then flipped him like a doll, pushing him backward and landing on top of the man with his knees, hearing the snap of breaking ribs.

A low moaning escaped Stedman's lips, and Sky got to his feet, breathing heavily. He stood there, looking down at the man who would have gouged his leader's eyes out. There was a savagery in Sky's face and a wildness in his eyes that none of the crowd had ever seen.

"Better crawl over to see the Doc, Jack," he growled. "And you'd best be ready to drive that team when we leave here—or I'll leave you for the buzzards." Then he looked around and stared at the crowd. "I should have stuck to the rule—it seems that I was right the first time. But there'll be no more of this. Until we get to Oregon City, what I gave Stedman is just a sample of what the man will get who says one easy word to a woman. No exceptions. You've just had your last frolic on this trip."

Dave stared at him with displeasure, but he said nothing. The silence of the crowd was sullen as they began to clean up the dishes, but no one dared to question Winslow. His treatment of Stedman had been brutal and harsh enough to put fear into them.

"Be glad when we get to Oregon City," Dave said to Tom later as they got ready for bed. "The fun's out of this trip."

Lake settled into his bedroll and said slowly, "I thought Sky was going to kill Stedman."

"He will if this happens again. Winslow's got his ideas of right and wrong, Tom, and when something breaks across—he'll smash it down, or die tryin'."

"That's a good quality sometimes—I guess it's what got us this far."

"Sure—but he's gone sour, Tom." Dave shook his head as he lay back and looked up at the sky. "Soon he'll be seein' things that aren't there." Lloyd's voice was heavy. The vicious outflaring of the fight had rattled his nerves, and he wished again that the trip was over.

CHAPTER SIXTEEN

WELCOME TO OREGON!

★　★　★　★

Stedman was driving his wagon two days after his fight with Winslow, nursing broken ribs and a burning hatred. He said nothing about the fight to anyone after it was over, except once to Leon Crumpler. "He can't watch his back all the time. When we get to Oregon City, we'll have a settling!"

October was on them by the time they reached the foothills of the Cascades, and the air turned bitter cold in a freak display of winter weather. Sky led them to a lava beach that was hard-pressed between a high bluff and the rolling Columbia River. The canvas tops of the eighteen wagons cast a pale glow against a gray flicker of sand and rain. They had come two thousand miles in just over six months, and now they faced the monumental task of building rafts and floating downriver the last ninety miles through the gorge of the Cascades.

They all got out of the wagons and stood staring at the river. *They've been whittled down quite a bit*, Sky thought, watching their faces. Summer's heat had boiled the confidence from them, and the daily grind of the trail had sapped their vitality so that most of them moved with the carefulness of the aged. The strength with which they had started the trip had been reduced to a dogged persistence that barely enabled them to make it through a single day.

Tom Lake was standing beside Edith, both of them dulled by the cold and depressed by the thought of what lay ahead. While Edith had little to say to him before the night he'd come to her wagon, after that meeting the two of them had been friends. Tom knew she'd been wounded deeply by Sky's carelessness, and he made it a habit to spend a little time with her each day.

He had gone to her wagon that night, thinking she was sick, and found her crouched over, her shoulders shaking uncontrollably. Pulling her upright to get a better look at her face, her eyes had met his with such a hopeless expression that he hadn't known what to say except, "Tell me, Edith—maybe I can help."

He had been shocked by the torrent of sobs that wracked her body as she flung herself against his shoulder; he'd held her until she had quieted down long enough to tell him what had happened. "I'm the hopeless old maid, Tom. I thought that Sky was going to ask me to marry him." She'd sniffled. "I guess I ought to be flattered that he picked me out of all the others to marry his best friend." Lake knew she had been heartbroken, so had taken special notice of her the rest of the trip.

Now he sighed and looked back at the towering pines that lined the high landscape of the bluff. "It makes me tired to think of making those rafts," he remarked wearily, "but Sky says there's no other way."

She looked up at the sky. "I hope a snowstorm doesn't catch us here."

He asked carefully, "Have you been thinking of the man Sky mentioned?"

Her face was drawn, and there was little of the vivacious light in her expression that had been there six months earlier. "No, Tom. Just getting there is about all I've got the strength for."

She might have been speaking for all of them. As the days went by, life settled down to a mind-numbing routine. A third of the men went to the woods to fell the timber, while the others drove the oxen to-and-fro, dragging the logs back to the beach. Sky, along with Lot Penny and Tom Lake, formed the rafts out of the fir logs, while the women did the cooking and washing. There was no letup from dawn to dusk, and all of them moved as if they were in a trance.

When they had finished the thirteenth raft, Lot groaned,

"This sure is a hard way to serve the Lord, Brother Winslow!"

Sky straightened up carefully, the backs of his legs aching with the strain of shifting the heavy logs into place. "Only five more to go, Lot. We've got to beat that weather that's building up over there." He sank the blade of his axe in a log. "Let's get some grub."

They walked along the beach to where the women had put together a table of rough saplings to hold the food. Over the tables they had erected a framework of sorts and covered it with canvas so it was possible to keep out of the fine drizzling rain long enough to eat. When Penny had commented on the constant rain, Sky had said, "You'll get used to it. The wetness around here is the saturatin' kind. When you get close to a stove, you'll stand around in a steam bath. You won't get entirely dry until spring, and you may get to feelin' like a book with the glue about ready to let go—but it'll feel normal after a winter or two."

After eating his meal, Sky got up from the fire and began to walk down by the river. Rebekah watched him as he disappeared around the bend behind an outcropping of rock. After all the men were fed, she checked on the baby, then fixed a plate for herself and went to sit beside Tom, who was holding Timmy. The boy was wearing so many clothes to keep the cold out that he looked like a ball, but he was still agile enough to pull at Lake's plate.

"I'll take him, Tom."

"No, you go on and eat. We're doing fine."

She watched as he played with the child, wondering at the transformation that had taken place in Lake. At the beginning of the journey, he had been just another driver—though less imposing than most of them. Failure had bent him physically and spiritually, so that his shoulders had drooped and he'd been unable to meet a gaze directly.

Now everyone marveled at how he had grown in assurance since he'd assumed his role as the trail doctor, causing Karen to remark, "Tom Lake didn't save three lives that day—he saved *four!*"

As Lake held up the baby, playing with him, Rebekah looked at his hands. "Your hands are in terrible shape, Tom!"

Setting the baby on his lap, he looked down at them, noting

the blue nails on the fingers that had been pinched by shifting logs and the cuts that scarred them, and nodded ruefully. "Guess there's no way to build a raft without getting a little beat up."

"But you're a doctor," she argued. "Your hands are more important than other men's."

"Don't take a vote on that, Rebekah."

"Well, it's so!" Her voice was indignant. "I don't think Sky ought to have you doing a job that will ruin your hands. What if you had to operate on one of us?"

Lake regarded her patiently. "Sky doesn't think that way. He always does whatever's needful at the moment. Stedman needed a whipping, and everything else stopped for Sky until it was done. These rafts have to be built to get the wagons down the river. That's the one thing that's needed—and until that's done, nothing else matters." He shrugged. "Even if all of us get our hands cut to pieces, he'll do whatever's needful."

She reached over and took Timmy from him. "You eat." Then she rocked the boy back and forth thoughtfully. "You're right, Tom," she said after a while. "Sky is like that. But he has to be. We wouldn't have gotten this far if he hadn't pushed us."

"Sure. I'm not speaking against him, Rebekah," Lake hastened to agree, rising to his feet and looking down the river. "I'm just saying he's not an easy man to live with. He's led a pretty hard life, and he didn't make it by giving in—he pushes himself harder than anyone else. What worries me is that someday he'll find himself in a situation where he can't get through with muscle and a gun. That's always been enough—up till now. But what'll Sky do when *that* fails him?"

A crease of worry formed on Rebekah's brow. "I owe him a lot, Tom. He took a chance bringing me on this trip. No other man would have done it."

He nodded soberly. "Sure. Me, too, Rebekah. I'd still be a drunk if Sky hadn't made me change." He started to leave, then turned to ask, "Is the baby still coughing?"

"Last night she did, but she's been a little better today."

"I'll stop by and look at her after supper."

By the end of the day two more rafts were finished. As Penny and Winslow tightened the last bolt, Lake said, "If we're about finished, I'd like to go have a look at Mrs. Riker before supper. She's feeling poorly."

"Sure, Tom." Sky took three more turns on the nut, then said, "That's good, Lot." He sat back on his haunches and watched Lake walk back to the train. "You know something? Tom's a different fellow these days."

"He's found his place, is all." Penny straightened and stretched his aching arms. "Somewhere in the good Book there's a verse about that."

"If there is, you'd know it, Lot," Sky replied with a touch of admiration. "Except for my pa, you know more Bible than any man I ever saw. What verse you talkin' about now?"

" 'As a bird that wanders from her nest, so is a man that wanders from his place.' " Lot thought hard. "That's in Proverbs."

Sky couldn't guess what Penny was talking about. "What's it *mean*?"

"Well, Sky, God didn't put a man here to be alone—He meant for him to be with other folks. And that's why God made Eve, remember? To be company for Adam."

"Yeah, but it seems to me that most of our troubles come from other people, Lot. Man out by himself in the woods can get killed by a grizzly or a rattler, but most of the miseries that hang on come from other people."

Penny loved to argue the Scriptures, so he settled himself against the raft they just finished and went on. "Why, sure, they do. But look at the other side of it. It ain't only our miseries that come from other people, Sky; we get our happiness from them, too. Man can't talk to a dog, can he?"

"I don't know, Lot—I had a smart old hound that had more sense than most men. I talked to him quite a bit," Sky argued. Truthfully, he was not paying much heed to the talk, for Lot could go on for hours. Still, it was relaxing, and he knew that soon he would have to get back to the burden of getting the rafts down the Columbia—which would be a dangerous and tricky job.

Lot Penny, though he had little formal education, was an inherently intelligent man who had spent a lifetime sharpening his skills at reading people. He had rarely met a man with more potential than Sky Winslow, and it grieved him that the man had never taken a strong stand for God. Penny never forced the issue, however; he knew that no man would force Winslow into serving God—or anything else! Still, he had prayed often that somehow he would be able to lead the young man into the ways of the Lord.

"God made all the animals to be subject to man," Penny said with conviction. "But a dog won't take the place of a human, Sky, and you blamed well know it! Anyway, that Bible verse's talking about something else. When a bird wanders from her place, she's not got anywhere to go. True enough, she don't have no little birds she has to feed—no responsibilities. But she ain't *complete*, don't you see?"

"I reckon she could get by."

"Sky, you know you don't believe that," Penny reproved him gently. "What about that boy you speak of—Joe. Ain't you yearning to see him?"

Sky nodded. "I love Joe—but his mother put me through hell, Lot."

"So you've had a taste of both heaven and hell, Sky. After you die, you'll be in one or the other—but on this earth, man's got some of each. Anyhow, *that's* what the verse is sayin': man needs a *place*. And that don't mean a house. It means people that love him, and more important than that, he needs to love people."

"I guess so."

"You're a smart feller, Sky. You know I'm right. And I can tell that you think the world of your ma and pa. There's another verse that says, 'Raise up a child in the way that's right, and when he's old, he won't depart from it.' " Lot laid a hand on the younger man's shoulder. "Brother, I've got the feeling that you've been out of your place for a long time, but I believe you're gonna find it again—soon. I'm trustin' God for it."

Penny's words stirred Winslow, reminding him that he had no one to share his thoughts with. The end of the journey was not something he looked forward to, for his problems with Joe would still be as critical then as they had been when he left months earlier.

"Lot," he said tentatively, "I haven't told many people this, but I've come on this trip for a couple of reasons. First, I wanted to help a friend find a wife. I hope now it'll work out for him, but there's something else." He hesitated, not wanting to burden other people with his troubles.

"What is it, Sky?" Lot's prompting seemed to encourage Winslow, and he laid the whole thing before Penny, including his difficulties with Joe. "I've got to have help, Lot."

Penny replied, "You ought to get married, Sky."

"No!" Winslow bellowed, and Lot blinked. "I've tried that, Lot, and it didn't work."

"But not all women are like *her*, Sky."

"Yeah, I know . . . but I'm not going to take a chance on going through that hell again!"

"You going to live like a hermit for the rest of your life, Sky? You can't shut people out like that and stay human. You'll fester inside and get mean." Penny hesitated, then said carefully, "I think a heap of you, Sky—but I'm honest when I tell you that I've seen some of that in you already. Unforgiveness does that to people. It don't hurt the one you hate so much—but it eats away at a man's insides until he's all empty. No love, no kindness—*nothing!*"

Sky wanted to believe the preacher, but in the end he shook his head determinedly and said, "It's all right for most, Lot, but I'm just not going to try it."

"Well, you said there was another reason for your coming here; what is it?"

"I want to hire one of these women to be a housekeeper for me and Joe." Now that the idea was out, Sky's eyes glowed as he went on to explain his plan, but he talked with a desperate animation that sounded to Penny as though Winslow had to convince not only Penny but himself. "I could move into town, Lot, buy a house and build a little house for the woman, just for her. She could cook and take care of the house for Joe and me, and I could pay her well."

Penny smiled sadly. "Son, these women didn't come all the way across the country to be servants. They want to be wives!"

"I know, Lot, but—"

When Winslow did not continue, Penny said, "Well, I can tell there's more. Spit it out."

"It's Rebekah. She's got those two children, and not many men would want to raise another man's kids. So I've decided to ask her if she'll do it. What do you think, Lot?"

"I think she'll say no." Penny shook his head. "You're foolin' yourself, Sky, and that ain't like you. Sure, some men will back off from those two children, but there'll be others who'll welcome them. Especially when they see how pretty Rebekah is."

Tired of the conversation, Winslow got to his feet. "Guess I've always had the idea that she was pretty well fed up with men. At any rate, I'm going to ask her, Lot." He walked away from the raft with a purposeful straightness in his back.

"Sure hate to see that boy get hurt—but he's headed for a bad fall!" Penny said to himself.

The crew in the woods worked late that day cutting enough logs for all the rafts; by doubling up on the oxen, they brought the last of the logs into camp by nine o'clock. All of the men were exhausted, but after a late supper everyone sat around the fire and talked about the descent down the river.

"How do we go about it, Sky?" Al Riker asked. "I don't see how anything can get through those rapids down there."

"Well, there's about six miles of white water," Sky explained. "We'll float the rafts through and portage around the rapids."

"What'll happen to the rafts?" Dave asked.

"Won't be hard to catch 'em in the calmer current. Then we load the wagons back on and take a thirty-mile drift to the mouth of the Sandy. From there it'll take two days into Oregon City by land."

"Don't sound too bad," Lake spoke up.

"Won't be—unless we get a big rain that fills the river up." Sky glanced upward at the black and ominous sky. "There's been lots of big thunderheads building up since yesterday."

"What if that happens?"

"It gets a little tricky. Have to have a boat and a couple of good men ready to catch the rafts."

Riker shook his head. "Wouldn't want that job—a small boat in a wild river tryin' to stop heavy rafts."

"It can be dangerous," Sky admitted. He looked up at the sky again, feeling the pressure of the rains building up. "Let's get some sleep. Maybe we can finish the rafts tomorrow or the next day and beat those thunderheads."

The men wearily shuffled toward their bedrolls, but Tom Lake went first to stand by Rebekah's tent. He listened intently for the baby's coughing but heard nothing, so he went to his blankets. He and Lot Penny had rigged up a snug shelter underneath the wagon Lot drove, lining the ground with canvas and raising a skirt of it to keep the cold air out. Lot was already down and snoring, so Tom crawled in beside him and went to sleep.

He slept fitfully, half-waking from time to time. Lot was a difficult man to sleep with, for he was either mumbling or snoring most of the night. Tom had just dropped off into a light slumber when he was awakened with a start. Something was scratching at the walls of their makeshift tent. Fishing beside his bedroll for his glasses, Tom reached out with his other hand to grasp the pistol he kept handy in the roll over his head.
"Tom! Tom!"

He sat up and promptly smacked his head on the underside of the wagon. Rubbing the sore spot, he looked over to see that Lot was still sound asleep. Recognizing the voice, he replaced the pistol, pulled his boots on, and moved the draw cover of the shelter aside. Rebekah stood in a drizzling rain holding a lantern, her face blurred in the darkness. "What's wrong?" he whispered loudly, crawling from under the wagon.

"Mary's worse." Rebekah's voice was tense with panic. "I can't stop her from coughing."

"Let me get my bag." He went around to the back of the wagon and picked up his medical kit, then followed her across the muddy ground to her wagon. He could hear the baby's racking cough even before he got there; he crawled inside the wagon and Rebekah followed. The baby was lying in a crib made of smooth saplings on top of some boxes. Sitting down on the bed beside the crib, he said to Rebekah, "Hold the lantern closer."

He examined Mary as carefully as he could by the dim light. Intently he listened to the child's chest, which heaved with the effort of breathing, hearing a rattle in the lungs he didn't like.

"Is it bad, Tom?"

"Well, I wish we could help her breathe. Let's water down some of this cough syrup and see if that will help."

Working together, they managed to get some of the cough mixture down the baby's throat. That accomplished, he said, "I'll just sit with you for a while."

It was well he did, for the child's temperature rose half an hour later, and the two of them worked tirelessly at getting it down by applying cool, damp cloths to the skin.

Tom was well aware that if the baby's temperature went too high, convulsions would follow—which could be fatal—so time passed unheeded. Finally he leaned back and exhaled a sigh of relief. "I think she's all right, Rebekah. Why don't you get Karen or one of the other women to watch her while you get some sleep?"

"I couldn't sleep, Tom. It must be nearly dawn anyhow."

"Well, I'll try to get a few winks. If she gets worse, come and get me."

"Tom—thank you." She clasped her hands together and smiled tremulously. Her hair down, she looked not only vulnerable but very beautiful in the pale light of the lantern. "If you hadn't been here. . . !"

"Get some sleep, Rebekah," he said quickly, then pulled the flap of the tent aside and stepped down out of the wagon. The ground was soft under his feet, and the cold rain was still falling, but the thin gray light of dawn outlined the forms of the other wagons. Wearily, he turned to go.

"Hold it right there."

The challenge took Lake off guard, but he peered intently at the man who had stepped out of the gray light. "Oh, Sky—it's you!" The thrill of fear that had touched him turned to relief. Winslow often kept a close watch during the early hours. "It's okay, Sky. Just me."

"So I see. Stay right where you are."

Lake was bewildered. "What's wrong, Sky? Some kind of trouble?"

"You're the trouble." The hard edge on Sky's voice shocked Lake, as did the raw anger that flared out of the light blue eyes as he moved closer. "You know the rule about being alone with a woman, Lake."

For one moment, Tom couldn't imagine what Sky was talking about, and then the implication hit him. "Oh, I can explain that,

Sky. Rebekah came to get me—"

"You're not going to blame this on her."

Sky hadn't lowered his voice, and from the other wagons came the sound of people moving, coming to see what the trouble was. "Sky, don't make an issue of this. The baby was sick. I went to see how she was."

"Don't give me that!" Sky snarled. "You've been in that wagon for nearly two hours. It doesn't take that long to doctor a sick child."

"What's up, Sky?" Dave Lloyd was standing beside the two men, his unshaven face rough. Behind him, others formed a circle a short distance away, watching intently.

Winslow said, "I caught Lake with Rebekah."

The tent flap opened behind Lake and Rebekah came down out of the wagon. "It's all right, Sky. Mary had a fever and I went to get Tom."

The set look of anger on Winslow's face did not change with Rebekah's explanation. He had risen in the middle of the night, which was not unusual for him, and told Mack Malone, who was on late guard, to go to bed. About an hour later he'd heard the noise as Rebekah and Lake had climbed up into her wagon, but had not been able to see who it was. Because he had no way of knowing what had happened, he thought at first it might simply have been Rebekah getting water for the baby, or some other necessary errand. But his caution prompted him to stay within range of her wagon.

When Lake had stepped down, Winslow was filled with an irrational, blinding rage. He did not stop to consider that as a doctor, Lake might have had a plausible reason for being in Rebekah's tent, nor would any other excuse have dimmed his fury. For in that moment, the memory of his wife's last infidelity swept across his mind in living color.

He had taken her and Joe, along with one of his partners, on a trapping venture on the upper Missouri. One night he had been delayed on one of the lines, and came back long after dark— and caught the man coming out of his wagon. After beating him senseless, Sky made up his mind to take Irene and Joe to Oregon in a futile attempt to change his wife's adulterous ways.

The memory of that moment had seized his mind so powerfully that he'd almost shot Lake as he climbed out of the wagon. Even now, he was not thinking clearly, and was unconscious of the others who had gathered around. Lake's excuses seemed weak, and the fact that Rebekah confirmed his story made no difference. In times like this, Winslow was a man of impulse more than conscious thought. That fact had always protected him before, and now it caused him to act immediately.

"Take a horse and what you need, Lake," he said evenly. "You can make it to Oregon City by yourself."

Lake stood still, not believing what was happening. "Sky, that's ridiculous! We've told you what happened. The baby had a fever, and we had to get it down."

Winslow didn't seem to hear. "Get out of camp, or I'll shoot you, Lake. That's what any man deserves that takes advantage of a woman on my train. But I'm giving you a break. Take it— or take a bullet."

"He means it, Tom!" Edith came to stand beside Lake, her eyes wide. "Take a horse and get out of here."

An angry mutter rose as the crowd grew larger, but no one had the nerve to stand up to Sky. Lot Penny had arrived at the scene just long enough to hear Sky's threat. "The lady's right, Lake. Right or wrong, you got to leave."

Tom Lake stared incredulously at Sky. The admiration and respect he'd felt for Winslow was dashed, and yet he knew that he had no show against the deadly westerner in any sort of fight. Adjusting his spectacles, he settled back on his heels and said, "If I go, it'd be the same as saying that Rebekah's a bad woman. She's not—and I won't be a party to your crazy jealousy!"

Sky had not moved, and there was something ominous in the stillness of his posture. Every soul on the train knew he was a deadly man with any sort of weapon, and they all were nervously eyeing the gun he had at his side. None of the others were armed, but even if they had been, no man would have had a chance against him.

"All right, Lake," Sky said through clenched teeth. "I tried to give you a break, but you wouldn't have it."

"Just a minute, Sky." Dave Lloyd moved to stand between the two men. He let his arms hang loosely at his sides with his usual air of lazy ease, but his eyes were bright with barely controlled emotion. "Sky, I guess I got as much respect for you as any man I know," he said quietly, "but you're wrong this time. Now let's just get this train down the river."

"Get out of the way, Dave."

Lloyd didn't budge. The rain had matted his coarse black hair to his skull, and molded his shirt to his huge shoulders and long arms. "Won't anything make you change your mind, Sky?"

"No. Get out of the way, Dave."

Lloyd sighed. "I'll have to take your gun away from you, Sky."

That cut Winslow like a blow. "You heard me, Dave! Stand aside! No man's taking my gun—and I'm not warning you again."

Lloyd said, "I don't have a gun, Sky, and wrong as you are about this—I don't reckon you'd shoot one of your friends cold turkey. C'mon—give me the gun."

He stepped forward and like a flash Winslow drew his gun and fired. The report shattered the morning air, and Lloyd felt the breath of the slug on his cheek, but did not even pause. He ignored the second shot as well, which grazed his shoulder. Quickly he reached out and slapped Sky's gun from his hand. It landed in the mud, and Sky made no attempt to get it.

"Okay, Sky." Dave said soothingly, his hands outstretched. "C'mon. Let's forget this and get to work. You're the leader of this train, and it looks like it's going to rain buckets. None of us can do this without you, so I'm your man all the way."

Sky still had not moved all this time, but stood there, his face pale. Then a ripple ran through his frame; he stared at Dave in unbelief, and covered his face.

"*Sky?*"

With an anguished moan, Sky turned from the group and stalked from the camp.

Rebekah retreated back into her wagon, sickened by the ugly scene and angry at Winslow's irrational and violent reaction. She covered her eyes and as she did so, she heard a voice say, "Sister, try not to hate Winslow too much."

She whirled to find Lot Penny peering inside the wagon flap in front of her. "He's a real mixed-up man. It was wrong, what he said—but if you knew how badly he's been hurt, you might see things a little different."

Rebekah turned away blindly, then whispered, "I'll be glad when I never have to look at him again!" At a loss for words, Penny silently drew the flap back over the opening and walked away.

Sky returned in an hour. During his absence his anger had subsided and he could think clearly. Why were his actions so volatile and unbending? Was it the pressure of his responsibility? Was it just because the rule had been broken—or because Rebekah was involved? Everything seemed so confusing to him. He resolved to change—but not now.

As he entered the camp, he saw Lake about ready to ride out, with Dave and the others gathered around him. Sky walked over and the rest stepped back. Coming directly to the point, he said, "Lake, Dave, I misjudged you. I want you to stay, Lake."

Sky Winslow faced the crowd unflinchingly. Only Rebekah had left, and the rest of them waited for his next move. Sky simply announced, "Let's get the rafts built."

Winslow turned without a word and walked toward the logs, followed by most of the other men. When he was out of hearing, Karen came up to Dave and said, "That man! He never does what you'd think, does he, Dave?" She hesitated, noticing his lack of response. "You mustn't feel bad about what happened this morning, Dave. Tom could have been killed—and you couldn't have done anything else to stop it. He won't hold it against you when he's thinking more clearly." She touched his cheek and said, "I was very proud of you, Dave!"

He watched her as she turned and walked away, and all day as he worked on the rafts, he thought about her praise with a warmth that almost made him forget about his encounter with Sky. He kept his eye on him, but said nothing. Penny uttered once under his breath, "I think more of Sky Winslow for this than anything else. It must be eating him alive—and for him to stay and help—why, that's a miracle, Dave!"

Lloyd thought so too, but it grieved him when Sky saddled his horse and rode off when they stopped work. He lay awake for a long time thinking of what Winslow must be feeling. As the night wore on, he heard him ride in some time after two.

They finished the rafts the next day, and the rest of the trip was anticlimactic. Under Winslow's direction, the wagons started on the portage. The rains stopped, but the river was high, so he told Lloyd, "Give us the rest of the morning, then push the rafts off at noon. Leave about ten minutes before you launch the next one."

It had gone perfectly. The rafts came floating down into the calmer water, and the crew pulled them to the bank and loaded the wagons. It took most of the day to tie them down; then Sky took four men ahead with him.

"Start the first wagon at eight tomorrow morning. Thirty minutes later, the next one. That'll give us plenty of time."

"The river's not so bad is it, Sky?" Dave said, hoping to see a break in the hardness of Winslow's face.

"It could be a lot worse," Sky answered blankly. He rode out with the others, and Lloyd turned away heavily.

The last leg of the Sandy River went as well as the portage. The rafts rode high and the only incident was when one of them got hung up on some driftwood, but two of the men quickly pulled it off.

It was nearly dark before they got all the wagons off, but the next day they left for Oregon City, and spent two uneventful days on the trail.

Now they had come into the place they'd risked their lives to reach.

It wasn't much of a town, Rita thought, taking in the muddy streets and the string of frame buildings that lined the main street, but the welcome they got made up for it. Men poured out of every doorway, and there was a high-pitched yelling as the crowd gathered around the wagons, pulling at the horses and waving their hats at the women.

As the procession stopped, Rita laughed, "They're a pretty rough bunch, aren't they? You find one who looks good to you, Rebekah?" She got no answer, and glanced at the other woman. Rebekah was staring at a young boy who had run out of a store and grabbed Sky Winslow around the middle. The two stood there, holding on to each other, oblivious of the crowd, and then Sky swung the boy around and saw Rebekah staring at him.

He stopped in his tracks, and his expression changed in a

way she could not explain. He held her gaze for one long moment before the boy pulled at him, and he looked down. When he answered the boy and looked back, a tall young man had come up to Rebekah, sweeping off his hat and introducing himself, unknowingly blocking Sky's view of her.

Her last sight of him was of the two of them mounting his horse and his spurring it down the muddy street, going at a fast run until she could not see him anymore.

Rita was being pulled toward a large building by anxious hands, but she resisted them long enough to draw close and say, "Forget him, Rebekah! Who needs a reluctant bridegroom when there's men for the asking all over the place! *Welcome to Oregon!*"

Rebekah suddenly felt more lonely in the midst of the shouting throng than she had in all the emptiness of the great plains. She shook her head at the tall fellow who was urging her to let him escort her to the hotel, and went to find a place of quiet in the wagon. "I don't want to go with them, Lot," she said and got under the canvas. She picked Mary up and cuddled her close, and allowed the tears to flow.

"Welcome to Oregon!" she whispered—and wished that she were anywhere else in all the world.

PART THREE

OREGON CITY

★ ★ ★ ★

CHAPTER SEVENTEEN

SKY MAKES UP HIS MIND

★ ★ ★ ★

The snowstorm caught up with Sky and Joe at the end of the first week of their trip north. When the sun shrank to a small, gray disk in the iron sky and the temperature plummeted, Sky said, "We're in for it now, Joe. Got to make for McKenzie's old place over by Sixpoint River."

By the time they reached the deserted shack, heavy flakes had padded the earth with three or four inches of snow. "You take care of the horses, Joe, and I'll get a fire going and fix some grub," Sky said.

"All right, Pa." Joe piled off his horse, took the reins from Sky and led the animals around back to a shed with a slanting roof branching off the main structure. He brought them inside, stripped off the packs and saddles, and dug out a small sack of feed. Pouring it into an old bucket, he gave each a turn, then went down to the river and brought back water. The horses emptied the bucket thirstily, and he went back to refill it. By the time he finished, the dark was closing in, and his hands and feet were almost numb as he stumbled to the front door and fumbled with the latch.

"Come in and warm up, Joe." The warmth of the flickering fire was a welcome sight, and the smell of the sizzling steaks in the frying pan that Sky held stirred the boy's juices. He stomped the snow from his feet, shut the door behind him, and sat beside the huge fireplace. "Glad we left that kindling and wood here last year, Son. Don't reckon there's been a soul here since we left. You get the horses fed?"

"Sure."

Sky was amused at the taciturn answer; he had noticed that Joe was out to prove himself grown up: avoiding boyish chatter and speaking briefly in as deep a voice as possible. There were times when he forgot—like when he'd brought down the six-point buck early that morning. Sky had put him where the boy would get the first shot; and if he lived to be a hundred, Sky would never forget Joe's wide-eyed excitement as he'd stood over the fallen animal, dancing and chattering loudly.

"Glad you got this fellow, Joe," Sky said idly, turning the steaks. "We'd be chewing hardtack if you'd missed." He cocked his head and allowed admiration to shade his tone: "That was a good shot."

Joe flushed with pleasure. "Wasn't much." Then he forgot his resolution to keep his words to a minimum, and began to talk with animation of the hunt. His flow of words was slowed only slightly by the steak that Sky put before him.

Boy's been dying for someone to talk to—never should have gone on that fool trip! Sky thought. During his brief talk with Sam Birdwell, he'd learned that Joe had not been happy. "He missed you a lot, Sky," Birdwell had said. "I tried to find things to do with him, but I'm a town man and he just naturally wanted to be outside, hunting and trapping. We're *both* glad you're back, Sky. Boy needs you."

Winslow leaned back and ate slowly, enjoying his son's company and pleased with the sight of Joe's lean figure and lively face. The months had stretched his body out. *He's going to be a big man—like his grandfather, maybe.* The thought of his father sent a wave of discontent through him, for much as he was enjoying the hunting trip, he knew he was only postponing the inevitable. A nagging sense of lost time disturbed him, for he was no closer to resolving the problem than before. By the end of the trail to Oregon, he had realized that getting a housekeeper was not feasible. And he could see nothing ahead for himself and Joe but more of what they'd had before—and it was not enough.

Joe was tired after the hard day, but he fought sleep as long as he could. The snow outside blanketed all sound, and it was satisfying to sit there beside the glowing coals. From time to time Sky would poke the fire, sending golden, fiery sparks up the chimney. Joe begged him for stories of his youth, and Sky managed to dredge up a couple he'd never told while he drank strong black coffee. As he told the stories, Sky was amused to see Joe manfully down a mug of the stuff, though he liked chocolate better.

"Better go to sleep, Joe," he said after the fifth story.

"Aw, Pa, we can't do nothin' tomorrow anyway! Tell me something about when you was a boy with the Sioux."

Sky poked at the fire, and the log shifted with a hissing sound. "Joe, do you remember much about your ma?"

An uneasy look passed over the boy's sensitive face, and he mumbled, "Oh, just a little."

"Pretty hard for a boy to be without a ma," Sky said offhandedly. "Lot of things a father can't do for a young'un."

"We do fine, Pa!" Joe insisted, rolling off his back into a sitting position. "Pa. . . ?"

"Yes?"

Joe bit his lip, then blurted, "Pa, you're not gonna marry up with one of them women, are you?"

"Hadn't planned on it, Joe. Why?" The thought leaped into Sky's mind that the boy was about to urge him to marry, but he saw relief on the thin face.

"Oh, Sam said once that he thought you might—but we don't need nobody, Pa." He grinned and twisted his head to one side in a starboard list. "We make out fine like we are."

Sky shook his head soberly. "We can't stay on a hunting trip for the next ten years till you're grown, Joe. You need education."

"I can be a trapper like you!"

"Time you're grown, trapping will be over. It's about that way now. Beaver's getting thin, and now they're using silk for hats in England. And the buffalo won't last—not the way they're being killed." Taking a deep breath, he asked, "What would you think of moving back to the Yellowstone country—back to where I grew up?"

"You mean with your ma and pa?"

"Yes. Be good for you to be around your kin—and the Mission's got a good school." He had already decided that it was the only course that made any sense, but he wanted Joe to like the idea, too, so he did not press the issue. "We'll talk about it," he said, then got up and stretched. "I'm tired. Let's get some sleep. Tomorrow we'll make some snowshoes and scout around a bit. Maybe get an elk."

For a week they roamed the hills on snowshoes, finding plenty of game during the day and spending the long nights in front of the fire. The only book in the cabin was a battered old Bible that had been left behind. It had been soaked until the book was thickened, and some of the last pages were missing, but Joe liked the stories of the Old Testament—especially the heroic exploits of David, Joshua, and Elijah. Sky was saddened when he realized how little the boy knew of the Bible. He himself had soaked it up from the time he was eleven, for either his father or Missy had often read it aloud to him. He grimly determined that he would remedy the gap in Joe's education, which was one more factor that tipped the scale toward his decision to move back to the Mission.

After a week had passed, he said, "Well, we'd better be headin' back, Joe." The boy ducked his head, disappointed, but the snow had melted enough for travel, and they made the return trip with no difficulty. Returning to the house was a bad experience, for it was dirty and damp with mildew. Sky silently surveyed the dirty clothes, the unwashed dishes with food hardened in them, and said, "We'll go to town tomorrow, Joe. I'm going to sell this place. Look at it!"

"Aw, we can clean it up, Pa!" Joe protested. While he had come to accept a move to some degree, the house was all he'd known, and the reality of leaving it grieved him. The months of town living had been hard on him, and now he was being asked to give up a life he loved for one he knew nothing of.

But Sky shook his head, and Joe saw that his father's mind was made up. "Got to be a better way than living like a couple of hogs!" he said, and from the determined look on his face, Joe knew that it would be useless to argue.

The next day they rode to Oregon City. The streets were thick ribbons of mud from the thawing ice; and as they went down

Main, Sky said, "Have to take care of some business, Joe. You got anything to do until I finish?"

"Mr. Emory said he'd have the new case for my rifle in a week. Have we got the money for it, Pa?"

"Sure." Sky fished several coins out of his pocket and gave them to the boy. "It'll do till we can get a Sioux squaw to make you the real thing. You can wait at Sam's when you get through."

"Okay, Pa."

Sky watched him spur his horse into a gallop, then made his way to Sam's store. He had an unpleasant chore to take care of, and he wanted to get it over with as soon as possible. Stepping inside, he was surprised to see Karen Sanderson behind the counter. He felt embarrassment redden his face, for she had not spoken with him since the Tom Lake incident, and he figured she was probably still angry for the way he'd behaved.

She saw his reaction and said evenly, "Hello, Mr. Winslow."

"Hello, Karen. Is Sam here?"

"No, he's out campaigning."

"Campaigning for what?" he asked curiously.

"He's running for mayor." She was a calm woman, but she shook her head disapprovingly, and her blue eyes were troubled.

"Mayor? I never knew he was thinking about politics."

"I don't think he wants it—but he thinks he's got to do it." She bit her lip. "I wish you'd try to talk him out of it, Mr. Winslow. He thinks a lot of you."

Sky frowned. "Matthew Poole and Rolfe Ingerson have had this town sewed up tight for a long time. Trying to get Oregon City away from them will be like taking honey from a mad grizzly. They play rough." Then a thought occurred to him. "Karen, have *you* married Sam?"

"No! He didn't ask me," she laughed. "But he's about the only man in this town who hasn't!"

"He's a good man. I'd thought once that you'd make a good wife for him."

"I know. You sized us all up for that job, didn't you? But the rest of us lost out to Edith." Amusement turned the corners of her broad lips up at his embarrassed reaction. "Oh, don't worry, Mr. Winslow. Edith laughs about it now—but it hurt her badly at the time."

"Is she married?"

"Well, let me give you a rundown." Karen began to name off the members of the train and what had happened to them since they'd arrived in Oregon. Most of them were already married, Karen said, then added, "But four of us are still spinsters. Care to guess the other three?"

"I'd rather hear why *you* haven't found a husband, Karen."

She looked him squarely in the eye. "I think you know, Sky. Dave and I are going to be married—just as soon as he gets a place. I'd marry him tomorrow, but he's stubborn."

Sky said quietly, "Congratulations—to you both."

"Thank you." The answer was polite but reserved, and he wondered if she was thinking of his skirmish with Lloyd. But she went on, "Rita is working for a saloon man named Dandy Raimez."

"I'm sorry to hear that—but can't say I'm surprised," he replied regretfully. "Edith is the third—who else?"

"Rebekah." Her face did not change expression, but there was venom in every syllable. *She's still angry at what I said about Rebekah and Lake*, Winslow realized. Not wanting to bring up the subject again, he said only, "I need to see Edith."

"She's teaching school in the community building. Lot Penny's got a church going there, too. Meets every Sunday."

"Tell Sam I'll be back, will you?" He turned and walked out of the store, digesting the news. He walked by the Silver Moon and was tempted to go see Rita, but instead went directly to the square frame building that sat on a side street at the edge of town. Smoke coiled out of the chimney, and he paused at the door to listen. There was a hum of voices inside, and he hesitated momentarily before pushing the door open and stepping inside.

Edith Dickenson looked at him with a startled expression, then turned back to the small group of youngsters who sat in front of her on puncheon seats. There were not over ten of them, and they ranged from one who looked barely able to talk, to a tall boy of at least fifteen who looked terribly embarrassed at having to sit with the smaller children. The boy looked up as she called his name: "Henry, please go over these spelling words while I speak with our visitor."

"Yes, ma'am." The boy took a book from her, and she came

across the room. "Hello, Sky. Let's step outside and talk," she suggested.

She picked up a coat and put it on, and Sky followed her outside. She took a few steps along the wooden walkway and turned to face him. "You've been gone a long time."

"Had to get reacquainted with my boy." He searched her face carefully and saw no sign of anger in her eyes. "I came to apologize, Edith."

"Well—do it then."

He ducked his head in surprise at her straightforward response, then grinned sheepishly. "All right—I'm sorry for the way I treated you. Back on the trail, I mean."

"I forgive you." Then she smiled wryly. "At least you got me to Oregon." She hesitated, and a touch of red flushed her cheeks as she said with an embarrassed laugh, "It's just that you're far too romantic, Sky!" His startled expression caused her to reach out and touch his arm. "Oh, you don't mean to be! But in those buckskins, you could turn the head of any girl—especially a spinster like me who's read a few too many Cooper novels! I guess I just got carried away."

"You seemed to have gotten over it, Edith," Sky responded dryly.

"Oh, it wouldn't have worked, anyway. It would have been awful, living with you, Sky!" she exclaimed. "I like order—and you're like the wind. Always will be, I reckon." She smiled. "I got thirty-two offers of marriage—enough to do me proud for life."

"Taking any of them?" he asked.

"Let me tell you." She turned, looked out across the town, then back to him. "I was never so bewildered in my life as I was that first week, with all those men running after me. After the first day or two, it was really terrible, Sky! I started hiding in my room just to avoid them. Then I remembered what you'd said about Sam Birdwell—and I kept waiting for him to come and get in line—but he never did."

"Not Sam." Sky smiled at the thought, cocking his head. "So what'd you do, Edith?"

"I went into his store early one morning and introduced myself." Edith's eyes brightened with humor as she related the incident. "He was real proper, but I came right out and said, 'Sam Birdwell, Sky Winslow thinks I'd be a perfect wife for you. What are you going to do about it?' "

Sky threw his head back and whooped with laughter until the tears ran down his face. "What'd old Sam say to that?" he gasped.

"Oh, he blushed and hemmed and hawed at first, but then he said, 'Well, Miss Dickenson, I've always admired Sky's judgment—so I guess I'll have to come courting'—and that's what he's been doing."

"He asked you to marry him yet?"

"No—but he will in a day or two. I can tell that he wants to—but I'll have to help him along."

Sky put his hand out. "He's a lucky man, Edith!"

"Thank you, Sky." She extended her own hand in a handshake.

"You'll have to talk him out of this mayor business. He could get hurt."

"You know him better than that, Sky." Edith shook her head. "Sam says it's a question of who's going to run Oregon City—the crooks or the decent people."

"Let somebody else do it."

"Try telling that to Sam! He says somebody's got to stand up against Poole. I wish you'd talk to him."

"Won't be here, Edith."

She stared at him. "You're leaving?"

"Got to do something about Joe." He told her of his plan to go back to the Mission, and added, "I'll try to talk him out of it—but I never had much luck talking Sam out of things." He looked at her with admiration. "I guess you can do more than I can, Edith."

He left her and went to the feed store where Mike Stevens, the owner, greeted him warmly. They had coffee, and Sky cut right to the point. "Mike, you still want to buy my place?"

"Why—I sure do, Sky!" Stevens had been buying up land on the outskirts of Oregon City. For some time the two men dickered over the price, but at last they agreed and shook hands. "I'll need a few days to get the cash, Sky." Stevens said. "A week from today be okay?"

"Sure, Mike."

Leaving the feed store, Winslow rode back toward the center of town. As he crossed over the muddy street, he heard his name called and turned to see Lot Penny approaching with a wide smile on his face. "Sky! When did you get back?"

"Just pulled in, Lot. I hear you've got a church started."

"Sure have! And we been havin' a real move of God. Come on, let's have some coffee and I'll tell you about it."

They spent half an hour over coffee at a small cafe, and half a dozen men greeted Sky as they sat there. Lot bubbled over with enthusiasm, saying happily, "I've been threatened with a beating if I keep on preaching, Sky!" He slapped his leg and laughed. "I shore do like to get the devil stirred up!"

"Who's threatening, Lot?"

"Oh, feller named Jim Rook."

"Rook? Bouncer at the Silver Moon?"

"Sure. Dandy Raimez got mad 'cause one of his fancy girls got saved and quit. He didn't say so, but I figure he's told Rook to see to it that none of his other girls get religion."

"Rook's a bad one, Lot. Kicked a man to death over in Portland before he came here to work for Dandy."

"So I hear," Lot replied, unconcerned, and took a sip of his coffee. "Sky, you was pretty hard on Rebekah—but I'm wonderin' if you heard what she's up against now?"

"Just heard she hadn't gotten married like most of the others." He looked at Penny and asked, "Is it because of her kids?"

"Not a bit! Larry Melton wanted to marry her—and I hear that he's a good man."

"None better. What happened?"

"You know a man named Carl Morton?"

"Don't know anything good." Morton was a savage man who lived in a shack ten miles out in the woods, with four small children who were shy as animals. He brought the half-clothed urchins with him from time to time, usually when he came to get drunk. He boasted of wearing out two wives and claimed he'd wear out half a dozen more. The huge Tennessean was of mountain stock, and when he drank he was dangerous. He had been in two shootings in Oregon, and the word was he'd come here after he'd killed more than one man back in Tennessee.

"He got to town last week, Sky. Heard about the women coming for husbands and swore he'd have one of 'em. Most of them was married already, but somebody let slip about Rebekah, and he just barged in and told her she was goin' to marry him—then went out and got roaring drunk. When he heard about Melton askin' Rebekah to marry him, he picked a fight with him. Beat him nearly to death!"

Sky's lips tightened. "Ingerson do anything about it?"

"Not likely!" Lot snorted. "Said it was a fair fight. But no man in this territory's got the nerve to stand up to Morton. He's the kind of man that'd ambush a man if he couldn't get him any other way. Rebekah'll have to go with him for sure."

"Sorry to hear that, Lot."

The answer displeased Penny. "That all you got to say, Sky?"

Winslow looked surprised. "Why, it's none of my business, Lot."

Penny stared at Sky, disappointment etched in his homely face, but he said nothing more.

"I'm selling out, Lot." Sky changed the subject. "Going to take Joe out of this mess!"

"I was hoping you'd stick around and give Sam Birdwell a hand. He's going to need all the help he can get."

Anger touched Winslow and caused him to say sharply, "Lot, I've got a boy to take care of. I can't be responsible for these people!"

Lot was not a man to give in that easily. "You mean you can't be your brother's keeper, Sky?" he asked quietly.

Winslow got up abruptly, his eyes flashing. He looked down at Penny, and his voice had a hard edge. "Charity begins at home—that's what the Bible says, doesn't it?"

"No, it don't say that. It says, 'Bear ye one another's burdens.' And I'm thinking you're less of a man than I figured, Sky."

Winslow glowered at him, then turned and left the cafe. Lot stared after him, mulling over his words. After a while he got up and left, his shoulders bowed and his eyes sad. "That boy's in a bad shape," he mumbled as he turned toward the church.

CHAPTER EIGHTEEN

"AS LONG AS WE BOTH SHALL LIVE"

★ ★ ★ ★

When Joe turned and looked over his shoulder at the house, there was a rebellious set to his shoulders that Sky did not miss. It had been a bad week for both of them; and as they made their way down the trail toward the main road that led to Oregon City, the doubts that had gnawed at Sky all week were stronger than ever. Joe had begged him not to sell, and he could understand the boy's reluctance to leave the only home he'd ever known; what had come as a shock was his own reluctance to leave. The house he'd built with his own hands had come to mean more to him than he'd realized, and as he'd put the place in shape for the new owner, a hundred times he'd found himself regretting his decision to sell it.

To his surprise, the memories of Joe's mother had ceased to be associated with the place itself. The bitter thoughts of her were replaced by memories of the good times he'd had with Joe here. It had become a citadel and a refuge for them both from the world. Now as they rode around the timberline and the house was lost to sight, he thought, *By the Lord—I hate to leave this place!* He could not bring himself to admit his feelings to Joe, telling him instead of the good times they'd have when they got to the Mission.

Rain had not fallen for a week, and the streets were dried out in town. "Let's go down and see Sam, Joe," Sky said. They found the storekeeper inside, sitting at his desk and staring at the wall with a worried expression on his face. "Sam, you look like you're goin' to a funeral," Sky remarked.

"Oh, hello, Sky. Hey there, Joe." Birdwell got up and turned to face them. "You still aiming to sell out to Mike?"

"Sure."

Birdwell chewed his lower lip and jammed his hands into his pockets. "Blast it, Sky, you sure picked an awful time to pull up stakes. We need every good man we can rake up to win this election. I was countin' on you to help."

"Wish you'd stayed out of that race, Sam," Sky replied, then went on with a doubtful look in his eyes. "In the first place, it's going to be hard to win—and if you do get elected, Poole will give you trouble. He's got a stranglehold on this town, and he'll fight with everything he's got before he turns loose."

"'Course he will, Sky—and that's why the rest of us were hopin' you'd be around to give a hand. He hesitated, then added, "Guess you haven't heard about our new candidate for sheriff."

"Who is it?"

"Tom Lake."

Sky snorted. "He's no lawman, Sam."

"Oh, we all know that, but he's made lots of friends in the short time he's been here—you know how people look up to a doctor. What Travers and Sellers and Clay Hill figure is that once Tom's elected, we can hire some toughs to be his deputies. They can do the scuffling and he can sort of do the bookwork. What'd you think, Sky?"

"I think you're all crazy! Why, all Poole will have to do is shove one of his hard hands at him. If Tom don't take him on, he's finished as a sheriff. If he does, he'll get killed! Did *you* think up this nutty idea, Sam?"

"Well—as a matter of fact it was Clay's idea—but we've got to have an honest man in the office."

"You'll have a dead man, Sam." There was utter finality in

Winslow's voice, and it had an effect on Birdwell. "Anyway, I think you ought to get out of the thing."

Birdwell was not an imposing man; Oregon City was filled with rough men who could have tied him in knots with one hand. But the firm light in his brown eyes did not waver as he spoke. "*Somebody* has to make this town a place fit to live in. I'm no politician, Sky—just like Tom Lake is no gunman. But a man does what he has to do. Maybe it's giving Poole and Ingerson a big laugh—two men like me and Tom standing up against him and his toughs. But somebody's got to care—and I *care* about this town, Sky. I want to live here the rest of my life. I want to have a family—maybe a boy like Joe here. Don't figure I could look at myself as any kind of a man if I didn't try to fight this thing."

Sky considered Birdwell intently. He had never seen the man so adamant, and until he heard the last couple of sentences, he hadn't understood why. "You gettin' married, Sam?"

A grin broke the soberness on Birdwell's face. "You know it! I feel like a young man, Sky! She's better than any woman I've ever dreamed of."

"I congratulate you both, Sam—but what does *she* say about this plunge into politics? Edith's sharp enough to see that it could be dangerous."

"Said she wouldn't have a man who wouldn't fight for what he thought was right."

Sky ducked his head and studied the floor. "You're makin' me look bad, Sam—but I've got Joe to think of."

"Ah, Pa, I *wanna* stay here."

"We've been through all that," Sky said sharply. "Well, I've got to go—"

"Sky, I've some bad news. You got pretty close to Lot Penny on the trip here, didn't you?"

"Something's happened to Lot?"

"Last night he was preaching on the street in front of the Silver Moon, and Jim Rook came out and beat him up."

Winslow looked startled, then angry. "Raimez put him up to it," he said bitterly.

"Sure. Him and Poole and Ingerson."

"Where's Lot?"

"Tom's keeping him at his place. Karen and some of the women are taking turns nursing him."

"Can you look after Joe?" Sam nodded, and Sky turned to his son. "Joe, I'll be back pretty soon. You behave yourself."

When he left, Joe kicked at the counter. "I don't *wanna* leave here!"

Sam put his hand on the boy's shoulder, but could think of nothing to say that would comfort him. "Let's finish that game of checkers, Joe," he said gently.

––––––

A sharp wind was sweeping out of the north, but Winslow ignored the cold as he walked rapidly down the street toward Lake's office. He had grown genuinely fond of Penny, which only intensified the cold rage he felt building inside him as he passed along Main. He'd discovered long ago that his temper was a wild and uncontrollable thing when it got out of hand, and so as he walked along he told himself that he had made up his mind to leave, that the affairs of the town were not his problem. In fact, they never had been; his world had been his small ranch and the far-flung traplines. Although he had come to town for supplies and to visit with a few close friends, the politics of the town had never concerned him. Until now.

Knocking on Lake's door, Winslow pushed it open and went inside. Lake was sitting on a chair, reading a thick book. He looked up from his reading and rose from his seat. "Hello, Sky." The guarded quality of his tone reminded Winslow of the wall that he himself had created between them. "Guess you heard about Lot."

"How is he?"

Lake looked worried. "Not good. He took some bad licks to the head. Rook used his boots on him after he was down." Anger flared in his black eyes, and he said, "I'm going to have it out with Ingerson about this! It's a plain case of assault and battery!"

"Can I see him?"

"Go on back. He's got a concussion—the pain's pretty bad when he wakes up."

Sky hesitated, trying to think of something to say to Lake about their confrontation on the trail, but nothing came to him.

"He's going to be all right, isn't he?"

"Can't say. He took some bad blows around the eyes. May affect his vision—and a concussion as bad as he's got is always tricky."

Sky stared at him, then turned and went through the door that led into a bedroom. Penny was lying in the single bed, and Rebekah was sitting in a chair by his side. She looked up at Sky and got to her feet. He waited for her to speak, but she did not.

"You don't have to get up," he said quickly. Going to stand by the bed he looked down at the battered face. Lot's features were swollen so badly that he could scarcely recognize him. His nose was flattened and his eyes were both swollen shut. Cuts around the eyes had been stitched and the mouth was distended. He had probably damaged some ribs as well, Winslow surmised, seeing where Lake had bound the torso with strips of white bandages.

Rebekah stood with her back against the wall. The sight of Winslow disturbed her, for she had lived the scene on the train over and over. She watched him as he sat down and stared at Penny's battered face. He took off his hat, and the pale November sun came through the single window, throwing the planes of his face into sharp relief. His eyes were half hooded, but she read the anger that burned in them clearly, and his lips were drawn tight. *He's mad enough to kill,* she thought. *Just like the time when he found Tom coming out of my wagon.*

There was, she realized, no middle ground with Sky. Other men saw gray areas, but with him it was different. *Why, he's like a powder keg ready to go off!* she thought. *Lot's his friend—and that's all that counts.* It made her go back to that moment when he'd accused her and Tom, and for the first time she saw the ugly scene from his side. *He liked me more than I knew—and that's why he lost control.* She'd had little experience with men, but she had known that he was attracted to her—not so much by what he said, but by the way he looked at her. Until that minute, though, she had no idea how much.

Now as he sat there silently, Rebekah saw that beneath his strength, there was a vulnerable area in Winslow. She had heard how his wife deceived him, and now she realized for the first time how deeply that had wounded him. It made his rage at what appeared to him to be another case of a cheating woman at least understandable.

He looked up and their eyes met. He held her gaze, thinking—as he often had—of her unusual combination of beauty and strength. He thought, too, of the ugly scene on the trail, but it never occurred to him that she would ever understand. He didn't understand it completely himself—except that it had been one of those moments when his ungovernable temper had exploded. He had relived that moment over and over, and regretted it, but he could not change it. One of the things that he had never learned to do was to fix the results of his actions. It was not a matter of swallowing his pride; it had simply never occurred to him that words could remedy what had been *done*.

"Lake's not sure he'll make it, is he?"

Rebekah answered, "He's been badly hurt—but I'm believing God will heal him."

The simple statement caused him to regard her intently; something in her words caught him and pulled him up short. He studied her face, seeking for a clue to the quiet faith that had always drawn him. "Seems like God lets the best people take the worst beatings." He tore his eyes from her face and rose to his feet. "I'll be back later."

"All right."

He went to the door, put his hand on the knob, then turned and said quietly, "It's none of my business, Rebekah—but what are you going to do?"

She faltered for one moment, and he saw the uncertainty in her eyes disturbing the placid serenity. "I—I'll be going back to the East."

He knew, instinctively, that it was not what she wanted. He wanted to press her further, to have her speak of Carl Morton, who was at the root of her problem. He recalled the intimacy between her and himself that had built up on the train, how she'd shared some of her hope with him—but that was gone now. He'd destroyed it himself, and now he could only say, "I'm sorry it didn't work out, Rebekah."

He left the room and found Dave Lloyd and Clay Hill standing beside Lake. "Hello, Sky," Clay greeted him. "Just heard you'd got in."

"Hello, Clay," Sky responded, then nodded to Lloyd. "How are you, Dave?"

A look of relief brightened Lloyd's face. He had just been saying to the other two that he doubted that Sky would ever speak to him again for embarrassing him in front of the wagon train. He returned the nod quickly. "I'm fine, Sky."

"We're going down and insist that Ingerson arrest Rook, Sky," Clay announced. He had a high color by nature, and the anger in him brought an added flush to his cheeks. "He'll do it, too—or I'll send for a federal marshal!"

"I'll just go along, Clay," Sky told him.

"You will!" Hill exclaimed. "Good!"

"Thought you were leaving town, Sky, " Lake commented.

"Sure—but I've got a little message for Mr. Rook."

The others looked at him nervously. "We're going to do this the legal way, Sky," Clay informed him.

"Go ahead" was all that Winslow said, with an implacable look on his smooth face. "I just want to ask the gentleman a question or two."

"So do I," Lloyd grunted.

They went to the sheriff's office and found it locked. "He'll be at the Silver Moon," Clay commented. "That's really his office, anyway."

The lawyer was correct, for they found Ingerson standing at the bar in the company of a tall, thin man who wore two guns. "That's Del Laughton," Clay said quietly to the others. "He's a bad one."

The Silver Moon was the fanciest saloon in town, and the proprietor, Dandy Raimez, was no less ornate. He was seated at a table playing solitaire, dressed—as always—in a white linen suit, a spotless ruffled shirt and a brightly colored vest. He was half Indian and half Mexican, his handsome face expressionless as he looked up at the three men. Beside him, Winslow noted, was Rita Duvall.

Her eyes widened as she saw Winslow, and turning nervously to study the face of Raimez, she cast her gaze covertly at the men at the bar. Raimez said something to her and she shook her head, but he spoke again, and she reluctantly lifted a hand and called out, "Sky—come have a drink."

Winslow went to her at once, ignoring the men at the bar. He recognized Jack Stedman along with a huge man he took to be Rook, but walked by them. "Hello, Rita." He gave Raimez a look. "How are you, Dandy?"

"Fine as silk, Winslow." The saloon man indicated a chair. "Have a seat." When Sky sat down, he offered, "Have a drink on the house."

"Too early."

Raimez took a drink from the glass in front of him, then gave Sky a brilliant smile. "I owe you one—for bringing me a beautiful present." He put his hand on Rita's bare shoulder possessively, his white teeth gleaming against his dark skin.

"Glad to be of service, Dandy."

It was not the answer Raimez expected, and his smile slipped. He turned to look at the other man offhandedly. "Hear you're leaving the country, Winslow." He tapped the table with a well-manicured finger. "Might be just as well. Things might heat up a little around here. Hate to see a good man like you get caught in the crossfire."

It was a veiled threat, and Winslow recognized it at once. He knew that Raimez, for all his fancy clothes and soft manners, was a hard man. He wore a gun at all times, and had used it more than once; a saloon man in a tough town like Oregon City had to be able to handle trouble.

"Didn't know you were so interested in my health, Dandy," Sky said; then he turned his head, as did Raimez and Rita, to watch the scene that was unfolding at the bar.

Clay Hill had taken a stand opposite Rolfe Ingerson and Matthew Poole. "Ingerson, I've got a deposition here. I want you to arrest Jim Rook on the charge of assault and battery."

Ingerson assumed a look of surprise. "Why, Clay, I can't arrest every man that gets into a fight in this town! Shoot, the jail wouldn't hold them—and they'd never get convicted."

A quiet laugh went up from the men around the bar, and Clay Hill flushed angrily. "This wasn't a fight, Sheriff. It was an unprovoked assault on a minister of the gospel by a known bully. Mayor, I expect you to support me in this thing."

"Well, now, Clay," Poole replied, "I've heard a different version. Way I hear it, the preacher got mad and threw a punch at

Jim. You saw it, didn't you, Del?"

The tall man with the cadaverous face nodded solemnly. "Hate to go against a preacher, Sheriff—but Rev. Penny just plain lost his temper and took out after Rook. Poor Jim had no choice but to defend hisself!"

The laugh that followed this was louder, and Hill snapped, "I'm calling in a federal marshal, Poole!"

Ingerson's bulk dwarfed Clay Hill, and he sneered, "Come on, Hill. You think they're going to send a marshal over one fist fight? Be sensible."

"Better take your marbles and go home, Hill," Dandy Raimez called out, smiling unperturbably at Rita. "This fine lady here says the preacher was after her and the rest of the women all the way from Independence, anyway."

Rita's head jerked up at that, and she started to protest, but she had no chance. Dave Lloyd whirled and said loudly, "You're a liar, Raimez!"

Raimez paled and his hand dropped to the gun at his belt. For one moment it appeared that he would draw on Lloyd, but he warned, "Be wearing a gun next time I see you."

Lloyd, who had been a professional fighter at one time, took a few quick steps and stood before Rook. "You're pretty rough on old men, Rook," he mocked. "Why don't you try it with a man under thirty?"

Rook's head jerked up at the abrupt challenge.

"Bust him up, Jim!" Raimez said.

Rook looked down at the smaller man, smiled, and pulled his gun out of the holster.

"Good thing you did that, Rook," Dave taunted. "If you hadn't, I'd have made you eat it!"

Rook gave a yell and threw a punch that would have torn Lloyd's head off if it had landed, but Dave shifted his head and let Rook fall into his arms. With a powerful motion he shoved him back with such force that Rook's back struck the bar and tore it loose from its moorings.

The big man bounced off the bar and stood with a bewildered glaze in his dull eyes. "Come on, Rook," Lloyd cried, "kick me in the head a little like you did Penny!"

This time Rook was more careful. He had felt the power in

Lloyd's arms, so he carefully planted his feet and threw a punch at the belly of the smaller man. With contemptuous ease, Lloyd turned the blow aside and with a lightning-like move, he drew his right back and drove a shattering punch into Rook's stomach. It made a solid booming sound and snapped Rook's mouth open as the breath was driven from his body. He grasped his arms with both hands, his face pale as he sucked for air.

Lloyd closed in and took one look at the helpless man. "Good night, Friend." He turned Rook's head to one side, and with a crushing right caught him in the mouth. Rook fell backward and lay there with his legs kicking the floor frantically for several seconds before they stopped.

A shocked silence fell, and Lloyd stood with his head lowered and anger shining in his eyes. "Tell him as soon as he's able to get up that I'll put him down again!"

Ingerson glanced at Poole, who nodded slightly. "I'll have to arrest you, Lloyd," the sheriff said.

"On what charge?" Clay Hill demanded.

"Disturbing the peace."

Hill laughed. "It won't wash, Ingerson."

"He's going to jail."

Lloyd wasn't about to play his game. "I can see it now. You'll get me in jail, shoot me, and then claim I was tryin' to escape. No soap. I'm not goin'."

Ingerson retorted, "You're just making it worse on yourself, Lloyd. Resisting arrest is a crime. I'm taking you in. Dead or alive, that's up to you."

Every man in the room knew that the sheriff was making an example of Lloyd; if he shot Lloyd, no questions would be asked later. Ingerson would never be penalized for it.

"Go along with him, Dave," Hill said. "I'll have you out by tomorrow."

"I reckon not," Lloyd replied, and stood there alone, eyeing the sheriff.

"You heard him," Ingerson stated. He moved away from the bar and planted his feet, his hand near his gun. "I'm giving you one last chance.

There was no surrender in Lloyd's face, and Lake, who had

taken no part in the action, pleaded, "Dave, don't be a fool—he'll gun you down!"

"I won't be arrested."

Ingerson heard this exchange with a gleam of satisfaction. Moving his right arm, he said, "All right, if you've got to have it—!"

"Hold it, Ingerson!"

The huge bulk of Ingerson turned quickly to find that Sky Winslow was standing on his left. "Stay out of this, Winslow, or you'll be sorry!"

Winslow had taken his coat off, looking dangerous in the light of the chandeliers. He wore a well-worn gun at his side, and a laughing light in his blue eyes. "Get this straight now, Sheriff," he said easily. "You're not going to arrest Lloyd and that's the end of it."

A gasp went around the saloon, and Ingerson's face grew crimson. "Winslow, I'm warning you—!"

"No, I'm warning you, Ingerson. You try to arrest Lloyd, and I'll nail your hide to the wall."

The stark simplicity of the challenge struck Ingerson like a blow, and left him caught in a no-win situation. If he let Winslow buffalo him, he was finished. On the other hand, Ingerson had heard, as had the whole town, tales of how tough the blue-eyed man was, and was unwilling to risk a fight with an unknown factor. Ingerson had used his gun more than once, and in most cases would have met the challenge head-on, but this time he was uneasy. And so, as pressure built, Ingerson decided to hedge his bets.

Poole said, "Winslow, you'll have to stand aside or take the consequences. The sheriff has to keep order in this place."

"Del," Ingerson barked, and the tall man came to stand beside him. "We got to take this man in."

"You need your mamma to help, Sheriff?" Winslow taunted. "Why don't you collect a posse? I'm only one man. You afraid to take me by yourself?"

Ingerson ignored the taunt and began to move away. As if by signal, there was a wild scramble as men ducked to move from behind Winslow and from the two men who were moving apart to make a harder target.

Del Laughton was enjoying it. He was a known gunman, and there was a predatory expression on his lean face. "I've got to take your gun, Winslow," he said.

"Come and take it, Del," Sky challenged. Looking at him, Rita saw that there was a slight smile on his face as if the scene amused him.

There was one moment's stillness, then Laughton's hands slapped the butts of his guns. Sky let him pull both guns almost clear of the holsters, then drew his own gun and fired with one fluid motion. He aimed low and the first bullet caught Laughton in the kneecap. Laughton dropped one gun, grabbing his shattered knee with one hand, his face contorted with agony, and lifted his other gun. Sky's second shot caught him in the shoulder, sending the other gun to the floor. The draw was so fast, and the explosion that rocked the room was so abrupt, that it stopped the sheriff's draw. He found himself staring into the muzzle of Winslow's gun and threw his hands up, calling out in panic, "No! I'm not drawing, Winslow!"

Sky lowered his gun and glanced back at Laughton, then ignored him and turned to face Ingerson. Dropping his gun into his holster, Winslow said wickedly, "Come on, Rolfe. Take my gun."

Ingerson shook his head and folded his arms in a gesture of surrender. His face was pale as old ivory. He looked at Poole and the two of them stepped back.

"Dandy, you want to take a hand?" Winslow moved to face Raimez, who had not moved from where he sat. Dandy's hand had dropped to the butt of his gun, but he seemed to reconsider and brought it back on the table.

"Not my game, Sky," he answered evenly.

"I'd keep it that way, Dandy," Winslow suggested. "You'll live longer."

Poole spoke up. "Winslow, you may be tough, but you'd better know that if it takes half a dozen men to handle you, that can be arranged."

"You make it hard for a man to leave town, Poole," Winslow said. "Here I was all ready to sell out, but now I've got to stick around." He saw Mike Stevens over by the wall. "Deal's off, Mike. I've got to stick around and see if Poole and his pack of yellow dogs can run me off."

He left without a word, followed by the other three men.

"He'll pay for that," Raimez whispered to Rita. Then he shouted, "Get that loser off my floor before he bleeds all over it!" He got up and walked over to where Poole and Ingerson stood. "You made your brag, Poole. Now you'd better do it."

"Get some tough boys lined up, Dandy," Poole said quietly. "He's only one man."

"It only takes one bullet," Ingerson gritted.

"It only takes one for you, too, Rolfe—or me." Dandy shook his head. "I've seen one man change the whole deal. Get Winslow."

Hill caught up with Sky outside, and said, "They won't let that stand, Sky. They'll put you down."

"I've got some business, Clay—but I'll be around."

Dave ran to catch up with the other two. "Thanks, Sky. I was a dead duck in there."

Lake said, "You're the one for sheriff, Sky, not me."

Winslow shook his head, "I'll be around, and if a man strikes at me, I'll go get him. But I'm not much for politics." He walked off quickly, leaving the three men staring after him.

The incident had dropped out of nowhere on Sky, but it had been characteristic of the man to change his plan at once to meet the new situation. He had been reluctant to leave to begin with, but the raw attempt to run him off caused him to change his mind. He knew that he could not leave the country now.

With an urgent restlessness, he made one fifteen-minute stop at the courthouse, then headed back for Lake's office. He pushed through the door to find Lake talking with Karen and Rebekah. From the way they glanced at him, he guessed that Lake had been telling them about the incident at the saloon.

Karen came up to him, her eyes wide. "Sky, I've had bad thoughts about you ever since your run-in with Dave. I—I was wrong. Thank you for helping him!"

Winslow's face was set and a little paler than usual. "He's a good man, Karen." Then he said with an effort, "Rebekah, I've got something to say to you."

She looked puzzled, for he was obviously uneasy. "What is it?"

He shrugged. "I'm glad Lake and Karen are here because this

is going to be hard." He was aware that they were all staring at him. "No way to say this right—but here it is: I'm going to stay here and raise my boy. But I've made a mess out of it by myself. He needs a mother."

Rebekah's heart beat faster, but she could not say a word. Lake and Karen were staring at Winslow, who was watching Rebekah intently. "You don't want to go back East, do you?"

"No," she whispered.

"You've got two children and no way to live. I've got a boy who needs a mother." He paused, his eyes enigmatic. "Looks like we need each other."

"Sky—!" she protested.

"Wait, Rebekah," he cut in. "I'm not wanting a wife—not in the usual way. I'll give you my name, and I'll see that you and the kids never want—but that's *all* I mean." His composure broke slightly, and he rubbed his cheek with the back of his hand. "We'll be legally married—but that's all. You'll have separate quarters and keep the house."

He stood there, his back straight. It had taken a lot for him to come, for he fully expected her to laugh at his offer. If she had, he would not complain; he had to play the cards he had.

Rebekah's face was pale, her eyes intent. His offer had dropped on her with a suddenness that took her breath away, but it offered her a gleam of hope. *I won't have to go back East.*

It was one of those moments that brings life to a crossroad, and for one fleeting moment Rebekah was swept with fear. With one brief prayer, she put out her hand with tremendous sobriety.

"I'll marry you—on those terms," she replied simply.

Winslow let out the breath he had been holding. "Can you leave today?"

"Yes."

"Get your things. I'll rent a buggy. Tom Mosley, the J.P. , does most of the legal business, so he can marry people. I'll pick you up in an hour."

"All right, Sky."

When he had gone, she turned to the other two. "I guess it sounds crazy to you two."

"I hate to see you do it, Rebekah," Tom told her, shaking his head. "It's not the kind of marriage you deserve."

"People won't understand," Karen said slowly. "*I* don't understand, Rebekah. If you don't love him. . . ?"

Rebekah gave a small smile as she moved to the door, "He's a reluctant bridegroom—but it's the door God's opened!"

Meanwhile Sky went to get Joe, and for the next fifteen minutes he carefully pointed out what he was going to do, stressing that Rebekah would be more of a housekeeper than a wife.

Joe had stared at him in consternation, but at least he agreed, saying, "It'll be better than leaving!"

Sky reached out and tousled the boy's head; he had expected no more than the response Joe gave him. Winslow rented the buggy, and the two of them went to pick up Rebekah. She was waiting with her few things packed. "Joe, drive the wagon down to the J.P.'s," Sky said, throwing her belongings in the rear floorboard. He picked up Timmy, and with Rebekah carrying Mary, they walked along the street. Several people stared at them curiously, but Sky kept his eyes straight ahead.

When they got to the two-story building that served for a courthouse, he broke the silence. "You can still change your mind, Rebekah."

"Do you want me to?"

"No," he replied. "But you're not getting much." He looked into her eyes. "It's not a marriage, Rebekah. You've got to know that."

She nodded and said, "I'll not complain."

A few minutes later they stood before Tom Mosley and he married them. He was a tall, thin man, the most avid gossip in town, and it was all he could do to keep from asking them about what they were doing, but something in Winslow's face warned him.

He read the usual legal marriage formula, but at the end he improvised a bit and included a phrase he'd heard used in the Episcopal church when he was back East.

"You are now married to each other," he said; "until death do you part—as long as you both shall live!"

He didn't ask for a response, but as Rebekah stood there, Sky heard her whisper faintly:

"As long as we both shall live!"

CHAPTER NINETEEN

A WARNING FOR WINSLOW

★ ★ ★ ★

"Sam, you think it's all right to barge in like this, with no warning?"

"Don't know if it's right or not—but blast it, I've got to know what's going on here!" Sam shook the reins, and the matched set of sorrels picked up their pace. A heavy layer of snow carpeted the road, and the only sound except for their muffled hoofbeats was the hissing of the sled runners. It had been fully two weeks since Sky had taken Rebekah out of Oregon City after the hasty wedding, and the whole town had buzzed with the affair, while Sam fumed with impatience.

"It ain't all that far to town, Edith," he said moodily. "It wouldn't have killed Sky to come and see us—just to let us know they ain't all dead."

Edith moved closer to Birdwell, then took his arm and smiled. They had been married only a week, and she was happier than she ever dreamed she could be. Two days after their wedding she had said to him, "Sam—I feel so *married*!" It had seemed silly to talk so, but his quick kiss had assured her that he felt the same way. In the few days since, she had learned to know him better than she had thought possible. "You're worried about Sky and Rebekah, aren't you?"

"Sure I am. This nutty idea of Sky's about 'hiring' a wife won't ever work." He shook his head, then added, "He said all along he was going to do it, so it didn't surprise me much—but I can't figure out why Rebekah would agree to such a thing!"

Edith studied the snowy tops of the evergreens lining the road. They wore conical caps of snow that glistened in the sun now peering over the mountains. "I think she's in love with him, Sam," she finally said. "We talked a lot on the trail. Sky was different then—or seemed to be. I didn't know about his former wife at that time, but I thought I saw something between him and Becky."

"Maybe so—but you don't know how stubborn that man is! Hangs on to his ideas like a snapping turtle! Guess he's had to be that way. Mountain men can't have a lot of sentiment, I reckon—but I'm thinkin' the whole thing is somehow *wrong*. Why, he's tried to *buy* a wife, Edith; that's what it comes to!"

"I've thought the same thing, Sam." Edith peered down the road. "There's smoke rising. Is that the house?"

"Yes." He shifted nervously and gave her a worried look, saying ruefully, "Now that we're here, I sort of wish we hadn't come. Seemed like a good idea to drive out and see about them—but Sky's mighty touchy sometimes."

"Well, we've got a good excuse. You don't get married every day, do you?" Edith smiled and squeezed his arm, then sobered. "But I'm worried, too, Sam. Rebekah's had a hard time. She's a very sensitive woman, and I'm afraid this 'marriage' is going to hurt her—if it hasn't already." The sleigh glided around a curve, and just off the road beneath a grove of towering firs sat a log cabin with smoke curling out of the chimney. "Let's not stay long," Edith suggested quickly. "But you get Sky and Joe out of the house so I can talk to Rebekah alone."

"All right."

Two dogs roused up and raced across the snow to snap at the heels of the horses as they pulled the sleigh toward the house. The door opened and Rebekah came out, with Joe following. "Buck! Bob! Get away from those horses!" Joe shouted. The dogs retreated, showing their teeth, and Rebekah stood in the doorway with a glad smile as the sleigh stopped. "Edith! Sam! Get down and come in out of the cold."

"Rebekah!" Edith let Sam help her out of the sleigh and the

two women embraced. "I've missed you so much!"

"Where's Sky?" Sam asked, looking around.

"Gone to feed some yearlings he keeps in a pasture about a quarter of a mile back from the house." Rebekah went to Sam and gave him a hug as well, which surprised him somewhat, for she had never been so demonstrative before. "Come on in," she invited, pulling at them. "He'll be back pretty soon."

Edith entered the house and looked about her. It was larger than most log houses, with a huge fireplace dominating one end. She walked toward it and warmed her hands at the cheerful blaze, taking in the sturdy furniture that contrasted with the frilly curtains over the windows. Everything was neat and clean, and she exclaimed, "What a nice house, Rebekah!"

"Sure looks different from what it did before," Sam remarked. "It always looked like a tornado had just gone through it. A woman's touch sure does make a difference."

"Oh, it's not hard to keep a house clean," Rebekah shrugged. Turning to Joe, she suggested, "Why don't you go tell your father we have company?"

"All right."

There was a surly look on Joe's face that neither of the visitors missed. The table was covered with books and paper; Sam remembered how Joe had hated to study. Joe picked up a thick coat and opened the door, but Rebekah plucked a fur cap off a peg and pulled it over his ears, saying, "You'd better wear your cap, Son."

Joe jerked the cap to a different position. "I'm not your son," he scowled and went through the door, slamming it behind him.

Sam took his cue. "I'll just go along. Need to stretch my legs a bit." The scene had accentuated the fears he'd carried about the situation. He caught up with Joe as the boy rounded the house. "Wait up for an old man, Joe!" he said. Then trying to erase the frown from the Joe's face, Sam began to talk about things in town as they made their way along the path that had been beaten flat by footsteps. He had learned much about Joe during the long months Sky had been gone, and he was aware that the boy was highly sensitive. Carefully avoiding any reference to Rebekah, he kept talking until finally the boy was smiling again.

"When I get elected mayor, Joe, I'm going to need a bright young fellow to help me with all the bookwork. Think you might like to get in on some of that?"

"Aw, Sam, I'm not any good with books. You know that."

"You're smart enough, Joe." Sam tossed out the next statement casually. "Now that you've got a good teacher, why, you'll be as good at books as you are with that rifle of yours."

Joe's youthful face hardened, and he said in a tight voice, "I don't like her, Sam."

"Rebekah?" Sam allowed surprise to shade his tone. "Why not, Joe? I don't know her well, but she always seemed real nice to me."

Joe shook his head stubbornly and said nothing. It was a way he had learned from his father, Sam realized. He walked along and did not break his silence until Joe blurted out, "Why'd he have to marry her, Sam?"

Sam replied quietly, "Guess you asked the right man about that, Joe—I just got married to Miss Edith last week." He smiled at the boy's surprise, then said, "Man gets lonesome with nobody to talk to. Guess I didn't know how lonesome I was until I got a wife to share things with. I've talked more in the week I been married to Miss Edith than I have in the last five years, I reckon."

Joe kept his head down, thinking of Sam's words. "Pa don't talk to her. He don't even sleep with her—him and me sleep in the loft and her and the kids sleep in the bedroom."

"Well . . ." Sam was taken aback by Joe's observations, but he said gently, "Takes a while for people to get used to each other, Joe. Some can do it quicker than others."

"He shouldn't have married her." The silence ran on for ten steps or so, and Joe looked at Sam with resentment in his eyes. "She ain't a good woman, Sam. I know what they say about her in town. The men make jokes about her—having babies without no husband." His lips grew tense. "I hate her, Sam. I wanna come and stay with you!"

Sam's heart sank. He had known it would be hard on the boy, but this was far worse than he had imagined. "Joe," he said, "I don't know as I ever liked anything more than having you with me last year. Made me want a boy of my own worse than I ever wanted anything—someday I'd like to have one just like you. But Sky's your pa, boy, and you've got to stay with him. He loves you better than anything else."

"It's her I hate—not him!" He turned to go, but Sam caught him and pulled him around.

"Joe, listen to me! Some things in this world are pretty hard—and you've had to grow up faster than most kids your age." He hesitated, knowing the boy's hurt was too deep to be healed by idle talk. He sighed heavily. "Joe, if your pa did wrong in marrying Rebekah, it was because he was thinking about what was best for *you*. And all I can say about Rebekah is, she's had a harder time than you or me—harder than any man is likely to have, for that matter. Lots of women would have run off and left those babies, but she stuck with them."

The boy did not respond, but at Sam's words he stopped in his tracks, his lips pressed together and his eyes hard. "The pen's just over that rise."

Sky saw them coming and ran to meet them. "Sam—you old reprobate!" He grinned and slapped his friend on the shoulder. "You come all the way out here to get my vote?"

"Nope. Came out to tell you Edith and me got married last week."

"You did!" A broad grin spread across Winslow's face. "I knew you was a goner, Sam—but you sure did get a fine woman."

"Guess we're both pretty lucky, Sky," Sam replied, then saw the smile fade from his friend's eyes, so he said hurriedly, "Say, you got a quarter of beef I could take back with me? Edith says that stuff we've been gettin' from old man Taylor is made of shoe leather!"

"Just butchered a fine yearling day before yesterday. It'll be your wedding present. Come on, Rebekah's made some chili that'll burn you down to your toes. Right, Joe?" He did not see the flash of resentment in the boy's eyes, but moved back down the trail, saying, "Tell me how the election's shaping up."

Back at the cabin, Edith had taken the baby out of the crib and sat rocking her as Timmy investigated cautiously. "She's grown, I do believe, Rebekah," Edith marveled. She poked the baby's fat cheeks and was rewarded by a loud burp. "She's like a little doll!" she laughed. "I can't wait to have a baby, Rebekah. All my life that's what I've wanted. "

Rebekah had pulled a chair around and Timmy ran to her. Pulling him up onto her lap, she squeezed him affectionately. Timmy sat staring at the visitor with round, curious eyes. "You'll be a wonderful mother, Edith. Now tell me about you and Sam. I wish I could have been there for the wedding."

"Oh, it wasn't anything grand. Sam just said one night after church, 'What are we waiting for, Edith?' And you know, neither of us could think of a single thing—so the next day, we did it. Lot Penny married us—he's doing much better than the last time Sky saw him." She paused and her cheeks colored slightly and she gave a half embarrassed giggle. "You know, I thought that Sam was a little slow—but when he goes after something—that man is downright determined!"

Edith saw that Rebekah was starved for such talk, and filled in the finer details of life in town as Rebekah hung on to every word. When Edith had finished, she asked, "Is Sam going to win the election, Edith?"

"I hope not!" Edith bit her lip and toyed with a curl that fell over Mary's ear, then whispered confidentially, "It's getting bad in town. Everyone knows that Poole is doing everything he can to win the election—and if he doesn't win, Tom says that they'll try to kill him and Sam."

"We'll have to pray for them," Rebekah said. "I've been reading the Bible a lot lately, and over and over it says that we can't get by without faith."

Edith feared that the men would come back, so she asked abruptly, "How have things been, Rebekah—with you and Sky?"

A shadow came to Rebekah's eyes. "All right," she replied quietly.

"I don't think so, Rebekah," Edith returned boldly. "I don't mean to be a busybody, but I care about you, Becky. You can tell me—it's been hard, hasn't it?"

Timmy squirmed, and Rebekah put him down. He crawled off into the bedroom, so Rebekah rose and went to look out the window. Her eyes fixed on the white landscape, she murmured, "I can't complain. I have a home, a place for my children. Sky is good to Timmy and Mary, and he . . ." She faltered for just one moment, then turned to face Edith. "And he's kept his part of the bargain with me."

"Rebekah!" Edith protested. "You and Sky have forty or fifty years ahead of you! When you married him, surely you must have hoped for more than—than just being a housekeeper!"

"It's what I agreed to, Edith." The words were emotionless, and she added quietly, "Don't worry about me, Edith. It's not easy—especially with Joe. He resents me so, and I can't blame him."

"He's jealous of his father, I suppose?"

"He's never had to share him, so I guess that's natural—but there's something I'm afraid of, Edith." Rebekah twisted her fingers together as the sound of voices outside came closer. "Sky can't see it, but his resentment against his first wife has rubbed off on Joe." The voices got still louder, and she rose, whispering hurriedly, "It's going to destroy both of them—all of us—if he can't resolve to forgive her!"

The door opened and Sky entered, coming at once to pull Edith to her feet. "Lord help you, Edith, having to put up with Sam—but he's so gone on you that maybe you can housebreak him!"

He reached down and kissed her on the cheek, then took the baby. "Now, how's this for a pretty one?" he asked, and the affection in his face caused Edith to give Rebekah a strange glance. "How about some of that chili of yours, Rebekah?" he asked.

"I wish we could do better than that for our first guests," Rebekah protested.

"Oh, we've got to get back," Edith interrupted quickly. "We really only came out to be congratulated and to invite you to the camp meeting that's going to start at the church."

"Camp meeting?" Sky asked. "In the middle of winter?"

"Well, it's an *indoor* camp meeting," Sam shrugged. "Tom got Lot out of bed and able to function, and he's determined to have a revival. I asked him how you 'revive' something that ain't never been 'vived' to begin with—but you know Lot!"

"It'll start next Saturday," Edith informed them firmly. "And nothing will do but that you all come." She moved closer to Rebekah and smiled. "Sam's rented me a house, and I need some help getting it fixed up, Sky. So you've just got to bring your family in for a few days."

Sky looked at Rebekah and asked quietly, "You'd like to go, I reckon?"

"I'd like it a great deal," Rebekah answered.

"All right," Sky said. "I can't promise I'll be at the meetin' myself—but guess a few days in town will be good for you and Joe." He looked slyly at Joe. "You probably can use a break from the books, can't you, Joe?" Once again he did not seem to notice the lack of response from the boy. "Well, let's see to that quarter of beef while Rebekah fixes our meal."

They enjoyed a good meal of rich, spicy chili, and shortly afterward Edith and Sam left for town. Neither of them spoke for a time. Finally Sam commented, "They're in a bad way, Edith—worse than I thought." He rehearsed the incident with Joe, then added in a discouraged tone, "Can't see how they can make it. What'd Rebekah have to say?"

"She won't say much—but it's killing her spirit, Sam." The sleigh hissed through the snow as she wracked her brain for some way to help, but nothing would come, so she moved closer to Sam, depressed by the visit.

The visit had lifted Rebekah's spirits briefly, but after the pair had gone, the house depressed her. Sky and Joe went hunting, leaving her alone with the children; and both of them had gone to sleep, so there was little for her to do. She had cleaned the cabin and taken care of the household work, but she needed something to occupy her mind. Pulling a chair in front of the fire, she took her Bible and began to read. After two hours her eyes grew tired and she tried to pray, but it was difficult. She remembered how easy it had been when she'd first been saved, when she'd had Mary to pray with and a church to attend.

She put her head back, thinking over the past two weeks, and a despair rose in her so sharp and painful that she could keep from weeping only by a force of will. For the hundredth time she asked herself if she had made a dreadful mistake by marrying Sky, the doubts gnawing at her mercilessly. Getting up, she paced the floor, remembering how Joe had rejected every attempt she had made to befriend him. She felt her failure keenly; and no matter how she looked at the matter, it grieved her to no end.

What she had expected from Sky, she could not say—but he had been different from anything she had seen before. On the wagon train, there had been moments when he had smiled at her, lifting her spirits. She thought often of the times they'd talked as he rode beside her on the wagon seat. She had felt his warmth then, but since that awful night he'd accused Tom of being with her, she had not seen that lighter side of him. Deep in her heart she wondered, *Does he really think I'm a loose woman—like his first wife?*

Restlessly she moved around, her mind confused and weary of the struggle. *He treats me like a servant*, she thought, *but that's what I bargained for. It may be enough for him—but is it enough for me?*

That was the question that was draining her deep down, for she knew she had expected more than that. He had made no promises, but she had hoped that eventually he would look at her as more than a woman to clean his house and help with his son. He had done nothing to encourage that idea, however. When they had arrived at the house for the first time, he told her, "You and the children will sleep in the bedroom. Joe and I will bunk in the loft." It was as if he were warning her at once that their relationship would be on that plane—nothing warm or personal.

Closing her Bible, she went to bed, though it wasn't late. She knew Sky and Joe would be in by dark, but she could not face another evening of Joe's coldness. Long after they came in, she lay there listening to them talk until she finally heard them go upstairs to the loft. They were laughing about something that had happened, and she felt cut off and left out. The utter isolation gripped her and the tears that she had been too proud to shed during the day burst forth and flowed unchecked down her cheeks.

"Well, we don't have a big meeting like Brother Finney has," Lot Penny said, "but it's a beginning." Satisfaction crept into his bright blue eyes as he looked over the crowd that had come out for the Saturday night meeting. Potbelly stoves glowed at each end of the room, sending waves of warmth radiating from their cherry-colored sides; those who sat closest to them perspired profusely, while those in the center drew their coats closer around them.

Sky surveyed the congregation. "Looks like you got a good start, Lot." He glanced over to where Rebekah was surrounded by a group of her friends who were admiring the baby. "Hope you have a good meeting tonight."

"Wish you'd stay for the service, Sky," Penny said sadly. His face was still scarred from the beating he had taken, but his spirit was as strong as ever. "Brother Truitt is a fine preacher—in fact, don't know if I've ever heard better."

"Maybe some other time, Lot," Sky replied. He had brought Rebekah and the children in three days earlier, but had gone back to the farm, claiming that someone had to watch the stock.

Penny didn't argue, for he knew the futility of it. He watched Winslow leave and saw that Rebekah's eyes had followed him as he passed through the door. She had been a cheerful woman on the trail, he remembered, but now there was a heaviness in her that dimmed all the gaiety. She met his gaze and he smiled at her, but she didn't smile back.

He went to the front and sat down beside Henry Sellers. "Well, I couldn't get him to stay for the meeting."

"Too bad! Too bad!" Sellers shook his head, taking out a red bandanna and wiping the perspiration from his brow. "Maybe when he gets settled into his marriage, he'll get more sociable. And I'm still hopin' he'll jump into this election and give Sam a hand."

"Maybe—but somethin's eatin' at his insides, Henry. He's out of step with God—and until he bends his neck to the Almighty, Sky Winslow ain't gonna have any peace." He would have said more, but the door opened and Rev. John Truitt came in and the two men rose to greet him.

"He sure ain't much on looks, is he now?" May Stockton whispered behind her hand to her husband, referring to the preacher. May had married a prosperous merchant named Larry Prince, but marriage had not changed her outspoken ways. She and her new husband were well satisfied with their match, though their personalities were quite different. Prince was soft-spoken and not at all outgoing, while May was sociable to the roots of her red hair. "I get him to goin'—and he puts the brakes on for me!" May had laughed when asked about her marriage. But Prince was pleased with his bride, and smiled at her observation.

Rebekah was sitting between Edith and May, and had overheard the remark about the preacher. "Beauty is only skin deep, May," Rebekah chided her friend gently.

"Well, let's skin him, then!" May giggled. "No, I'm just joking, Rebekah. He's just about the best preacher I ever heard—not that I ever heard many!"

Edith and Sam listened as May and Rebekah talked, and when the song leader got up, Edith leaned over to her husband. "Try to get Sky to come to the meeting, Sam. It'll mean a lot to Rebekah."

"I did everything but put a gun at his head. He's a hard case, Edith—but I haven't given up."

Outside, Sky made his way down Elm Street toward the center of town, aware that he had been the target of almost every eye in the church. There had been much pressure to get him to attend services, but he had known it would be one of the penalties he'd have to pay for being in town. Passing Seth Long's blacksmith shop, he wondered if he should move the family into town for good. He'd never lived in a town, and the decision to move would be solely for Rebekah and the children. As the time grew near when he'd have to decide, he had the feeling that life was closing in on him. He put the thoughts aside for later as he walked along the plank walk.

To his amazement, he was greeted by almost every man he met. He had never been involved in the activities of Oregon City, and had known these people only through his rare visits. He realized that the recognition was because of the way he'd faced Ingerson down and out-gunned Del Laughton, though the thought gave him no pleasure. Politics had never held any interest for him, and now he was being drawn into the heated cauldron of political warfare that stirred the entire town. It was another pressure that pushed at him, and he shook his shoulders angrily, determined to avoid getting more involved—yet knowing he would probably be drawn deeper still.

He stopped at Mike Stevens' house, and found no one at

home. He remembered then that he'd seen Mrs. Stevens at the meeting, and made his way to the Silver Moon. As he'd suspected, he found Mike at a table with Judd Travers and Clay Hill. Hill's face lit up, and he kicked a chair back with his boot. "Sit down, Sky, and help me pound some sense into this hide-bound Yankee!"

Judd Travers was a staunch abolitionist from Boston, and his verbal battles over slavery with Clay Hill, who was from Georgia, were legendary. He snorted disgustedly and waved a bony hand at Hill. "How a man can be as smart as you are in some things, Clay, and be so infernally *dumb* in a thing like slavery is beyond me!" Travers was not religious, but he was a zealot over the antislavery cause. His deep-set black eyes glowed as he pounded the table with a hard fist. "England had sense enough to set her slaves free—and sooner or later in this country we'll do the same!"

"Not without a war, you won't, Judd," Clay shrugged. He took a drink from the glass in front of him. "The South will pull out of the Union before *that* happens."

"Pull out of the Union!" Travers scoffed, declaring fiercely, "That would be treason!"

Clay smiled at the older man, but there was a dead seriousness in his eyes. "There's a good precedent for it, Judd," he pointed out. "The thirteen colonies pulled away from England because they didn't want anyone telling them how to run their business. I don't see any difference between the king of England trying to put a tax on me, and some abolitionists in New England telling me what I can or can't do. No, the South won't be ruled over by the North. It'll mean war if you folks push it."

"Don't believe it," Travers stated flatly. He turned to Sky. "Your people—they're from Virginia, didn't you tell me, Sky? What'll *they* do if it comes to a fight?"

"There's some Winslows in Virginia—but there's some in the North." As he thought, the dark streak of fatalism in him knit his brow. "Hate to see it come. Be brothers against brothers all over this country. Families split right down the middle."

Clay said, "I'll worry about that war when it gets here." He took another drink, then added, "We got a war on right here, Sky. I'm set on winnin' it before I take on another one."

"Think Sam will win?" Sky asked.

"It's up for grabs right now." Travers took an ancient pipe out of his pocket, then filled and lit it. When it drew well, he looked around the room. "Here's the bunch that wants an open town. The other side's in church, I reckon. Always like that: the black and the white."

"You and Clay and me, Judd, we're here," Mike Stevens remarked pointedly. "Sky, too. Are we the sheep or the goats?"

"We're not saints," Travers decided flatly. "But we're better than Poole and Ingerson and their lot."

They bantered back and forth for two hours, and slowly the tension drained out of Winslow. The men around the table were not outdoorsmen, but there was a solidness about them, and Sky knew their word was good. They started a mild poker game and the time passed unnoticed. Their group made a little island in the saloon, and once Sky noticed Dandy Raimez staring at him from his place, but Sky paid no heed to it.

He was not a drinking man, but the others were; and although he drank only one to their five or six, by the time Hill and Travers got up and left, Sky was feeling the effect of the alcohol. "No more for me, Mike," he said when the other offered him the bottle.

Stevens hiccoughed loudly. "I'd not be walking the streets alone if I were you, Sky."

"Why not, Mike?"

"The word is out." Stevens looked at the bar where Poole and Dandy were still engaged in talk. "Poole is going to pull out all the stops to stay in power. You made an enemy out of Ingerson when you faced him down—and Raimez, too. Way the talk goes, they'll stop your clock if you stick your oar in."

"They're welcome to try."

"What about your family if you go down? You thought about that?"

"I won't go down."

"You won't go down." Stevens got to his feet and rolled his eyes. "You're tough, man—but anybody can die. Don't get me wrong. I'm against Poole and his crowd all the way—but just be sure you count up the bill before you jump in."

He turned and walked out of the saloon without looking

back, leaving Sky wondering. Stevens had not been so outspoken earlier, and his new belligerent attitude seemed to be a warning. *Things are getting warmer*, Sky thought. *I must be crazy getting myself pulled into this thing.*

He rose to leave, and a voice said, "Hello, Sky. Got time for a drink?"

He turned to find Rita standing just behind him; her presence was like a physical touch. She was wearing a red dress that set off her figure, and her smile brought back old memories that stirred him. "Guess I'd better not, Rita. I'm an old married man now."

"From what I hear, you're not all *that* married, Sky," she retorted with a crooked smile. "Sort of an in-name-only sort of thing, isn't it?" She saw his jaw harden and said, "Dance with me, Sky. Please—I've got to tell you something." She stepped closer and he had no choice. They moved to the small dance floor where half a dozen other men had claimed partners from the Silver Moon's girls, and the two began to move across the floor.

"Be careful, Sky," she whispered, moving closer to speak in his ear.

He didn't like the way her perfume and the slight pressure of her body against his stirred old hungers—it made him dissatisfied with himself and angry at his weakness. "Be careful of what, Rita?"

"I guess you know. I was hoping you wouldn't be involved in this, but everyone knows that you're Birdwell's friend. And any friend of his is in Poole's little book."

"I'm not running for office."

She pulled back so she could look at him and asked, "And if they go after Sam Birdwell with guns, what'll you do, Sky?" She saw his reaction. "See? It's not in you to run out on a friend. But you don't have a chance, Sky. I'm Dandy's girl now, and I hear things. And what I hear is that anyone in Birdwell's camp will be killed—if that's what it takes to keep 'em in line."

Sky knew all this, but he asked quietly, "Why are you telling me all this, Rita?"

She didn't answer at once, but just as the music stopped, she whispered, "I'm a fool for a man I like." She turned and left, saying, "Get out of it, Sky!"

He walked back to the table, laid down the money for his drinks, and left the saloon. When he got back to the church, the service was over and most of the crowd gone. Going inside, he found Rebekah talking to Edith. "Ready to go?"

Both of the women were looking at him in a peculiar way. "I'll get the children," Rebekah replied quietly.

Edith waited until she left. "You're a fool, Sky."

"What?" He was taken off guard by her harsh words. "What's the matter?"

"You come into this place for your wife, half drunk, smelling of cheap perfume, and with this—" She reached out and pulled a long black hair from his shirt collar. She glared at him. "If you have to go to that woman, you could at least clean yourself up before Rebekah sees you!"

The attack was so unexpected and the anger in her face so strong that he could not think of an answer. Turning, he left the building and waited until Rebekah came out carrying the baby. Joe was with her, holding Timmy. Sky got them inside the wagon and started for home. Rebekah said nothing, and soon the children were all asleep—Joe bundled up with Timmy on the floor and the baby held close in her mother's arms. The lights of the town faded as they moved into the thin timber. A quarter moon threw faint silver beams on the snow, and the horses' hooves made squashy noises in the half-melted slush.

Sky had rarely felt so uncomfortable. Edith's words burned in his mind, and even if he knew that his intentions had not been bad—at least as far as Rita was concerned—he felt guilty. Winslow looked at Rebekah. Her face was sharply outlined by the faint moonlight, and he admired the classic simplicity of her face, though he could not see her expression. After several miles of silence he could not stand it anymore, and made his apology.

"I shouldn't have come into the church after drinking, Rebekah." He wanted to say more, to explain to her what had happened, but her silence built a wall, and he could not go on.

She thinks I've been with Rita, he thought, and for a long time he tried to find some way to tell her what had happened, but he couldn't. Not only that, the memory of how Rita had stirred his longings grated against his conscience. Finally he settled down to the long ride home.

Rebekah was waiting for him to speak again, and when he didn't, she steeled herself against the mounting silence. One word from him, and she would have turned at once with understanding—but he did not say that word. He helped her get the children inside, hoping at the last moment to find a word to ease the situation, but nothing came.

They went to bed without speaking to each other, and long afterward, Sky heard the mournful cry of a timber wolf far off in the woods. The sound stirred him deeply. He lay there thinking of what the days ahead held, but found nothing to soften the blank wall of despair that shut him in.

CHAPTER TWENTY

CHRISTMAS GIFT

★ ★ ★ ★

A week of false spring freed the frozen brooks and turned the crisp snow into slush, but Winslow knew winter still lurked up in the Cascades. He rose early one morning and said to Rebekah, "I'm going over to the lower pasture and get some of that big oak that fell. Be back before noon."

"All right."

The shortness of her reply struck him, but he hitched the team to a sled and drove down the slope that led to a bottom section. For two hours he hacked at the tough white oak that had fallen the previous year in a storm, loading the sections on the sled. The sun came up, heating the small meadow, and he soon took off his coat.

The physical work was pleasant, for he could expend his energy against the wood, see the pile grow on the sled, and take satisfaction in the small accomplishment. He enjoyed the simplicity of the work as well because he had been struggling against things that had no simple answers. Since the night they had returned from Oregon City, Rebekah had been different.

Their marriage was not the usual, he realized. From the start her manner had been subdued, yet he had become aware of part of her that was waiting—for what, he wasn't quite certain. But he recognized it, and he'd had something of the same expectancy in his own mind. Despite his talk of her being "just a house-keeper," somehow there had been a knowledge that such a relationship could not go on forever. More than once they had looked at each other, and a keen awareness had leaped out in a way that alerted them to the fact that they were more than just master and servant.

But that had passed—at least from Rebekah. She cooked, sewed, and maintained the house, but kept to herself, speaking for the most part only of necessary things, the ordinary affairs of keeping house.

Sky had been aware, too, of Joe's growing resentment for Rebekah, but had not found any way to curb it. Both he and Joe enjoyed Timmy and Mary. It was the one thing that had gone right with their arrangement. Every night Sky would come in from work and spend time playing simple games with Timmy, and often he would hold Mary, rocking her to sleep or marveling at the finely made features that were beginning to take form. Joe did much the same, and his interest in the children made Sky feel better—but he was aware that both he and Joe were shut out from Rebekah more firmly than ever.

Now as he pushed the one-man crosscut saw through the stubborn oak, his head was filled with thoughts; and when a voice spoke right at his side, he almost panicked. His years in the mountains with danger constantly around had given him catlike reactions, but the years spent away had blunted those. Even as he whirled, throwing himself to his left where his rifle lay propped too far away against a stump, he knew he was too late.

"Whoa, Hoss! Don't get your dander up!"

Sky blinked at the figure who had appeared from nowhere. Recognizing the man, he whooped loudly and threw himself forward, beating the man on the back. "Jim O'Malley!" he shouted. "Blast you! I oughta shoot you for sneaking up on me like that!"

A smile broke across the broad lips of the visitor. "I knowed you'd go to pot if you left the mountains! Good thing I wasn't a Cheyenne buck, ain't it now?"

"Jim! Where in the world did you spring from?"

"Brought my furs to Oregon City, Sky. Thought the price

might be better—and anyway, your pa told me you was here, so I thought we might split a bottle and see which one of us could tell the biggest lies."

Jim O'Malley was two inches taller than Winslow and much thicker through the body. He was wearing a worn set of buckskins, which seemed molded to his body, and a pair of handmade elkskin boots. A coonskin cap failed to hide the reddish thatch of hair that grew down past his ears, and he held a Hawken rifle as if it were an extension of his body. He had steel-gray eyes, deep set and watchful, and his face was heavy and durable like the rest of him. The two men were about the same age, and had spent several years trapping together on the upper Missouri.

"Jim! By the Lord, it's good to see you!" Sky exclaimed, slapping his thighs and crowing with pleasure. "Let's go to the house and get something to eat."

"Stopped by and met your wife and kids," O'Malley said. "You sure done yourself proud, Sky! Don't see how an ornery coon like you could talk a fine lady like that into marryin' the likes of *you*."

Sky looked for something in the man's face that would imply a hidden meaning, but he saw only the fine humor characteristic of O'Malley. He hesitated, then said, "It's kind of a funny thing, Jim. I'll tell you about how we got married while we walk back."

But it was not as easy as he had expected. As he tried to put into words the history of his marriage, it sounded artificial even to his own ears. He was also aware of the sidelong glances O'Malley gave him as they made their way back to the house.

Finally the trapper said, "Well, I knew that Irene cut the heart out of you, Sky. I didn't know she was dead until your folks told me a year back when I went by the Mission to get word about you."

"Joe needs a mother, Jim. I went east to hire a housekeeper and teacher—but Rebekah was in a fix, so I thought we could work out something that would help us both."

"How's it workin' out?" O'Malley asked.

Sky reflected for a moment. "Well, it's hard, Jim. I've had some doubts—and I reckon she has, too." Soon he grew tired of talking about his own problems, so he changed the subject. "What's on your ticket, Jim?"

"Why, you're looking at a man with a hitch to settle down, Sky," O'Malley smiled. "I met up with old Charlie Dugan last month—you remember Charlie?"

"Sure. Thought he was dead, though."

"Oughta been. He's only about fifty, but he looks seventy, Sky! Living alone in a little hut outside Fort Laramie—plumb wore out! And I can remember when Charlie Dugan could walk the legs off any man in the mountains!" O'Malley shook his head. "I decided right then to sell out, get married, and raise myself a dozen kids!"

Sky laughed loudly. "Can't see you in that light, Jim. And you've come to a mighty poor place for finding a bride. Just told you how I had to bring a bunch clear from the East."

O'Malley waved his hand. "That's no problem for an Irishman," he announced grandly. "I've got a pocketful of money, and with my charm and good looks, finding a woman will be a small matter."

"Well, good luck," Sky replied, thinking that the man was telling the truth. Jim O'Malley was the finest looking man he'd ever seen; and in their years together, it was always the Irishman who managed to get the inside track on every pretty girl that appeared.

When they got back to the house, Joe was waiting on the doorstep, his eyes taking in the big man, who won his heart by saying, "Joe, is it? Well, now, I've got an idea that the two of us might get along. You got a rifle?"

"Sure!"

"Well, I hope to teach you how to shoot it," O'Malley commented with a grin at Sky. "I remember once your pa and I was penned in by a Crow war party, and he said right there, 'Mr. O'Malley, if we get out of this thing alive, I'm going to take shooting lessons from you.' "

"Gosh! Is that right, Pa?"

"Sure is," Sky smiled. "Guess you're looking at just about the best shot in the West—with a rifle, that is."

"Now your pa is being too modest, Joe," O'Malley protested. "I can maybe shade him with a Hawken, but there's no man who could come close to Sky Winslow with a pistol."

"We can brag on each other later, Jim," Sky grinned. "You're stayin' with us, so get your plunder unloaded." He hesitated as Rebekah stepped outside. "You say you've met my wife?"

"Yes." O'Malley smiled and pulled his hat off. His teeth gleamed white against his bronze skin, and there was a gentlemanly grace in his manner as he bowed. "Don't want to be any trouble to you, Mrs. Winslow."

"Why—you'll be most welcome, Mr. O'Malley." Rebekah's heart thumped, for the presence of the man was strong. His gray eyes danced with life, and she felt his admiration. "We're a little short on meat, Sky—"

"Why, I'm your man, Mrs. Winslow—and by the way, Mr. O'Malley, he's my pa. You can just call me Jim." He put a hand on Joe's shoulder. "Why don't you and me go out and try to find a buck, Joe?"

"Can I, Pa?" Joe begged.

"Take Jim down to Big Owl Creek, Joe. Deer been feeding in the river bottom there. Try to get a nice tender doe."

O'Malley and Joe left at once, the man holding the boy's attention by some tall tale. As Sky watched them go, he said, "Sure is good to see Jim."

Rebekah's mind was on the problems of taking in an extra guest. "I suppose he'll sleep with you and Joe," she said, a faint flush rising in her cheeks as she turned to enter the house. "I'll find some extra blankets." She hurriedly found two thick blankets, and took them up to the loft, which was built much more solidly than in most cabins. The ceiling sloped up so steeply that there was plenty of room for the two single beds that Sky had built for himself and Joe, as well as a table and two chairs. After she had put the blankets on one of the beds, she was about to go when she saw a sheet of paper under the table and bent to pick it up. Thinking it was one of Joe's exercises, she held it to the light and read a few lines before she realized it was a letter Sky had been working on. Her face paled and she tore her eyes from the page. Looking down, she saw several other sheets on the table. She put the sheet she had retrieved with the others, then went downstairs. The few lines she had read fixed in her memory:

I should have written you before, but I had hoped things would get better. I told you of my marriage in my last letter. It was for

Joe's sake that I married Rebekah, but I've come to realize that is not enough to make a marriage. Joe has taken a dislike to her, and the whole thing has been difficult for everyone. If I had only hired her it would be much simpler, but I've married her . . .

Rebekah's eyes burned so badly that she had trouble finding her way down from the loft. When Sky came in a few minutes later, he saw her pale face and asked, "What's the matter?"

"Nothing."

"You look like you don't feel well. Not getting sick, are you?"

"No. I'm fine." She turned away from him and busied herself in the kitchen. "If you'll milk the cow, I'll churn the butter and we can have sorghum with our biscuits tonight."

He left and Mary began to cry. She brought the baby into the warm kitchen and began to nurse her. The words of the letter attacked her brain like knives, and tears formed in her eyes. She felt trapped, cut off from all help; and no matter how hard she tried, nothing came to her in the form of escape. Joe's dislike had broken her spirit, and now that she was certain that Sky was already sick of his bargain, her spirit was wounded deeply.

She thought again of the way Sky had come for her at the church, and was more certain than ever that he had been with Rita. Finally, when the baby was fed, she put her in a cradle that Sky had made of smooth saplings, and began pulling the elements of a meal together.

Two hours later Joe and O'Malley came back with a doe, and the men dressed the animal expertly. O'Malley came in with a pile of steaks in his big hands and gave them to Rebekah, saying, "If you can spare a little hot water, I'd like to come out of hiding, Mrs. Winslow. I'm a sight for sure."

"You can call me Rebekah," she smiled. Then she studied his beard and said, "You'd better let me trim the worst of that off before you try to shave."

"Don't want to be a bother."

"Oh, I'm the official barber around here, Jim." She pulled a pair of shears from a peg on the wall. "Why don't you sit on that high stool?"

When Joe and Sky came in, they found Jim perched on a chair, and Rebekah, having already trimmed the man's beard, was cutting his hair. A pile of reddish locks lay on the floor, but it wasn't an easy job cutting straight, for O'Malley was telling her a funny story about a bear hunt. "Jim!" she laughed, pulling the shears away, "you've got to stop that or I can't finish the job!"

O'Malley looked at Winslow and said, "Sky, I was just telling Rebekah about the time you and me and Sam Hawkins got cross-ways with that bear; you remember—up in Dawes Canyon? But you probably told that tale a hundred times, I bet."

"No, I never did," Sky replied. "You go on and I'll correct your lies, Jim."

O'Malley sat on the stool, sometimes spreading his hands wide to illustrate a point, and soon Joe and Sky were as engrossed in the tale as Rebekah. The man was a natural storyteller, and though they had both been there, Sky enjoyed the tale as much as Joe.

"Hey, Joe, why don't you throw those steaks on the skillet for your ma?" Jim said. "Soon as I get out of all this hair, I'm gonna be ready to eat hair and hoof!"

"Sure, Jim!" Joe leaped to the task with an alacrity that made Sky exchange a startled look with Rebekah. The boy had helped her only when forced to, and to see him so eager made Sky realize that he had been remiss in training his son.

Rebekah worked carefully on O'Malley's mop of auburn hair, shaping it expertly around the ears and his well-shaped head. He sat quietly after the story was finished; and once when she was working on the front, their eyes met, and the look of admiration in his dark eyes made her feel warm inside. "That's the best I can do, Jim," she said when she was done. "There's plenty of hot water if you want to shave."

"Best haircut I've had in twenty years," he smiled, admiring himself in the small mirror she handed him. "Didn't know what a good-looking fellow I was!"

He moved over to a small table in the living area and carefully shaved while Rebekah went over to the stove. "That's good, Joe. Thank you for your help."

Joe muttered, "Aw, that's okay."

O'Malley went up the ladder to the loft, and when Rebekah called supper twenty minutes later, he came down wearing a pair of gray pants and a soft pearl-colored shirt with a sky-blue neckerchief. "Well—" Sky commented in surprise as the big man came down the ladder, "if you drop dead, we won't have to do a thing to you, Jim!"

O'Malley shot a grin at him as Rebekah said, "You can sit down; it's all ready."

"It looks mighty good," O'Malley complimented her. Joe and Sky sat down promptly, but Jim moved quickly to pull Rebekah's chair out.

She stared at him uncertainly for a moment, then sat down with a slight flush in her cheeks and said "thank you" in a quiet voice.

The unexpected act of courtesy made both Sky and Joe feel awkward, and well aware of the fact that neither of them had done a thing like that for Rebekah. Sky looked at the table and saw that Rebekah had put on a fresh white linen tablecloth and the good plates and silverware.

O'Malley looked the smoking food over. "Been many a day since I sat down to a table like this, Rebekah." He cast a sly look at Sky. "You fellows have it made, blast your hides! Us poor bachelors getting dyspepsia from our own sorry cooking, and here you get served like you were in a fine restaurant in St. Louis!" With a wise gleam in his eye, Jim went on. "Well, you're the preacher's son, Sky, so I guess you do the thanks over the grub. Wish you'd make it a quick one, 'fore I fall out!"

It was an embarrassing moment for the three of them, and Sky admitted, "Guess I've gotten out of all the good habits that Pa and Ma tried to put in me when I was younger."

There was another awkward silence before Rebekah bowed her head and prayed, "Lord, thank you for this good food—and for our guest. In Jesus' name."

She looked up to find O'Malley staring at her. "I hope there's enough for everyone," she said quickly.

She had made fresh biscuits, with sorghum, opened some canned green beans and carrots, and prepared baked potatoes with gravy to go with the sizzling steaks. For dessert there was apple pie, and everything was washed down with fresh milk and cup after cup of steaming black coffee.

An hour later, O'Malley pushed back, and with a regretful shake of his head said, "Only thing wrong with this meal is that I can't eat another bite!"

"It was good, Rebekah," Sky echoed; and Joe piped up, "It was the best supper I ever had."

It was the first compliment that Rebekah had gotten from Sky and Joe, and she knew it had been forced by O'Malley, but she enjoyed it anyway. Standing up, she said, "You men can talk while I do the dishes."

"I reckon *not!*" O'Malley leaped to his feet and began to pile the dishes into a stack. "Don't you try to stop me, Rebekah, because nothing won't do me but to give you a hand—then we can all sit and talk."

As O'Malley began to help Rebekah, despite her protests, Sky and Joe moved to the other end of the large room, feeling awkward. Joe stared at the big hunter as he kept up a running line of talk, making Rebekah laugh from time to time. Sky knew what was bothering the boy; he had men's work and women's work neatly divided into two compartments, and now his piles were being mixed up. He had never seen a man he admired more than O'Malley, except his own father. If O'Malley had been a weak man, he would have despised him for doing a thing like washing dishes. But his father had told him briefly of a few of the exploits that had made Jim O'Malley a legend among mountain men—and yet there he stood, holding a delicate china plate in his large hand. Obviously *he* thought nothing of doing a woman's work!

The dishes done, O'Malley stepped back to allow Rebekah to go first; then after she was seated, he said, "Well, folks, I came out of the mountains with the idea of gettin' a wife. If I had any doubts about it, tonight took care of them!" He looked around the room and sighed, "Yep, you had the right idea, Sky. This is the way a man is supposed to live!"

Sky smiled and suggested, "You might miss the freedom a mite, Jim. You've never been tied down."

"Freedom to stay cold and hungry!" O'Malley lifted his hands in disgust. "Freedom to take a Sioux arrow in the liver! That's all right for a young buck, Sky, and I'm glad we done it—but the good trapping days are gone. Beaver's played out, and now it's time for Mrs. O'Malley's boy to settle down—just like you."

They stayed up late, and O'Malley did ninety percent of the talking. He was filled with raw energy, and he managed to draw his captive audience out—Joe included. Sky saw that Rebekah's eyes were happy as the big hunter skillfully included her as well.

Late that night, after Jim went up to the loft with Joe, Sky paused long enough to say to Rebekah, "He's a charmer, isn't he?"

Rebekah's eyes wandered over to the place he had been sitting with a gentle smile on her face. "Is he always like this?"

"Jim's pretty much what you see. Don't think he'll have any trouble finding a wife. If anybody's got a pretty young daughter, you better tell them to lock her in the cellar till O'Malley's gone."

"You don't think he'll stay?"

"Jim?" Sky shook his head and smiled. "No, he'll be going back to the mountains as soon as he gets bored with town living."

O'Malley's visit stretched out for three days, then a week; yet he showed no signs of restlessness as Christmas drew near. He made several trips to town, once with Sky, then by himself, and he made more acquaintances in those scattered visits than Winslow had made in years. When Tom Lake commented on the redhead's ability to make friends, Sky remarked, "He's always been like that, Tom. I've ridden into an Indian village with him, and inside of a day, it seemed like he knew every papoose in the camp."

"Hope he'll stick around," Lake responded. "He's been talking to Sellers about buying a sawmill. He's got some money saved, and I think the bank will back him."

"Another vote for you, Tom?" Sky smiled.

"No, I reckon not. He won't meet the residence requirement." He looked at Sky and asked, "You think I'm a fool for getting involved in this election, don't you?" He waved aside Sky's protests, adding with an air of agitation, "But I'm not doing this for me, Sky. I've wasted a lot of my life—*now I want to do something that counts*."

When Winslow thought about that remark later, it cut deep. He had been a loner for so long that when he added up the things he had done to make the world a little better, his list seemed woefully inadequate. He thought of how his father had spent years to see a few Indians come to know Christ; yet Sky had done nothing for anyone except himself.

Later that day O'Malley came out of Birdwell's store with his arms full of bundles and nearly collided into Winslow. "I'm playin' Santa Claus, Sky," he announced. "Haven't had a Christmas with a family since I left home, so I aim to use your family— if it's all right."

"You shouldn't be spending your money like that, Jim."

"Aw, you know how tight I've always been. Well, I've got a pile and I'm gonna spend it. Bought myself a sawmill this afternoon, and I still got enough to buy a bunch of stuff for the kids."

O'Malley loaded the gifts into the wagon with some supplies, and when they reached home, he hid them in the barn while Sky unhitched. The two of them went inside, carrying the groceries that Rebekah had asked for, and found Joe at the table studying his books. He was scowling as usual, but after O'Malley sat down and went over some of the arithmetic, the boy soon brightened up. "How come you know all about figures, Jim?" he asked.

"Got snowed in with a feller who was a schoolteacher, Joe. We got so bored that I let him teach me that stuff—and it's a good thing, because I'm going to need it now that I'm a businessman."

"A businessman, Jim?" Rebekah asked, looking up from the potatoes she was peeling. She listened carefully as he told about buying the sawmill; then she nodded and said, "I'm glad you're staying here."

Studying her intently, O'Malley had an odd expression on his face. "I was hoping you'd feel that way, Rebekah."

Uneasy, Sky sat very still, his attention fixed on the faces of the two in front of him. He had noticed that Rebekah relaxed when O'Malley was around, that she seemed much happier— more peaceful—than she was with Joe and him. O'Malley was quiet for the rest of the evening and retired early, taking Joe with him.

Sky played with Timmy, who was driving his chubby legs into a walk. Rebekah settled into a chair to feed Mary. "Christmas is day after tomorrow," Sky remarked.

"We'll have that turkey Jim killed. Ought to be good with some corn-bread dressing."

The words in themselves were normal enough, but the lack of warmth in her tone reminded him of the wall that lay between them. He lifted Timmy high in the air to cover his feelings. "Saw Tom Lake today. He says he'll win the election."

"He shouldn't even be in it. He's not the man for that job."

"Guess not—but he's made up his mind." He put Timmy down and watched him crawl along the floor. The silence rattled his nerves. "Rebekah, I've got something to say to you," he said with a tight voice. She lifted her gaze and he said hastily, "I've been noticing how Jim acts around you."

"What does *that* mean?"

The sharpness in her tone caught him by surprise. "Oh, just that he's always helping you with things—like with the dishes."

"Does that bother you, Sky?"

"In a way." He put his hands behind his back and squeezed his arms to his sides. "I should have been doing some of those things."

"You don't have to."

"No, but . . ." He paused, unable to tell her how he felt. In the letter to his folks, he'd explained further on that the marriage was going bad because he'd never learned how to treat a woman right. With a touch of embarrassment, he'd admitted:

> I've been a bad husband—none at all really. Rebekah has tried hard, and if she'll give me a chance, I'd like to show her another side of me.

If Rebekah had read that section instead of the first one, she would have felt far differently. But because she believed that he despised her, she refused to rise to his words. "We've got a bargain, Sky. I keep the house and you see that the children are taken care of."

"Is that all it is?"

She looked at him steadily. "It *was* what you wanted."

He didn't answer her, feeling the hopelessness gnaw at the pit of his stomach. After he'd gone upstairs, she put the children to bed, then got out her sewing and worked on the small Christmas gifts she was making. Her hands worked busily, but once she stopped and stared up toward the loft, wondering at the conversation she had just had with Sky. Then she thought for the hundredth time of what he'd said in the letter, and her lips grew firm as she continued sewing.

Christmas morning the cabin was full of paper and ribbons. Joe stared, wide-eyed, at the fine hunting knife Rebekah had bought from Sam. "Gosh! I—I didn't think you knew I wanted it," he said to Rebekah.

"You mentioned it enough, Joe," she smiled. Then she opened the package Sky had given her and found a set of fine carving knives from England. "How nice!" she exclaimed, testing the edges. "Just what I need. Thank you, Sky." She handed him a package. "I wanted you to have this."

He opened it, then looked up with surprise. "It's a book!" He opened the cover and exclaimed, "Why, it's WINSLOW'S JOURNAL!"

"What kind of book is it?" O'Malley asked.

"It's a journal that one of my ancestors, Gilbert Winslow, kept," Sky replied softly. "He was on the *Mayflower*. My pa has a copy of this, but it's almost worn out. He used to read it to me when I was just a kid. But I haven't seen a copy in years." He looked up at Rebekah and asked, "How'd you come by this?"

"It was a gift from a friend of mine—before I met you."

The nameless ghost of her past seemed to fill the room, but Winslow said quietly, "Guess if you looked the world over, you couldn't have found anything that would please me more."

After all the presents were opened, Jim said, "Well, now that the family's all done, it's *my* turn to play Santa Claus."

He disappeared outside and was back in a few minutes with his arms loaded with packages. "Had lots of fun buying this stuff," he said when Rebekah rebuked him for spending too much on them. "Most of it Edith helped me pick out."

Sky was pleased with a new fishing rod he'd often admired in the store window. It was a tiny thing, but strong as steel. "Watch out, fish!" he exclaimed, trying it out.

"You won't catch any more fish than you do now, Sky," Jim grinned, "but you'll *look* like a sportsman. This is for you, Joe."

Joe opened a heavy package and unwrapped a perfectly balanced .32 revolver. "You're too young for that now, but your dad will teach you how to use it. Thought you'd like it just to look at for now, and dream about the time when you'll wear it."

Joe caressed the weapon with fingers that trembled, and his eyes were filled with wonder.

"Probably shoot himself in the foot," Sky grinned. "See what this prodigal son Jim got you, Rebekah."

Rebekah opened a box, carefully moved some tissue paper away, and then stopped. She sat, unmoving, for so long that even Joe tore his eyes away from his gun long enough to say impatiently, "Well? What *is* it?"

"Why, it's—it's a dress," she murmured softly. Carefully she pulled a royal blue dress out of the box and held it up. She fingered the white lace collar. She looked as if she were going to cry. "How'd you find out I wanted this so bad, Jim?"

"Asked Edith, of course," O'Malley grinned. "Go try it on, Rebekah."

"Oh, not now."

"Hey, now," Jim urged. "I want to see Joe shoot that gun, and I want to see Sky catch a fish—*and I want to see you in that dress!*"

"All right," Rebekah relented, and ran to the bedroom, closing the door. She was back in five minutes, wearing the dress, and her eyes were bright with pleasure. "How does it look?"

O'Malley exclaimed, "Why, Mrs. Winslow, you look *beautiful!*"

"Gee!" Joe said quietly, for he had never seen Rebekah in anything so pretty. "I didn't know you looked so good!"

"Well, now," Rebekah smiled, "that's good to hear. I'll have to wear it to clean house in, Joe, if you like it that much." She turned and put her hand out, "It's the most beautiful dress in the world, Jim! Thank you so much!"

Sky opened his mouth to say, "Why didn't you *tell* me you wanted the blasted dress!"—but stopped in time. *I should have asked Edith what Rebekah wanted,* he thought, but it was too late.

He stared at Rebekah, noting how her hazel eyes were turned almost blue by the rich color of the material; he also noted how she had regained her figure, for the dress was well-fitted. Her auburn hair caught the light of the morning sun that now streamed through the window, but most of all he was struck silent by the light air of pleasure that emanated from her eyes as she moved around the room, admiring O'Malley's gift.

Later on, after breakfast, the two men took Joe out for target practice. On their way back, Jim said, "Guess I went overboard on the presents, Sky—but I sure have gotten attached to your family. Makes me want my own awful bad!"

"You'll get one, Jim," Sky assured him. He was still feeling downcast, for the morning's activities had depressed him. He looked at O'Malley. "Guess you'll be moving to the new mill pretty soon."

"Oh, I don't take over for a month or two, Sky," the big man said cheerfully. "Guess I'll impose on your hospitality for a little longer—if that's all right with you."

Winslow didn't know what to say except, "Glad to have you, Jim."

CHAPTER TWENTY-ONE

JOE'S MA

★ ★ ★ ★

The warm weather that came in the middle of January thawed the frozen crusts of the earth and filled the streams with melted snow water. Oregon City's streets once again became rivers of thick mud, and as the temperature soared, so did election fever. Sam Birdwell and Tom Lake campaigned strenuously as the Poole machine spent money recklessly. Now, a few days before the day of the election, there was still an air of uncertainty concerning the outcome.

Sky brought five yearlings into town, and Noll Turnage, the butcher, bought them all. As he counted out the cash, he said, "These won't do me, Sky. You got four more you can bring me next week?"

"Guess so, Noll." Sky put the gold coins into his pocket. "Business must be good."

"Oh, these are for Mayor Poole. He's throwing a big barbecue on election day. All the food you can eat and all the liquor you can hold." Noll observed dryly, "Gonna be hard for Sam to top that, Sky. Don't rightly see how him and Lake got a chance to win this one."

Later that day, Sky stopped by and got some supplies from Sam. He found the two candidates and their chief supporters having a war council in the back of the store. "Come have a drink,

Sky." Clay Hill waved him into the circle. Sky got a cup of coffee out of the pot, and Hill sat back, his thin face florid. "Tell these birds we're losing this blasted election, Sky. I've talked myself hoarse, and it's like casting pearls before swine."

Sky looked around, noting that none of them looked particularly happy. "I take it the saints are losing out to the sinners?"

Birdwell slammed his fist down on the counter. "We ain't licked yet, Clay! There's more folks in this town who want law and order than you'd think."

Hill shook his head gloomily and took a drink from his glass. He was finely tuned to the politics of the whole state, and the others were disturbed by his fatalistic attitude. "We're going to lose," he said quietly. "Poole has spent a bundle on this race, and by election time he'll have every no-good and deadbeat in the county so filled up with promises and booze that we won't have a show. Lots of good folks will just stay home—and those are the only ones who could put you in office, Sam."

Sky sat by the window sipping his coffee, not taking part in the talk. He still felt like an outsider; while he trusted the men in the small circle, the larger aspects of government left him cold. After a while he'd had enough and got up to go. "Got to get home."

"That fellow O'Malley still roosting at your place?" Henry Sellers asked.

"Sure."

"Tell him he can come by and sign the papers on that mill any time." Sellers paused and added, "They've been ready for a week. I'm surprised he's not been by to close out."

Sky shrugged, "Oh, Jim's that way. I'll tell him what you said, Henry."

He left the store and, throwing the sack of supplies behind his saddle, rode slowly out of town. Passing by the Silver Moon, he had an impulse to go inside and see Rita, but turned away from the thought at once. *Just what I need—for someone to tell Rebekah I've been going by to see her.* He could not shake off the gloom that had plagued him for the last week. *Life used to be a lot more simple,* he thought, spurring his horse down the streets onto the main road that led north. On his return journey to his ranch, he thought of his carefree days in the mountains with a mixture of regret and longing.

When he got close to the house, he caught the sound of a rifle and froze in his saddle, pulling his mount up. He quickened his pace, for there were still a few Indians roaming the foothills who had been known to attack lone settlers. *Although,* he conceded with a grin as he urged his horse down the muddy road, *it'd be a sad Injun who tried to move in on James O'Malley!*

O'Malley had risen early that morning and gone squirrel hunting with Joe. They returned at eleven, and Joe had rushed into the house, holding up a sack and shouting, "Look at this! Jim shot them right through the head—and I got two myself—not in the head, though!"

Rebekah looked at the furry bodies that Joe began pulling out of the sack, and smiled at his excitement. "Better take them outside, Joe, and I'll clean them for supper."

"Why, I expect Joe will want to do that little chore for you, won't you, boy? We do the killing and cleaning, and your ma does the cooking." O'Malley let his large hand fall on Joe's shoulder and gave him a warm smile.

"Sure, Jim," Joe said instantly. He whipped out his pocketknife and dashed out, crying, "I'll have these varmints ready 'fore you know it."

Rebekah smiled at O'Malley. "He'd stick his head in the fire if you told him to, Jim. For a bachelor, you have a real way with boys."

"Guess I'm still about his age on the inside, Rebekah." He leaned over and picked up a dry cloth from the counter and wiped her cheek. "You've got some flour there."

"Oh, I'm making an apple pie—your favorite." She had no idea how fresh and pretty she looked. The morning sun caught her hair, the rich auburn shade redder than usual. Her cheeks were glowing from the heat of the stove, and the shapeless brown work dress could not conceal her womanly figure.

"Wish you always looked as happy as you do right now, Becky."

She looked up in surprise, and saw that he was studying her intently. His sleepy gray eyes were now sharp under his bushy eyebrows, and she thought again what a handsome man he was.

But his statement brought a flush to her cheeks, for she was sure that he was commenting on the strange life she and Sky led.

"Don't worry about me, Jim," she replied quickly. "I'm not unhappy."

There was a gentle rebuke in his answer. "Reckon I've got eyes, Becky." She dropped her head suddenly, unable to meet his gaze; and he reached out and put his finger under her chin, forcing her to lift her head. "Your eyes are like windows—clear as light, Becky—and when I look at you, it grieves me to see you sorrow."

He was a big man, and she felt very small as she stood there looking up at him. "Jim, don't—don't pity me," she whispered. She retreated a few steps backward. As his hands fell to his sides, she saw that her own were trembling. Holding them together to conceal her weakness, she said, "Sky and I made a bargain. He's kept his end of it, and I'll do the same."

O'Malley shook his head, stating flatly, "You're not a house-keeper, Becky. You're a beautiful, desirable woman, and for that to be wasted—why, it's a sin!"

He took a step toward her, but she stopped him. "No, Jim. I'm Sky Winslow's wife." Her lips trembled, but she spoke firmly. "You're a good man, Jim. Go find yourself a wife and forget about me." He started to argue, but she interrupted him. "If you want to do something for me, teach me to shoot a rifle."

"*Teach you to shoot?*" The corners of O'Malley's eyes crinkled with concern. "Sky never taught you?"

"No. And there've been a few times when I've wished I knew how, Jim. Once a wolf came after a calf when Sky was gone."

"Come right with me, young woman," Jim grinned. She followed him outside, and he called out, "I'm going to the clearing to give your ma some shootin' lessons, Joe. You stay clear."

For the next half hour the two of them stood beside a large stump, and he showed her how to prime and load the rifle. Placing a can on another stump fifty feet away, he showed her how to hold the rifle. It was too heavy for her, but she closed her eyes and pulled the trigger. "Did I hit it?" she asked hopefully, rubbing her shoulder.

"No—but if it'd been a varmint, you'd have given him a scare," O'Malley said cheerfully. He loaded up again, and showed her how to take a rest on the fork of a convenient sapling. "Now, try to keep your eyes open this time, Becky," he admonished; and when she fired, he cried, "Didn't miss it by more than a couple of inches!"

"This is fun, Jim!" she exclaimed. "Let me load this time."

Once his pupil had gotten down the basics of loading and shooting, O'Malley began showing her some of the finer points. "You're pulling to the right, Becky," he told her. "Most folks do that at first. Let me show you how to cure that." He handed her the rifle and said, "Take a bead on that can, but don't fire."

She put the rifle in the fork of the tree, as he had shown her, and peered down the length of the barrel. He came to stand behind her and put his left arm around her, his hand on hers to steady the rifle. Reaching around to put his hand on her right, he said, "Now, this time, aim at that can, dead center—but don't *pull* at the trigger. *Squeeze* it, real slow."

His voice was in her ear; locked in with his arms around her, she could not concentrate on the target. Although she tried to keep her eye on the can, the muzzle of the rifle began to wander. He laughed softly and held her a little more firmly, whispering, "Steady, Becky. Remember—don't *jerk* the trigger, just *squeeze* it, real easy—"

"A little shootin' lesson, Jim?"

Rebekah pulled free and looked around to see that Sky had approached and was regarding them soberly. "Oh, Sky," she said quickly, "Jim was just showing me how to shoot."

"So I see." The words were even, but his voice was flat. "You should have told me if you wanted to learn how to handle a rifle, Rebekah."

"I—I didn't want to bother you."

"She's got a pretty good eye," O'Malley said, his gray eyes fixed on Sky. "Thought it might be a good idea, Becky learning to shoot. Never can tell when she might need to let off a shot."

Sky's nod was almost imperceptible. "Maybe so, Jim," he said, walking away.

O'Malley watched him walk back toward the house and said regretfully, "Sky's a little jealous, Becky."

"No! It's not that, Jim," she assured him, knowing that such words were useless; he knew Sky too well to be fooled. She handed Jim the rifle. "I'd better go get supper started."

That night Sky had little to say, except to relate the news from Oregon City in as few words as possible. After supper he picked up the Winslow journal and read while O'Malley entertained Joe with tall tales of the mountains. When Rebekah finished cleaning up, she said, "Joe, we need to work on your geography tonight."

Joe scowled rebelliously. "Aw, I don't need to know that stuff! I know the woods around here like the back of my hand. I ain't never gonna go to China—so why do I need to know where it's at? It's dumb!"

Sky looked up from his book, frowning. "Boy, you do what Rebekah tells you or I'll cut a piece out of your hide, you hear me?"

Joe glared at Rebekah sullenly, then went to get the book. When he sat down at the table, rebellion was written in every line of his thin young body. Rebekah began going over the lesson, but he stubbornly refused to answer when she asked him questions. O'Malley watched the scene without comment. The dissatisfaction on the boy's face, he thought, was a mirror of Sky's, and Rebekah's valiant efforts to engage Joe's attention soon flagged in the face of his stubborn refusal to answer.

"Now, Joe, we went over all this yesterday," Rebekah sighed tiredly. "Don't you remember *anything* about where the first people from England settled in this country?"

Joe did not even bother to shake his head, and Jim suddenly had an idea. "Hey, Sky, this is something you could help with. Didn't some of your ancestors come over on the *Mayflower*?"

"Two of them did—Edward and Gilbert."

Jim waited for him to continue, and when he saw that was all Sky intended to say, he urged more strongly. "Well, come on! I reckon most of my ancestors came over on a cattle boat, but if one of those Pilgrim gents was *my* relation, I'd be shoutin' it all over the place! Come on, Sky, give Joe a hand here about those days."

Sky had been fuming ever since he had found O'Malley teaching Rebekah how to shoot, though he had tried to convince himself he was overreacting again. He envied the way Jim could bring Rebekah to life—and the fact that Joe had followed the man around constantly ever since their visitor arrived. O'Malley was able to do the things Sky wanted to do, and felt that he could not; this was the final straw. "I'm not the schoolteacher around here!" Sky snapped. "That's what I brought Rebekah here for."

As soon as he said it, he could have bitten his tongue off, and he saw that his reply hurt Rebekah and even shocked Joe. Sky got up, tossed the book on the table, and left the house without another word.

"Gosh!" Joe said uncertainly, "what's he so mad about?"

"He's probably worried about the way things are going in town, Joe," Jim replied quickly. "Look, I need to brush up on some of this stuff myself. Would it bother you if I sort of sat in for this lesson, Pardner?"

"Gee, no!" Joe would have enjoyed anything that involved him with O'Malley, and soon the three of them plunged into the lesson. Joe discovered that Rebekah had been to the very spot where the Pilgrims had landed, and asked, "Does Pa know you've been there?"

"No. He's never asked," she answered quietly.

When the lesson was over, Rebekah sent Joe to bed. Timmy began to cry, so she went into the bedroom to get him and he quieted at once. She carried him into the living room and began to rock the little boy as O'Malley sipped a cup of coffee. "He has bad dreams sometimes."

"So do I, Becky," he said softly. "Mostly I dream about how I'll wind up an old man, all alone and old, with nothing done and nobody to care whether I live or die."

"I doubt you'll come to that. You'll marry and have a dozen red-headed Irish kids," she laughed.

He started to speak, but seemed to change his mind; his thoughts set his eyes close together in a sleepy look. Getting up, he said, "I'm going into town for a couple of days. When I come back, Becky, I'll be a respectable citizen—not a roughneck mountain man."

"You'll do well at whatever you take on, Jim," she told him. "Look how you managed Joe! He'll do anything for you. Will you come back and see us sometime?"

"Yes—I'll do that, Becky." He rose and climbed to the loft, and the next morning he was gone before she got up.

When she asked Sky the next morning why his friend had left so abruptly, Winslow said, "Jim's like that. Gets a notion and cuts loose." He meant to apologize for the way he'd snapped at her, but she seemed preoccupied, so he said instead, "I'm going over to Little River and see if I can locate some beaver. May stay a couple of days if it looks good."

"Will you take Joe?"

"No. He needs to study." Again the words were on the tip of his tongue, but he could not bring himself to say them. Gathering his traps, Sky pulled out, saying, "Tell Joe I'll take him next time if he studies hard."

"All right, Sky."

She watched him through the window as he rode off into the timberline. As she went about her work that day, a spirit of gloom pulled at her. Joe got up, and was angry when he discovered that he had been left behind. "I'm sick of those old books, Rebekah!"

"Your father wants you to learn, Joe."

"It ain't been no fun around here since you come!" he said spitefully. "I don't see why Pa ever married you!"

He whirled and ran out the door, and she did not have the heart to call out for him to stop. He went to the barn, threw a saddle on his horse, and galloped out in the same direction Sky had gone.

Mary was awakened by the slamming door, and Timmy came crawling out, fussing. It was a relief to have something to do, for Joe's behavior had been a climax to the fears that had kept her awake most of the night. Her mind was a blank as she fed the children, for she had gone over and over the problem until there was nothing left to consider.

She had asked herself a thousand times, *Why did I marry him?* And time after time she had offered Timmy and Mary as her reason. But now that both Sky and Joe were gone, she admitted out loud the reason that had been deeply buried in her heart.

"I thought I could make him love me."

Now it was out; turning her back to Timmy so he could not see, she allowed the tears that she had choked back so many times to flow freely. But the release did nothing to lighten her heart; the prospect of the string of loveless years ahead oppressed her, and there was a heaviness in her spirit that would not go away.

She spent the day playing with the children and asking herself, *What will I do when he comes back?* She had failed with Joe just as much as she had failed with his father, and now there was nothing to look forward to but a dreary existence in a house filled with anger and bitterness.

The day wore on past noon, and the shadows of the tallest firs were beginning to shade the kitchen windows when she heard the sow give a piercing squeal. She had asked Sky to let her raise some pigs, and he had built a stout pen and bought a sow that had been bred. The piglets had been born two weeks earlier, and she had delighted in the antics of the pink-nosed porkers. Maybelle, the sow, was fiercely protective of her brood, and Rebekah's first thought was that one of the dogs had gotten into the pen and was after the small pigs.

Opening the door, she ran toward the pen, which was fifty yards from the house in a grove of oak saplings. "You dogs get away from—!"

Her words were cut off like a knife, for as she moved closer, a massive form reared upright beside the pen, and she saw the huge hump and fierce beady eyes of an enormous grizzly. For one second she stood paralyzed; then the bear gave a hoarse *whuff!* and dropped to all fours, lumbering in her direction. She whirled and raced across the yard, breathing a prayer. She dashed inside the house, slamming the door and dropping the sturdy oak bar just as the weight of the bear crashed against it.

She picked up the baby and soothed Timmy, who was wailing. She held her breath, but there was no other attempt on the door, and soon she heard his claws scratch on the small porch as he moved away. She put the baby down and leaped up to the window in time to see the animal loping back toward the pigpen.

She tried to still her racing heart as she heard the sow squeal. The pen was built to hold a large sow, but the powerful grizzly would crumble it like a toothpick with a single swipe of its paw. She had heard Sky and Jim tell about the almost unbelievable strength of the animals, and she knew that the pigs were doomed.

Her eyes fell on the rifle that was over the fireplace, and she ran to get it down. It was a much heavier weapon than the one she'd used the day before, but it was of the same type. She carried the weapon over to the shelf where Sky kept his powder and balls, and awkwardly loaded it. She had no idea how much powder the large rifle required, but poured a steady stream down the muzzle, put a patch in with the rod, then one of the balls, then another patch. With trembling hands she added the flint and moved back to the window just as the squeals of the big pig were cut short. The grizzly had got the mother sow.

She prayed that the beast would carry his prey into the woods, but when she opened the window she could hear the animal grunting as he ate. *He'll go away when he's finished*, she thought. She put the gun down and went to comfort Timmy, who was still sniffling. He held on to her, then was reassured and went toddling off to the bedroom. Rebekah was about to pick Mary up when she heard the faint sound of a horse approaching.

Throwing the door open, she saw Joe riding into the yard. *He'll go to the barn!* she realized with horror, and she ran out into the yard, crying as loudly as she could: "Joe! Joe! Don't go to the barn!"

Her cries frightened his horse, which shied away from her, almost throwing Joe out of the saddle. He lost one rein and was struggling to keep his seat, for the horse had scented the grizzly and was out of control, kicking and whinnying wildly.

Out of the corner of her eye, Rebekah saw something move. *Oh no!* The grizzly loped into the clearing and headed straight for the horse. "Joe!" she screamed as she whirled and dashed into the house. She snatched the rifle up and bolted outside, holding the weapon awkwardly. Joe had seen the bear, but he clung to the back of the horse, trying to get control.

The bear picked up speed, covering the ground faster than a horse. He plunged straight at the horse, reared up, and lifting one huge paw, struck the animal alongside the head, sending Joe catapulting to the ground. The blow drove the animal's head to one side and raked bloody furrows through the hide. The grizzly roared, striking the horse again and again on the head and neck, and the animal fell heavily to one side, blood streaming from a dozen deep wounds.

Joe was scrambling to get away when the horse crashed on top of him, pinning his legs. He smelled the rank odor of the bear and saw the bloody claws rip and tear at the dying animal. He could have reached out and touched the huge head as the bear opened his jaws and tore out the throat of the horse in one bite.

Joe lay there with his eyes frozen on the bear, which had straightened up, licking his bloody chops. As the animal moved his head, the beady eyes fixed on him! Joe screamed with fear, and the noise seemed to confuse the grizzly; for he suddenly reared up again, bobbing his head from side to side.

Still clutching the loaded rifle, Rebekah began to walk toward the fallen horse. Joe saw her and cried, "Look out!" struggling wildly to free his legs.

Got to get so close I can't miss, Rebekah thought, praying with every step, *Oh, God, save Joe!* Her approach caught the attention of the grizzly, and he moved in a circle, coming at last to face the woman. His eyes were red, the bloodlust strong, but she did not think of danger. All the world seemed shut off—except the monstrous form of the bear now shuffling toward her.

The animal was so large that he cut off the light from the sky, dark and strong and rank, as he loomed over her. She lifted the rifle as he reared, paused for one brief second, then pulled the trigger. The explosion of the rifle was deafening, and the recoil of the weapon so powerful that it drove her backward. She dropped the gun as she fell, and saw that the bear had fallen to the ground as well. Struggling to her feet, she could see the bear's mighty limbs twitching feebly, but the entire front of his face had been blown away.

She staggered over to Joe, and he reached out to her as she fell beside him. "Ma!" he cried, tears running down his ashen cheeks. He held to her so tightly that she could not get her breath. Over and over he cried, "Ma! Ma!" His body was racked with sobs, his tears mingling with hers. The pressure of his thin arms around her and hearing the name he had called her made Rebekah hold him even more fiercely until finally his sobbing ceased.

When he was quieter she said, "See if you can get your legs out while I push." With a mighty effort he yanked free and scrambled to his feet, then wiped the tears from his face with his sleeve and stared at the dead grizzly. He reached out and touched her arm hesitantly, and when she looked at him, she saw a look of wonder in his eyes.

"Ma—you done it! He would have killed me for sure! And if you'd missed—he'd have killed you, too!" Then he looked again at the huge animal. "Bet not many women would stand up to a grizzly like that! Most women would have been too scared to come outside—and you let him walk right up to you!"

Rebekah was weak from the ordeal, but she managed a smile and put her arm around Joe's thin shoulders. "God was with us, wasn't He, Son?"

The boy felt the warmth of her arm on his shoulders and awkwardly put his arm around her waist, hugging her. "Sure was," he nodded, and said again loudly, "He sure was, Ma!"

CHAPTER TWENTY-TWO

A DEAD WOMAN'S HAND

★ ★ ★ ★

" . . . an' then that big ol' grizzly reared up, Pa, and he was so big I couldn't even see Ma—but she let fly with that rifle gun and just plain ol' blew that bear's head off!"

Sky leaned over and set another three-foot-thick section of the oak tree on end, thinking: *Now he calls her his ma like he's been doing it all his life.* He lifted the splitting maul and struck; the two sections fell as splinterless as a cloven rock. Joe scooted forward and pulled one section upright, and Sky said, "Guess she saved your bacon, Son."

Joe's dark eyes glowed, and he nodded vigorously. "You're mighty right, she did!" With that, he launched into yet another detailed account of the adventure with the bear, lauding Rebekah to the skies.

Sky had heard the story at least ten times since he had ridden in that morning, but he let the boy speak, glad that the wall he had raised against Rebekah had at last been broken down. He had ridden in to find Joe trying to skin the bear, and making a pretty bad mess of the job. Seeing his father, Joe had run to him, telling the tale so excitedly that at first Sky could not understand what had happened. "*What* happened, Rebekah?" he had asked.

"Oh, the bear came for the pigs, and I shot it," she had answered.

"Aw, c'mon, Ma!" Joe had cried, "let *me* tell about it!" Sky had immediately noticed the word that now came so easily to the boy's lips. *Ma.* By the time Sky had the story straight, he saw that Rebekah had earned a place in the boy's heart.

He and Joe worked all morning, dragging the dead horse to a gully to be burned, skinning and dressing the bear, repairing the pigpen, and searching for the piglets that had escaped. Carrying one of the little pigs back, Sky found Rebekah standing by the pen, looking down at the two they had already located. "Sorry about Maybelle, Rebekah," he said, putting the squealing pig into the pen. "I'll get you another one from Taylor."

"All right."

Sky noticed her lack of enthusiasm and tried to cheer her up. "You did fine—killing that bear. Joe thinks you're just about the best thing going." She shrugged and walked away from the pen. Her attitude was beginning to frustrate Winslow. He knew that his remark to O'Malley had hurt Rebekah, and he wanted more than ever to make it up to her. With a sigh, he ran to catch up with her and fell into step as she was nearing the house.

Carefully he tested out the waters. "I'm grateful to you, Rebekah. You saved Joe's life."

"Anyone would have done it."

"No, that's not right. You did a very brave thing." He took her arm, and she turned to face him—reluctantly, he thought. "You risked your life for Joe. It would have been hard for an experienced hunter to walk up to a grizzly like that—and for a woman who's not had much experience with a gun, why, it's—"

"I'd rather not talk about it, Sky." She pulled away from him, saying, "I'd better get to work."

Helplessly he watched her go into the house, shutting the door behind her. Winslow slapped his hands together in an angry gesture. *Why is it I can never say the right thing to her?* he asked himself, turning to go back to find Joe. *She's changed, I reckon— or maybe it's me that's done the changing.*

All day as he worked around the place, the sense of frustration grew, and Joe's enthusiasm only aggravated him. At supper he ate silently, listening as Joe kept up a running conversation with Rebekah. Afterward, when the two put their heads together over a book, he felt left out, so Sky played with Timmy until the little fellow grew sleepy. Putting the boy down, he picked Mary up and rocked her, admiring the creamy complexion and bright eyes. Finally she grew fussy, and Rebekah rose from the table and came over to him. "I'll take her now."

"I don't mind keepin' her while you two study," he said.

"We're finished—and she's hungry."

"Guess I can't help with that," he said, handing her over. Soon Timmy went to bed, and the house was quiet, so he took up the book Rebekah had given him at Christmas. He had already read *The Journal of Gilbert Winslow* through several times, and had found the account fascinating, but a restlessness filled him and caused his attention to wander. Letting the book fall on his lap, Sky glanced over to where Joe was working torturously at his lesson. On the other side of the room, Rebekah nursed the baby, and he wondered how the scene would appear to a stranger who knew nothing of their situation or the tension that existed between them. *Guess we'd look pretty good*, he thought ruefully. *Man and his wife. Children all healthy and happy. Plenty to eat. It would all look almost perfect, I guess, to most folks.*

Rebekah lifted her eyes from the baby and looked across the room at him. Caught off guard staring at her, he flushed and got up. "Guess I better go check the pigpen—see if it'll keep those little fellows up tight," he said. He waited for Joe to ask to go with him, which was his custom, but the boy was scribbling furiously on his tablet, so Sky left the house.

The air was crisp, and overhead the stars glittered coldly in the sky. The pigs began squealing as he came close, and he murmured, "Reckon you miss your mama, don't you?" He leaned over and rubbed their wet snouts as they nudged each other to get at him, nibbling at his fingers hungrily. His thoughts went over the past months, but there was no pleasure in thinking of such things, so he straightened abruptly and moved away from the pigpen, walking across to the path that led through the woods. The tall firs shut off the starlight, but he groped his way through the woods to the small stream that surrounded the house like the crook of an elbow, and came at last to the deep pool where he and Joe had often come to catch the thumping red-ear sun perch that nested underneath a huge fallen log.

Sitting down on the log, he listened to the night sounds and smelled the odors of the woods that crowded in on the house. The peaceful quality of the woods relieved the strife that marked his life in the busy world, and for nearly an hour he absently toyed with a stick, keeping his mind away from the problems that awaited him at home.

Later, he rose and tossed the stick into the stream, watching as something nudged at it—a big bass, he thought, or a snapping turtle. He wrenched his mind away from the peace of the woods to thoughts of Rebekah and their future. He was reminded of a passage from *The Journal of Gilbert Winslow* which he had read so often that he could remember it almost word-for-word. The brief passage had been written by Gilbert Winslow concerning his bride, Humility, shortly after their marriage at Plymouth:

> It is late, and Humility is abed as I write this. We have been man and wife three months tomorrow. After so short a time, we should be blissfully happy, but my heart is grieved tonight, for at supper we quarreled—our first quarrel since we married. It was a little thing (if any quarrel between two who love can be little!) and I spoke to her harshly. Her sweet face, so joyful these last months, grew pale, and her lips trembled. She said naught, but rose and left the table, and went to bed soon after.
>
> Now I sit here, the biggest fool in Plymouth! With a wife fit to stand beside any man, I let my accursed tongue say words that cut and burned! For two hours I have tried to find the courage to tell her what a fool I was—but cannot do it. I can face death in a duel or in battle, but I cannot bring myself to say the simple words—*I am sorry!*
>
> By heaven, I will do it yet, though the words choke me! Shall I be cut off from all that is sweet in this world to me because of my pride? Like the prodigal son, "I will arise and go!"

Sky thought of the next line with a smile. The brief note was poignant; from it he had learned that Gilbert Winslow was a lover as well as a fighter:

> It is early morning. I have swallowed my pride—and my Humility received me with open arms—quite *literally!* We are newly married, praise the Lord!

Why should I be cut off from all that is sweet in this world because of my pride? Winslow rose and walked back down the path determined to speak to Rebekah, to tell her he'd been a pig-headed fool. Just how he would manage to say it was beyond him, but the thought of the sweetness he'd known in her on the trail was strong. *I'll just say it right out! It won't kill me to say I've been wrong.*

But he got no chance to make the speech that night, for when he entered the house, he found that she had gone to bed. Joe looked up from the table, yawning. "Ma said she was a little tired." He got up, stretched and said, "You 'bout ready for bed, Pa?"

"Sure."

The two of them went upstairs, and after they were in bed, Sky said, "I was glad to hear you call Rebekah your ma, Joe. It's what I wanted for you to have."

Joe's voice was a little awkward as he replied, "Aw, she's sure something, Pa, ain't she?"

"Sure is."

There was a moment of silence.

"Pa?"

"Yes, Joe?"

"You reckon—?"

When the boy broke off, Sky rolled over and looked across the room. The moon had come out and he could see Joe's face faintly. "Do I reckon what?" he prodded gently.

"Do you reckon you'll ever—ever love her? I mean, like a *real* husband?"

Sky lay there, knowing what the boy was asking. After a long silence, he said quietly, "I reckon you'd like that, wouldn't you, Joe?"

"Sure would!"

"Well—I guess I would, too," Sky admitted. Neither of them spoke again, but a determination formed in Winslow's mind.

Maybe she won't want me as a "real" husband—but I'm blamed well going to give it a try!

In the morning he rose and went downstairs determined to speak with Rebekah alone, but his plans were spoiled at breakfast when a cloudburst produced a heavy rain that did not let up until nearly ten. Joe sat down to read a book, while Timmy followed Sky all over the house, clamoring for attention, and Mary cried incessantly, cutting a new tooth. Seeing that there was not likely to be any privacy for a while, Sky left to do the chores.

When he came back at noon, Joe asked, "Pa, can I go squirrel hunting after we eat?"

"I guess so," Sky nodded as they sat down to the dinner of bear steak. Joe bolted his food, then grabbed his rifle and disappeared into the woods. After dinner Sky pushed back his chair, saying, "Bear steak's not as good as buff'lo, but it's nice for a change."

"It's too strong for me," Rebekah said. She started clearing the table, but Mary began to cry.

"I'll do this," Sky offered, picking up his plate. "You see if you can get Mary to sleep."

She looked at him in surprise. "That would be a help."

As she rocked the baby, Sky washed the dishes, noting that the stepping stool that Rebekah used in the kitchen was broken, tilted on three legs against the wall. *Guess I have time to fix it for her 'fore the kids fall down,* he thought. *Maybe that'll sweeten her up a little.*

Hoisting the broken stool, Sky went outside, calling over his shoulder, "Be right back, Rebekah." Moving to the barn, Winslow settled at his workbench and began to hammer busily, so intent on his work and the thought of what he would say to Rebekah when he got back that he did not hear the sound of O'Malley's horse approaching.

Pulling up to the house, O'Malley dismounted, tied his horse to the rail, and stepped up on the porch.

Rebekah had put Timmy and Mary down for their naps and opened a window to let in the rain-washed breeze. Hearing his knock, she ran to the door and opened it. "Why, hello, Jim. Come on in. Sky should be back in a minute."

"Hello, Rebekah. Actually, it was you I've come to see." He took off his rain-soaked hat and coat and went to stand in front of the fireplace, making small talk. "Sure was a toad-strangler of a rain, wasn't she now?"

"Yes," Rebekah agreed, then paused. "Did you say you wanted to tell me something?"

O'Malley took a deep breath, brought his hands out and lifted them in a plaintive gesture. "Becky, I know how unhappy you are. It ain't no secret—everybody who knows you talks about it." He lifted his hand as she tried to speak. "Wait now, let me have my say—then you can answer me."

"Becky, you wasn't meant to be a servant. You're a healthy

young woman, pretty enough for any man—and straight enough to do them proud. Sky done wrong to bring you here—and you done wrong to agree to it."

"I needed a home for my children," Rebekah whispered. His charge had stirred her guilt, for she had been telling herself for days the same thing O'Malley said. She *had* been wrong to marry Sky!

"That ain't good enough, Becky, and I think you know it."

Just then Sky returned from the barn, repaired bench in hand, and overheard O'Malley's next words through the open window.

"I've got my own mill now, and can take care of you and the kids. This mountain man is ready to settle down." He paused and took her hand. "Becky, I want you to marry me."

Outside, Sky could barely contain himself, but somehow he managed to hold himself in check long enough to hear her answer. Inside, Rebekah withdrew her hand and stammered in confusion. "B-but, Jim! I *am* married!"

"I've been talking to the judge and to a lawyer," O'Malley said evenly, his eyes steady on hers. "They say that since your marriage ain't never been a *real* marriage—ain't never been what they call *consummated*—why, you won't even have to have a divorce. It can be annulled. Be just like it never took place."

With a roar, Winslow crashed open the door, took two steps forward, grasped O'Malley's arm, and threw him toward the door. Jim, who had not expected the attack, nearly fell down, but caught himself in time. *"I ought to shoot you!"* Sky bellowed. "What kind of a man are you, O'Malley? Coming into my house and talking like that to *my wife!*"

"Sky," Jim said, his huge shoulders tense as he faced the smaller man, "Becky *ain't* your wife!" He raised his voice and asked, "Can you tell me you've been a *husband* to her?"

"That's none of your affair!"

"Sky, if you loved her—if you was a real husband to her—I'd kill any man that tried to come between you two. But this is different." He turned to Rebekah, who looked as white as a sheet and had backed up against the wall closest to the bedroom. "Rebekah, I'm telling you that I'll make a good home for you and your kids. I've never seen a woman I admired more than you—

and if you'll marry me, I've got my mind set to be a *real* husband. Don't aim to brag, but most men who know me would tell you that when I set out to do a thing, it gets done! I'll love you and take care of you—*and you'll be more than just a servant*—"

His words were cut off by Sky's fist. The blow caught him in the mouth, driving him backward. He bounced off the wall and raised his hands to catch Sky, who attacked him with a fury Rebekah had not seen since the days of the wagon train when Sky had confronted Tom Lake. She knew the man was capable of this kind of battle, but had never actually seen him fight. She stood by helplessly as Sky rocked O'Malley's head with a series of blows so rapidly that he could not defend himself at first. Then with a muffled roar, he shoved Sky backward, shouting, "Wait a minute—!"

But Winslow was in a red battle rage and came roaring back, striking Jim in the stomach with a terrific blow that brought a gust from the big man's lips and drove him to a sitting position. Winslow dove at him, and in an instant the two were rolling across the floor, locked in a fierce embrace. At first O'Malley tried simply pinning Sky's arms to stop the fuselage of blows that rained on his face, but failed, so he threw one arm around Winslow's neck. Holding him there, O'Malley struck him in the temple.

The blow sent red spots to Sky's eyes, but it had no other effect on him except to enrage him further. With a mighty wrench, he tore free from O'Malley's grip and tried to get to his feet, but Jim caught him in the chest with a numbing right hand, and he fell over backward. Instantly O'Malley was on him; it was like being grabbed by a grizzly, and only when Sky landed a series of blows against O'Malley's throat did the grip loosen enough for Winslow to slip free.

Both men were now totally unaware of Rebekah, who was crying out for them to stop as the furniture was splintered by their violent thrashing. O'Malley was easily the stronger of the two, but Winslow's slashing blows were like lightning, and both men's faces were marked and bloody as they careened into the wall and fell to the floor, striking and kicking wildly.

Rebekah tried to pull them apart, but she was like a feather in a whirlwind until her eyes fell on a bucket filled with the dirty water she'd used for scrubbing the floor. She ran and picked it up, then carefully brought it to where the two men were rolling on the floor. Sky was on top, but as she approached, Jim threw him to one side, so that for one moment they lay side by side. She dumped the contents of the bucket right in their faces.

Immediately both men fell away from each other, sputtering and coughing, for the dirty water had caught them with their mouths open. Sky struggled to his feet, and O'Malley rolled over on his face, gagging horribly.

"Get out of here!" Rebekah cried. Sky coughed and wiped his eyes, which were burning from the lye soap. To his amazement, he saw that she was weeping. "I hate you both! I won't be fought for like—like. . . !" She whirled and ran to the wall. Pulling down the rifle, she pointed it wildly in their direction.

Jim had struggled to his feet by that time and now found himself looking down the barrel of the weapon. "Now, hold on, Becky—!"

"Get out! Get out!" she shrieked.

Sky lurched backward, yelling, "Rebekah—you're going to kill somebody with that thing!"

"I wish it had two barrels so I could shoot you both!" She pulled the hammer back, and both men backed out the door as fast as they could go. "If you're going to act like dogs—I'll treat you like dogs!" she shouted after them.

Once they were outside the door, she hurled Jim's hat and coat out after them, slamming the door with all her might. She dropped the gun, which went off, sending the ball through the window and bringing a yell from O'Malley.

"Now see what you've done!" Sky yelled at O'Malley.

"I ain't sorry, not a bit, Sky," he retorted, glaring angrily. Blood streamed down his face from a cut eyebrow. "She's going to have to get away from you sooner or later—and I don't aim to let her be without a place to go."

Winslow glared back at the other man, his own face beginning to ache from the pounding it had taken. Whipping out his handkerchief, he wiped the blood from his mouth. His hand, he noticed, was trembling; he held it out and studied it. "Look at that! A Crow war party couldn't have made me shake like that! And you've done it with your foolishness."

"It wasn't *my* foolishness." O'Malley took a deep breath, and the anger was replaced with sadness. "You were wrong to make a slave out of that girl. You're wrong to try to keep her from having a real home. You're just downright wrong."

Sky had heard enough. "Get out of here, Jim."

"I'm going," O'Malley said quietly. "But this ain't over. Becky's heard the truth, Sky, and she ain't gonna go on being no servant." He tugged at an ear thoughtfully. "Sky, whatever in this blue-eyed world made you even *think* you could use a fine young woman like you been doing? I always thought you had a headful of sense . . ." He retrieved his hat and coat, then turned and said quietly as he left, "But I don't think so no more!"

As O'Malley rode out of the yard, Sky drew a bucket of water from the well and, pulling his handkerchief from his pocket, began to wash the blood from his face. His knuckles were raw and it hurt to breathe. O'Malley's blows had been devastating, and now the pain began to come in waves. He made a fist, grimaced at the raw knuckles, then moved back to the house. The door, he discovered, was bolted, and he walked to the edge of the porch and slumped down.

He was still there an hour later when Joe came back from hunting.

"*Pa!* What happened?"

Sky looked up with one eye closed and the other one half shut. He was trying to think of a way to tell Joe about the fight when the door behind him opened. He turned to see Rebekah come outside wearing her heavy coat. Her hazel eyes were cold as she announced, "I'm going to town. Joe, will you hitch up the light wagon for me?"

Joe stared at her, then at Sky's battered face. "What's the matter, Ma?"

"I'm taking Timmy and Mary and going to town, Joe."

His mouth fell open. "You mean—for good?"

Rebekah saw the stricken look on his face and put a hand on his shoulder. "I'm sorry, Joe. It's a shame I have to leave just when you and I have learned to like each other. But your father and I have decided that we can't live together."

Sky started to argue, but the look on her face stopped him. He clamped his lips together. "I'll get the wagon."

While Sky hitched up the team, Rebekah tried to make Joe understand, well knowing that it was an impossible task. "But, Ma, you *can't* go away now!" he wailed. "You're married to Pa!"

"It just didn't work out, Joe. Grown-ups do stupid things sometimes—and our getting married was one of them."

"But—what'll you do?"

"Don't worry about me, Joe," she said, managing a weak smile. "I'll be all right. And remember this—I'll always love you, no matter what!"

Sky drove the team up and got down. "I guess you'll want your things."

"Yes."

The three of them moved to the house. When the wagon was loaded Rebekah went in and came out with Mary in her arms. "Will you please get Timmy for me?" she asked Sky quietly.

Sky went inside, picked up the boy and put his coat on. Timmy laughed, thinking it was a game. The sound brought a lump to Winslow's throat, and it went down hard when he handed the boy to his mother.

"I know you don't want me along," he said evenly. Turning to his son, he added, "Joe, drive them to town. But wait . . ." Going into the house, he came back out with a pouch of coins and handed it to Rebekah. "This is for your hotel. Joe, you stay in town with Sam and Edith tonight. Now, I want a word with Rebekah. Go get your heavy coat."

As soon as Joe left, he said, "You don't have to go, Rebekah. I know you won't believe this—"

"Sky," she interrupted, "it's over. It's my fault as much as yours—or maybe more." Her voice was low and weary. "I know it was just a bargain—but I dreamed that we'd find more than that." Her voice was intense, her eyes angry. "But you'll never love anyone again, will you, Sky—?"

"Rebekah. . . !"

"You're too filled with bitterness and hatred for Irene," Rebekah went on relentlessly. "You're bound by a dead woman, Sky. She's been in her grave for years—*but you'll go to your grave hating her.*"

Joe came out and, glancing at them both nervously, got in the wagon. "Don't come after me," Rebekah warned, climbing in as well. "There's nothing left for us. Drive on, Joe!"

Sky Winslow stood there, helplessly watching the wagon until it disappeared around the bend of the road, his eyes vacant and his mouth tense. His shoulders slumped, and he sat down hard on the steps of the porch and stared at the ground. He had been in tight spots many times, but now there was an emptiness inside that sickened him. He was beginning to get cold outside, and he was still wet from the soaking, so he got up and started into the house, then stopped. Thinking with dread of the silent rooms inside, he turned and walked rapidly away into the woods, his head down, his shoulders stooped over like an old man.

CHAPTER TWENTY-THREE

SHOOTOUT AT THE SILVER MOON

★ ★ ★ ★

Joe returned the following day at noon. Sky helped him un-hitch the team, waiting until they got inside the house to ask, "They get in the hotel all right?"

Joe shook his head, and there was an air of stubbornness in the set of his shoulders as he answered, "No. Sam and Edith took 'em in." For the next three days, Joe talked to Sky only when he was forced to, and then only with monosyllables. He did his work, but went off into the woods hunting every afternoon. At night after supper, he would climb to the loft, leaving Sky alone.

Once Sky tried to explain the thing, but even as he spoke, he saw Joe's eyes harden. *Can't blame him much,* he thought sourly. *I don't admire myself—so why should I expect Joe to understand?*

The house went to seed quickly without Rebekah's touch, and after the good food that she had served, neither of them had much appetite for the hasty meals they put together. Sky encouraged Joe to keep on with his studies—but that was a failure as well. Worst of all was the wall that Rebekah's leaving had created between him and his son. *Got to get away from here,* he told himself. *He'll never get over his feelings as long as we stay here.*

By the third day he had made up his mind to sell out—as he had once intended—and go north. He had it in his mind to tell

Joe at noon that they'd be leaving, but while they were eating, they heard a wagon approach. Getting up and looking out the window, Joe said, "It's Edith and Miss Karen."

Thinking they'd come on some sort of mercy mission, Sky frowned and got to his feet as the women came in, prepared to cut the visit short. One look at Edith's pale and swollen face, however, and he realized that there was another, more terrible reason for their visit. "What's wrong?" he asked urgently.

Edith spoke in a tightly controlled voice. "It's Tom Lake. He's dead."

Shocked, Sky stared at her, his eyes narrowing. "Sit down, Edith."

"No, I've got to get back to Sam."

"What happened?"

Though Edith's voice was even, he saw that she was near the end of her endurance. "The election was yesterday. Sam won somehow. Nobody expected it, but the farmers and church folks worked night and day, and Sam and Tom won." She paused, and her voice grew hard. "I was afraid, because I knew that Poole and Ingerson wouldn't let it go at that—and they didn't!"

"Who shot him, Edith?" Sky asked quietly. He thought of the gentle man who had been such a friend to him, and knew he could not let it go, either. The anger that filled him was not a blind rage, but a calculated and icy feeling; he swore to himself that as long as he could walk he'd go after the men responsible.

"Oh, it wasn't Poole or Ingerson," Edith replied wearily. "They're too clever for that. It was one of the new men they've been hiring—name's Roy Hart."

"Heard of him," Sky said. "Got a reputation in Seattle as a gunman."

"He came up to Tom in the street this morning and there was an argument. He claims Tom drew on him, but that's a *lie*! Can you imagine Tom Lake using a gun on anybody?"

"No, I can't." He thought for a long moment. "I reckon Sam's got the idea he'll have to arrest this Hart?"

Edith nodded, unable to speak, and Karen spoke up nervously, "He's made Dave sheriff, and the two of them are going to go arrest the man."

"Just what Poole and Ingerson would like them to do," Sky murmured softly.

"I've tried to talk Sam out of it," Edith said desperately, "but he's got this thing about honor. Says he's got to do it for the good of the town."

"Dave is the same way, Sky," Karen nodded. "They've tried to get support from the townsfolk, but everybody is scared. They're afraid to face that gunman—and now Ingerson's hired some more men besides Hart—all of them practically criminals!"

"When are they going to make this arrest?"

"They were trying to get some help when we left, Sky. I got Sam to promise me he'd wait until I got back. Sky, he's going to get killed if you don't do something!"

Karen and Edith were both looking at him with a desperate intensity, and Joe put their thoughts into words. "Pa, you're not gonna let Sam fight them all alone, are you?"

Sky turned and met Joe's gaze. "I'll have to go in and lend a hand, Joe. But I don't want you anywhere near when we go to arrest them."

"Sky!" Edith breathed, and a faint color came into her face, "I came to ask you to help—but it's a lot to ask."

Sky shrugged. "Sam Birdwell's been a good friend, Edith." He looked at Karen and said with feeling, "And Dave, too." Then his face darkened with sobering thoughts. "You take care of Joe," he told the two women. "I'm going to ride in quick as I can."

"Pa, let me go with you!"

Sky looked down at Joe thoughtfully. "All right, Son—but you'll have to stay clear of the action. Go saddle your horse."

"We'll start back now," Edith said, and turned to go, but he stopped her with a word.

"Got one thing you can help me with." He went to the cluttered desk, found a sheet of paper and scribbled a few lines. Holding it up, he said, "Like to have both of you witness this."

Edith came closer and looked at the paper, then up at Sky with a startled expression. "Why, it's a will!"

"Never know about a thing like this," Sky commented. "It leaves this place and everything I've got to Rebekah. Guess she'd get it anyway, but sign this and I'll give it to Clay Hill."

"All right, Sky," Edith replied, and the two women signed

the paper. As Sky put it in his pocket, Edith warned, "Be careful, Sky, and—God be with you!"

They hurried out, and Sky strode over to the walnut cabinet where he kept his guns. He ignored the rifles and the shotgun, but laid out all the revolvers he owned. He chose two worn .44's, and after carefully loading them, put them in a belt with double holsters. He'd always despised two-gun men, but now he buckled the weapons on, then pulled his hat from the peg and left the house.

A short, stocky puncher came through the double doors of the Silver Moon. Hurrying down the long room, he pulled up and said excitedly, "I just seen that Winslow feller, Mr. Poole. He come in and went down to Lawyer Hill's office."

Poole said swiftly, "Get back there and keep an eye on him, Fred. I want to know what he's up to."

As the man wheeled and left the saloon, Dandy said, "You don't have to wonder about what Winslow's going to do, Poole." He took a drink from the glass in front of him and added, "He'll come along with Birdwell and Lloyd to arrest Roy."

Roy Hart was a slender man, with long yellow hair that fell to his shoulders and a pair of muddy brown eyes. He was something of a dandy, judging by the way he dressed, but the frilly shirt and fancy vest did not conceal the hard edge of his character. He wore two guns strapped to his thighs, and even as he spoke his hands caressed the butts of the weapons.

"This Winslow," he remarked carelessly, "he's supposed to be some sort of gunfighter?"

Ingerson's huge bulk filled the chair he sat in, and his heavy shoulders leaned forward for emphasis. "Don't make any mistake about this fellow, Roy. He went up against Del Laughton— and beat him. And you know Del."

"He let Laughton go for his iron first," Dandy put in. "Let Del get his guns clear—then draw and put him down."

"I haven't seen a draw that fast since Speedy Langsdell was around," Poole commented, and his brow clouded. "This thing is mighty tricky—on the razor's edge, I tell you! We got a lot of support in town right now, *but if we don't play our hands right, we're all finished.*" He studied the slender gunman carefully. "Roy, I think you'll hang if they ever take you. The townspeople are pretty scared right now; but if Birdwell can get you locked up, it'll put some steel in their backbones. I'll be finished here—but you'll be stretching a rope."

Poole's words did not seem to worry Hart. Pulling one of his guns from the holster, he spun the cylinder and purred, "Guess I can take Winslow out." There was a deadly quality in the man that seemed to satisfy Poole.

"All right. I figure they'll be coming here as soon as they get all the help they can. They'll come through the front door, so you stay right at this table, Roy—make them come to you. Ingerson, you be at the bar close to the door. Let them walk by you so that you're behind them—that way they'll be in a crossfire."

"We got to get Birdwell!" Ingerson grunted. "He ain't gonna quit as long as he's alive, Poole."

"That's right," the ex-mayor said. "But if we can wipe him out, we can call for another election—and I'll be in office until that happens."

"And I guess there won't be too many candidates for mayor after the town sees what happened to Birdwell, right, Poole?" Dandy sneered. "I'll get my rifle and get on the landing." He waved at the long landing that ran overhead on one side of the saloon leading to the rooms where the girls lived. "I'll cut down anybody *you* miss, Roy."

"That's it, then," Poole said, rising to his feet. "If I had my way, I'd be here for this thing—but I've got to stay clear of it. You boys understand."

"Sure," Dandy smirked. "Take a little vacation, Matthew. I figure in an hour or so, you'll be the official mayor of Oregon City." With a crooked grin, he watched Poole leave. "He'll take care of number one, Roy—you can bet on that." Taking another drink, he said, "Don't think we'll have too much trouble. These townsmen are sheep. I figure Birdwell won't be able to deputize more than three or four, if that."

Clay Hill was passing along the same thought to Sky inside his crowded office. Sky had come in unexpectedly and tossed an envelope on the lawyer's desk, saying, "Here's my will, Clay, and that deed you worked up for me. Change the name on it to Rebekah Winslow."

"What's this, Sky?" Hill asked in bewilderment. "She's your wife, so she would get the place if anything happened to you."

"I want it to be hers free and clear. I'm leaving the country, but I want her to have the place. And here's a check—see to it that she and the kids get what they need. Make that legal, Clay, and hurry."

"All right, Sky. It won't take much doing." He sat down and quickly made a few notations, then said, "Sign right here." As soon as Sky had signed the paper, Hill asked, "You're pulling out, Sky?" His thin face was etched with disappointment. "Didn't figure on that. You know about Lake?"

"Edith came out and told me."

"You going to give Sam a hand?" Clay asked hopefully.

"You don't even have to ask—do you, Clay?"

Hill's face brightened, and he clapped his friend on the shoulder. "'Course not! What am I thinking of, asking you a fool question like that?" Then he frowned doubtfully. "It's going to be close, Sky. No volunteers rushing to join up. They're afraid of Roy Hart. All of 'em."

"Can't blame them much," Sky shrugged, then lowered his voice. "We've got to keep Sam out of this thing, Clay. He's never even fired a pistol, far as I know."

"Maybe not—but there's no chance of keeping him out of it." Hill bit his lip, adding, "I've tried to get him to wait until we can get a federal marshal here to arrest Hart—but he says it's now or never. And I reckon he's right, Sky. If we don't take care of Tom Lake's murder, we'll never have anybody willing to go up against Poole and Ingerson."

"I know that, but what good will Lake's death do if Sam gets killed as well? The whole thing's on his shoulders, Clay." He paused and asked, "Is he down at the sheriff's office?"

"Yeah, hoping for some volunteers—which he won't get."

"Here's what we'll do—I'll send him over to see you on some excuse, and while he's here, we'll arrest Hart."

Hill listened carefully and a grin touched his lips. "He'll never forgive us if we do that, Sky."

"He'll be alive, though," Sky answered dryly, standing up to go. "I've got one little errand, Clay. You go on and I'll be with you in fifteen minutes."

He walked out of the office, then swung into the saddle. "Are you going to arrest that gunfighter now, Pa?" Joe asked. His face was pale as he scrambled into the saddle and turned his horse to follow Sky.

"Joe, I want you to promise me something." Sky twisted in his saddle to look at the boy, ignoring his question. "I've been through some pretty tight scrapes in my day. A few times I was sure I'd lose my scalp. This is one of those times, Son—it's going to be pretty tough. That's why it would please me if you'd make me one promise."

Joe's throat thickened with fear, and he had to wait until it cleared before he said, "What—what is it?"

"Son, I married Rebekah so that you'd have a mother. She's a fine woman. I reckon you know that, don't you?"

"Sure, Pa!"

Sky dropped his gaze and was silent as they made their way down the street. They passed several citizens who gave Sky a startled glance, then scurried off quickly. One burly miner said audibly, "Wal, so Winslow's come to town! That oughta make this here thing more even!"

Sky didn't seem to hear the man; looking again at his son, he said, "I've made a heap of mistakes in my day, Joe. But the way I've treated Rebekah—that's the worst of them all. She's true grain, Son—and I made a servant out of her."

"Aw, Pa, she won't hold it against you!"

"This is hard, Joe, but one day you'll learn that some mistakes don't wash out." A hard line creased Sky's lips, and regret made his voice tight and low. "It's too late for Rebekah and me to get back together. I'm pulling out of here if I make it through alive."

"Where we going, Pa?"

"That's what I want you to promise," Winslow replied. "I want you to say that you'll stay here with Rebekah and the kids. They'll need some help—and you're gonna have to grow up in a hurry." He hesitated, then said, "I expect Jim will marry Rebekah—and if he does, there's no man alive I'd trust to be a dad to you more than Jim O'Malley."

"Pa—!"

"I'm asking you to do this thing, Son," Sky said quietly. "You've got to have a home—and I've proven I can't give you one." Sadly, he looked away, for he saw the tears glistening on the boy's cheek and could not bear to see him cry. They rode along until they came to the Birdwell house, where Sky dismounted and waited until Joe did likewise. "It'd make me feel real good, Joe, if you'd give me your word on this."

Joe wiped the tears from his face, and said with a timid but solemn voice, "I—I promise, Pa—if that's what you want."

At that, Sky reached out and pulled the boy close. He had not been demonstrative toward his son, but now held him tightly, feeling the thin body shake with sobs. *Should have done this a long time ago! Would've been much easier!* he thought uneasily.

O'Malley had been visiting Rebekah at Edith's when he saw two horses coming down the street. "Rebekah, here come Sky and Joe. I reckoned he'd come when he found out about Tom."

Rebekah stared at him, her face pale. "He'll be in the fight, won't he, Jim?"

"You know Sky, Becky." The burly hunter shrugged with a worried look on his dark face. "The word is that Poole and Ingerson got a small army over at the Silver Moon. It'd take maybe ten good men to put up a scrap with them—and from what I hear, this fancy gunfighter has scared off most folks."

"We've got to do what Clay says—wait for the marshal to come!"

"Never knew a single soul who had any success in making Sky Winslow wait for anything, Becky. He's fool stubborn when he gets his mind set."

A knock punctuated his words, and Rebekah opened the door. "Come in, Sky . . ." she said, taking in the two guns strapped in his holster. Jim was right—nothing she could say would change what he was about to do.

"Jim, I need a word alone with Rebekah if you don't mind."

"Sure. Be waiting outside."

Sky waited until O'Malley stepped out; then he turned to her, his eyes intense. "Rebekah, I wish things were different between us—but words don't change things."

"Sometimes they do," she argued.

His face was stretched taut, his features emotionless. The high cheekbones and the faint coppery tint of his complexion revealed the blood of his Sioux mother plainly as he stood before her.

"I've got a little chore to take care of," he said evenly, "And then I'm riding out."

"Where are you going, Sky?" Rebekah asked.

He shrugged. "Haven't thought much about it—but what I *have* thought about is you and the kids. I've asked Joe to stick around for a while—and he's agreed. Now I'd like a promise from you."

"What—what is it, Sky?"

The only sign of his tension was the fact that his hands were clenched tightly at his sides. "Take care of Joe."

She saw that he was counting himself a dead man, and she could not speak from the fear that rose to her throat. She nodded silently, and reached out to hug the boy as Joe turned his face away, trying to hide his tears. "Yes, Sky. I'll do that."

Winslow relaxed visibly. "That's it, I guess." As he turned to go, he halted. "See Clay Hill today. He's got something for you."

He hesitated, looked fondly at his son and quickly pulled him into one last bear hug. Feeling the thin arms around his neck, once more he wished he'd been able to do this earlier. Winslow looked over Joe's head at his wife and said, "Rebekah—for all I've done to you—I'm truly sorry."

Then with a sudden move, he pulled Joe's arms from around his neck and passed out of the room before she could speak. The scene had paralyzed her, robbing her of words, as the impact of what Sky had said hit her full force. She looked at Joe, who ran to her and buried his face in her shoulder. Holding him, she realized for the first time the real reason Sky was doing this foolhardy thing. Breaking away from Joe, she ran to the door.

"Sky!" she cried out, but he and Jim had mounted their horses and were already well on their way to the center of town. She heard Joe come up beside her and told him, "Joe—watch out for Timmy and Mary!" Then she grabbed a coat and began walking rapidly toward the cluster of buildings that marked Main.

Sky and O'Malley spurred their mounts to a run, and it was

not until they dismounted in front of the low building with the SHERIFF'S OFFICE sign that Sky asked, "You sure you want in on this thing, Jim?"

"Always liked to tree coons, Sky," O'Malley shrugged. "This here sounds like quite a coon hunt."

"Likely to be more coons than hunters this time," Sky remarked. Then he stopped with his hand on the door. "I'm pulling out of here when this thing is over, Jim." He hesitated, searching for the right words. "You were right about Rebekah, Jim. I was dead wrong. I hope that whatever happens, you'll take care of her."

"Sky—!" O'Malley protested with a startled look on his face, but Winslow set his jaw stubbornly. He opened the door and found a small group of men standing in the center of the room.

"Sky!" Sam Birdwell's face brightened, and he looked relieved. "You come to join the party?"

Sky saw Dave Lloyd to Sam's left, and to his surprise Al Riker and his son Pete stood over to Birdwell's right. "Glad to see you, Winslow," Al said, coming to shake his hand. "Don't mind tellin' you, I feel a lot better with you in this thing."

"This is Omar Skates, Sky. He's a good man." Dave motioned to the final member of the group, a hard-faced man who nodded curtly toward Sky. "You in on this, too, O'Malley?"

"Always wanted to be a lawman," Jim commented with a sly look in his eye.

"I'll deputize you then," Dave decided, drawing some badges out of a drawer. Handing them to Sky and Jim, he said, "It's official; now you're both deputies."

"How we going to do this, Sheriff?" Pete Riker asked. He held up his steel hook, saying, "If Tom Lake hadn't been there to cut my arm off, I figure I'da been dead on the trail. But I got one good arm, and I don't aim to let Poole and his crowd by with it. Somebody's going to go down for Tom!"

Sky said quickly, "Before we get started, Clay wants to see you at his office, Sam."

Birdwell frowned. "It can wait."

"No, he's got some sort of idea that may help us," Sky insisted. "Clay's pretty sharp, Sam. Go check it out while Dave gives us some idea of the plan."

"Well—all right. Be back as soon as I can."

He hurried out of the office, and as soon as the door closed, Sky said, "Dave, me and Clay set this up. Sam has no business in this thing."

Dave Lloyd looked mildly surprised, but agreed. "I tried to tell him that, but he wouldn't listen." He shifted his weight nervously. "This is new to me, Sky. You got any ideas?"

"Just one—every mob has a key, Dave. Get him, and the rest will fold."

"And you figure Hart's the key?"

"Sure." Sky looked around at the small group and said, "They're primed and ready to blast away. We've got to do something to get them rattled."

"Bet you've already got that little item in your conk, ain't you, Sky?" O'Malley grinned and slapped his thigh. "Reminds me of the time over in the Teton foothills at Horse Creek. Remember when that Flathead war party got us pinned down in that canyon?"

Sky smiled, and the heaviness that had been in his face lightened. "Shore, Hoss! We were gone coons that time. But I figure we can lessen the odds a mite." He nodded at Dave and instructed, "You four walk right down the middle of Main so that Ingerson's bunch gets advance notice you're coming. They'll be waiting inside the Silver Moon; and I figure they'll have men planted, so when you walk in don't stay in a bunch. Move around until you're scattered. Dave, you're not much of a talker—but this time, you'll have to be."

Lloyd looked curious. "I'll talk my head off, Sky—but what's going to even things up?"

"You just keep talkin', Dave, and Jim and me will find some way to get them rattled." He took a deep breath and let it out in a big sigh. "It's not going to get any easier, so let's get 'er done!" He took off his heavy coat and touched the butts of his weapons. O'Malley grinned as if the whole thing pleased him. "Let's see the way she goes."

"We'll go the back way, Dave," Sky directed. "You keep talkin' your head off—but don't pull a gun until you hear from Jim and me."

"All right," Dave murmured. His face was a little pale, but he replied strongly, "Let's do it."

As the four men passed out into the street, Sky said, "My guess is that Ingerson's got a man watching pretty close. Let's see if we can sneak up on these birds, Jim." He went out the back door into the alley, which was deserted.

Clouds covered the sun, and as they made their way down the long alley, Sky was thinking hard. As they came to Elm, he said, "If they spot us crossing, we're goners, Jim." He peered out cautiously, and saw only an old woman with a cane making her way painfully along, her back to them. "All right," he murmured, and the two of them dashed down Elm, turned the corner and whipped into the alley backing the line of saloons on Main. There they saw only one man, a drunk who was just getting to his feet after a rough night. He took one look at the two of them and ran clumsily away, disappearing around a corner.

"This is it," Sky said, stopping to look up at the three-story frame building. He put his hand on the knob. "You ready?"

"Let 'er flicker," O'Malley answered, his eyes alive with the sense of danger.

Sky tried the door, found it open, and stepped quickly inside. O'Malley followed him into a store room dimly lit by the light that filtered through the single window. The sound of voices drifted through as Sky moved carefully across the floor and turned the knob on the door very slowly. He cracked the door and heard Dave's voice.

" . . . violated the law, and you've got to give him up."

Ingerson's voice followed, and Sky held his breath and pushed the door half open. The door opened directly into the saloon, and he saw at once that the tension was high, ready to break.

Dave had advanced halfway to where Rolfe Ingerson and a slender man sat at the rear of the room. Al Riker and Pete had moved to the outer edges of the room, and the man called Omar was just behind Dave, his eyes fixed on the two men. One glance and Sky realized that the four men were surrounded by several roughs he knew to be in Ingerson's pay, including Jack Stedman.

"You got the wrong man, Lloyd," Ingerson was saying. "It was a fair fight. Lake drew on Roy here, and we ain't lettin' you take him." Then he said roughly, "Where's the mayor? I thought he was going to be in on this arrest." He got to his feet, and Hart stood up as well. "You're here to make trouble, Lloyd, and I don't aim to stand for it."

Sky knew that it was some sort of a signal, for out of the corner of his eye he saw Stedman and another one of Poole's men drop their hands to their guns, ready to draw.

He shoved the door open, letting it swing wide; and as it banged against the wall, Ingerson and Hart jumped and wheeled to face Sky. "You're not going to stand for it, Rolfe?" Sky said loudly. "Well, maybe you better sit for it then—watch your hand!" Ingerson's hand had dropped to his gun, and Sky's words froze the action.

Ingerson looked around, catching Hart's signal, then moved to his right. "That badge means nothing here, Winslow," he taunted. He looked around the room and added, "You're not taking Hart in."

"So this is Winslow, the gunfighter." Hart laughed and stepped forward, his thin lips twisted in a parody of a smile. "Heard about you—but I think I heard lies."

It was clear to Sky that they were ready to open up, and he said quickly, "Jim, bring that Greener in here."

"I'm all dressed up for the party, Mom," O'Malley replied cheerfully. He stepped past Sky and laid the muzzle of the shotgun on the six Poole men who stood at the bar. "Just think," O'Malley mused, "all I have to do is touch this trigger—and the undertaker will sell six nice new coffins!"

Jim's threat knocked them out of the action, Sky saw. They stared at the blunt muzzle of the shotgun, and knew that if for any reason O'Malley pulled the trigger, they'd be blown to bits by the weapon.

"Easy with that thing," one of them pleaded.

Dave and Omar wheeled to their right, not having to fear the men frozen out by O'Malley, and Dave called, "Al—Pete!" And the Rikers moved to stand beside them.

Jack Stedman and the other four men who were along that wall found the odds had changed. Omar Skates had a shotgun, and the muzzle of it was weaving back and forth, lined up on the five men against the wall. "Rolfe—!" Stedman choked. "They got us boxed!"

"We just want Hart, Ingerson," Sky said in a reasonable tone. "No sense dying for *him*, is there?"

Ingerson glanced around and saw that his plan had failed. "You better go along with them, Roy," he told him. "We'll take care of you."

The words struck Hart like a whip, and he cast a hateful glare at Ingerson's bulky form. "You'll take *care* of me? *You'll let them hang me, Ingerson!*" Then he cried, "Winslow!" His voice was high pitched and desperate as his hands darted for his guns.

Sky saw at once that the man was a much faster draw than Del Laughton had been—a draw he could never beat. Desperately he threw himself backward, pulling his guns as he hit the floor.

Hart had not counted on Winslow's fall, and his bullets went high. He never got a chance to fire again, for Sky got one gun free and sent a bullet that caught Hart in the chest, knocking him down. He rolled over once, gave a gurgling cry, and was still.

Ingerson had pulled his own gun and got off one shot that caught Sky in the thigh. In response, O'Malley's shotgun roared, and the charge of it caught Ingerson in the chest. He was driven backward as if struck by a mighty fist, and ended up in a ball on the floor, lifeless.

"Hold it! Hold it!" Dave Lloyd shouted. He had drawn his own gun, as had the Rikers, and the five men along the wall threw up their hands at once. "We're out of it, Lloyd!" Jack Stedman shouted. The men at the bar put their hands up as well, for the deadly muzzle of O'Malley's shotgun had swung in their direction.

"Sky! You all right?" Dave called out.

"Okay, Dave." Sky struggled to his feet and looked down at the blood on his thigh. "Got me in the leg." He glanced at the two dead men, then said wearily, "I guess we got off pretty cheap at that."

"Better get that slug out, Sky," Dave suggested. "Jim, you take him down to Doc Ellington's while we put this scum in the jail."

"Better go tell him to come here," Jim suggested, looking at the wound.

"No, I'll make it." Winslow's pride was stronger than his sense, and he limped toward the door. The leg was numb, but the pain would come soon, he well knew.

He was almost to the door when there was a scuffling noise over his head, and he heard a woman's scream. He turned to see Rita struggling with Dandy Raimez on the landing. He had a rifle in his hands, and Rita grasped it with both hands, crying out, "Sky—look out!"

He whirled and the sudden action made his wounded leg collapse. He fell, and as he struggled to his knees, he saw Raimez knock Rita aside with one blow of his fist, then swing the rifle toward him. Sky tried to draw his gun, but the explosion of the rifle and the blow in his chest came at the same time.

So this is what it's like to die! he thought. Just as he was swallowed up by the vast, empty pool of darkness, he heard one last explosion—and then, nothing at all.

CHAPTER TWENTY-FOUR

PILLAR OF FIRE

★ ★ ★ ★

Sometimes a light would penetrate the darkness of the depths, and he would try to go deeper, but always there was a voice, a familiar voice, but one he could not identify, and it would plead with him to come back and face the light. Over and over this voice continued to call, pulling him out of a cool, comfortable place into a world of noise and pain, and he would mutter and twist, trying to slip back into the tarry darkness.

Time was nothing. Seconds and years were all the same, but he measured only those times that the voice and hands pulled him toward the light. Visions drifted by with terrifying reality, and more than once he found himself crying out as the past rose up and filled his mind—a faceless, mindless specter that tore at him with white hot talons. At those times the voice would be there, soft and gentle, and the hands that touched him—holding him as he fought to dispel the visions—were as gentle and firm as the voice.

Sometimes, though, the voice was different, and the hands as well. One voice came from far away, far back in time, and he felt comfortable when that happened. The other voice was no less gentle, but it frightened him, and he would shrink back from the hands that went with it.

He awakened suddenly while the first voice was speaking to

him. Coming out of the deep pit of blackness with a rush of consciousness, he opened his eyes to see a woman's face bending over him.

The room swam, and he quickly closed his eyes again. The faint movement must have caught the attention of the woman who was doing something to his chest. "Sky? Are you awake?"

He opened his eyes, squinting painfully against the brilliant sunshine that filtered through a window to his left. He tried to say something, but his lips were parched.

"Here—drink some water."

A strong hand lifted his head, and he gulped thirstily at the cool water. Lying back, he whispered, "Missy? Is it you?"

"Well, praise be to God and the Lamb forever!" Missy lifted her hands into the air as she spoke, her eyes wet with tears. She put her hand on his forehead, saying, "Like Lazarus back from the dead! How do you feel?"

He tried to sit up and was amazed to discover he couldn't. "What's the matter with me, Missy?"

"Well, you were shot twice—and caught a bad case of pneumonia that would have killed most men," Missy said as she caressed his forehead. "But your fever's broken at last. You're going to be all right—though you've caused Chris and me a sight of prayer!"

"Help me sit up." He struggled and, with her help, got into a sitting position with a pillow wedging him upright. The room tilted crazily, and he shut his eyes until it stopped rolling. When he opened them, he looked around the room, then back at her. "I remember that Dandy Raimez shot me from the balcony."

"He's dead, Sky," Missy informed him. "Jim O'Malley shot him."

"How long have I been here?" He felt a pressure on his chest and touched the thick bandages. "How bad was I hit?"

"The bullet was angling down, Sky," Missy explained. "It hit you in the chest and ran into some ribs. Broke several of them, but they saved your life. Dr. Ellington says if the ribs hadn't deflected the bullet, it would have gone right to your heart." Missy looked intently at him, saying, "God saved you, Sky."

"Guess so," he replied weakly, adding with a slight smile, "Reckon Jim O'Malley had a little to do with it."

"God uses what He can get," Missy replied firmly.

"Maybe so. Can I have another drink, Missy?" He took the glass, holding it with both hands, and drank all of it.

"Now," she said, taking the glass from him, "how about something to eat? I'm tired of wrestling broth down your throat, so if you can sit up, you can feed yourself." With that she got up and left the room. After she had gone, he looked around, trying to get back into the present. When she came back and put the soup bowl into his hands, she said, "I'll go get Chris, Sky. He's sat beside you so much he's just about worn himself out." She smiled. "Lots of people have been doing that, Son. You've got many friends here. This is Mike Stevens' house. He insisted that Chris and I use it as long as you need help."

She rose to go, and he asked quickly, "Missy, did you take care of me all the time?"

She stopped short. "I had some help from time to time. Why?"

"Oh, nothing. I was just dreaming, I reckon." He began to eat the broth, and she left the room. The first bite awakened his hunger, and then he could not spoon the hot soup down fast enough. When he was finished, however, he was so sleepy that he could hardly sit up. He managed to put the bowl on the table, then slumped back in the bed and fell fast asleep.

He was awakened some time later by the touch of a hand on his arm. "Sky? You all right?"

He opened his eyes and struggled to sit up. "Sure, Pa. I'm fine." He looked up at his father, adding, "But you look terrible!"

The craggy face of Christmas Winslow, though worn and pale with fatigue, was reamed with a smile and a glad light in his eyes as he protested, "Blast you, boy! We come all the way to the coast to see you, and you pull a stunt like this! Ought to bust your britches."

"Wouldn't be too hard to do right now, Pa," Sky mused, holding up a hand that trembled slightly. "Got no more strength than a newborn calf."

They were interrupted by Missy, who announced, "Have another visitor for you." Before she could say any more, Joe rushed in and ran to the bed.

"Pa, you gonna be all right?" he asked anxiously.

Sky put his arms out, and the boy immediately hugged his dad. "I don't look like much, Joe, but I'm gonna make it."

Joe stepped back, the past forgotten for the moment, and said accusingly, "You never told me all the things Grandpa did! Why didn't you ever tell me about how he raided a Pawnee camp to get you and your mother away? And you never told me about how he hung at the pole—!"

"Whoa up, boy," Chris laughed. He put his heavy arm on the boy's shoulder and winked at Sky. "Reckon I can embroider my own tales—but this here is my idea of what a grandson ought to be. He's already agreed to come for a visit with his grandparents—if it's okay with you, Son."

"We'll talk about that later!" Missy interrupted. "Now you two get out of here and let me get some more food into this poor boy. Why, he's nothing but skin and bones!" She shooed Chris and Joe out of the room, then came back with another bowl of soup. "Eat this, Sky. When you've finished, you get right back to sleep. For a few days, I'm your ma again, just like when you had chicken pox!"

Sky smiled, and ate the broth. Settling back into bed, he asked drowsily, "How's Sam doing? What happened to Poole?"

"Don't you fret about that, Sky," she replied firmly. "You'll have plenty of time to catch up on politics when you get better." She peered at him, satisfied that he was already asleep before she turned and left the room. Chris was seated at the kitchen table with Joe, and she said, "I'm going to tell Rebekah that he's awake."

She put on a light coat and walked out of the yard toward the Birdwells'. The last of winter was gone, and in a few more days it would be April. The relief over Sky's dramatic improvement put a joy in her heart, and as she passed under a plum tree with a small bird perched in the top branches, singing his heart out, she smiled. "I'd sing like that, too, if I had a voice." Instead, she settled for a silent prayer of thanksgiving that lasted all the way to the Birdwells', where Edith met her at the door.

"Come in, Mrs. Winslow," she said eagerly. "Is Sky better?"

"Yes, praise the Lord!" Missy smiled. "He woke up a little while ago, and the fever's gone. The doctor will be checking in on him, but I'll have to tell him plainly that it was the Almighty God who did the healing!"

"Oh, I've got to tell Sam!" Edith cried. "He's been going crazy, worrying over Sky!" She yanked a coat from a rack and ran out the door, calling as she went, "Rebekah's in the kitchen!"

Missy went through the parlor and walked into the large kitchen, where Rebekah was stirring something in a pot at the stove. Rebekah heard her come in and turned to see who it was. When she saw Missy, she panicked and dropped the spoon. "Missy! Is he—?"

"He's fine!" Missy replied with a broad smile, and when Rebekah turned back to the stove abruptly to hide her face, Missy understood and went to put an arm around her. "It's all right, Rebekah—God has spared him."

"I've been so afraid. . . !" Missy held the girl close until Rebekah drew back and began to dab at her eyes. "Thanks for coming to tell me," she said. "I'll bet Joe is hopping for joy."

"He is," Missy beamed. "Maybe you'd like to go over and see Sky, Rebekah?"

"Oh no! I don't think I ought to."

There was something fearful in Rebekah's face, which puzzled Missy. "Why—it would be good for him, Rebekah," she insisted. "You've done as much of the nursing as I have."

"I know—but he didn't know I was there." Rebekah clasped her hands and walked over to the window. "He doesn't want to see me, anyway. We've done nothing but hurt each other since the day we got married."

"Come and sit down, Rebekah. I want you to tell me everything—all about yourself and your marriage."

"You've heard most of it, I expect!" There was a defiant look in Rebekah's eye, and she colored slightly. "Our grapevine works pretty well here in Oregon City."

"Rebekah," Missy reproved sternly, "I don't give a sow's ear for that sort of talk. But I've been talking to Rev. Penny, and he tells me you're a Christian. Is that right?"

"Yes. I was saved at a meeting in New York, but—"

"Come and sit down, then, and begin as far back as you want." Missy led her to the parlor, and after they were both seated she said, "God is going to do a work in my son's life, Rebekah. Now, you tell me all about yourself—then we'll know how to pray for you *both*."

Her gentle words and kind face put Rebekah at ease immediately, and soon she found that it was not difficult to share her life with Sky's mother. She began with her family history; then as Missy listened quietly, Rebekah told her something that she had never revealed to anyone else—how she had been betrayed by Tyler Marlowe.

By the time she was finished, the shadows were growing long, and both women were misty-eyed. "Sky was so good to the children—to Mary and Timmy," Rebekah whispered. "Just like they were his own. But he's got such a bitterness for his first wife. . . !"

"I know," Missy responded gently, "and that's what we've got to pray about—that he'll be able to forgive Irene. Do you believe God can change him?"

Rebekah nodded slowly. "For a while I thought that Sky *had* started to change—" She broke off, thinking that she should not bring up the Jim O'Malley incident now. "But it didn't last. Oh, Missy, I've been so alone! I guess I've just stopped believing in anything!"

"Then *start!*" Missy fell on her knees and began to cry out to God, and soon both women were engaged in such fervent prayer that they did not hear Edith come in. Seeing them there, Edith, too, began praying for the man who'd saved her husband's life.

———

Missy allowed no visitors the next day, but within three days Sky's room was filled with a constant swarm of company.

Jim O'Malley took up his station in a straight chair across from Sky's bed, and laughed when Sky marveled at the number of people who came by. "Why, it's the fate of a hero, Sky. You'll run for office now for sure. Little fracas like you had, why, it ought to be enough to get you elected to Congress, at least!"

"I'd settle for a pair of pants and a chance to get out of this place, Jim," Sky complained. "I appreciate folks being so nice, but to tell the truth, I'm feeling sort of hemmed in. Why don't you get my clothes, and we can hightail it out of here?"

O'Malley grinned and shook his head. "You think I'm here because I like your company? Nope! Your ma made me promise to keep you in that bed. So, don't even *think* about leaving until she says it's all right."

"Don't know what I'd do without a good friend like you, Jim," Winslow grumbled. "First you come and steal my wife—now you nominate yourself as chief guard to keep me from getting away."

"Oh, I'll give you your britches—soon as Missy tells me it's all right. For now just lie back and enjoy it."

Sky shook his head. "You got the bulge on me now, O'Malley," he replied stubbornly. "But in a week, I'm headed for the mountains—if I have to shoot you in the foot to do it. Got a yen to see Yellowstone country again—maybe get a few beaver."

"I don't think so, Sky," O'Malley commented. "They're all gone. It was good while it lasted, but a man's got to know when to make a change. That's why I come out of the mountains to the coast."

"Maybe I'll go to Canada," Sky said dreamily.

"Why go anywhere, Sky?" O'Malley asked, his dark eyes fixed on Sky's. "This is new country here. Biggest track of forest on the continent. There ain't nothing better over the hill."

Sky didn't answer. O'Malley stared at him keenly, then went back to reading a book on sawmill operation. When Penny came into the room, Jim was more than happy to be relieved of his guard duty—besides, he was hungry.

"Boy, you look strong enough to chop wood," Penny teased. "How much longer you gonna stay in that bed?"

Sky looked at the muscular preacher. "Lot, you want to help me?"

Lot smiled warily. "I want to help you find God, Sky—but I been warned by your ma that Oregon won't hold me if I let you outta this room." He laughed at Sky's crestfallen expression and sat down. "Doc tells me you'll be up and about in a couple of days, anyway—so just enjoy it."

"Not much fun staring at the ceiling, Lot—thinking of all the mistakes I've made."

"We all got our pasts to live with, boy," Penny said quietly. "But God's got a short memory for some things. He can't remember nothin' that's under the blood!"

"You really believe that, don't you, Lot? My folks do, too." A pensive look crossed Winslow's face. "Wonder why some fellows have so much trouble thinkin' that way? I've heard about Jesus most of my life—and I don't doubt a word of the Bible—but it's never helped me. I've done nothing right since—"

Penny was listening intently. "Since you married a woman who let you down—is that what you were fixing to say?"

Sky grunted with irritation. "Everybody knows my business, it seems. Don't you folks have anything better to do than sit around and discuss *my* problems?" Then he caught a glimpse of Penny's face and regretted his words. "Sorry, Lot. Guess I'm just touchy these days."

"It's all right, Sky," Penny replied soberly. "But what you don't see is that you've got the whole world right in the middle of your hand—and you're too stubborn to take it!"

Sky shook his head. "It's not that easy, Lot. I've got hard feelings toward Irene—and they've been with me so long, I can't just cut them out and throw them away." Penny didn't say anything, so Sky added angrily, "Don't you think I'd like to?"

"Hatred gets to be sort of a pleasure after we let it live in us for a spell," Lot commented. "Don't know why that is—but it's so. My daddy was a hard man—a no-good man, everybody said. Many a time he beat me so bad I couldn't walk. When I left home, I had two dollars and a heart full of hate. Took me twenty years to get rid of it—but when it was gone, it was like coming out of a deep cave into the sunlight!"

Sky studied the man's honest face, then asked quietly, "How'd you do it, Lot?"

"I stopped looking at my pa and started looking at *me*." Penny's smile was crooked as he added, "When I saw some of the sorry things I'd done, why, Pa's orneriness didn't seem near so bad!" Penny got up to leave. "I been talking to your dad a lot. Don't know as I ever met a man I took to any more. He's been telling me all about the Winslows. Seems like most of 'em had a real struggle getting God in their lives. But they all made it—so I'm bettin' that you'll make it too, Sky."

Soon after the preacher had gone, Missy came by and brought Sky a snack, then left him reading Winslow's journal.

He waited until the house was still. When he knew it was safe, he got up and moved gingerly to the hall. For a couple of days Sky had practiced walking, and now felt much stronger than he'd thought possible. Carefully, he pulled his clothing from pegs in the hall where he'd seen Missy hang them, and dressed in the darkness. He left the house, making no more noise than a Sioux on the prowl, and went to the barn, which was fifty yards behind the house. His horse nickered when he entered, but he calmed it by speaking quietly, and with some effort he saddled the animal. It was a struggle to pull himself into the saddle, but he made it, and left the yard at a walk, turning the horse's head toward the home place.

He had brought just two items in the saddlebags—a Bible and a copy of *The Journal of Gilbert Winslow,* but his mind was set on only one thing—finding peace. The ride had not been easy, and it took all the strength he had to make it to the house—almost falling off the horse once. He pulled the saddlebags off, left the horse standing free, and staggered inside, dropping heavily on the bed. Five hours later, he awoke, his wounds aching and his lips dry with thirst.

After getting a long drink from the well, Sky went to the kitchen and ate a little canned meat. His thirst and hunger satisfied, he took the two books from the saddlebags and spread them out on the table. Sitting there with an air of finality, he stared at the books for several minutes. Then with a sigh, he bowed his head and prayed softly, "All right, God—I'm here!" He waited quietly before continuing. "You know I hate Irene," he said. "It's been eating me alive for years. Now, I can't seem to change that—but folks who know you tell me that you can do it. So here I sit, Lord. If I'm not willing to be what you want— why, you'll just have to *make* me be willing!"

Slowly he pulled the Bible toward him, opened it, and began to read. He read until the sun came up; then he blew out the light and continued to read, though his vision was blurred. With determination he said stubbornly, "Lord, I'm waiting for you." Sensing no response, he went on reading.

All morning long he sat there, and finally at noon he dropped to his knees and began to call on God in a broken voice. He felt as though God were breaking him in two with mighty blows, and he cried out in great choking sobs.

When his strength gave out, he lay prone on the floor, shaken

by the waves of pain and regret. It was as if his whole life un-
rolled before him, and he saw things he'd forgotten—how he'd
wronged this man, and betrayed the trust of another. Each time
he saw a wrong, he'd cry bitterly, "I'm sorry about that, Lord!"

Then he saw Irene's face. He thought of how she'd deceived
him, how she'd spurned his love in so many ways. As scene
after scene flashed before him, the hatred that had been lying in
his heart for years leaped up like a live flame.

He forced himself to recall those agonizing years with her;
then he directed his full attention to his own life just like Lot
Penny had done. As he saw the ugly sordidness of his past, the
miracle happened. The full weight of his sin fell upon his conscience, and he cried out as though he'd been stabbed, "Oh,
God! I forgive her! I forgive her—I'm worse than she ever was!"

The words were barely out of his mouth when a peace came
over him. It was as if he'd been in a raging storm, with wild
winds knocking the boat to pieces—and suddenly, the waves
stilled and the wind became soft and gentle.

He lay there for a long time, weeping—but now for joy. After
a while, he rose to his feet. The house seemed too small, and he
left, taking the path to the creek. When he got to the deep pool,
he sat down and began to pray again, but this time it was a
prayer of thanksgiving, not of despair.

He didn't know how long he'd sat there before he became
aware of someone calling his name. Getting to his feet, he started
toward the sound just as Rebekah came running down the path.
When she saw him, she stopped abruptly, staring.

"Rebekah!" he cried urgently. Going to her, he saw her ashen
face. "What's wrong? Are the kids all right?"

His question made her heart warm. "Yes, Sky, they're all
right," she assured. "But *you* scared us all to death," she chided.
"Everyone's out looking for you!"

He dropped his eyes sheepishly. "Why, I never thought of
that, Rebekah. I just had to get away."

"Couldn't you at least have told Missy?"

He seemed not to hear the question. "Rebekah, are you going
to marry Jim?"

The unexpected question made her lips open slightly with a
startled look. Silently she searched his face, then shook her head

with certainty. "Of course not! That was all his crazy idea, Sky. He doesn't love me—and I don't love him."

Sky took a deep breath and exhaled with relief. "Well, if you're not going to marry him—would you marry me?"

For one moment, Rebekah thought he'd lost his mind. He was waiting for her answer with an eagerness she'd never seen before. "Why, Mr. Winslow!" she said pertly. "I *am* married to you!"

"Not yet, you're not," he countered, taking her by both arms.

"What are you doing?" she whispered, her eyes luminous with a mixture of wonder and perplexity.

"Proposing," he replied firmly. The joy in his blue eyes reflected the fullness that welled up in his heart. "I want a wife, not a servant! And I want Lot Penny to marry us—like people should be married, with a preacher praying over them. And I want Joe to be your son—and Timmy and Mary to be my kids. And I want—!"

"What's happened to you, Sky?" Rebekah cried excitedly.

He pulled her close. "Lots of things, Rebekah. I've got some sense at last. I've learned to let Irene rest in her grave, for one thing!"

Rebekah lifted her head and her lips parted. "Are you sure, Sky?"

"Yes, I am—and there's more! I've been on God's trail all night, Rebekah—and just a little while ago, I found Him! Well, I guess it's more like He found *me!*" he added with awe. "I've been searching how to find God for a long time—and now I don't see how I could have missed Him! He's like a pillar of fire! You can't miss Him—if you'll just look in the right place!"

"Sky!" Rebekah cried, and tears sprang to her eyes. "I'm so glad!"

His arms tightened around her, and he bent his head to touch her lips. He kissed her gently, firmly, possessively. The mixture of joy, response and surrender was like nothing either of them had ever known. The anger and fear that had separated them were gone, and when he pulled back, his eyes searching hers, he whispered softly, "I didn't know a man could love a woman like I love you, Rebekah! It's going to take a whole lifetime to explain it to you."

She bracketed his face with her hands and kissed him passionately, all the pent-up longing rushing through her. As they drew apart, she looked up, her face aglow with new life, and smiled joyously, "Oh, Sky! I've got a lifetime to spare!"